J. A. Kerr Bain

The People of the Pilgrimage

First Series: True Pilgrims

J. A. Kerr Bain

The People of the Pilgrimage
First Series: True Pilgrims

ISBN/EAN: 9783337291679

Printed in Europe, USA, Canada, Australia, Japan

Cover: Foto ©Andreas Hilbeck / pixelio.de

More available books at **www.hansebooks.com**

THE PEOPLE OF THE PILGRIMAGE

AN EXPOSITORY STUDY

OF THE

"PILGRIM'S PROGRESS" AS A BOOK OF CHARACTER.

FIRST SERIES

TRUE PILGRIMS

BY

REV. J. A. KERR BAIN, M.A.

EDINBURGH:
MACNIVEN & WALLACE.
LONDON: HODDER & STOUGHTON.
1887.

To the Memory of

WILLIAM BRUCE ROBERTSON, D.D., of Irvine,

THIS WORK,

WHICH HAD A PLACE AMONG THE LAST OF HIS
EARTHLY THOUGHTS, AND WAS COMPLETED
IN THE AFTER-LIGHT OF HIS FERVENT
INTEREST IN ITS WELFARE,

Is tenderly dedicated

BY THE

AUTHOR.

PREFACE.

IT may be felt that this book owes a good deal more of "apology" for itself than the great book which it seeks to expound. Probably it would not have taken existence but for the counsel of some whose judgment it should have been affectation to disregard. It was thought that room is still left for a work which should deal with the Allegory of Bunyan in a way more critical and thorough, even if therefore less popular, than has been usual hitherto; and the writer could not but acknowledge that he had at least something of the indispensable leisure for so congenial a task.

More especially it was considered that the field of exposition of the Allegory is at present but scantily occupied in its department of Character; and this consideration gave its weight to individual predilection in limiting the exposition almost entirely to that department. Indeed, some limitation is plainly desirable in a field so rich; and we shall find, that no limitation as to the line of our study of the book can well exclude a sense of its whole contents.

It is hoped that the book may be acceptable to the more thoughtful in our Churches, and perhaps even to some whose earnest intelligence does not associate itself with evangelical things; for while Christianity cannot dispense with dogma, it yet can afford to put character in the front, and dogma in the rear, at least as fearlessly as any system which has taken a place among men. Nor may it be too bold to hope that younger brethren in the ministry, whose materials on the subject have not had opportunity of gathering, may find hints in these pages which can be turned to use—for their people if not for themselves.

The book owes something perhaps to every important work which has appeared with the " Pilgrim's Progress " for its theme; but it owes nearly everything to Bunyan himself, whose mind it would fain interpret freely and at first hand. And the study which this involves only heightens one's esteem alike for the author and for the man whose finest legacy is the Allegory which these pages are honoured in contributing to unfold.

Among those to whose kindness the book is more or less indebted, thankful mention ought to be made of the late Dr Robertson of Irvine; the Rev. R. J. Sandeman of Edinburgh; the Rev. John MacKnight of Whitburn; Thomas Chalmers Hetherington, Esq., of Rangoon; and the Rev. John Kennedy of Liff, Dundee, whose casual suggestion, offered more than half-a-dozen years ago, was the germ out of which the book ultimately sprang.

LIVINGSTON, *October* 1887.

CONTENTS OF FIRST SERIES.

CONTENTS.

INTRODUCTORY.

BUNYAN—HIS ALLEGORY—CHARACTER IN THE "PILGRIM."

BUNYAN is one of the few original men who have been given to the Church. What was more essentially original about him, whether as a man of literature or as a man of religion, was due to a genius which would have done much to assert its own form and method whatever might have been the circumstances that chanced to press upon it from without. Yet we should omit from our reckoning not a little which went to the making of him as we actually know him, if we failed to take account of two forces more external—the one, the impact of an age which was in many ways remarkable ; the other, and by far the greater, the handlings of a personal discipline, for the most part spiritual, which was of such peculiar strength that it wrought a fashioning, almost a fusion, through his whole being and destiny.

His life of sixty years— from 1628 to 1688—spanned one of the most eventful periods in the history of the country. The year of his birth was the year of the Petition of Right, and of the installation of Laud as Bishop of London. The year of his death was the year of the Revolution. Between those two years lay the Parliamentary War, the execution of Charles I., the Commonwealth, the Restoration, the reign of Charles II., and the fragment of a reign which James II. was hastening to its doom when the Dreamer was dying of exhaustion and fever in the house of a friend at Holborn Bridge in London.

Bunyan's lifetime thus coinciding with what can be more strictly called the Puritan period, we shall expect to find it as notable for its men as for its events. In politics we may look for Hampden and Pym, for Cromwell and Blake and Falkland, for Sydney and Russell. In theology we may look for Owen and Howe and Charnock, for Baxter and the Henrys, for Jeremy Taylor and Thomas Fuller, for Cudworth and South, for Chillingworth and Tillotson. In philosophy we may look for Hobbes and Locke, and in science for Isaac Newton, though the "Essay" was not published till 1690, nor the "Principia" till 1687. And the period was equally rich in general literature, since in poetry alone we may look for Herrick and Cowley and Waller, for Butler and Dryden, for George Herbert, and for John Milton; while at the birth of Bunyan, Shakespeare was but twelve years dead.

The author of the "Pilgrim," whose name we need not shrink from adding to this brilliant roll, was the son of a working brazier, or "tinker," who had his home in the village of Elstow, within a mile of the town of Bedford. The son, having received a slender measure of schooling, became the assistant of the father in this lowly trade, which continued to be his own until his election to a settled pastorate.[1] For what particulars of his youth we possess, we are largely indebted to the autobiographical work to which he gave the title of "Grace Abounding to the Chief of Sinners." It is a record of his spiritual experience during the first thirty years of his life, with incidental references to his outward career. From this account of himself, which must be held to be substantially unimpeachable, we gather that his youth was one of determined godlessness, only falling short of abandoned immorality. Yet happily falling short of this; for no fair interpretation of Bunyan's strongest language concerning his early behaviour need

[1] Note A.

shut us up to the belief that he was ever positively vicious. He was a leader among unprincipled companions; he was addicted to Sunday sports; he was an enthusiast in the pastime of bell-ringing; he uttered lies; he swore perhaps more blasphemously than any of his class. But his conscience—as ill-informed as those of his companions, yet more keen and active than theirs — was often casting him into alarms such as they could little comprehend. The intensity of his religious nature, working together with his ignorance and with the vividness of his imagination, gave him a spiritual history which furnishes an extraordinary record of pain and conflict. It is almost needful we should recall the leading lines in that history.

Even in his childhood he was wont to be scared by "fearful dreams" and "dreadful visions." Throughout his boyhood "the thoughts of religion were very grievous to him;" yet his "spirit trembled" when those who "professed goodness" did wickedly, and we do not find that he himself was unusually precocious in evil. About his seventeenth year, when the Parliamentary War was still a few years from its close, his knowledge of the world, both as to evil and to good, was being extended by a short period of service as a soldier;[1] and it greatly impressed him that the man who took his place at the siege of some town was one night shot dead—a circumstance which he reckons among several escapes from death that struck moments of thoughtfulness into his reckless youth.[2]

His first faint regard for religion took rise after his marriage in his twentieth year. His young wife, the daughter of a pious father, read to him from her scanty stock of religious literature, and "would be often telling him of how

[1] Note B.   [2] Note C.

godly a man her father was." Thus he "fell in very eagerly with the religion of the times," "yet retaining his wicked life "—"overrun with the spirit of superstition." A sermon against Sabbath-breaking " did benumb the sinews of his best delights "—only for a season ; but on the Sunday when he resumed his sports, he was startled by a voice that seemed to fall out of heaven into his soul—(this became a prevailing feature of his experience)—whereupon, concluding his hope was cut off, " he resolved in his mind he would go on in sin," and was seized with " a great desire to have his fill of sin." But this resolve and desire were unexpectedly overcome. An ungodly woman so reproved him as he was swearing outside her door, that he was smitten with shame, and " wished with all his heart that he might be a little child again, that his father might learn him to speak without this wicked way of swearing ;" and he never swore afterwards. Further, an acquaintance now led him into a habit of reading the Scriptures, and he began to find some pleasure in the employment.

He made a distinct moral advance when next he set himself to " keep the Divine commandments," and to ask Divine forgiveness whensoever he "broke one." He thought " he pleased God as well as any man in England," and earned some repute for a godly life, of which he was not a little "proud." Dancing he reluctantly abandoned ; his conscience fought a winning battle with his desire to "look on " at the "vain practice" of bell-ringing, and at last he fled from the steeple in terror lest it should fall upon him. Soon there came a clear crisis in his spiritual career; for he "was all this while ignorant of Jesus Christ."

One day, in Bedford, he joined a group of " three or four poor women sitting at a door in the sun," engaged in religious conversation. He was himself "a brisk talker " on religion ; but the talk of the women was so radiant and real that he felt beside them as if he knew nothing of the subject. "They were to him as if they had found a new world." His "heart shook as he bethought him" of his ignorance of what they assumed to be fundamental verities —regeneration, faith, inward sin. Henceforward, he was not able to withhold himself from the company of these good people, and his thoughts came to be fervently concentrated upon God and heaven. "The Bible was very precious to him" then. He resisted the influence of "the Ranters," by which many fell into looseness of doctrine and life. But it now became his absorbing anxiety whether he had faith; and he just escaped the hazardous experiment of commanding a petty miracle on the roadside to test his possession of it. In his trouble he had a vision which encouraged him :—his godly friends were grouped on the sunny side of a mountain, and he was shivering in the cold on the shadowy side ; a wall ran along between, through which he strove hard to force his way, and at last succeeded, and came beside the others into the full sunshine. Possessed by a "vehement hunger of desire to be among that number," he was ejaculating prayers wherever he went. Next he was "driven to his wits' end" by two questions which alternately haunted him—Was he "elected"?—Might not the day of grace for him be past? But one day a "sentence fell with weight upon his spirit;" and though, "after a year's search, he was somewhat daunted" to find it was from the Apocrypha, he had the good sense to "take the comfort" of it. He was "all in a flame to be converted to Jesus Christ;" and such as he thought to have been thus changed—to his eye "they shone, they walked like those who carried the broad seal of heaven about them." For many months he feared "the Lord would not call him," though he longed day and night that He should.

Human guidance now entered more directly into his history. Constrained to open his mind to his godly friends, they drew the attention of their minister to his case. This was John Gifford, once a royalist major of desperate character, but now a pastor of high Christian esteem in Bedford. The minister "spoke to him," and invited him to be a listener while he conferred with others at his house. The first effect of all this took him sorely aback. He seemed to lose out of him all longing after God, and was clogged in every duty. No promise was anything to him. He "saw that he had a heart that would sin, and that he lay under a law that would condemn." He "was driven as with a tempest." His heart was shut fast against Christ, though he cried that it might be opened. But as to the act of sinning, he was never more tender than now. "*For some years together*" he continued thus—in full "sight of his own vileness," and "deeply in despair." It struck him with amazement to see people make so much of the things of this life, the things of his soul were so tremendously momentous to himself. Yet concerning this consuming trouble he "should cry, 'Lord, let it not go off my heart but the right way, but by the blood of Christ.'" He came to be sorry that God had made him a man, for he "feared he was a reprobate." He envied the sinless beasts that he saw in the fields on his journeys. A sermon on Christ's love filled him for a while with "comfort and hope," and rays of this light continued to visit him when he was "questioning all again." A "very great storm" of temptation, of which he was strangely warned, now broke upon him, and he was goaded to touch even the confines of atheism. But in the midst of this incessant tempest of dark suggestions, he felt—at least, as he says, "when God gave him leave to swallow his spittle"—that he did not entirely make them his own. "These things," nevertheless, "did sink him into very deep despair." He bore all this for a year—his most sacred duties infested with vile thoughts, and mingled with almost sensible strugglings against "the devil," yet his heart sometimes powerfully affected with "apprehensions of God" and of His Gospel. At last "the temptation was removed, and he was put into his right mind again, as other Christians were"—not wholly at once, but by advancing steps.

The period that followed was a bright one. "Travelling into the country once," he was enabled to see vividly that "God and his soul were friends" by the blood of the Cross. Another day, at his fireside, he "was ready to swoon as he sat," so overpoweringly he realised that Christ had "destroyed the devil," and had "delivered from fear of death." Mr Gifford's public teaching was now of priceless service to him. His "soul was led forth from truth to truth of God," under manifest illumination from the Divine Spirit. His personal assurance of salvation was clear and strong. Luther's book on "Galatians" fell into his hands after he had been longing to "see some ancient godly man's experience;" and now he seemed as if he were reading his own. At length "he found, as he thought, that he loved Christ dearly." But the clouds of tempest were to gather yet again, and in "a more grievous and dreadful temptation than before:" he was tempted "to sell and part with this most blessed Christ."

This temptation, so remarkable for its tenacity and vehemence, was laden with anguish for him because of his failure to perceive how much it was a matter of suggestion from without, and how little it was a matter of compliance from within. For long he kept saying in response to every solicitation, sometimes with muscular "pushings and thrustings," "I will not." But at last he "felt the thought pass through his heart,—'Let Him go if He will,'" and immediately he "was like a man bereft of life." He supposed he had committed the unpardonable sin. Those days were terrible. The strain seemed to threaten his health; indeed it is amazing that either mind or body could endure it.

But, by-and-bye, relief dawned upon him, "as he was walking to and fro in a good man's shop:"—"Suddenly, there was as if there had rushed in at the window the noise of wind upon him, but very pleasant, and as if he heard a voice speaking, 'Didst ever refuse to be justified by the blood of Christ?'" This struck at the root of his misconception on the subject, and "commanded a silence in his heart." He was still tempted fiercely not to pray to Christ —tempted to believe he had forfeited all personal benefit from Christ's atonement. But voice after voice, and Scripture after Scripture, came to his help like successive waves that would float him off "the rocks" upon which he was "jostling." He saw his "sin" was not wilful; he had "fallen," he imagined, but he had not "fallen away;" he had not "despised his birthright." And now "the thunder was gone beyond him; only some drops did still remain, that now and then would fall upon him," and "every touch would hurt his tender conscience." The word of final deliverance was, once more, no quotation from Scripture, though he grasped it as precious truth—"Thy righteousness is in heaven." Now his spirit was flooded with a sense of the glory of Christ—His fulness, the mystery of union with Him, the grandeur of His representative dignity; and he speaks of such powerful apprehensions of the grace of God, that he thinks "if that sense of it had abode long upon him, it would have made him incapable of business."

He puts on record several other instances of sharp temptation; but, in comparison with those we have recounted, they were inconsiderable and brief.

In following this inward history of Bunyan, we have outstripped his outward history by several years. It was at the age of twenty-five, and when all this spiritual vicissitude was in mid-course, that he became a member of the church in Bedford. About four years afterwards—he himself has it "about five or six," but those would be long years to him—"some of the most able among the saints with us," he says, "desired me, and that with much earnestness, that I would be willing, at some times, to take in hand, in one of the meetings, to speak a word of exhortation unto them." This staggered him; but at length he was prevailed upon to speak at two private meetings—"with much weakness and infirmity," yet so as to constrain his listening friends to "give thanks to the Father of mercies for the grace bestowed on him." Next, in accompanying more experienced speakers when they went to hold a private service in the country, he would venture to address the people, and with the same warm recognition of his power. Ere long he was "more particularly called forth and appointed to a more ordinary and public preaching of the Word." To this he "did evidently find in his mind a secret pricking forward," and he "could not be content unless he was found in the exercise of his gift." "Wherefore," he says, "though of myself of all the saints the most unworthy, yet I, with great fear and trembling at the sight of my own weakness, did set upon the work." He had not preached for long till he had to "begin to conclude it might be so, that God had owned in His work such a foolish one as he." "I went myself in chains," he affirms, "to preach to them in chains, and carried that fire in my own conscience that I persuaded them to beware of. . . . Yet God carried me on, but surely with a strong hand, for neither guilt nor hell could take me off my work. . . . I have been in my preaching . . . as if an angel of God had stood at my back to encourage me. . . . I never endeavoured to, nor durst, make use of other men's lines (though I condemn not all that do), for I verily thought, and found by experience, that what was taught me by the Word and Spirit of Christ could be spoken, maintained, and stood to by the soundest and best-established conscience. .... I felt myself more blessed and honoured of God by this than if He had made me the emperor of the Christian world. .... My great desire in my fulfilling of my ministry was to get into the darkest places of the country." Assaults of Satan, oppositions of churchly power, slanders of his character, troubled him with little intermission, but did not daunt his courage or move his constancy.

At the end of his first year of evangelistic labour, Bunyan issued the earliest fruit of his pen,—as if he must needs make haste to give earnest of the double weapon he was destined to wield. His little book, emboldened with a preface by the youthful successor of Mr Gifford (himself now dead), went forth to grapple with the doctrinal ignorance and folly which he encountered among the people of the villages. The book, which bore hard upon Quakerism, provoked the attack of a Quaker champion, to whom Bunyan replied with some spirit in a book almost equal in bulk to the book it was vindicating. A year later he published a second work, and one of more decided power: its theme was the Parable of the Rich Man; and it ventured forth under a warm preface by " J. G.," probably Mr Gibbs of Newport-Pagnell. About two years afterwards his work on " Law and Grace" appeared, and gave proof of a ripening in mind and spirit which could well dispense, as it did, with the commendatory prefaces of friends.

Bunyan was already known beyond his own county as a gifted preacher when he was taken from the midst of one of his religious meetings in name of the new king. For over twelve years thereafter the county prison of Bedford was his "home"—so, with scarcely conscious irony, we find him calling it. During the course of his imprisonment he enjoyed periods of comparative liberty, succeeded by periods of more rigorous restraint : for his jailors, as if they would belie Overbury's description of "A Jailer" as much as their prisoner belied his description of "A Tinker," treated him with a hazardous kindliness which sometimes challenged the interference of those who inspired the policy of the day. Indeed, his long imprisonment would seem to have been divided into two equal portions by his entire release for six weeks, after which his confinement would appear to have been more strict until, in the summer of 1672, he obtained his liberty. He immediately entered upon his work as pastor of the Bedford congregation—an office to which he had been appointed several months before. Three years afterwards, however, as his latest and best biographer has proved, he was a prisoner again, and now in the town jail of Bedford, for half a year.

The proceedings of the Crown, in as far as they affected Bunyan, were more than usually shortsighted. To his imprisonment we owe some of his most influential works. Among these were "The Holy City," "Grace Abounding," "The Strait Gate," and, suggested by this last, the First Part of the "Pilgrim's Progress."[1] To the First Part of that work we owe at least the Second Part. Indeed, it may not be too much to say that if Bunyan had not been thus early made a prisoner, he might never have become an author of abiding distinction. His brain and hand, as well as his heart, were still free. Writing became the solace, if not even the necessity, of his unsought leisure. His fingers might be busy at the tagged laces by the making of which he earned a pittance for his family; it would not stay the ferment of his thoughts, nor obstruct the current of his desire to reach the hearts of men. There was nothing but likelihood that he should just feel his way as he did to easy familiarity with an instrument which should prove still more potent, and greatly more enduring,

[1] Note D.

than that voice which the intolerance of the Court had seen meet to silence.

This irrepressible prisoner, it is true, judging him conventionally, was little of a scholar. The reading and writing he learned at school, when they had been wellnigh lost, had been more than recovered to him by the assiduous encouragement of his young wife. That young wife was gone, and Bunyan was married a second time to a noble woman, before the years of imprisonment set in; but it is probable that the world owes more to that almost unknown girl than very clearly appears upon the surface of the history. She evidently took unwearied interest in all that touched the higher welfare of her husband. Before the time of his arrest, as we have seen, that interest had already borne good fruit, and now it was to yield such results as could not have entered into her brightest anticipations. Nor need it be doubted that Bunyan's short period of labour as a preacher had been not only a time of privilege for those who crowded to hear him, but also a time of invaluable schooling for himself. Stimulated as he was by the eagerness of his audiences, and sustained by his own lofty estimate of his task, it could not fail to abridge many of his deficiencies of training,—enriching his mind, broadening his views of truth, developing his gifts of expression, inducing precision of thought, and, above all, carrying forward that saturation of his faculties at the fountain of his vernacular Scriptures which made him the most purely biblical author that ever wrote.

Even still, however, as men commonly speak, he was a man of the meagrest education and the narrowest culture. He had no doubt read a good deal in those later years, but he had read it all from a very few books, and had read as much of it from his Bible as from all other volumes together. Must we then account him ill equipped for taking rank as a powerful religious writer? In an ordinary instance we well might, but we should err if we did so in the instance of Bunyan. With his vividness of imagination he combined great natural vigour of intellect, and with his rare susceptibility of moral nature he united an unusual wealth and play of feeling. His judgment was robust; his observation was wide-eyed and accurate; and his inborn tact, when brought to bear upon literary production, had much of the regulative influence of a taste which had been elaborated by culture. Chief of all, perhaps, even in this relation, we must bethink us of that spiritual experience in which his strong mind was constrained to travel its bitter way across the lonely waste of almost every religious uncertainty and misconception until he reached for himself the truth that lay beyond. That experience was to him a theological curriculum of wide range and of keen reality— not moral and spiritual only, but strenuously intellectual besides; and now it was all crowned by a clear vision and a large grasp of evangelical truth as he conceived the Divine Book to teach it. His fervent nature burned to make that truth equally real to men to whom it was but a scheme of shadows, and his earnestness was already moulding for itself a fitting vehicle in a masterly command of that homely but adequate English which his mother and his Bible had given him.

We have made passing mention of Bunyan's faculty of observation. No faculty could have been of more indispensable service to a man who was to be the author of as many books, large and small, as there were years in his life, and who was nevertheless to be a reader of perhaps fewer books of other men than he had written of his own. And no faculty of Bunyan's had been exercised to better purpose than this. His opportunities of seeing men and things had been limited, and before his life had passed its fourth decade he had been severed for eight years from any regular intercourse with the world. But all he had looked at he had really seen, and all he had seen he had absorbed into his masculine understanding and tenacious memory. We know that his inherited occupation, which brought many callers to the village-workshop on market-days, had also led him to make many journeys about the neighbourhood; and we can guess how rich his months of soldiering might be in what should replenish his mind through eye and ear. His writings bear traces enough of the kind of reminiscence with which these employments would supply him. But it was in the sphere of religious life that his gifts of observation gathered their choicest fruits. And here again we have to bethink us of that spiritual force which seldom ceased to draw and to drive him from childhood onwards. With a business on hand which was often so urgent as to cast his tinkering into the shade, it would be a gaze of intentness and scrutiny which young Bunyan would bestow upon every character that came well within his view. And we must give its due place to that year or two of evangelising as a busy harvest-time of his surprising knowledge of human character on its religious side. Yet no more than its due place. Doubtless there are few situations within the range of human affairs which afford a reflective man better advantages for penetrating into the core of human character—for analysing motives, for tracking tendencies, for appreciating the true, and valuating the false—than that of a messenger of the Gospel. But he almost had need to be working in a settled pastorate, and Bunyan was not. Time, too, he must have—time in the form of duration, and time in the form of leisure; but that itinerant shepherding of Bunyan's gave him little of either. Indeed, it looks as if it amounted to a presumption in favour of the theory which brings down the composition of the First Part to the date of his second imprisonment, that his education for the task would then include all his experience of men during his twelve years among fellow-prisoners, and also during the three years of pastoral occupation which intervened,—not to speak of the greater maturity of his powers. Still, on any theory, the wealthy truthfulness of the book in this matter of character can only be accounted for by a rare combination of grace and genius.

A good deal of what we have said as to Bunyan's preparation does not so fully apply to the Second Part of the "Pilgrim" as it does to the First. This Second Part, which is still more rich in character than the earlier part, was published at the beginning of 1685. The seven years of varied contact with men which the interval supplied him are not lost when the author dreams again. It was the most popular of the works which streamed from his pen during the productive decade between 1678 and 1688, in which he gave a score of books to the publishers, or an average of two in each year. In 1680 had appeared "The Life and Death of Mr Badman"—a vigorous work, which seems to have embodied his first conception of how he ought to furnish a complement for the picture of the life and death of his good man as painted in the "Pilgrim." Two years later had come "The Holy War." No fewer than six works, headed by the "Jerusalem Sinner Saved," left his hands during the first half of the year of his death, —the last of them only appearing when he had been three weeks in his grave at Bunhill Fields. But the Second Part of the "Pilgrim"—the book of character pre-eminently among all these, and indeed among all Bunyan's works together—is the book which has taken its place inevitably by the side of its companion, not in subject only, but also in fame.

If we look in upon the prisoner in that Bedford dungeon of his,—a place comfortless enough, judging by the average prison of the time,—we shall find a plain-looking man, tall and broadset, with complexion ruddy, " hair inclining to red," and eyes that sparkle as they turn to greet us. His expression may wear a little of sternness, and his words may be somewhat few till we gain something of his confidence ; but his severity then relaxes into modesty, and his reticence into a mild affableness which even a certain roughness of manner does not render unpleasant. His lace-making has been laid aside for the evening, and writing-materials are lying before him, with many leaves of crabbed manuscript. In this study of his the library is not extensive :—his Bible, and those three volumes not far off, on the title-pages of which we read, " History of the Acts and Monuments of the Church," more commonly abbreviated into " Foxe's Book of Martyrs." There is no other literature within the four walls—unless we count in that manuscript itself, as indeed we may. It is a sheaf of one or other of those works which had his dungeon for their birthplace. If we are visiting him in the latter months of his shorter imprisonment, it is pretty sure to be a bundle of the " Pilgrim's Progress." The written leaves are falling fast from evening to evening : he may not be able, however, to complete the precious pile in this place of durance ; for the time of bondage, though he is not likely to know it, is already nearing its close. The syntax of these sheets may not be perfect, and the spelling may not be controlled even by the indeterminate fashion of the age ; but those are blemishes which the printer shall by-and-bye remove, when the days of liberty shall have permanently returned. Bunyan shall yet see twelve distinct editions of this book, or more than one a year, before he dies.

The modest author himself was as much surprised as any one at the success of his " Pilgrim." He did, indeed, defend its method against the timid prejudices of some of his Baptist brethren, for he believed the book was fitted to do good, and to do it entertainingly. But there was an element of adventure in the publication of a religious book of so new-fangled a construction, and his expectations were perhaps not greater than his fears. Whatever should become of the book, however, he had already enjoyed his reward in the making of it. Its genesis is interesting, and affords some confirmation of the saying that there is no truly great book but " makes itself." He was not contemplating the allegorical method, and was engaged on a work of a different cast—a work in which the figure of a pilgrimage, apparently in the form of metaphor only, became familiar to his pen while he wrote. Whereupon, as he tells us in the hearty lines of his " Apology," he found another book was starting growth unbidden. " I," he says,

> " *Fell suddenly* into an *allegory.* . . .
>   Nay, then, thought I, *if that you breed so fast,*
>   *I'll set you by yourselves,* lest you at last
>   Should prove *ad infinitum,* and eat out
>   The book that I already am about."

And the literary impulse did not degenerate as the work itself proceeded :

> " I only thought to make—
> I know not what ; nor did I undertake
> Thereby to please my neighbour : no, not I ;
> *I did it mine own self to gratify.*"

He had struck a living spring, and he had only to set about the recreation of building it into a well. Or, to take his own homelier figure,—

> " For, having now my method by the end,
>   Still as I pulled it came."

We should have welcomed any stray beam of light as to how this great amateur in the art of book-making went to work in the planning and developing of his masterpiece. As it is, we can only guess what the order, rather than the process, of its growth may have been.

The thought which underlies it all, is the reality of a Christian life as such, together with the momentousness which gives weight to its reality, and the changefulness of experience which gives interest to its momentousness. The germ of the particular literary form is the metaphor—a course, a journey, a pilgrimage. Next, a destination—a starting point—a way extending between : the metaphor has already spaced itself into allegory. Immediately the outline begins to fill with glimpsed fragments of analogy. Then there begin to loom here and there, out of the mist which yet enshrouds the landscape, a tract, a spot, an object—a hill, a river, a slough, a valley, a palace—which takes first "a local habitation," and next "a name." Incidents meanwhile are taking shape—happenings of danger, of conflict, of failure, of joy, of triumph. And all through this thick coming of materials there is implied a pilgrim— one at least : he may be alone, or he may, from first to last, or at intervals, be in the company of other pilgrims. Those pilgrims may be true, or they may be false. Nay, he may meet with those who are not themselves on pilgrimage at all—persons who are better than human pilgrims, or are worse. Here enters that element of Bunyan's Allegory which shall most engage us. The Pilgrimage now "lives and moves" as well as "has its being." Character begins to interweave itself with place and incident. And it is just here, in that special region of embellishment which would probably be the last to suggest itself, that we have the most surpassing evidence of the author's genius, scarcely less in the conception than in the working-out of his Allegory. Already, indeed, has the indispensable figure—that of the pilgrim himself—introduced this element of individual character, and offered opportunity for the execution of a careful and masterly study in this department. Nor can we doubt that even if Bunyan had unhappily confined himself to this single study, he would have done it well—so well that his Allegory should still have been eminently readable and valuable. But we have only to imagine the canvas empty of all human figures but this one, however true in colour or vivid in drawing it might be,—we have only to let our fancy dismiss from the stage all the other actors who give it animation and variety without crowding it,—that we may realise how much this central figure itself has gained, and how incalculably much the quality of the whole work has been enhanced, by the more sumptuous treatment which commended itself to the affluent sagacity of Bunyan.

It is therefore in this feature—not in this alone, but in this most strikingly of all—that previous attempts to work out the figure of a pilgrimage are found to stand defective and poor beside this spontaneous book of Bunyan's. Perhaps the most noteworthy of these—noteworthy in itself and in its resemblances to Bunyan's work—is a poem bearing the title of "The Pilgrimage of Man," and written about 1330 by a French Cistercian monk, Guillaume de Guileville. The resemblances we are safe to regard as purely accidental, since we cannot think it was of much account to Bunyan that the old French of this poem had been turned into old English two hundred years before the Restoration. But the particular resemblances, whether accidental or not, only serve to accentuate the general contrast. The dreaming,—the vision of the heavenly city,— the beautiful Lady Grace and her house,—the needed scrip and staff,—the donned armour,—the giant Temptation,— the hag Sloth, with her axe Weariness of Life,—the snares Vain Hope and Despair,—the crone Flattery,—the valley of Old Avarice, six-handed, hump-backed, lame, and ragged, —the hunter Satan,—the House of Holy Scripture,— Mercy, of pleasing countenance, holding the string of Charity,—the "wicket gate" of the city, where Grace comes to his aid for the last of many times ;—all this contains coincidence enough to be interesting to readers of the "Pilgrim's Progress." But, with a monotonous fertility in personifying abstractions, the author introduces us to no being of genuine flesh and blood but the adventurer himself. There are many characters, but there is no character —scarcely even in the typical "man" of the pilgrimage. The traveller goes forward through strictly allegorical regions, where he meets none but strictly allegorical personages; and a dull, dreary, depressing way it is on which we follow him—always unnatural, often weird, sometimes grotesque. Indeed, with fewer marks of mediæval superstition than we might have looked for, the contrast with the everyday lightfulness, the dramatic livingness, the various humanness, and, withal, the poetical charm of Bunyan's treatment, is complete. Nor ought we to withhold the admission that in the author's own companion-allegory of "The Holy War"—so much more compactly consistent in its allegoric framework than the "Pilgrim" is—we find a comparative poverty of this element in which the "Pilgrim" is so rich.

Indeed, in the "Pilgrim's Progress," character is not an ornament merely, nor an adventitious excellence, but a constituent substance. Christian truth itself is scarcely more fundamental to its structure. If truth be the warp which already waits in the loom, character is the woof which the free hand of the worker plies according to his pleasure, so making the fabric. Or, if we may press the matter to further analysis, the substance of the woof is character strictly so called, and the colour of it is conduct —both of them obedient to the artist's choice. Of course the warp and the woof are akin; truth and character are for each other : are they not compacted into this homogeneous unity which grew under the shuttle of the inventor? The creation and management of character, then, is a foremost aim of the book as a work of art. We can accurately speak of it as a poem. Offor apostrophises its author with a not unreasonable enthusiasm—"Thou art the prose poet of all time!" "The 'Pilgrim's Progress,'" says Dean Howson, "is the poetical result of the experience of the man who wrote it;" and twice he quietly calls it "this poem."[1] "The Pilgrim's Progress," affirms Mr Green, "is among the noblest of English poems. For if Puritanism had first discovered the poetry which contact with the spiritual world awakes in the meanest souls, Bunyan was the first of the Puritans who revealed this poetry to the outer world." "Bunyan's work is the poetry of Puritanism"—so the *Edinburgh Review* had said in 1838. M. Taine tells us that "the 'Pilgrim's Progress' is a manual of devotion for the use of simple folk, while it is an allegorical poem of grace;" and he speaks of "the last two poets of the Reformation"—Milton and Bunyan.[3] But, above most poems, it is a poem of character. Its finest scenes either promote character, or display it, or reward it. Its verities impinge upon character on every side. And it is the grandest distinction of this poem of character, that while the poet lavishes his art supremely upon man, and upon character as that which is most intrinsically significant in him, he fearlessly casts down the conventional barriers of time with which more worldly poets have limited their subject and their genius—quits the shallower margins of men's dispositions and motives, and launches forth into the deeps,—never witting, indeed, but to treat of human character in the whole profundity of its sources, and in the whole sweep of its issues, as the great subjective factor in an immortal destiny which the Good One desires should be a destiny of loftiest well-being.

The more specific qualities of Bunyan's character-paint-

---

[1] "Companions for the Devout Life—'The Pilgrim's Progress.'"
[2] "Short History of the English People," chap. ix. section 2.
[3] "English Literature," book ii. chap. v.

ing shall command our attention as we proceed. We shall have occasion to mark not only the great number, but the wide range, of his character-studies. We shall find that with lively contrast between different characters there is a truthful consistency in each with itself, thus furnishing each with a degree of valid individuality which is remarkable when we consider the narrow scope of incident, and the scanty setting of circumstance, of which he is able to avail himself. We shall see that in almost every character there is a life-like reality, which sometimes is nearly startling, and often is holding the reader under the illusion that he is perusing an account of living men. We shall note that even in the instance of characters which do little more than flit past the eye, the impression of distinct actuality which they usually leave upon us is such that their longer stay within the story would not so much deepen the impression as merely illustrate it. If we shall meet with nothing of the soft amplitude of Spenser, we shall meet with much of the incisiveness of Chaucer, and with even this condensed. The characters, moreover, are never either conceived or depicted with a primary view to the amusement of the reader, but to his instruction—to the comprehensive set- ting forth of those experimental verities which the Allegory is laying itself out to display; yet they rarely fail to in- terest him as if they had been designed to do nothing besides. They instruct after this interesting manner not only by what they are seen to be, but also by what they are heard to speak. Indeed, with true dramatic instinct, Bunyan makes more copious use of dialogue than had ever yet been the wont in English narrative literature, and usually permits the character to do the most of its own un- folding in the free interchange of talk, the character fre- quently becoming at once lesson and teacher. In this way of hearing as well as seeing in his dream, the author, scarcely ever but veiling his own personality even where we might excuse its obtrusion, manages to pour along his pages a luminous stream of teaching, enriched by more of humour and tenderness, and quickened by more of penetrative efficacy, than could easily be possible in the instance of any method less impersonal and picturesque than that which he has chosen.

We might set the " Pilgrim's Progress," therefore, at the head of all those books of entertainment which have been written, as the critics speak, " with a purpose." Of his purpose, however ingeniously he may have draped it, Bunyan is not ashamed. It was the purpose of his life. In the prosecution of that purpose, which was no advantage of his own, he was led in a happy hour to lay down the pen of exposition, to stay the tones of appeal, and to take up the brush of representation—the picturing of that which he had preached, and would preach again. The picturing is as earnest as the preaching. The subtle play of fancy, or the homely ease of style, need not deceive us. The spiritual energy is conserved although it has passed from exhortation into invention ; it has changed its form rather than its force. In a better sense than "the preacher" of Ecclesiastes signified, "a dream cometh through the multitude of business." It is still the Evangel he is unfolding, and it is still the Lord of the Evangel he is serving. The fervour of his convictions may seem as if it were in abeyance, but it is this very fervour which in large measure reappears under the new garb of stirring incident and life-like character. And it is to this spiritual intensity, scarcely less than to his purely mental endowments, that we owe the demonstration of how enchanting a theme an ordinary Christian life had from age to age contained the capacity of becoming—whenever its true prophet should appear.

No one who knows anything of allegory as a literary form will look for absolute harmoniousness in the structure of the "Pilgrim." A perfect allegory, as Macaulay sixty years ago reminded the literary world in claiming a lofty place for this book, is by the nature of it an impossibility.[1] If the current of analogy, flowing so far in a prescribed direction, were to meet with no rapids or falls or compelled deviations in its course, this good fortune would imply a "pre-established harmony" between the things of facts and the things of illustration which would wellnigh preclude both the task and the merit of invention. And Bunyan's work has all the difficulties, as well as all the advantages, of being at once an allegory and a dream. As an allegory it is unquestionably loose in its general structure, and provokingly unconcerned about its consistency in details. Yet, all things considered (for perfection in respect of its particular form is not in the front rank of qualities), the whole that sanctified genius is capable of doing has probably been done by Bunyan in this work of his. Captiousness, moreover, feels itself out of place, and even fair criticism is not wholly at ease, in presence of the unpretending temper of a book which displays on the whole such exquisite execution. We read it, and its honest realism, its hearty love of truth, its loyal catholicity, its manly good sense, conspire with its fascination to postpone the critical attitude till we have perused it again and again. We read it, and it is scarcely well with us if it does not so enchain our sympathies that we yield ourselves the willing scholars of so genial and true-hearted a teacher. We read it, and perhaps we do not hesitate even to take our part in the thankfulness of the Christian Church that she has such a book in possession. For it is to be accounted among the most notable things in Christian history, that there has come into its course a book which has held its way to a diffusion so immense, and has carried its quickening and

----

[1] *Essays:* "Review of Southey's Edition of the 'Pilgrim's Progress,' with the 'Life of Bunyan.'"

guiding, its warning and cheer, into so many myriads of homes and hearts around the globe. When we would estimate the moral forces which have taken sway in the world since the revival of evangelical truth in the 16th century, we cannot overlook that this book is being read to-day in eighty languages; that, in its countless editions, the rich man reads it decked in all the sumptuousness of art, and the poor man takes it down from his shelf of cheapest literature; that to many in every latitude the geography of the "Pilgrimage" is better known than the geography of their own country, and that during every generation for two centuries the story of Christian's way-faring has set multitudes upon treading the same path as his, till the same path led them at last into the same felicity. And it is a significant fact in modern evangelism, no less than a noteworthy fact in literature, that this book, which has so long been a far-going messenger in a world that deeply needs its message, bids fair to wield an influence that shall only increase with the "increasing purpose" of the ages.[1]

[1] Note E.

<h1 style="text-align:center">II.</h1>

THE CHARACTERS OF THE "PILGRIM": AN OUTLOOK.

IN accordance with the method on which we propose to study this Allegory of Bunyan's, our eye must be set upon the figures in the story much more than upon the incidents in it. Our business shall be with men and women who are moving in a region of incident,—this rather than with a system of incident in which men and women are bearing their part. It is incident, doubtless, which carries the greater measure of the doctrinal wealth of the Allegory, and it is upon this mainly that the weight of exposition has usually been thrown, and thrown most justly. But the figures themselves yield abundance of teaching, and are able to sustain not a little of interpretation.

This must appear probable to us the moment we remember that the figures, for the most part, are not figures only, but are also characters, and characters which are drawn with a firm and wisely-guided hand. Each figure has argument in it as well as fancy. The least important character is a compressed treatise of truth bound in living human form, and the more important characters are the living equivalents of volumes of treatises. Each has a meaning for us, and a message,—is the unconscious bearer of a prophetic burden for us, whether he may have in him a heart that would rejoice at our wellbeing, or one that would smile at our calamity. It is our part to cast a heedful eye upon the messenger, that we may make out his message, and may question him, if need is, concerning the credentials he carries, and the quarter from which he hails.

While, therefore, we shall strain after no artificial riddance between incident and character,—an aim which would bear unreality on its face, and would be undesirable even if it could be successful,—we shall not hesitate to turn the full front of our regard upon the persons, the *personæ*, with which the enlightened fancy of the Dreamer has peopled his book for us. In doing so, the tissue of event may seem now and then to suffer at our hands by disregard, and we may miss something of the force which depends upon the uninterrupted sequence of occurrences ; but for the reader to whom the Allegory is already a not unfamiliar book,—and there must be few readers indeed to whom it is a strange one,—this shall be no serious disadvantage. And perhaps the disadvantage is balanced by the degree in which the study of the characters casts light upon the occurrences themselves, and by the successive points of view from which the same occurrences have need to be looked at in tracking the characteristics of those who have taken part in them. But, above all, we shall expect compensation for many disadvantages in the clear impact which each character is thus permitted to make upon us, as an embodied phase of that actual life in which all doctrine, whether by way of illustration or of contrast, is put into mechanism and motion.

If now, in imagination, we select for ourselves a position from which we can enjoy a bird's-eye view of the line of pilgrimage ("as straight as a rule can make it"), and of all the near-lying country which is fenced-off from it, yet out of which surreptitious paths and lanes sometimes slide in upon the way, we may not be struck with much sense of multitude in the figures which fall into places here and there among the inanimate phenomena of the road. But if in imagination we go further, and embolden ourselves to

gather all those figures into one various throng beneath
our nearer gaze, we shall find, not only that their number
is very considerable, but also that each individual of the
number has an effective significance. We can now estimate that we have a good deal on hand when we take to
ourselves the task of considering each of them more or less
in detail. But now, too, we are able, though not perhaps
without a suspicion of taking undue liberty, to dispose
them in some such way as may simplify our consideration
of them.

In the foreground, then, we can afford to set *Christian,*
who by himself is sufficient to form a category. Behind
him, but not far off, we find place for *Faithful* and *Hopeful,*
who make up the scanty category of his companions.
Next, we cannot longer delay recognition of *Christiana
and her Family—his* family, tracing their father's footprints,
after the feet that made them have stepped on out of
earthly sight ; and into this group, or close upon its margin, glides *Mercy*, with all her earnest gentleness in her
face. For the same line of pilgrimage is travelled twice,
and our summoning of figures must have comprehended
all whom we have ever seen upon the way. The date of
the travelling is not paramount with us ; nor, indeed, is
travelling itself quite indispensable to a claim upon our
attention.

And just here we may take breath in our classifyings
till we have adjusted our perceptions a little as to the
diversity of the contents of this remarkable gathering.
There are those before us whom we must account to be
pilgrims, and there are manifestly those whom we cannot
account to be such. Among the pilgrims themselves, there
are those whom we recognise to be true and good, and
there are those whom we cannot but reckon to be false
or evil. Among the true, our eye falls upon a notable
number who are weak although they are good, as well as

upon a few who are both good and strong. And hovering in the background all the while, neither pressing for acknowledgment nor altogether evading it, are a scattered company of pilgrims—and, indeed, of others too—whom we have only heard of by report, and have not with our own eyes seen upon the Pilgrimage.

Then, when we pass beyond this great order of the actual pilgrims, we find diversity still prevailing. Here, again, we have the good and the evil, which is the dominating division everywhere. Among the good, some we can distinguish as Helpers; and of these, one or two are about upon the Pilgrimage, while the others are resident, and at least two of them may be more specially described as Hosts. Among the evil, some we can best designate as Deceivers, others we must regard as open Enemies; nor need we overlook a class who are not strictly either, since they continued to be dwellers in the aboriginal city. And complicating somewhat this untravelling order, we are brought face to face with a distinction between the human and the superhuman—even between both and the Divine; and the complication is nothing cleared when we recognise that there are human characters who are indubitably and merely human, and human characters who seem scarcely more than allegorically so.

This arranging of things, however, rudimental as it is, has brought some aid to us in our work of assortment into manageable categories. It is now easy to call forth from the assemblage a category of pilgrims who are efficient men, reminding us of those who are already standing apart in their places of honour; and it is not difficult to summon *Honest*, and *Valiant-for-truth*, and *Standfast*, to form it. Next we may look for the weaker pilgrims, when a group of some interest begins to gather—*Feeble-mind*, *Ready-to-halt*, *Despondency* and his daughter, with the more shadowy forms of *Little-faith* and *Fearing*. Then a numerous and noble category claims to be brought together . it is that of the Helpers of pilgrims.   In the front of these stand *Evangelist* and *Great-heart,* each of them in trim to travel.   Near them is clustered a group who have come forth from their blessed dwellings of help, bringing an air of mingled gravity and beauty to their gathered company : they are *Good-will* and *The Interpreter,* with the *Ladies of the Palace,* and the *Shepherds* of the happy Mountains, and the *Gardener* of the land of maturity.   At the side of these *Gaius* is greeting his brother-host *Mnason,* who shall soon introduce him to those friends of his who are visible behind him.   Less conspicuous in the shadow, but not unworthy of our regard, we observe *Sagacity,* and can make out *Tell-true.*   Clearer to the eye than these, unless when they dazzle us with unearthly light, are a varied company, among whom we recognise *Help,* and the *Three Shining Ones,* and *Secret,* and the *Reliever,* and *Skill,* and *Great-grace* with his son ; also, perhaps especially here, we look upon ONE incomparably supreme among all others, ever adorable, ever blessed, Whose wondrous condescension, when He comes upon the way with personality unenveiled, must move us only to silent reverence.

We have now before us the entire population of the twice-travelled Pilgrimage that are true and good.   But this is only the smaller half of the People : the larger half are untrue and evil.   We must brace ourselves therefore to fill up less attractive categories, and may begin with those who are False Pilgrims.   As we seek about for these, the crowd that masses itself is surprisingly great, but many of its individuals are little more than distinguishable by us in their motley obscurity.   Into the front come *Talkative* and *Ignorance,* and close behind them the generation of *By-ends* and his clique, with glimpses of that gentleman's kindred.   At their hand we discern such brotherhoods as that of *Simple, Sloth,* and *Presumption,*

of *Formalist* and *Hypocrisy*, of *Timorous* and *Mistrust ;*
and we are faintly sensible of several separate figures in the
rear of these, among whom we can reckon upon *Self-will*,
and *Not-right*, and *Vain-confidence*, and *Turn-away*, and
two *Heedlesses*, with *Brisk* giving himself airs in the nearer
neighbourhood. Meanwhile a group is jostling itself into
its place—not pilgrims of any kind, since they have come
from the city where " Graceless " dwelt : of these *Obstinate*
and *Pliable* are the chief, and a little crowd of women are
claiming the unhappy right of their protection. Still less
cheerful work remains to us as we muster before us the
Deceivers of the Pilgrimage, headed by *Worldly-wiseman*
and his confederates, and filled up by *Atheist*, *Demas*, the
Flatterer, and such shapes as *Wanton, Adam the First,
Discontent, Shame*, and the notable *Madame Bubble.*
From these we boldly proceed to marshall the undisguised
Enemies of pilgrims, when a portentous aggregation of
hideousness gathers to us at the names of *Apollyon* (whose
names and forms are various), and the many *Men of
Vanity*, and the gigantic company which includes *Despair*
and *Diffidence, Grim Bloodyman*, and *Maul*, and *Slay-good*,
with the ambiguous *Monster* who in the latter days made
havoc in the city of the Fair, and *Pope*, and the hovering
shade of *Pagan :* nor must these overshadow out of sight
the more ordinary bulk of such miscreants as *Faint-heart*,
and *Mistrust* the second, and *Guilt*, or the *Two Ill-favoured*,
or the other gang whom we know as *Wild-head* and
Inconsiderate and *Pragmatic.* And then the gathering is
complete.

As we now look forth upon the aggregate of personalities
who are thus classified for our closer acquaintance, it
becomes clear that they do not all of them claim our
attention with the same urgency. There are not many of
them, it is true, whom we should feel it easy altogether to
dismiss from our further consideration ; but there are

many, at least within the order of non-pilgrims, who cannot well demand of us any prolonged notice, unless that notice is to be more of a critical than of a practical kind. While, however, we are unwilling to acknowledge any imperative that would deter us from looking critically at these creations of Bunyan's, it is yet our purpose that the practical should predominate in our study of them. Plainly, therefore, the best part of our attention shall be invited by the order of pilgrims—by those to whom the book assigns the vocation of travelling towards the heavenly City. These, at least, are men and women of flesh and blood as we ourselves are, and this vocation of theirs is the vocation of many of us, as, in its true pursuit, it had need to be the vocation of us all. The importance to us of any non-pilgrim character himself is nearly altogether determined by the place he takes in working prosperity or adversity to those who are set upon pilgrimage. On the side by which we approach the book, if not on every side, it is pre-eminently a book of pilgrims.

A book of pilgrims; but, above all, of true pilgrims. The true alone are normal there: the false are abnormal. They are more; they are almost an awkward element, very nearly an impertinent intrusion, in the story. The Allegory is immensely enriched by their presence, in respect both of instruction and of interest; nevertheless, the Allegory is somewhat strained to admit them at all. Strictly regarded, this road that conducts to heaven,—a road which is essentially a spiritual one,—never feels the foot of a pilgrim who is not made a pilgrim by a renewal of his will and heart. But the Allegory must permit the true pilgrims to have the possibility of meeting untrue pilgrims on that road, "straight" and specially constructed though it be, else there is left no possibility of their meeting them at all— save by their leaving it; and that is a device which Bunyan feels he must very sparingly employ. And we have reason to congratulate ourselves, that in this matter, as in others, Bunyan did not allow the Allegory to fetter him further than was consistent with a generous and natural treatment of his theme. For the false pilgrims, who really exceed in mere number the true pilgrims themselves,—as truth demanded then, and might still demand,—give us not only the artistic effects, but the ethical insight and the practical guidance, which only contrast can afford us. The differences which prevail among the true pilgrims, indeed, are themselves great; but these differences appear rather those of comparison than of contrast, the moment we introduce pilgrims who are false. And the differences among the false pilgrims are even greater than those among the true,—as if Bunyan had designed to indicate to us, that there is a wider range of variety within the class of mere professors of Christianity than there is within the class of genuine Christians, and that the unrestrained scope of motives which false religiousness permits is sufficient to create a diversity which is happily impossible within the holy confines of the "liberty of the sons of God."

While, therefore, we should be shutting from ourselves a great part of the treasure which this book holds for us, were we not to bestow our study upon at least the principal figures among the pilgrims who are only false ones, it still appears that the true-hearted pilgrims must take the first place in our attention, as they have the first in our esteem. And among these the largest share of our consideration is undoubtedly due to the prime *persona* of the book—to him whose history the First Part is, and whose history the Second Part still reflects and celebrates—to "the pilgrim" (so Great-heart calls him), the man whose name among men for two centuries has been, and for all centuries to come shall continue to be, "Christian"—the most picturesque symbol of the whole contents of the word which has ever been given to human keeping. It is with him that the genius of the

Dreamer is mainly, and most fondly, engaged. Any other character is most of all for him : even the figures which stir so freshly in the Second Part are only those of his long-left family and their friends, and many of them are friends of his own. The book, through all its rich variety, is still the story of the life of Christian and his family, as distinguished from that of Graceless and his. And Bunyan loves the man, and feels the task of his story upon him. He writes like one who is entrusted with the biography of a friend, and who is making faithful use of the materials which have come to his hand fragrant with the living memories of one departed. The man is real to him, and therefore he has made the man real to us. That man went that way—we know, till we correct our fancy by cold rationality. He has had as real an existence to many as any one of the family-ancestors whose names and features they bore. We go with him to the end, and we have a sense of bereavement when he passes out of our sight. There are not a few of us who shall almost look for him in heaven, that we may tell him of our sad interest in all that he endured, and of our satisfaction in all that he accomplished, and of our thankful content that he is folded safe, with staff and armour laid away, within the City of his King. We shall see him ; but he shall be many—"a great multitude whom no man can number, out of every nation, and of all tribes and peoples and tongues."[1]

In a general way, the superior claim which the purely pilgrim order has upon us, as distinguished from all the other various *personæ* of the book, may be stated as consisting in this—that it is they who are the real characters, the actual presentations of character in its manifold phases of false or true religious life. Yet this statement of the case admits of some modification. We bethink us of the Helpers of the pilgrimage—some of whom are men and

---

[1] Note F.

women—are indeed pilgrims, and most true ones, according to the deeper laws of the book, although they are not pilgrims according to the laws of its outer machinery. They are pilgrims whose function it is to hover or abide about the road for the sake of the more ordinary way-farers—pilgrims mostly of surpassing efficiency, like Evangelist and Great-heart, who are entrusted by the King with generous service, and are doubtless reserved for generous reward. They will somehow reach the heavenly City, notwithstanding that the story permits but few of them to approach it very near, since it is in the earlier stages most of all that their services are needed. They are men of Beulah whose spirits only are dwelling there while their busy feet are distant. It is another of those frequent instances which almost tempt us to say, that great part of the wealthy truthfulness of the Allegory is begotten of its departures from strict allegorical consistency.

But this mere attitude of outlook—it is not one to be prolonged, and least of all when it has revealed to us that much ground lies before us to be traversed. Yet as we disperse our several groups about the way again, and gird ourselves for moving somewhat freely to and fro along that line of pilgrimage which they so enliven, it will not impede our purpose if we look once more at the throng as they retire, that we may mark how much those figures are truly and wholly characters, and not by any means caricatures. The earnest religious aim of the author secures that they are this. It comes back upon us as something almost singular in this species of literature, that he is painting in the interests of truth, and not of amusement, and that, when he does amuse, it is by means of the truth, and for the truth's sake. The same can be said of but few books of character. In great part they are but books of carica-ture, in which the determination is predominant that the reader shall at any rate be amused; wherefore it is but

the harder for some of us to get much amusement from
them. Excesses, defects, foibles, are projected in such
obtrusive boldness of relief, that proportion and perspective are sacrificed, and sometimes very laboriously, to
provoke at all hazards a sense of the ludicrous. The
pictures are to the life, and more—as much more as is
needed to draw forth the coveted smile, or to move the
enchanting laughter of the reader. Unfortunately, it is in
professed books of character that this exaggerating of
features is perhaps most usual, as it is at least in these
that the fault is most deliberate. It disappoints us in
the thirty sketches of the Greek Theophrastus, whose
characters, besides, are all of them vicious ; and it impairs
the value of those of the French La Bruyère, who first
translated, and then surpassed, his Greek master ; while it
stands as an abiding blemish upon those of the English
Overbury, and Earle, and Butler, who have much of the
Frenchman's vigour of handling, if little of his delicacy of
touch. But, indeed, if we except the powerful presentations of character, by deed and dialogue, which abound in
the more serious dramas of ancient and modern times,
pre-eminently in those of Shakespeare,—and if we except,
as we readily do, an occasional figure in our first-rate
works of fiction,—there is not very much of soberly
truthful delineation of character in existing literature.
Even in the work of such masters of character-drawing as
Molière, and Schiller, and Goethe, and Holberg,[1] there is
not seldom a one-sidedness which suggests insufficiency of
moral conviction, or slenderness of moral purpose. And
in these qualities our homely Bunyan was sufficient and
strong.

The three Englishmen whom we have named—Overbury, Earle, and Butler, each of them a clever pen-and-ink
draughtsman of character after his own manner—were

[1] See Martensen's "Christian Ethics (Individual)," Section 26.

filling their portfolios with their sketches during the same age of sharp individuality in which Bunyan was filling his humbler portfolio with his. The fact almost compels us to comparison, within such limits as are fair and just. For Bunyan is not making detached portraits, nor have these three contemporaries of his the surroundings of narrative to give their pictures atmosphere and bearing and breadth of light. But not many will question that the superiority remains with Bunyan, if we confine our comparison to truthfulness and fulness of drawing, or to lively permanence of interest. Bunyan's characters are satisfying without excess. They are to the life, and no more. He holds himself free from the elegant drudgery of entertaining for its own sake, even at the expense of fidelity; and in reward for his loyalty first and most to truth, she herself becomes our entertainer in his hands. We are amused without ridicule, and satire itself has its strength from verity. We admire worth, and we despise worthlessness, but only as a healthy moral nature must admire or despise them in an actual world of immortal men.

TRUE PILGRIMS.

TRUE PILGRIMS.

III.

CHRISTIAN : HIS BOOK—HIS CONSCIENCE—HIS MORAL
EARNESTNESS.

IF there be a plot in the " Pilgrim's Progress," then the
hero of it is Christian. The progress is his. We shall not
say he is the greatest character in the book ; but he is the
typical one, and the one to whom all the other characters
are only accessory, whatsoever be their own attractiveness
or strength. This is directly so in the First Part ; and it is
so, by implication, even in the Second.

Should it happen to occur to us, however, as unpromising, in view of the large measure of attention we propose to
bestow upon this character, that the character is only after
all an average one, it is obvious to reflect that this is one
of its strongest recommendations to our sympathy and
study. Are we not, most of us, average people? And is
not, in truth, the average, as Christian represents it, an
average high enough to leave to many of us some room for
our own aspiration? Yet it is well that the average is not
pitched so high as to render our aspirations hopeless.
Indeed, here on the threshhold of our meditations upon
the characters of this book, it meets us as an evidence of
admirable wisdom that the " Christian " so called, and so
signified, is not a prodigy of grace, nor a marvel of one or
two gigantic virtues, but is a man of well-mingled and well-
balanced ordinariness—fulfilling his part nobly withal, but
just as any of us may be rightfully expected to fulfil our
own.

At this point we are touching a question of some importance to our subject.   Is the "Pilgrim," at least in the character and history of Christian, a book of autobiography? How far is the figure of Christian but the figure of Bunyan himself projected in allegory?   Not so far, perhaps, as some have been disposed to find.   Our author had already penned a vigorous account of his spiritual history, and the "Pilgrim," it need scarcely be said, is far more than "Grace Abounding" clothed in allegorical dress.   Bunyan knew both his art and his theme too well to make it only this.   Diligence will naturally enough be rewarded by detecting coincidences in history, and correspondences in character, as it ponders the two books side by side.   But, at the most, the "Pilgrim" is "Grace Abounding" generalised, mellowed, altered.   Lights and shadows of the real history do fall across the allegorical one; but they are shortened or lengthened, lightened or deepened, and transposed with the freedom of art and truth, in order to compose the picture which his purpose demanded.   That picture was a picture of the Christian, and not of Bunyan the Christian: still less was it the picture of Bunyan the un-Christian; though it is this which the earlier book, happily for us, takes up one-third of its pages in describing. "Grace Abounding" is experience alone; the "Pilgrim" is observation interpreted and vivified by experience. Christian is representative of the Christian man as Bunyan knew him; we have only need to consider, that the Christian man he knew best was himself.   This is sufficient to account for the fact, that Christian is more like Bunyan than any other character is; and it serves to explain a special complexion in the picture of him, even an occasional exaggeration of incident in his history, which is less generic than it is personal to the author, whose experience in these respects was apparently more exceptional than he quite realised.   Yet this personal element in the delineation, which could not be altogether suppressed, and in its due measure and function is one of the powers of the book, does not by any means bulk so largely in the " Pilgrim " as we might have anticipated. If Christian is an ordinary Christian, Bunyan was not an ordinary one. To be truthfully representative, he had to create a typical character who was lower in stature, and feebler in make, than himself. Consciously or unconsciously, he has done so. In the name of ordinary Christian fact, he has displayed a candour in his delineation—a faithfulness in depicting faults, and failures, and weaknesses—which brings into lives like our own a breath at once of truth and of consolation ; and he has done this with such an air of brotherhood with us, that we may be ready to forget how much the imperfections, as imperfections of the Christian, are rather our own than his.

Accepting the book, then, as on the whole a normal spiritual biography, it is noticeable that we have scarcely a hint of the kind of life which this man had been living in that city of doom—whether it was worse than that of his neighbours, or better. This silence not only gives a sharpness to the opening of the narrative as professedly a narrative of pilgrimage, but it leaves the main fact to press the mind of the reader with its full weight—the simple fact, that he was dwelling here at all. The question of locality transcends all questions of behaviour, as long as the man is content to be a citizen of that city.

The first glimpse we get of the man, therefore, is a glimpse of one who is already ceasing to be a citizen. He is not so much dwelling in the place as leaving it. His attachments to it are being strained to the point of snapping. We see him hovering about the outskirts of the city —ragged, burdened, restless, tearful, afraid—his heart not in the city, but in his " book "—his thoughts not on the present, but on the future—his interest drawn off from community and household, and concentrated most of all upon himself. His disorder is too profound and too far-reaching to be soothed by common appliances. Judgment is in the air : he has been already too long in that region. "What shall he do?"—"What shall he do to be saved?" His perplexity is gradually narrowing its scope, but is only deepening its intensity. A little more of this intensifying, and he has torn himself away from his home and family because those he loves best are minded to abide in the city—has quitted the place with strong intent to go some-whither, if only he knew what direction it were safe and right to take.

Without question, what we have most to note in this first sight we get of Christian—what the eye may fix upon as the most efficient and the most characteristic thing which meets it—is that BOOK which he is holding in his hand. When we are looking for the forces which have given shape to character, we shall do ill to pass lightly the influence that may have been wielded over it by books. One powerful book, if it be permitted to sustain a living contact with the mind, will enduringly colour a man's life, if it do not even determine its entire direction and form. Let the power of such a book be a power of truth and wholesomeness, and its beneficent efficacy will go on with a man like an angel of happy guiding. It is in deep harmony with this, that the Christian religion, from its first daybreak in history, and not less from its earliest dawn in the individual spirit, is inseparably associated with "a book." Christian is a reader from the first moment we see him, and before he is yet entitled to his name. All his disquietude—all that distinguishes him as he comes before us—is the result of reading and thought, and of reading and thought of which this Book is the object. He is permitting the power of the Book to touch him, and it is grasping him as we see. Its plain great affirmations are being realised, and are striking his moral nature with the effect of fresh tidings which concern him as nothing has ever concerned him. In view of these, he is bound, as being the reasonable man that God has made him, to set about an absolute change of life—indistinctly and perplexedly it may at first be, yet resolutely and without delay.

For, as every strong book is sensibly a book and more —is a book and its author,—so it is transcendently with this book of Christian's. The man is in contact with eternal Holiness and eternal Might, not yet seen to be eternal Love. It is the Author, rather than the Book, that is at work with him. The Book is but a voice, and the voice is filling his ear with the vast echoes of infinitudes, that seem to have left their far-off serenities, and to have become personal to himself, and urgently near. He is awakening to what he himself is—unholy and immortal : he is awakening to what God is—holy and supreme. The great Book is only fulfilling its function : its infinite Author and its sinful reader are meeting together over it. We will not wonder that so sovereign a Book was seldom afterwards very far from this man's hands. It is little to say, that among all books it stands alone. It is not much to affirm, that its power rises peerless in the midst of all book-power that ever has been. We may dispute about the circumstantial matters of the Book ; we may disagree concerning methods and authorships and dates and interpretations ; we may mistake the truest friends of the Book for its enemies, and may think we feel the stability of its revelation trembling because our own knees are feeble. All the while, the essential potency of the Book abides, untroubled and unstayed—is still calmly working, blessedly conquering ; and one thing at least is ever going further off from the range of legitimate dispute: it is this,—that the human spirit who commits himself to the influence of that Book, believing it to be God's, shall meet abundant proof in his own life and character that his belief has not deceived him.

It may be felt as if this first impression we get of Christian, tenacious as first impressions are found to be, were not on the whole a very auspicious one for a hero. Perplexity is not dignified. Tears are not heroic. Fears, most of all, are little fitted to command our respect. But let us not be too superficial, lest we be unfair to the character of this man as he starts into our acquaintance here. His trouble goes deep; and it is deeply reasonable, howsoever we may imagine that his reason is the one faculty which is least in operation with him. For his trouble is a moral one—is *the* moral one—and touches the entire range of his nature and destiny as a man. By the discovery he has made, he is guilty—has been wrong, and has been doing wrong, throughout the whole of his past, under the eye of a judge, and beneath the impending arm of law. The judge is omnipotent, and the law is eternal. It is the CONSCIENCE of the man—a most manly faculty as well as a most puissant energy—that is on its feet within him. "Conscience does make cowards of us all:" it may therefore be permitted for a while to make a coward even of Christian. For this cowardice—let us call it so—is the noblest sentiment of which the man's condition admits. He has been living in wrongness, and he is now in throes of solicitude how to direct his way to perpetual rightness. It is just what is unmanly and mean that is sinking out of his life as he comes before us: it is just greatness of soul that is struggling into dawn. The tears and fears belong to the terribleness of the situation as he is beginning to know it, and not to the weakness of the man. Moral eyesight cleared, and moral sensibility quickened,—these bring him consciously in front of verities which must overpower any man, if he be not less than a man, or more. He is letting his Conscience have its way; and we see that he is courageous and resolute enough—with his rending of attachments, and his adventuring on untried paths in the teeth of entreaties and enticements and scorn—to go at once whither Conscience impels him. That is the only form of magnanimity which his past and his present have left to him; and we have to allow its full significance to the fact, that this first glimpse we get of him is a glimpse, above all, of intensest earnestness to have his destiny and his life set right, because he has made certain that both are radically unsound, and therefore insecure.

Now, these traits, in the deeper lines of them, are not transient in this man, but permanent. We see only the first of them here, and not the last. This sway of Conscience shall distinguish the character, and regulate the conduct, of Christian till that journey has closed which now he knows so little how to begin. It is Christianity under its purely ethical impulsion, and controlled by its strictly theological facts—Christianity short of its distinctive and crowning verities, which are the "god-spell" of still higher ethical law. It is the original motive-power of religion simply as such, and therefore of every form of religion which can sustain any pretension to the name. But the religion of Christian has a way of its own in dealing with this ineradicable element in the man as it finds him. Other religions are content if they only appease it, get it to sleep, and to sleep in the dark; for light disturbs it in its slumbers. It is the glory of Christianity, and a remarkable evidence of its supernal source, that it does not flinch from dealing with Conscience as awake—nay, insists upon keeping it awake, upon nursing it into healthy tenderness under the full sunlight, upon taking it as an intelligent guide and cheerful ally along every step of a man's way through time into eternity. Does not this straightgoing ethical fearlessness—this masterful inexorableness which will grip its way down to the granite of our being that it may set its foundations plumb upon the everlasting rock,—does it not prepare us for the conclusion, that the Author of the Conscience and the Author of Christianity are one? But if it be possible still to doubt with only this before us, doubt must surely melt away in presence of the result by which this searching thoroughness is crowned—crowned within the consciousness which resigns itself to the Christian method of rectifying moral unrest. This one Author, preserving the dominance of Conscience intact at the level at which He finds it, sets over it, at a higher level still, a principle which dominates Conscience itself, but dominates it in the way of utmost harmony. The righteousness which Conscience desiderates, which it lives and moves to demand—*that He brings*, as something fulfilled by none other than Himself, and with all the overflowing sufficiency which this ensures. Wherefore it comes to pass that Conscience, relieved from the pressure of bygone misdeeds by a just forgiveness, goes forward as a party in all the subsequent issues—goes forward no less open-eyed, at the least, than ever it was, but only watching henceforth, with fondest interest, how this righteousness, at first for the most part objective, is gradually wrought as a subjective restoration into the spiritual fibre of the man under his new and magnificent conditions.

This starting pilgrim, then, constrained as he is to yield himself and his life once for all to the dominion of the moral sense within him, finds that dominion to be a somewhat pitiless one in the earlier period of its conceded sway. It is no happy condition in which Evangelist discovers him upon that suburban plain. But from the moment at which Evangelist introduces for him the new

element of ongoing and aim,—" Flee "—to yonder wicket-
gate which he can see by its glow of pure light,—the
man not only becomes a pilgrim, but is making for sure
rightening and relief.

The most persistent symbol of Conscience in this first
stage is the " burden "—a simple but picturesque emblem
of a sense of guilt. It is on him, though behind him; it
is oppressive, though it leaves his limbs all free for
action or advance; it is rather felt than seen. Somewhat
characteristic it is of Christian that this burden of his is
" great." When Pliable in his light-going eagerness would
hurry him on, " he cannot go so fast as he would, by reason
of this burden that is on his back." When they were both
plunging in the Slough, Christian " began to sink " because
of it. He touches the more literal aspect of the case when
he tells Help, out of the midst of the mire, that "fear followed him so hard that he fled the next (the nearest) way,
and fell in." Worldly-wiseman, looking more phenomenally upon the affair, remarks his " laborious going," and
twits him on his " burdened manner,"—constructing, too,
his whole seducement upon the just assumption that the
burden is by all means a thing to be got rid of. Christian
lets forth upon this stranger a flash of candid manliness
when he tells him that the burden is "more terrible to him "
than all the dangers and discomforts that may be flaunted
before him as awaiting him on his way. He very precisely
" knows what he would obtain," only he yields to make
trial of obtaining it by a method that is human, forsaking
the method that is Divine. " By that hill you must go,"
said the man of the world; and by that hill he went. " The
burden now seemed heavier." It was a place of threatening cliffs, of scorching fire-gleams, of sweat and quaking.
" Words of fire " came forth from the deep cavern-throats of
the mountain; and even in his contrition before Evangelist
he still "looked for nothing but death." Plainly, the

human plan did not meet the case. He resumes his way, bitterly instructed, to the Wicket-gate. "Here," says he to Good-will, ere the gate is opened —" Here is a *burdened* sinner;" and before he set forth upon his journey by the way that was "straight and narrow," "he asked him if he could not help him off with his *burden.*" He is content to be assured that by-and-bye it shall fall from him, and he shall go free. For if it be characteristic of Christian that this burden of his is "great," it is also characteristic of him that the burden remains with him for no small part of his really pilgrim way. The sense of guilt clings to him, and the spot and hour of relief are postponed. He has still his burden on him when he is following the wise Interpreter from scene to scene in that academy of superbest philosophy. Nor did that philosophy leave out of account the faculty which felt the burden. The parlour full of dust, which only the sprinkled water of God's Gospel prevails to make cleansable—the frightful spectacle of the man of Despair in his cage of iron—the awful narrative of the shuddering Dreamer of the Judgment,—these were impressive lessons in the science of Conscience, shedding more copious sun-shafts of intelligence into the moral instinct which impelled him. And when he had left all this, and was going forward along the way between the walls of salvation,—" up that way did *burdened* Christian run, but not without great difficulty, because of the *load* on his back."

That load, at last, was soon to be no longer his. Conscience was to pass out of this earlier stage ere his running had well ceased. So sure is the man to arrive at peace of Conscience who keeps to God's appointed path—the moment that God knows it to be best. It was the realising of a fact which cut the strings of this soul-burden—rather still the realising of a Person concerning whom the fact spake unutterable things. A Cross upon which One had hung—a yawning sepulchre-pit hard by,—-these stood right in his way while he was thus hasting on. "Just as Christian came up with the Cross, his burden *loosed* from off his shoulders, and *fell* from off his back, and *began* to tumble, and so *continued* to do till it came to the mouth of the sepulchre, where it *fell in ;* and I," says the Dreamer, " *saw it no more.* Then was Christian glad and *lightsome.*" Is it not the successive chapters of a volume compressed into a sentence,—-even as the fact is a lifetime compressed into an hour ? It is the hour of the triumph of Conscience ; and the triumph is threefold : it is a triumph of God, as guiding Conscience ; it is a triumph of Conscience as God-guided ; it is a triumph of the man as having submitted himself to the guidance of a God-guided Conscience. Nothing outside of the man had changed. The plan of God's salvation had only broken upon his mind in the heart-moving radiance of its grand simplicity. Now he saw what before he only knew ; now he felt what before he only believed. He " came up with " God's mind about himself and his sin —"came up with " God's heart concerning both,— let in the flood of the Divine purpose upon his whole being,— took to himself that Divine-human Saviour, and that sin-bearing work of His, with all the affection for himself that they so amazingly signalised. Henceforward, gratitude and love poured themselves around his Conscience ; and the ethical impulse resolved itself into the obedience of Christ, his endeared and stupendous Friend. Sense of guilt faded away into sense of undeservingness, which yet was taking hold of splendid inheritances of affinity with the Man of the Ages. Consciously, he was " made the right-eousness of God in Him."

As we might well expect, the vision of this supreme hour, the vividness of which was almost as characteristic as its delay, lingered in the heart of Christian like a shekinah, holding about him a perception of Divine friendliness, and shedding through him a tender regard to the Divine will. This on the whole, and this as his prevailing condition. But he was still imperfect. Conscience, modified and enriched as now it was, could not afford to lay down its sceptre or unbuckle its sword, or abdicate one jot of its lofty function. His moral nature, no longer burden-ridden, was more active and articulate than before. Its motives, which had been changing into new and greater ones, were now deepened and steadied in their force. Duty—duty to Christ—self-abandoning service of Christ—the pleasing of the higher self through the pleasing of Christ,—this was the platform of ethics to which he had clearly arrived. As a rule he kept to that platform,—sometimes on its more elevated levels; oftener, perhaps, on its lower levels. But now and again, for an unhappy season, he even slipped from it wholly; and then, the tenderness of Conscience, which made its smile the sweeter when he did well, made its frown the darker when he did ill. And always, now, there was the element of a personalized disloyalty and ingratitude which sharpened the fangs of self-blame.

In all the after-journey of Christian, then, we find him holding himself under correction of his emancipated moral faculty. To trace the influence of this faculty throughout, would be to track every step of his way; for it was at work always, and at work when it gave no view of itself above the surface. It was not absent even when feeling was the more immediate propelling power;—as when, in the sheltered hollow which he reached only a little way past the Cross, he came upon the three fettered sleepers, and failed in his efforts to arouse them: it went with the current of that endeavour; and it gave compensation, by its glow of approval, for the dull disappointment with which the endeavour was chilled. It entered where the intellect might be thought to be mainly engaged;—as when, in the interview which followed with the two who had "come tumbling over the wall," he stood upon the steadfast consideration—"I walk by the rule of my Master." It appears more fully still when duty must take the form of resistance, and wayfaring must pause for conflict;—as when Apollyon strode down upon him in the Valley of Humiliation, and he was put upon his mettle to make good his liberty as now a servant of the better King. Not less is it present when action must suspend itself, and faith, and patience, and hope, must become the work of the hour; — as in the Valley of the Shadow, and in the city of Vanity. It is very visible in his general dissatisfaction with his spiritual attainment;—as when he admits to Prudence that he has "borne away some of the things" out of the old life "greatly against his will," and that he is "weary of his inward sickness." Its more morbid states are figured in Apollyon's catalogue of misdeeds and blunders; and its recuperative energy no less in the masterly stroke of evangelical logic by which Christian shivers the catalogue to atoms.

But it is in periods of wrong-going, and most of all when the wrong-going took rise in his own will alone, that the undiminished sway of Conscience is best perceived. There is more in Christian's mind than the sense of hazard and loss when, for instance, he goes weeping back to the Arbour, while the sun is getting low, in search of his roll of citizenship. · So, when he has prevailed upon his companion to get over the stile into By-path Meadow with him, there is a rain-storm within his breast, comprising other feelings than fear, which goes out to meet the black night and the rising floods around them, and the thunder-riven heavens overhead. So, also, when the irresistible Giant bestirs them in the morning while they are asleep upon his grounds, and herds them before him to his Castle, they "had little to say, for they knew themselves in a fault"; and when they are shut up with their own thoughts in that dungeon of abominable darkness, Christian has "double sorrow" on account of the self-reproach which crushes in upon his spirit. Nor is this at all the morbid judgment of a mood that is passing: it will survive the circumstances, and will bear the revision of calm moments hereafter;—as we see while we stand with them on the Delectable Mountain called Caution, and gaze far down with them upon the eyeless men who are groping for ever there among the tombs, and hear the Shepherds tell, that these are men who climbed over a certain stile into the territory of one Despair, who made them to be thus :—they "looked upon one another with tears gushing out." And if, none the less, they forget ere long the counsels and the way-map of the Shepherds, and go meandering after the Flatterer till they get fastened in his net, Christian will say, "Now do I see myself in an error"; and the whip of the Shining One will be almost welcome to him ere again he goes forward, more "softly," upon his true pilgrimage. Ay, even in the bridgeless River itself,—after abiding for a while in the country of Beulah, where there was "abundance of what they had sought for in all their journey," and among those things a most peaceful companionship of Conscience,—this same Christian, in an interval of weakness, with the moral balance disturbed in him by the loss of a consciousness of the Friend he saw upon the Cross, will seem to be suffocating under "thoughts of the sins that he had committed both before and since he began to be a pilgrim," until the sight of the Crucified One hastens back to lift up his head, and to firm his footsteps with something of triumph.

A man of Conscience, then, was this Christian. He judged it wise and well to find the fast friendship of this incorruptible friend within him, and to keep that friendship when he had found it. This was no scrupulous or fantastic principle of living; it was much rather the principle which a man is made to live by, as a clock is made to beat its tiny march to the great footfall of Time by the regulative time-principle which is incorporated in its structure.   Men will sneer at the punctiliousness of a man who goes by his Conscience; they do not sneer at the punctiliousness of their watch when it goes by its structural controllings, which themselves go by the sun.   To go right is a characteristic as invaluable in a man as it is in a time-piece; but a man, to go right, must also abide by the peculiar potential energy of regulation that has been given him.   And the principle of the Eternal Will is how much more than the principle of Time is !

It is almost a common-place to say, that the width of the interval by which a man has lapsed from his true nature may be accurately gauged by the amount of disregard he manifests for the guidance of his Conscience.   Is not the lapse, then, very notably great in many?   How seldom are we refreshed by meeting a man who desires even to have the darkness and rubbish heaved off from the face of his Conscience, that it may breathe and speak as the monitor of his existence !   How much of a rarity is it to alight upon a man who has set it before him as a life-task to educate his Conscience, and to give fair and full play to its grand capabilities !   Is there more than one in a thousand who has quite made up his mind to follow only, and to follow always, whither his Conscience leads?   A Conscience easily offended, yet void of offence,—it is almost a curiosity in the crowding world of men.   A Conscience well-nigh brutalised by ill-usage,—degraded to follow rather than to lead—to follow, snarling and snapping, at the heel, till it becomes maddened by some surpassing affront, and springs in its strong fury upon the man in the bulk of him, and throws him trembling beneath the astounding momentum of his own moral self ;—that is not so unwonted a sight on the highways of the world.   And far more frequent still is the alternate starving and drugging of this royal faculty, until it sinks into a precarious imbecility, from which it may well be set free when earthly conditions have been ruptured. This is all palpably wrong, in every degree of it—wrong, even to monstrousness. Indeed, there are few but know it is wrong. For the worst of men, when they drive aside for a moment the nonsense by which they cajole themselves, and for that moment look at the great facts of things in simple seriousness, do not fail to acknowledge, at least in their own bosoms, that if you must come to real earnest truth about this existence of ours, Conscience is that which a man is bound to respect in all things.

In unchristian lands there have always been consciences, known to the All-knowing, which somehow had risen above that point of rudeness at which their religious systems could any longer satisfy them. It is a spiritual predicament which must deeply move our interest and our sympathy. It would seem as if their life must henceforth be a struggling in the moral vacuum which it is the design of Christianity to fill. Toiling beneath the burden—shedding the tears—going down in the Slough,—without a Wicket-gate and without a Cross! In the absence of a human Evangelist, we shall hope that they lifted up their eyes and saw the Divine Help. But Christian peoples—(we concede the name),—is it not marvellous, that so few men and women of them have risen to any appreciation of the advantage they enjoy, as living beneath the smile of a religious system like ours—a system which permits the cultivation of Conscience to any degree of enlightened refinement, yet makes haste to open its arms, in the plenitude of its Divine suitableness, when a man finds that his conscience has pushed forth beyond all satisfaction with the delusions that have been mocking it hitherto? And is it not even more marvellous, that the Divine Spirit should be often urging men towards that Divine suitableness, and they only stir around the suburbs of the deadly city, or turn in with the knaves who keep house in the neighbourhood of the hill of lightnings? And is it not most marvellous of all, that pilgrims themselves, so unlike the Christian of our story, should sometimes covet but little what our hero calls "the content of a good conscience,"—that they should pass the Wicket-gate and the Cross, and go on to feel as if they were now in some sense done with Conscience,—that they should mortify, not the flesh, but the faculty of everlasting rectitude in them, and of rectitude made so touchingly sacred by the holy agony and the sin-hating love of their Divine Restorer? They are mortifying as they can the very life of their spirit. They are pilgrims without progress—as long as this flaccid habit of soul is on them. *Are* they pilgrims? They had some need to see to it. Might it not be, that they should save time, and perhaps a very great deal besides, if for a space their progress were to be backwards—back to the Cross—back to the Wicket-gate itself,—that they may begin to do with thoroughness, and with a regenerated tenderness of moral touch, what they are now doing with so perilous insufficiency and obtuseness! This book knows of genuine pilgrims that are weak in faith, or weak in courage, or weak in hope; but it knows of none that are weak in moral feeling.

We have lingered thus long upon that characteristic of Bunyan's hero from which we now pass, because our two centuries of advancement have not carried us beyond the danger of forgetting how tenaciously Christianity takes up the moral into the spiritual, and takes it on with it through all progress which has eternal felicity for its goal. This matter of Conscience, too, has points of living contact with the whole circumference of Christian character. It can be regarded as the root of much, and it lies hard by the root of nearly everything. The grasp of Conscience may not lay hold directly of the heart of a man ; yet, like the grasp

which the angel took of the hand of Lot, it takes the whole
man with it, using a gentle force which does the double
work of guiding and of urging—of guiding onwards and
of urging on. For Conscience is not being allowed its
entire function if it only regulates, and does not also impel.
The propeller works very close to the rudder: in spiritual
navigation they work according to the ideal when they
work as one blended force. Hence we find in Christian,
that his moral sensibility is not a mere thing of discrimi-
nations, or of faculty for the points of the compass, but
gathers to itself a habit of steadfast motion and ongoing
power: he is a man of MORAL EARNESTNESS.

Nothing strikes us more, perhaps, in this hero of
Bunyan's, than the downright, straightforward, business-
like air of the man throughout the whole of that chosen
course of his. It is significant that Bunyan's pen twice
puts down this sentence word for word—"Then Christian
began to gird up his loins, and to address himself to his
journey." This was his ordinary temper from the first—
sure, then swift. He is standing in the fields near his
native city in great trouble, and Evangelist is at his side.
Evangelist bids him flee. He does not start off at the
words, but stays still on the spot. "Looking upon Evangelist *very carefully*," he "said, *Whither* must I flee?"
Evangelist asks him if he sees the Wicket-gate. The man
said, "*No.*" But once astart he goes on with speed, holding his face towards the shining mark,—sweeping on his
two neighbours, like pilgrims themselves, with the strength
of his steady earnestness, and, when both are gone back,
scrambling out of the Slough on that side which was
"farthest from his own house," because that was the side
"next to the Wicket-gate." The temptation of Worldly-
wiseman squandered his earnestness by misdirection.
That happily past, we read—"So he went on with haste,
neither spake he to any man by the way; nor if any man

asked him, would he vouchsafe them an answer." Not the less, this same Earnestness, which is too deep to be mere hurry, and too genuine to drive on in terms of self-will, holds him at a stand when it is God that must work, and not he. At the Wicket-gate he "knocked more than once or twice," as afterwards at the Interpreter's house he "knocked over and over," with a mind so well made up, that it was not soon to be discomposed or daunted, even by delay.

Indeed, without staying to consider how much of this Earnestness of character might be due to natural constitution in the man, and how much to purely supernatural influence, it is instructive to keep our eye upon it as it takes on its divers forms, and plays its consistent part in his varying circumstances. It concerns us to mark, for instance, how thorough a learner it makes him. When he is moving to and fro with the Interpreter, we overhear his eager words, "What meaneth this?" (five times repeated)—"Expound this matter more fully to me" —"May we go in thither?" So, when he and Faithful meet Evangelist, before they reach Vanity, it is Christian who "would have him to speak further to them for their help the rest of the way." So, too, when he is walking with Hopeful from mountain to mountain under the teaching of the Shepherds, it is Christian who thrice again puts the old question, "What means this?" And the Earnestness of hearing, let us note, is all the while straining towards the Earnestness of doing, till the doer almost threatens to overmaster the learner. "Now let me go hence," he pleads to the Interpreter; and when at last he gets hence, he "runs," which the third of the Shining Ones at the Cross—the Divine Spirit, whose relations to the Interpreter shall invite our future consideration—seems to have observed and approved, since he "bade him look on" the sealed roll "*as he ran.*"—But the Earnestness changes its aspect, and we see it inspiring him in the work of evangelising men, as he bends amazed over the sleepers, and implores them, in words that might be set for the motto of every one who would rescue souls in Christ's name—" Be willing also, and I will help you off with your irons."—Or we see it moving him to the task of warning fellow-Christians, under the powerful sanction of personal experience, as he sets up the pillar, with its engraven information, in front of the hapless stile.—It changes form again, and we note the fervour it gives him in religious intercourse, and Church-fellowship, and worship :—"With a very good will," he says to Piety when she proposes discourse ; "and I am glad that you are so well-disposed,"—a fit keynote to all his converse with the people of the King, onwards to the end.—It changes aspect once more, and we are stirred as we witness what absorbing reality it puts into his conflicts. " I never saw him all the while give as much as one pleasant look, till he perceived he had wounded Apollyon with his two-edged sword ; then, indeed, he did smile and look upward :" so speaks his biographer as his recollection hovers around " the dreadfullest sight that ever he saw." And when afterwards the warrior is urging his way through the thick of "things that cared not for Christian's sword," that stern Earnestness gives proof of how it can adapt itself without diminution : he "betook himself to another weapon, called All-Prayer ; so he said in my hearing," says Bunyan vividly, " O Lord, I beseech Thee, deliver my soul ! "—Elsewhere we find the same Earnestness working as decision. " Not a step farther," said he to By-ends, "unless you will do, in what I propound, as we ;"—no venting of a narrow exclusiveness, as some would hasten to call it, but a sharp declaration of existing incompatibility, and a clear assertion of liberty in the choice of companionship.—Elsewhere, again, we see it wearing the guise of unswervingness. " Then," said Christian to Hopeful, when this estimable pilgrim was wavering under the wiles of Demas, " let us not stir a step, but still keep on our way."—Elsewhere still, we recognise it under the dress of watchfulness, as throughout that remarkable journey across the Enchanted Ground.—And it has not gone out, but has only mellowed into the complexion of the time, when, in the bright land of Beulah, " Christian with desire fell sick."—But it surely was quenched—once, and quite —during that dismal season when he went into the way of Despair? No, we must trace it still, in its garb of dust and darkness,—holding our breath as we see its hallowed momentum staggering in upon the spirit itself, and becoming sheer load and strain, because the soul has stranded everything in a mood of relaxing waywardness. So the steamship, set round a few points upon the wind to ease her, because there is not the mood just then to expend the engine-power needful to keep her to her course, will start to her full engine-power, reversed, the moment she grates upon the surf-beaten beach in the night; then the racking of her timbers, instead of the brave headway of her voyage, will be proportioned to the power that is in her,—until the power proves fruitless, and the racking passes into the dead weight of the machinery in which the power reposes. What if no spring-tide came round, to lift her with all the strength of the sea, and with so little of her own !

We look around us in this time of ours, and we see it to be a time when Earnestness is not awanting—less awanting, perhaps, than in any previous time that we are able to recall. Triflers are few, and in small esteem. Earnestness, eagerness, strenuousness, are borne with or applauded. Our century has had its apostle of Earnestness, at once interpreting and teaching his age. Yet much of the Earnestness itself is little else than eager bustle. It is too seldom reckoned, that Earnestness, if it is to be great, or even to be very true, must be the Earnestness which gathers its volume, and controls its current, out of the Invisible, whereby alone is scope enough yielded for the setting-in of a strong calm stream of Earnestness such as befits the destiny of a man. The Earnestness which achieves so much as a thing that begins and ends with our banks and counting-houses, our markets and wharves, our laboratories and libraries, our courts and legislatures, is not the Earnestness which is most worthy of us. The Earnestness of moral purpose, and spiritual motive, and eternal outlook --this is a thing at once loftier and mightier and more beneficent ; yet a thing that is not unhomely with all its greatness, and not unearthly with all its heavenliness. The work of our desks and our counters, of our farms and our factories, should be as well done as ever under the sway of this, and should be done with less of the frenzy which consumes the nerve-force, and less of the selfishness which shrivels up the spirit. All the secular businesses of life should then find their happiest place, because then they should be subordinate to the pre-eminent business for which our life is the wondrous opportunity—the earnest faring of the soul, which God's Son has saved, towards the transcendent moral inheritance to which He has saved it.

IV.

WHEN we have set ourselves to the work of analysing any character, even if we stay our decompounding process when we have separated its more primary elements only, it is well to keep the fact before us, that the process after all is largely an artificial one, based upon convenience, and upheld by logic. A man's character is a unity—before analysis, and after it,—a unity as his face is, and with subtler blendings of its parts. Features of character shade into each other—interpenetrate, interwork, grow out of each other and into each other—in such a way as to put a constant limitation of actuality around our endeavours after an ideal sharpness of division. The very naturalness of Bunyan's delineation, therefore, presenting us with the concrete character in all the complexity of real life, leaves the more of the analysing to be done by ourselves, and may be thought to imply an appeal to our good sense that we should not overdo the task. But the unit of personality always does act itself out, nevertheless, in very distinguishable directions; and these, as long as we hold ourselves within the hinted limits, it cannot but be legitimate and profitable to trace.

This reflection concerning the interdependent oneness of character, and of Christian character, had some occasion to occur to us even while we were making a commencement with our analysis in the last section. We saw how Truth, striking its rays from the Book through the mental percep-

E

tion of the man as Tidings, and stirring his Reasoning Faculties on its way, reached the slumbering energies of Conscience, and awoke them into an activity which put his Will, Himself, into motion towards relief. But the relief he was impelled to seek, and found, was relief from wrongness. No such relief as this could take end with itself, and die down into passivity. The getting rid of wrongness is the getting into rightness—not a thing of negatives only, but of positives, and not a thing of condition only, but of action, and of action which calls every faculty into new play. The relief was the liberty to do right by being made right—made right by being brought into harmony with the nature and will of the Righteous One. Had he only been relieved from the wrong that he had done, and nothing more,—even then his gratitude, working together with his Conscience, would have pressed his Will into movement like a new force ; his Love, going in the line of his Conscience, would have lifted on his Will as if the old gravitation had ceased ; his Joy, welling around his Conscience, would have floated his Will onward as if the old friction were done away. He would have experienced the mightiest benefaction that his life had ever held, or ever could hold : he could have started clear of the past, with his heart set upon his Benefactor, to make what better he could of the future. But this, great as it should have been, is no adequate account of what had come into this man's lot. The remission of the crushing past was rather the seal than the substance of the new possessions of his spirit. In coming into the way of God, and into very contact with Him, the Divine effluence had touched his whole being with renovation—had swept every chord of his nature with a hand that at once healed and inspired it, tuning it to the key of unselfishness, and raising it to the pitch of an active sympathy with the eternally true and good. Now, a change so comprehensive could not but be a change that

was complex—complex in its elements and in its issues—
though it might be as simple as a stroke of miracle in its
coming to pass.

Within the great new-creation of character, then, to which
our last section introduced us, there were wrapt up many
elements of character which we have not yet noticed, and
indeed, in germ at least, every element of character
which it is possible to discern. Some characteristics, in
particular, kept so close to our hand while we were engaged
with the traits that are more strictly moral, that we could
not but sometimes be conscious of a deliberate postpone-
ment of them for a more formal and full consideration.
Chief of these was the FAITH of the man, or his new sense
of the spiritual. It was alongside of his moral rectifying,
or rather through and through it, that this quickened perception of the spiritual universe grew. An immense gap
in front of the man's development was then filled in, when
the lower perception which makes out material things, and
the higher perception which realises intellectual things,
stood graded in the rear of the highest perception of all,
which carries contact with the phenomena of spiritual and
eternal things. For Faith may in general be defined as
the perceptive function of the religious faculty—the seeing,
hearing, handling, tasting, by the soul, of what is of God
and eternity. It is a function which lies dormant in every
man till the Spirit of God thrills it into capability in the
act of its human exercise ; and it is dormant unto death
without this combination of Divine and human arousing.
The Godward sense—it was this, most of all, which the
human soul lost out of it by the deadly shock of sin.

This Faith, when we look into it, is itself seen to contain
elements which are sufficiently distinguishable to bear unfolding. First we distinguish Credence, or belief reposed
in authoritative declarations which are recognised as truth,

Close to this we distinguish Trust, or reliance reposed upon a person who is recognised as true and good and strong. Intimate with this we distinguish Vision, or the inward and onward observing power of the spirit within the region of its Credence and Trust—the bringing near of the invisible in respect of space. And blossoming out of Credence and Trust and Vision, bearing hues of each, is Hope, or the bringing near of the invisible in respect of time. It may be best to follow up each of these strands of the fourfold cord by itself, as we endeavour to estimate the place which Faith occupies in the character of this typical Christian of Bunyan's.

In the moment when Christian took orders as a pilgrim, and forsook the false settlement of his city life, he abandoned the seen in quest of the unseen. We only translate the Allegory when we say, that he gave himself henceforth, in spirit, to the life and business of Faith. Faith is dawning when we first see him; and the dawn we behold is of the same essence with the day. That dawn consists mainly in what we have called *Credence*—an accepting of the authority of a certain book, and a dealing with it as in truth a revelation from the unseen. He has many misgivings, but he has none about this; indeed, all his misgivings take their rise out of his certainty here. If he has had preliminary doubts concerning the revelation, they have utterly vanished before we know him. His book moves him like the seeing of the eye: its communications come to him as knowledge from which there is no appeal. Its statements are conclusive arguments :—" Read it so, if you will, in my book," says he, with fine simplicity, to Obstinate the denier. Its disclosures are too wonderful to be told save in its own language :—" I will read of them in my book," he says to Pliable, who is pressing him fussily for information. Long after he has entered by the

Wicket-gate, and the book is no more represented as being " in his hand," his Faith in it as a revelation of safety and of duty is by no means gone. " Know ye not that it is written," is the key of the remonstrance he addresses to Formalist and Hypocrisy. " Will it not," he suggests to them, with some self-repression—" will it not be counted a trespass against the Lord of the city whither we are bound, thus to violate His revealed will?" Nothing but what is conformed to this is firm enough to "stand a trial at law." And he lives in full accord with his theory. All the direct teachings which he himself enjoyed, whether previous to this, as in the House of the Interpreter and in the Palace Beautiful, or subsequent to this, as on the Delectable Mountains, derived their value and strength, if not their very possibility, from the unshaken Faith he had in " the Word of God "—" the Word." So he calls it, many times over, in his final interview with Ignorance. That interview was towards the close of his own journey, and after he had tried " the Word " of his early belief through every vicissitude of experience. Bunyan is true to Christian fact when he pictures his hero's loyalty to the Scriptures as gaining rather than losing in its incisive energy while he grows in spiritual maturity and stature. This man Ignorance is lurking under the spiritualistic fallacy—" My heart tells me so." " 'Ask my fellow if I be a thief!' " retorts Christian. " Thy heart tells thee so! Except the Word of God beareth witness in this matter, *other testimony is of no value.*"

And in this mind the pilgrim goes on to the City. There the verification of the testimony upon which he has ventured the ordering of his life, after having hitherto been brightening onwards with every reach of the way, breaks into a gathered splendour of verification which is other than the testimony only as it so greatly transcends it. Christian was wise to stretch his faculties as he could to the measure of those pre-intimations, and to let down his soul upon them with its weight; for they were defective in nothing but in saying less than the truth, since the whole of the truth would only have baffled its own purpose by bewildering. But when he has come to be at home among the unutterable realities of the City of his citizenship, it may fetch into his spirit one more drop of felicity, that from the first he had grasped the witness of his Book with a hand of certitude, as the very witness of his God.

"Without certitude in religious faith," says one, "there may be much decency and profession and observance, but there can be no habit of prayer, no directness in devotion, no intercourse with the unseen, no generosity of self-sacrifice."[1] "Without certitude in religious conviction," says another, "no religious life is possible."[2] Bishop Earle, in his "Microcosmography," which he must have published about the time when Bunyan was born, has "a Sceptic in Religion" for one of his portraits:—"A man guiltier of credulity than he is taken to be; for it is out of his belief of everything that he fully believes nothing. Each religion scares him from its contrary; none persuades him to itself. . . . He finds reason in all opinions, truth in none; indeed, the least reason perplexes him, and the best will not satisfy him. . . . He cannot think so many wise should be in error, nor so many honest men out of the way; and his wonder is double when he sees these oppose one another. . . . In short, his whole life is a question, and his salvation a greater, which death only concludes, and then he is resolved."

These are witnessings, from somewhat different quarters, to the value of this attainment which Christian had reached. Our own time is not remarkable for the Credence it reposes in revealed truth, or for the religious certitude which that Credence brings; rather, a mild scepticism is

---

[1] Prof. F. W. Newman.   [2] Dr W. G. Ward.

usually twinned with culture, and "dogma" is used to carry such unkindly ideas as narrowness, ignorance, vulgarity. Not only is a large proportion of our intellect and literature infected with this fashion, but it is doing more damage than a "killing time" within some of our churches by its radiation from the pulpit itself. It must be frankly conceded, that upholders themselves of Christian dogma have not been without blame for this result; yet liberated intellects might be expected to consider, that truth makes claim to stand by its own validity, and not by the wisdom of its defenders. It may be a reassuring reflection, that in the course of the historical cycle of truth, every age bears forward its own contribution to the final issue, and that the loosenings of our own age may be leading up to the rivetings of a finer reconstruction; nevertheless, the historical drift of the age does little to repair the present disaster to individual men and women which is wrapt up with their religious uncertainty. Even Christians feel more frequent invasions of this incertitude than are consistent with spiritual vigour. It is not hard to discover causes which go far to account for this prevailing weakness of faith in the facts of Christianity. Thought has become more active and free and fearless. Knowledge in science, which men persist in regarding as a natural storehouse of anti-Christian weapons; an acquaintance with other religions which is rather theoretical and sentimental than profoundly just; a reaction from tradition which doubts every doctrine, and an activity in scholarship which sifts every Scripture, —these are external causes which are inducing relaxation and suspension of faith. But those external causes would not be sufficient for this effect apart from an internal one —apart, as we think, from a lack of that moral earnestness which we found to actuate the hero of Bunyan's poem of faith. We are safe to connect this man's religious certainty very closely with his earnestness of soul. He may be a comparatively simple man, though he is far from being an unintelligent one ; he might be troubled with few of the intellectual difficulties which thwart the Credence of men in our time.   But—not to say that we have more confirmations of our faith than Bunyan's Christian knew of—it is plain that his sense of the nature and needs of the spirit within him, and his perception of the spiritual world and the spiritual One that touched him with conscious adaptation from without,—both of them effects as much as causes of his earnestness,—did more than all other arguments could do or undo, and kept him true and sure in his faith. Let our moral enthusiasm but be as strong and steady as his, and we shall go undetained through many of the thickets which hold us back, and shall bear a momentum in our march which not even all the litter of surrounding scepticism, so seldom earnest, shall greatly impede.

Christian was well advanced upon his journey when he and Hopeful were met by Atheist, who had gone far enough to "see" that the City "is not."   That is negative dogma—blank vision.   The men could meet it with positive dogma, with legible vision.   "Did we not see from the Delectable Mountains the gate of the City?" So cries Hopeful here, when Christian puts the firmness of his faith to the test.   "As for this man," says Christian himself, " I know that he is blinded by the god of this world.   Let thee and me go on, *knowing* that we have *belief* of the *truth*."

Upon this incident it would be easy to step from Credence to Vision in our consideration of Christian's Faith.   But first it is needful we should bring into view that underlying element of it to which we gave the name of Trust.   This was so intertwined with his Credence as to be practically almost inseparable from it.   "The Word " —that holds Credence ; " of God "—that reaches on into

Trust. He first believed the Word as God's ; this led him on to believe in God as the God of the Word, and as no other than the God whom the Word displayed. Every step of his acquaintance with God, from the moment that he gave credit to the true attitude of God towards him, was a step in which belief in the document was made living and strong by belief in the Three-One Being to whom the document bore witness. The Word and the Credence were the means of which God and Trust were the end : this at first, and this all through.

This great habit of personal reliance upon the Supreme, though it may not give itself easily to pictorial projection under the limitations of Bunyan's method, we nevertheless feel to be the very soul of Christian's religion. Trust of God, made so kindly a thing when it could take the mould of trust in the Divine-human Christ,—it was this above all things which constituted the subjective difference between Graceless and Christian. It was this which gave him to God, and which gave God to him—brought him under all the saving and sanctifying conditions upon which God communicates Himself to sinful men as a recovered universe of possession. Being the ruined man he was, the committing of himself to the Good One, upon whom all wellbeing must everywhere depend, had need to take the special form—the marvellous form, as he keenly perceived it to be—of committing himself to the Divine way of redeeming him. When his Faith went forth after the Voice which spake to him, and when it touched the Unseen Arm, and when it leant its everlasting burden upon that tenderness of great power, it was a lost man finding God again on the footing of a redemption—a self-ruined son finding a Father who had overmatched the intricacies of his ruin with startling ingenuities of love. The form of his trust was therefore, in the point of it, a settling of himself upon the stupendous method of his salvation—of his pardon, of his affiliation to the Divine, of his guidance, of his help, of his discipline, of his ultimate home-bringing and complete restoration. This form it takes and keeps, yet still with the Divine Lord Jesus evermore at its centre.

Though we are able to discover, even at the setting-out of the pilgrim, the early presence and workings of trustfulness, and can see the wholesome grasp of fear relaxing until it lets him all but free when the Wicket-gate has been closed behind him,—still, it is only at the Cross that his trustfulness gathers its due liveliness and strength. The load of sin-consciousness dissolves before the hold which his soul is there enabled to take of the unchallengeable completeness of the riddance from guilt which is accomplished by Christ, and accomplished by Him within that Divine plan of love which the pilgrim, as being a genuine pilgrim, has already accepted. The sealed roll of citizenship, therefore, gotten there with the coat and the mark, thenceforth goes with him as the definite pledge that his individual Trust is answered by outward and everlasting reality in respect of God's purposes with himself. At the settle in the bower he loses this, or at least the sight and touch of it—lets self-indulging heedlessness bereave him of the animating certainty, the witness of the Divine Spirit within him, that those purposes do indeed apply to his own personal destiny. But, by honestly and diligently addressing himself to the emergency, he recovers it soon ; and this sensitive linking-point of his Trust he is never represented as having lost again. For, whether lost or found, and precious always, this " assurance," this " evidence," did not traverse the whole extent of his Trust —not now, any more than before it was received at all. His very anxiety to recover his lost consciousness of being folded within the redemptive love, his unhappiness in every situation in which this consciousness was clouded,

sprung from a deep underground foundation of Trust in
God which these accidents on the surface did not much
disturb. He is resting himself back upon this main mass
of his Trust, or levering his efforts of soul upon it, in some
of the finest passages of his history. He is fighting as if
behind the rampart of it in that dread duel of his with the
Destroyer; and when he is treading his wary way through
the living darkness of the still more terrible Valley, he is
held up and held on by a reserve of Trust, upon the crest
of which he is groping among those doleful things as mere
circumstances, while he is keeping his grasp upon God as
the strong Substance of all. It is by this fund of Trust
that he and his companion are made heroes—if not more
really, yet more visibly, heroes—among the perils and
persecutions of Vanity Fair. And if at last the very sub-
stratum of this Trust in a redeeming God seems to tremble
beneath the fall of his faith in his personal safety, among
the billows of that River which is "deeper or shallower as
you believe in the King of the place,"—then, the cheerful
constancy of his trustfulness while he was on pilgrimage
must point us to some hidden cause in mind or body, or
in the final malignancy of fiendish onset, which overcame
for a passing hour the steady habit of his spirit.

Spiritual *Vision*, so essential an element of Faith, was a
faculty in which this Christian was strong, perhaps beyond
the average of Christian experience. That keenness of
spiritual eyesight brought a clearness and definiteness into
his spiritual life which is often meeting us in his pilgrim-
history. He was scarcely yet on his way when we find him
saying to Pliable regretfully, "Had even Obstinate himself
but felt what I have felt of the powers and terrors of what
is yet unseen, he would not thus lightly have given us the
back."—We have a striking instance of the vividness of
his perceptions in the whole scene at the Cross—a scene

which suggests to us, by the comparatively advanced stage at which it was beheld, that his Vision was probably less quick to see than it was intense when it did see.—When "they sat down to meat" at the table of the Palace Beautiful, where there is enjoyed a kind of after-vision of that surpassing scene, the picture they make, and the conversation they sustain, have a realism in them which signifies that all the company, and Christian himself not least, are seeing vividly both the Person and the Work they are remembering so fervently.—The same seeing-power is turned into retrospect, though near, when, looking back at break of day in the second valley, the dangers through which he had passed "were discovered to him." And may it not be, that the very keenness of his Vision, so precious in better circumstances, did something, when he was amidst the dangers themselves, to people the air for him with objects of terror which duller perceptions might never have seen?—On the other hand, soon afterwards, there occurs an opportunity of near prospect, when he reaches "a little ascent, which was cast up on purpose that pilgrims might *see before* them." This is the wiser and the finer attitude of spiritual Vision.

The dominant foreseeing of the Pilgrimage takes naturally for its normal form the sighting of the City of Destination. The topographical cast of the Allegory provides a sort of necessity for measuring the progress by the visibility of the point at which it shall be consummated. That point is not always under the actual Vision of the pilgrim; but here and there, from an early period of his journey, he catches glimpses of the region of the end, which impress him, and impress ourselves, with the compassable nearness of it all. These glimpses are only obtained at elevated stages of the way, and, even then, perhaps only if the air is clear; for they are conditioned, as all vision is, by more than the mere faculty of vision itself, though still by this mainly. The story, however, is not copious in its instances of this furthest foreseeing. Three typical stages of it are given, each wearing its own features, and all of them betokening well-marked advance alike in faculty and view. The Palace Beautiful stands on high ground, the ascent of which is with "difficulty," and the descent of which is with danger. From the palace-top, then, the pilgrim is first shown, not yet the City indeed, but those Delectable Mountains, touched with the beauty of the better clime, from which the City itself shall certainly be seen. Thus the journey is made manageable to the mind, and the sense of remoteness is conquered, by dividing the remaining way into two great portions. So many memorable incidents intervene before the first portion is accomplished, that we have almost let slip the possibility that those Delectable Mountains, when they are actually reached, are the very heights upon which the eye of the pilgrim had formerly rested, outstripping so long the slow ongoing of the foot. On Mount Clear, it is the City itself that is beheld, or at least its gates ; and more now depends upon the Vision of the onlookers themselves, and less upon the opportune transparency of the atmosphere, which seems here to be a settled factor in the prospect. The looking is done now through the Shepherds' "perspective glass," and is only done with effect "if they have skill to look through" it. Their skill is not so considerable as it might be, and they are disconcerted by the self-convicting sight they have just seen from Mount Caution. "They tried to look," but their hands were unsteady; "yet they thought they saw something *like* the gate, and also *some* of the glory of the place"—enough to send them away singing. This glass must be the Word of Revelation, to which the onlooking eye of the pilgrim betakes itself ever the more for true sight of the unseen as the speeding years diminish the interval between him and its unimaginable realities. The settled clearness of air must be the purer life of the soul, as distinguished from its moods and occasions—a life clarified by increase of knowledge, and cleansed of mists by the gathering energy of Faith.

Between the Delectable Mountains and Beulah there appears to lie much less of space and time than had lain between the Palace and the Delectable Mountains. In Beulah, however, the perception of the City has ceased to be a thing of occasional glimpses, and has passed into a thing of practicable habit. "Here," says the story, "they were within sight of the City they were going to"—within hearing, even, of voices which floated towards them with great words; and still, as they drew nearer, "they had yet a more perfect view thereof," so that they could in some sense describe it. When they have left behind them the vineyards of Immanuel, the telescopic method of descrying the City is now belittled by the use of "an instrument" through which the lustre of the place is shorn for them of some of its dazzling strength, that they may still look upon their future home, yet without the overpowering of their faculties. And ere long they cross the River, where the Vision of Faith, or of some capability which transpires between Faith and Presence, rapidly blends itself with the immediate Vision of the Soul, and in that is lost.

Doubtless, however, we should miss not a little of the evidence of this clear foreseeing of our pilgrim if we should limit our attention too exclusively to this more phenomenal method which Bunyan adopts for the picturing of it. Much of it lies less obtrusively in the bosom of the narrative. It is nothing else, for instance, but a steady Vision of the unseen, even among the attractive visibilities of Vanity Fair, which prompts Christian and his friend to "set very light by all their wares," and to say to the importunate booth-keepers, with the air of traders who are intimate with better markets and with finer merchandise, "*We* buy the truth." The whole conduct and bearing of the two in the city of Vanity is inspired by a calm fixing of the eye of the soul upon the regions of the better City. How otherwise this brotherly hope of each that the fate of martyrdom would be his?—this unanxious, uncomplaining endurance, nevertheless, under the dark uncertainty of the time, "until they should be otherwise disposed of"? Their realisings are far ahead of Vanity, with its rule and its rulers that are thus loading with harassment all the nearer contacts of sense. For the better City has also its better King, who is more to them than the City itself is, and is present even now to their Faith, which carries a consciousness as real and potent, if not so sharp, as their consciousness of Beelzebub and his constabulary of cruelty. "When we come to *the King*," said Christian to Demas: this was already their hearts' refrain as they lay in their dungeon, or stood meekly in the cage, of the heartless god of worthlessness. It was so with Christian to the end; for it is a kindred tone which makes the key-note of his recovered triumph when he is just "coming to the King" at last, though the mere City is already sunning the air with its splendour—"Oh, I see HIM again!" And he has never lost sight of Him since.

Thus, almost imperceptibly, we have been moving in upon the sphere of *Hope*, with all the passive strengths of submission, and patience, and godly content. It is the nature of Faith to advance from seeing the unseen into holding the unseen. Holding the unseen is scarcely different from being held by it. In the apostolic figure of the anchor (if we may take "hope" subjectively in the passage), we have both. There is a pull upon the soul from the fastenings which are in the unseen and future, but it depends upon the fastenings which are on board of the soul itself. When these too are secure, Hope is doing her work. That work is a steadying, staying, and withal an onlifting work; for the metaphor begins to fail us if we would include all the efficacy of that which it figures. The sense that those eternal things, so visible and near, shall soon be reached and enjoyed,—this is a sense which gives onbearing no less than upbearing power to the pilgrim-spirit in which it dwells. The anchor-chain is also an electric cable, which charges with heavenly energy the soul it is holding fast. And Christian had no lack of Hope, and seldom had lack of manifest hopefulness. The anchor-chain, as we know, was well-nigh torn overboard once; but the strain of the weather just then was extreme; and after the storm was over, its hold was only the more tenacious henceforth.

Thus rich, then, are the contents, and thus efficacious the qualities, of evangelical Faith as we see it in this man. Plainly, it fits itself well upon a human character, and can make large room for itself there. It is a principle almost absolutely new when it enters, and it creates a whole group of new characteristics in a man. It brings a strength and dignity, an integrity and unselfishness, which nothing else can provide, because it travels for these beyond all that is human, and on to all that is Divine. It stretches outward the horizon of our knowings, our experiencings, our purposings, our confidings, with an unboundedness of amplitude which leaves the expanding-power of all other principles quite behind comparison. It deals with sureties, and brightnesses, and grandeurs, on the one hand, which lift a man with them into a higher zone of life; it deals with disclosures and awfulnesses, and ineffable purities, on the other hand, which correct and regulate a man along the clear line of his destiny. Each one of its elements, how-ever severely we may analyse it, shall still be found trans-cendent of its kind.

Men trust,—trust things warily—trust men and women

reservedly or dubiously ; for the reeds have snapt ere now, piercing the trusting hand with future cautiousness. But to trust with all the weight and mass of our being, and to be able to school ourselves into the verity, that the more we trust, the more right and reasonable and happy are we,— this is trust in God.

Men ply their intellectual vision, and sometimes ply it nobly — penetrating mysteries, ordering confusion into science, looking down the ages of time as through a vista of atmosphere, and on through the universe of space as if it were a landscape around their homes. But the untimed and the unspaced, the eternal,—that is so often left out as if it were not to be reckoned ! Yet, when vision is denied to this, it is denied to the ever-abiding universe of the spiritual, in which all the efficiency of existence dwells. Far more than this : it is denied to the Unbeginning Spirit, supreme in everything of grandeur and loveliness, within whose eternity all universes have gotten their borrowed being and abode. Sadder still : it is denied to those surpassing sources whence all helpfulness must flow which is great enough to raise our nature and fortune out of the collapse that has befallen them, and denied to those wondrous consummations to which the eternal Fatherliness would lead us on. And it is denied, in great measure at the least, to the Divine Man, the hope and glory of our race, the upbuilder of our ruined possibilities, who has brought Godhead into the living heart of human history.

Men make out to hope, and to brighten life with their hopings—brave hopings often, in the face of hopes that have been shattered. But the hope which has not Christian's faith for its root is clearly too slight and too unsteady to serve the needs of a human spirit. All the stabilities, do as we may, are beyond the veil of sense : all our great futurities—the nearest possible to all our futurity whatsoever—lie outside the world. Defect of Christian hope comes of defect in realising ; defect of worldly hope comes of realising too well. Therefore, mere earthly hope is a decreasing force as life advances : strong in youth, and gilding all things with a mist of beauty, it fades down with the years which gather up the realities. But the hope of gospel-faith is an increasing force as life proceeds : feeble, it may be, in the youth of the Christian life, it goes on to draw strength around itself as Christian manhood fetches the realities nearer.

It were not good for any Christian to have less vigour and fulness of Faith than this pilgrim had : it were right good for him to have more. "According to our Faith" it is "done unto us" ; according to our Faith it is done by us : according to our Faith, it may almost be said, we are precisely the Christians that we are. It is the strength, and it is the sanctifying, of the soul. It is the nerve through which our feeble spirit touches the All-sufficient, and is thrilled in hand, and foot, and eye, with the holy energies and steadfastnesses of the higher world of our hope. With its blended belief and trust and vision, any one may give everyday reality to the picture of the poet :—

> " Far 'yond this narrow parapet of time,
> With eyes uplift his soul would ever look
> Into the endless promise, nor should brook
> One prying doubt, to shake his faith sublime." [1]

We may well hold our gaze to the grandest things, when the faculty and the opportunity are given us. " We gain more by looking on what is perfect," says one, " than by striving against what is imperfect." [2] In this there is deep truth—truth that to some of us might come with the power of a new gospel, yet the old gospel still. And well may

---

[1] Russell Lowell.   [2] Canon Carter.

we urge onwards our toil in the way of our gaze, when hope is beckoning us forward towards all excellence, and death itself scarcely makes an obstacle in the far-going path. "Dum spiro spero,"—that too is the Christian's: "Dum expiro spero"—hoping while we live, and hoping while we die,—that is the Christian's alone.[1]

[1] "Aids to Reflection," xlv.

V.

CHRISTIAN : HIS HUMILITY—HIS COURAGE.

WHEN now we take another step in our endeavour to expound the character of Bunyan's hero, we feel there is not left us any possible characteristic so great or so comprehensive as that from which we have just passed. Nor shall we find almost any feature which the character of the pilgrim exhibits in fuller proportion. He is not more a man of Conscience than he is a man of Faith. The play of his Conscience, indeed, went on within an atmosphere of belief and vision—went on with growing freedom and invigoration as this atmosphere gathered more richly around it. Conscience thus bore witness to Faith and its validities, finding them profoundly congenial to all the undeceivable exactitudes of its nature : so, too, Faith cherished Conscience with the vital air of a higher region of reality and purity and peace.

An age of Faith, if the Faith has not sunk into credulity, is an age of moral power, and of unimpeded moral energy in word or deed. To cast off credulity, as the greater part of Europe did three hundred years ago, is to cast off childishness ; but to cast off Faith, as so many in Europe are certainly doing now —or to starve it by a merely intellectual gymnastic in presence of the loftiest truths, as is too manifestly common among us,—is to use the privilege of manhood to expel the most uplifting force which manhood can embrace. An Agnostic suspension of Faith, or a Positivist exclusion of it, may seem to work little moral mischief in the few who first betake themselves to those dreary regions as regions of theory, or in the fewer still whose natural elevation of character, largely borrowed from Christian Faith, can withstand or surpass their theory. But such faithless systems, were they to spread their influence over the general mind and heart of a people, would work a moral disaster so wide as to precipitate a catastrophe of immorality and crime.

If, in turning to seek for other characteristics of this typical Christian, our eye first falls upon his HUMILITY, it falls upon what may well be accounted a simple product of Christian Faith. We look for Humility in a man who bears the name of Christian, and for much of it in a man who otherwise well sustains the name. We need scarcely watch to find it in any other than a Christian, — Humility, that is, of genuine temper—Humility without meanness and without fear; self-respectful, self-knowing,— recognising adorable heights, and estimating self in terms of measurements that lie infinitely upwards.

Yet it might appear as if Faith, being the thing we have found it to be, would not readily have lowliness of spirit for its product. It might be thought that the man who claims friendship with the eternally Greatest,—who rests his trust upon Omnipotence,—who believes himself to be loved by the Divine Man as a very brother whom He has ransomed with His life,—who holds fellowship with the unspeakable Unseen through the presumed indwelling of the Divine Spirit, and looks onward with the eye of a citizen to the very home of God ;—it might be thought that such a man would go on with lofty step and uplifted head, as beseeming a mortal who is exalted, and exalted above so many of his fellows, by a privilege and destiny so sublime. But it is not so. It might be so if the privilege and the destiny did not make but a magnificent foil to his own unworthiness. The consciousness of his exaltation,

of his eternal enfranchisement within the community of
God, gets birth and growth by the side of a consciousness
of what stands to this as a most sobering antithesis. There
comes with it a deepened sense of his own lostness, of his
own weakness to good, of his own depraved strength to
evil, of his own utter dependence upon the merciful favour
of the One he has wronged ; and all of this is penetrated
by a quickened sense of the sacred majesty of Him by
whose "gentleness" his own condition has become so
"great." The balance drops to the side of Humility with
a decisiveness which is very much the measure of the
Faith which realises the honour into which he has come.
Every objective item of his dignity, indeed, makes a subjective motive to lowliness of spirit : nay, his subjective
dignity itself, the conscious advance of spiritual royalty
within his being, is only a more touching and a homelier
motive to the Humility which it actually includes.

The characteristic to which we are giving the somewhat
general name of Humility, when we look at it a little, splits
itself into many shades of colour, which it is well to distinguish if not too finely. One group of these may be
represented by Reverence, another by Confession of Sin,
another by Lowly-Mindedness, another still by Gratitude.

When a sense of God sets in upon a man, all his capabilities of *Reverence,*—hitherto slumbering, or only lifted
unsteadily and to the comparatively trivial reaches of
human greatness,—begin to get upon the wing for soarings
unknown till now. The Father, the Son, the Holy Spirit
—each in His own Divine place, and each and all as
incomprehensible God—receive a habitual heart-worship
which is now and again tided into adoration. Whatever is
of God is mantled for him with sacredness. There grows
in him a Reverence for the Divine words, the Divine
works, the Divine symbols, the Divine day, the Divine
names—for whatsoever carries associations with the excel-

lency of Godhead—which is pained by profanity, and disgusted by flippancy, wheresoever he meets them. And this Reverence, not being an unsubstantial sentiment which can evaporate its existence, gives practical manifestation of itself in submissiveness to the Divine will, in resignation under Divine dealings, in childlike obedientness of spirit, in meek acceptance of mystery in the Divine ways. Indeed, it is more easy to illustrate this element of Humility, in the instance of the pilgrim, by his acts and deportment than by his recorded words. We discern it in nearly all of his conversations, but rather in their pervading tone than in any quotable sentences of them. We recognise it, very specially, in his whole bearing as a guest at the Palace Beautiful, the emblem of the holy sociality of church-fellowship and service. It beams upon us in the meekness of manner and the resignedness of spirit which so impressed the gay beholders at Vanity Fair. Sometimes, as here, it had regard to the Divine will as bearing mainly upon temporal condition; sometimes it had regard to that will as bearing mainly upon spiritual condition,— notably in the early instance of his unmurmuring readiness to toil onwards with his burden until it should be removed. There is a "godly fear" at the root of this Reverence, though it is conscious of no slavishness—at least when its sense of God has not been deranged by wrong-doing. The discourse of Christian to Hopeful on the subject of "true or right fear," when they were cherishing their wakefulness across the Enchanted Ground, suggests to us how much of his own "great Reverence for God, His word and ways," was "begotten and continued" by the fear which haunted him so sorely when his pilgrimage was beginning.

From what has been said of Christian's habit of Reverence as an element of his Humility, some light may be cast upon a certain sharpness, as some may feel it to be, in his manner with one or two of the false pilgrims whom he encounters on his journey. It may appear to betray an absence of Humility, but it really confirms the presence of Humility. It is Humility on its Godward side—Humility as tender Reverence for God and His truth—prevailing above the conventional marks of Humility on its manward side, and throwing them into temporary abeyance. For if ever there be a shade of harshness in Christian when he is face to face with those unhappy men, it is instructive as well as fair to note, that there is little trace of this, but oftener a tone of lowly charity, when he is speaking of them to others.

Confession of Sin may be reckoned as the counterpart of Reverence. The sin of a soul that is conscious of God is the wrong done by that soul to all which it reveres. The inherent sinfulness of such a soul is its supremest trouble. Bowed down with the sense of the wrong, weighted with the weariness of the trouble, it is urged, by every godly and manly motive, to unbosom the tale of its unworthiness to the God who abundantly pardons. The perception of the purity and the love which are for ever blended in the Three-One Godhead, and which are brought to touch the soul by the contacts of the Spirit, even as they stand incarnated before the eye of the soul in the sacrifice of the Cross,—this, when it is clear, will even overwhelm a man with an urgency of Confession, as the least thing of all which the deplorable circumstances demand. The exercise implies Humility, and fosters it. This Confession is made to God alone: the same temper, working within the human range, takes the form of a ready admission of faults, and a prompt appeal for the forgiveness of inflicted injuries.

There is evidence enough of the Humility of Christian on both of these levels of Confession. He is standing with Good-will, who is leading him to recall his spiritual history up to this point of decision and safety, on the inner side of the Wicket-gate. The case of Pliable is in question. "Truly," adds the burdened man, "I have said the truth of Pliable; and if I should also say all the truth of myself, it will appear *there is no betterment betwixt him and myself.*" And with much simplicity he recounts the story of his mishap at the hands of Worldly-wiseman, by whose persuasions he "also turned aside to go into the way of death." Again, he is in conversation with the Porter in front of the entrance to the Palace Beautiful, at the hour of dusk. Why does it happen he has come so late? "I had been here *sooner*," explains Christian, with a contrite copiousness, "but that, wretched man that I am, I slept in the arbour that stands on the hillside. Nay, I had, notwithstanding that, been here *much* sooner, but that in my sleep I lost my evidence, and came without it to the brow of the hill; and then feeling for it, and not finding it, I was forced with sorrow of heart to go back to the place where I slept my sleep; where I found it, and now I am come." Further on, he and Hopeful are full of grave reflections in the midst of the gleaming night-floods on By-path Meadow. "Good brother," implores Christian, "be not offended. I am *sorry* I have brought thee out of the way, and that I have put thee into such imminent danger: pray, my brother, *forgive* me; I did not do it of an evil intent. . . . I am glad I have with me a *merciful* brother." And very touching are his utterances of his sense of unworthiness in his darker hours,—as in the Dungeon of Despair, and in the River of Death,—when Humility, bereft of the strong buoyances which keep the bowed head still high enough to catch the radiance of the eternal smile, becomes a weight to press him down, for a season, beneath the reach of sunlight.

The middle tone of Christian's Humility is his *Lowly-Mindedness*—his modest esteem of himself all round, as one in the wide world of men, and in the narrower world of Christian men. It is his Humility in its most habitual and observable form. It is the every-day result, the working average, of the survey which his Faith affords him, and of the sensitive unselfishness which that survey brings. He strikes a low key about himself from the first :—"Such an one as I am," he says at the Wicket-gate. It deepened, however, and settled, with his increasing experience of himself and of the life on which he had entered. It grows as his knowledge grows. Under the teaching of the Interpreter, his docility of attitude intensifies visibly, and he goes from the temple of learning a humbler man, very much because a wiser man, than he came. The sights and tuitions of the Shepherds, though they evidently hold a lower rank than those of the Instructor at the earlier stage, are received into a heart which is more than ever a teachable and impressible one. There could be no finer evidence of the manly Lowliness of Mind which grew upon Christian than in the closing paragraphs of his conversation with Hopeful concerning Little-faith. "But for such footmen as thou and I are," he says, "let us never desire to meet with an enemy, nor vaunt as if *we* could do better when we hear of others that have been foiled ; nor be tickled at thoughts of our own manhood : for such commonly come by the worst when tried. . . . O my brother, if HE will but go along with us, what need we be afraid of ten thousands that shall set themselves against us? But without Him the proud helpers fall under the slain. I, for my part, have been in the fray before now ; and though, through the goodness of Him that is best, I am, as you see, alive, yet I *cannot boast of my* [another reading, *any*] *manhood.* Glad shall I be if I meet with no more such brunts ; though, I fear, we are not yet beyond all danger." This to a fellow-Christian. The same temper appears in his conversations with un-Christian pilgrims ; as when Ignorance affirms he "has left all for" God and heaven, and our hero replies—

"That I doubt; for to leave *all* is a very hard matter; yea, a harder matter than many are aware of." His eye is on his own achievement in this regard, which he will not claim to be complete. And at last, at the sad moment in the River, we are witness to the deep chords of pathos which this Lowly-Mindedness can touch, when we hear him assuring his companion, who "has been Hopeful ever since he knew him," that it is for him only, and not for Christian, that the "men" are standing waiting about the City of Glory.

Gratitude holds some such place in respect of Humility as hope holds in respect of Faith. Gratitude is the flower of which Humility is the root: they are not organically separable. Gratitude is a ready thing with us in proportion to the lowliness of our estimate of ourselves as the receivers of benefits, and in proportion to the loftiness of our estimate of those who are the givers of them. Gratitude is a profound and constant thing with us in the measure of what we feel to be the magnitude or the constancy of the benefits. Christian's pilgrimage, then, from the point of its assured beginning, was a pilgrimage of thankfulness. "But oh!" he cries, when he knows that now he is shut in upon the path of salvation—"what a *favour* is this to *me*, that yet I am admitted entrance here!" That day a fountain of Gratitude welled up within the clefts which had been made in his spirit,—as rock-springs will bubble upwards out of the depths which the shudder of earthquake has split, and will fill the rents with living water that never shrinks far below its mossy margin, and is oftener overflowing it. Christian's thankfulness is so frequently brimming over into thanksgiving, that we seem invited to infer that his thankfulness can seldom have been very much in ebb.—At the Arbour on the Hillside, when he has recovered his roll, we find him "*giving thanks* to God for directing his eye to the place where it lay."—The two strands of his thankfulness, the greater and the less, are laconically expressed to Charity in the Palace—"Now I thank *God* I am here, and I thank *you* for receiving me." —In the Valley of Humiliation, or of Humility,—and we cannot but regard the fact itself as highly significant,—he had to make good his passage through it by conflict and victory. "So, when the battle was over," according to the record, "Christian said, 'I will here *give thanks* to Him who hath delivered me out of the mouth of the lion—to Him that did help me against Apollyon.' And so he did." —When the light broke upon the pitchy darkness of the next Valley, revealing the perils he had passed, "Now was Christian *much affected* with this deliverance from all the dangers of his solitary way."—The Shining One with the whip in his hand is departing : "So," we read, "they *thanked* him for all his kindness"—though some of it was bitter.—His grateful regard for Evangelist, which is overborne by concern in the two earlier interviews, is free and fervent in the last :—"Welcome, welcome, my good Evangelist; the sight of thy countenance brings to my remembrance thy ancient kindness and unwearied labours for my eternal good."—Thus the Humility of our pilgrim keeps breaking forth into blossom of thankfulness—to God, and to men.

"All virtues together," it is said somewhere, "are a body whereof Humility is the head."[1] If this may appear to challenge some qualification, we must fully accept the wise verdict of Augustine : "Well nigh the whole substance of Christian discipline is Humility." It was a great part of the "discipline" of this "Christian" of Bunyan's. It does not seem to have been so natural or so easy a virtue with him as it is with many—if we may judge by the battle in the Valley, and by the slips upon the downward slope which are connected with it as its cause. Indeed, we can reckon, from the general make of the man, that he would have

____
[1] Quoted by Dean Perowne—Psalm cxxxi.

somewhat to do with himself ere he secured this virtue as a firm possession. But he did secure it. He got its rudiments as a grace; and these he wrought into a gracious virtue, under the givings of grace and the trainings of Providence. His progress in practical learning was very much a progress in Humility—a steady levelling-down of his estimates of himself and his sufficiencies, to which even his exultant experiences ultimately contributed. The result was altogether a wholesome one, for it was one that was essentially truthful. The deep experience of himself which he gained, and was meant to gain, by his vicissitudes, was an experience which held among its contents a sense of his inherent feebleness, and of his profound dependence upon the Power which grew greater to his view the oftener he was urged to draw upon its merciful resources. If this adjusting downwards of his measures of himself was weakness, it was a weakness which was a root of strength ; and if it was degradation, it was a degradation which kept step with the total uplifting of his character. For the better a man he became—that is, the holier and the stronger and the greater—he was all the while becoming the more humble. And he was becoming the more happy ; because this growing Humility was a principal element in the restoration of the lost harmony between his own heart and the reality of things which has its centre in God.

It is too often assumed that there is little else than contrast and incompatibility between Humility and COURAGE. There is something indeed of contrast, but it is on the surface only : of incompatibility there is nothing. When Lowly-Mindedness is true, it is not even enough to say that it consists with Courage ; it gives to courage positive nurture and development. There is a courageous habit of mind created in the very act of accepting and confronting the truth about ourselves, regardless of what humiliation that truth may bring. This habit of mind, besides, has steady accession of strength from the correlative elevation of our sense of the Divine greatness, as a greatness with which, notwithstanding its exceeding grandeur, we are summoned to sustain an unbroken intercourse. This inter course, again, is able to embolden itself, and a good deal which is not itself, with the ever-deepening conviction, that the immeasurably Mightiest is in truth our mightiest Friend. And nothing perhaps demands more firmness of texture in the spirit of a man than simply to hold down his estimate of himself in the midst of his fellow-men, and against the appeal of his own natural self-love, in such a way that his lowliness shall still retain its reality, and he his self-respect.

As Courage is a stronger and deeper thing than mere bravery, which is often but a very flashy and flimsy quality, so Christian Courage is human Courage at its strongest and deepest. It likes a soil of natural Courage out of which to grow; but it is capable of engendering its own soil,—imparting Courage of the highest kind to a character in which a natural Courage had scarcely existed. The sentiments and motives of Christianity are precisely such as go to brace the joints of timidity and cowardice, and to knit the soul into heroism. It not seldom happens, that hesitancy and fear are the result of a limited acquaintance with things—an exaggeration of what is encountered, which largely arises from having a field of view too small to bring down the affair into its own proper place of comparative insignificance: Christianity widens a man's view both of space and duration—gives him a consciousness of the Infinite One, and quickens his sensibility to the unseen; so that what is only seen, and creaturely, and transient, he can meet with a steadier step and a calmer eye. Again,— it greatly nerves the Courage of a man, more especially in the article of conflict, if he have within him a keen sense of his interests, a penetrating consciousness of his personality, and a vivid insight into the consequences which hang upon his dauntlessness: Christianity, like nothing else, works in upon a man a conviction of the vastness of his personal concernments, and the momentousness of acquitting himself so that the best issues shall be achieved. Once more,—it sustains the Courage of most men, and bears some men on to do and to dare great things, if they feel assured of the sympathy of those whom they revere, and the good wishes of those whom they love : Christianity reveals a sympathy which is wholly unique in its tender greatness, and good wishes which are more than the good wishes of all human love united—the sympathy and good wishes of the Godhead, and by the side of these, and dim only in the splendour of the other, the sympathy and good wishes of a universe of holy fellow-beings. Yet again,—it makes for intensity of Courage if a man is confronting hostile strengths not merely under the impulse of self-preservation, or under the higher inspiration of a sense of right, but also in the service and at the word of one whose name and cause are justly dear to his heart : and Christianity, in its very essence, is loyal-heartedness to Jesus Christ, nurtured by a gratitude which need have no limit, and by a devotion which is only the more reasonable the more intense it becomes,—nerving the will, and fortifying the heart, beyond all other sentiments, when dangers and toils are in hand for the honour of the Lord that bought us.

But all this, it will be noticed, applies only to Courage of the purest and noblest quality. The first thing we have named, for example, as promoting Courage—the expansion of the field of view—does nothing for Courage of the slenderer sort, which often indeed depends for its very being upon a limitation of view—upon obliviousness to the magnitude of the peril and the gravity of the issues; whereas it is one of the distinguishing ethical features of

Christianity that it fosters our Courage by the very means of expanding our knowledge of all which existence comprehends. And so with the other aids to fortitude which have just been indicated.

Bunyan therefore, in evolving the character of his typical Christian, finds place for not a little that is of heroic quality. When the pilgrim is put to it, there is seen to be very manly mettle in him. And it is his fortune, perhaps even beyond the normal experience of Christians, to be put to it sorely on some occasions. But usually he bears the brunt with credit to himself and with honour to his King. On such occasions, Christian exhibits Courage in its three most obvious stages : he displays Resolution, which we may regard as Courage simply awake and self-conscious; he shows Fearlessness, which we may think of as Courage on its feet and at work; he manifests Fortitude, Constancy, Endurance, which may be described as Courage holding on its way.

It gave space for his Courage to be detained in its more passive form of *Resolution*, that commonly Christian had due intimation of his oncoming seasons of effort. The storm loomed more or less ominously before it broke. The bravery of hot blood was precluded; and he had to reason his way, by a moral logic which was not of necessity so slow as it was sure, into a calm resolvedness of mood.—He has attained the top of the Hill Difficulty, amid some self-gratulations, when Timorous and Mistrust come upon him in breathless haste from the opposite direction, and have only time to tell him that they are speeding back from dangers which cannot be safely encountered. The reasoning process begins :—Its first step, "You make me afraid"; its middle step, "I must venture"; its last step, "*I will yet go forward.*" And although they were two, and he was but one, the distance rapidly increased between them as "Christian went on his way."

Nor did the long strain upon his resolvedness which supervened—the missing of his roll, and the tedious search that followed—prove sufficient to slacken the tension of his purpose.—Again, when in the Valley of Humiliation his eye falls upon that daunting vision of "a foul fiend coming over the field to meet him," the mental process, now more limited for time, is essentially the same: first, "he began to be afraid," and indeed to waver; last, "*he resolved to venture, and stand his ground,*"—adding significantly, "*Had* I no more in mine eye than the saving of *my life*, it would be the best way to stand." And in the subsequent parley with the monster, which is conducted on both sides with such adroit cogency and such fell spirit, the pilgrim is only amplifying his process, and clenching it with hammered application to the circumstances,—emphasising the step of clear resolvedness in the loyal exclamation— "O thou destroying Apollyon!—to speak truth, I like His service, His wages, His servants, His government, His company, and country, better than thine; therefore, leave off to persuade me further: *I am His servant, and I will follow Him.*" And when at last the fiend, failing to make a breach in the purpose of the man, fiercely assumed the offensive, "then did Christian draw, for *he saw it was time to bestir himself;*" and we are witness to the precise point of transition between Resolvedness and its more active consequent; while we are made spectators of an unflinchingness which is too profoundly settled to seek the battle before it comes. At last the battle is over, and we might expect his firmness of spirit to be somewhat relaxed by reaction. He is now on the borders of the more dismal Valley. "Two men" meet him hurrying back in a scare of thankfulness that back-going is still left to them. There is a sturdy insistence in the interjected questions of Christian:—"Why, what's the matter?"—"But what have you met with?"—"But what have you seen?" To them "the

Valley itself" is enough to have seen—"every whit dreadful, being utterly without order." Christian's attitude in
prospect of this new experience is all that we could wish:
—"I perceive not yet, by what you have said, but that
this is my way to the desired haven." "So they parted, and
Christian *went on* his way."—And this staying-power of
Christian's Resolution has not diminished when we note it
at work further on in his journey; as when he and Faithful
keep their way undauntedly after the sombre predictions
of Evangelist respecting the fate of "one or both" of them
in the city they were nearing, and after they have come in
full view of that city, and see it throbbing for them with
all irreconcileable hostilities.

It is plain that a temper like this needed no more than
the summons of confronting necessity to rouse it to a high
pitch of active *Fearlessness*. A mind made up so firmly
will withstand a good deal, and it will dare even to the
verge of romance before it yields. Christian never did
yield when he was squarely met by opposing power—that
is, when his Courage had occasion to get to its feet. He
appears nowhere to more advantage in the story than when
he is exhibiting, almost unconsciously, the highest order of
Fearlessness. Our concern for his reputation need not be
greatly disturbed at those points where we find him
stricken for a moment with dismay or terror. This natural
recoil from danger is part of the force with which he has
to do battle. It is in great measure a mere insubordina-
tion of the body; and this, swept in with the rest of the
hostile elements, is borne down before the massive prowess
of his spirit. The affair of the lions, as an instance, does
reveal something of weakness, and we should resent it if
the story were set to magnify the mere physical bravery of
the hero; but when he frankly fears and trembles at what
appears to him to be his appalling risk, yet accepts every
encouragement to go on, and does actually go on though

as yet comparatively defenceless, we may rather think of the physical fear as heightening the moral Courage which drags that fear as a burden behind it.

The chapter of the pilgrimage to which we naturally turn for evidence of Christian's valour is that narrative of the day and night and morning,—though the chronology is a little confused,—which he spent in the two Valleys after he had just left the House Beautiful. We are scarcely prepared for such intrepid militancy when we see the meek docile man bidding farewell to the hostesses whose gentle ways have been creating an atmosphere of such kindliness around him,—even though they have thus buckled him into armour, and sent their guest forth as a warrior who had come to them only as a wayfarer. Their experienced insight, though it has a tender reticence in it, seems to inspire them with confidence that Christian shall acquit himself well. We almost wish them to be onlookers with us, that they may see the flash in his eye, and the soldierliness in his bearing, when there ring from him the words which close the verbal encounter that prefaces the battle with the Fiend—"Apollyon, beware what you do, for I am on the King's highway, the way of holiness; therefore *take heed to yourself.*" It was a speech of good omen in the face of the unearthly mass of living frightfulness that towered before him as he spoke, among these lonely fields. There is no repenting of his words when the fiend straightway took position of combat, and "straddled quite over the whole breadth of the way," flaming with purpose to "spill his soul." The stern reality of the engagement is affirmed by the sway of doubtfulness there is in the conflict as the hours advance. The man is triply wounded, and "gives a little back;" the fiend "therefore follows his work amain;" but this only nerves the man to "again take courage, and resist as manfully as he can." By-and-bye, resistance will not be enough. The man becomes spent and weak. The fiend presses his advantage,—closes,—grapples his stubborn foe, and manages to give him "a dreadful fall." His "sword flees out of his hand," and all seems over. But it is only over for the enemy. Christian's Courage, thus pent up into a jet in its channel, becomes fleet, and starts for once into prompt agility—a thing of noteworthy rarity with him. Catching cleverly at his sword, and bounding to his feet, he delivers at the monster "a deadly thrust," beneath which he staggers back with signs of harm. Christian "makes at him" with redoubled energy, linking words of victory with thoughts of his all-conquering King.—We see the "dragon's wings" hoisting their grimy canvas, and shadowing for a moment the glance of the pilgrim's weapon, until they lift the fiend beyond the arm of the man whom he has simply found to be more than his match, at least in open contest.

This appeal to open combat concludes, as it begins, the purely military career of Christian. His armour, henceforth, slips out of the story; and the artists must be puzzled as to whether or not they should picture him afterwards in the attire of a mere pilgrim again. We see him going "with his sword drawn in his hand" after he has recruited himself from the weariness of battle, and once more as he is nearing the second Valley; but in that valley he is "forced to put up his sword," and the act puts a period to this picturesque mode of representing the strenuousness of the heavenward pilgrimage. This appears perhaps the more remarkable when we bethink us of how fully and fondly our Author has worked out the military system of figure in his " Holy War."

But, undoubtedly, the Courage which is evoked in the Second Valley is of a still higher order than that which we have seen displayed in the first. In his description of this place Bunyan puts forth all his strength of vivid imagination. It is pitchy dark, and earth and air are crowded for

the pilgrim with dangers and horrors. On his right runs a
" ditch," with death in its depths ; on his left lies a " quag,"
miry and bottomless ; betwixt them is his path, just broad
enough for the foot. Midway in the Valley, the mouth of
hell fumes and blazes, striking live flame across his way,
and sending forth into the night an intermittent torrent of
eerie sounds and heart-piercing voices. The rush of im-
palpable presences convulses the lurid darkness around
him, and overpowers him with a sense of tremendous
imminence of peril. He has gone on for " several miles "
when the multitudinous sough of fiends seems to mass
itself into a battalion of invisible onset, and he comes to a
pause that he may hold debate with his own being. Fearlessness is going back upon Resolution under the gathering
stress of his danger. " He resolved to *go on* ;" and when
he went on, he probably touched the highest single point
of his career in respect of this department of virtue. The
phalanx was all but on him ; but "he cried with a most
vehement voice, ' I will walk in the strength of the Lord
God.' "—The onmoving storm of assailment, as if smitten
by the fronting power of a holier tempest, recoiled, and
was gone.

These powerful pictures of the strivings of the Christian
soul with hostile forces external to itself, and of its victory
over those forces, would not have been complete without
some representation of a phenomenon which Bunyan's own
experience forbade him to overlook. The external forces
sometimes succeed in worming their way into the internal
consciousness, and in mingling their own activities with
those of the soul which is in dead earnest to oppose them.
In the Second Valley, therefore, the " confusion " of the
place managed to pierce the pilgrim himself : he appeared
to inhale something of the bad chaos into his heart. He
seemed to himself to be now and again taking side with the
fiends—thinking their thoughts, expressing their sentiments,

phrasing their profanities. "He did not know his own
voice": his deeper consciousness had sometimes to work
through a zone of more superficial consciousness which
wore the temper of the fiendish atmosphere with which he
meant to be at war,—and yet seemed his own consciousness still. He had not expertness enough to penetrate the
illusion. But his historian has :—"Thus *I* perceived it:"
—a more audacious fiend would take possession of his
ear unperceived, and would drop blasphemies into the
current of his consciousness—things which no more
belonged to that consciousness than the flames which
belched from the cavern of woe. The device had the
effect of demonstrating how the man's Courage could
maintain its buoyancy beneath a pressing incubus of perplexity—nay, could then increase its own inherent energy,
as it needs must do, when it seemed to be half-forsaken
even by himself. We may regret it as a needless strain
upon his valour; but since it did not crush him, it does
illustrate to us the undoubted fact in Christian life, that
inexperience itself, if only the soul be of honest fibre, may
develop a spiritual intrepidity, in the earlier stages of a
religious career, which stands as capital of character in the
stages that succeed.

Along the subsequent history we recognise this Fearlessness less in distinct instances, and more in the general
bearing of the pilgrim. It becomes articulate, however,
once and again,—sometimes self-evidenced, as when he
appeals to Hopeful at that troublous hour in the dark
swamping Meadow—"Let me go first, that, if there be any
danger, I may be first therein;" sometimes witnessed to
by others, as when Hopeful, who had occasion to know
him well, reminds him, amid his depressions in the dungeon
of Despair, that his companion is "a far weaker man by
nature" than he himself is.

The incidents already quoted have here and there come

very close to that fullest development of Courage at which
we have yet to glance. Even if we had evidence of no
more than of the Resolution and the Fearlessness which
we have seen in Christian, we could not fairly withhold
from him the merit of Courage. Still, the absence of
steadier qualities of heroism—*Fortitude,* Constancy, Endurance—would leave upon us a sense of shortcoming and
incompleteness. As the journey advances, however, this
passive Courage—the heroism that bears and waits—gets
ample opportunity of manifestation, and responds to the
opportunity well. Christian not only toils and fights ; he
endures. And Endurance is but stored Courage: it is
the strength of spirit which before rose high in detached
moments and minutes, now lifted to a continuous high
level during days and weeks and years.

Even in the earlier parts of the story, hints are not
wanting that the blossoms of his Courage were ready to
ripen to this ; but we have no unseasonable precocity in
this Christian, and we must look further on for their
maturity. Our eye falls first and chiefly upon Vanity Fair.
This is the paramount period of Christian's display of
Fortitude, though he was not the more forward figure of
that period. But though it was not he who made the
strong defence at the trial, nor he for whom the heavenly
chariot stood waiting near the stake, he was in mood to
suffer all that his comrade suffered, and had besides to
bear the pain of separation from him, and of the uncertainty which followed respecting his own fate. More to
our purpose even than this : he bore himself, throughout
those bitter days and nights, with at least all the firmness,
flowering as it did into a sober strong beauty of meekness,
which Faithful himself exhibited. Indeed, we are led to
imagine Christian, having perhaps less of defiance and
hardness in him than Faithful, as doing even more than
his companion did to soften with relentings the better-

hearted of the citizens, when they saw the uncomplaining self-possessedness with which those solitary strangers went through the ferocious ordeal—the beating, the besmearing with dirt, the exposure in the cage, the manacled imprisonment, the torture in the stocks, and the insolent sham-trial which brought matters to a crisis. As we keep our eye on Christian, we are preparing to feel the force of Hopeful's personal reminiscence afterwards, when they were together in the darkness of the Castle—" Remember how *thou* playedst the man at Vanity Fair, and wast neither afraid of the chain nor cage, nor yet of bloody death."

Unquestionably it was Christian's theory from first to last,—and he seldom belied it by his practice,—simply to hold on his way, come what might, and to force his way when that was unavoidably needful. He must keep forward, even though it be, as he described it to By-ends, " against wind and tide." His pilgrimage, comprehensively considered, was one long Constancy and Endurance. He struck the keynote of his enterprise at the outset, when he said to the two neighbours who had hastened after him to persuade him to go back—" *That can by no means be.*" And so, up to the River-side, and beyond it, he held out, and held on, when many would not have matched themselves with one-half of the difficulty that encountered him as he went. Even in the Giant's Castle itself, where he paid so dear for the violation of his theory, and where we may think of his passive Courage as collapsing, he was still one of the two concerning whom " the old giant wondered that neither by his blows nor his counsel could he bring them to an end "; and he was the one of the two who held out thus while a load of constitutional despondency, aggravated by a galling conscience, was crushing him more grievously than either the dungeon or the cudgel of the tyrant.

The Christian, then, as Bunyan understands him, is

neither a weakling nor a craven, but is really something of a man. And indeed, by his account, there is demand upon all the manhood there is in him, and upon all the manhood he can train himself to attain. Christianity, when it is true, is a thing for stout hearts; and it is a thing which makes stout hearts stouter still, both by its incidents outside of a man, and by its influences within him. There are foes to his Christianity and him—foes seen, foes unseen, foes that touch the outward comfort of his lot, foes that smite at the inward weal of his spirit; and not seldom those foes are desperate and deadly. He must have a source of Courage that is at once accessible and inexhaustible; and he has it. His faith keeps a current flowing in upon him from that source: it is the consciousness of an illimitable Strength which for him is personally friendly and protective, and to which his own heart is loyal; for it is the Strength that redeemed him into all his great hopes. His is not a kind of Courage which at all strikes the careless eye with a sense of its true measure, or with a due appreciation of its high quality: it works too much within the sphere of the spiritual for this. In a world which is largely misled by appearances, too little account is taken of the brave chivalry and heroic constancy of which many a Christian heart is the hidden field. It is not that men are tardy to recognise Courage, or slow to praise it. Resolution in affairs, Fearlessness in warfare, Endurance in the exploration of untravelled lands, Constancy in an arduous intellectual pursuit,—they are prompt to pour upon these their torrents of well-earned applause. But the Courage of the Christian is too deep for their observation, or it is too lofty for their sympathy. They are scanning the wide world for heroes, and wit not that their Christian neighbour, whom they are meeting every day as a mild man of scrupulous ways, may be carrying himself through a course of heroism which in the

eye of the All-seeing has every element in it of the heroism
which they are waiting to hail with honour. They would
hail even this man's heroism if it happened to give itself
the mode of an outward and common-world bravery,—as
it often costs it comparatively little to do. Our Havelocks,
long before the earth is filled with their fame, have done,
and borne, and fought, and conquered too, with a Courage
which to their own consciousness is as great and real as
anything which has stirred the plaudits of the world. And
it may be well that it is so. Christians too are but men.
It may keep their Courage genuine, and may inure it into
finer strength, that they live and die as heroes of eternity
rather than of time, and pass, with what of heroism God
has given them, into the Presence where it is as grandly
acknowledged as it is intimately known.

But it is possible for the Christian himself to have less
of spiritual Courage than he might—to have less, indeed,
than it is his necessity to have if he would deport himself
in a manner that is worthy of the name he bears. He has
much of Courage, or else he is little of a Christian. He
has probably displayed something of Courage once ; if he
never did, it is hard to conceive how he ever became a
Christian at all. But his Courage may have spent itself in
his initial efforts, and it may have died down—not because
there have been no occasions which ought to have called
it into vigorous play, but because he has nearly lost out of
him the temper of resistance, and has tamed persistency
into languor, and exertion into ease. Then there must be
backgoings and shameful defeats instead of ongoing and
manful conquest. For without some degree of dauntlessness in him, the strong world around shall have its way
with him, and potent demons shall have their will with
him, and the lurking vitalities of his old nature shall repair
their broken sway over him, until all may be nearly lost.
It is a spectacle which would make a sad picture in a

Pilgrim's Progress. "You mistake," says Jay, "if you suppose that holy Courage is only necessary for ministers and missionaries in their work. Why, every Christian is called to do and suffer the will of God; and without this Courage, in some instances, he will be sure always to fail."[1] The habit of failing—with a rank and a destiny like his! And it is the Will which gave him these that he is too silly-hearted to do and to endure! Nay: the transient powers of the world that now is, and the powers of darkness whose time with him is not less brief, must begin to stand aside and make way for him in his march, as he treads onward under the holier powers of the world to come.

[1] " Sunday Morning Sermons," v.

VI.

CHRISTIAN : HIS TENDERNESS—HIS SINCERITY.

AS we advance in the survey of the pilgrim's character it appears the more evidently desirable that we should secure ourselves against confusion while the number of characterising qualities increases upon us. We have need to gather-in the multiplying branches around their root, and to get them in hand as a cluster which traceably unifies itself in this. The radical thing in this man's character, as the Christian he has become, is his Faith in God. That Faith, as we have seen, let in upon his consciousness a universe of momentous verity, and began to bring his whole being into tone with the universe which had thus grown so actual to his spiritual senses. Its earlier glimpses, working by his Conscience, drove him on to a larger and keener beholding, and so gave current to an Earnestness which took with it his whole will and aim. Its moral revelations, as they augmented and sweetened, infused into his estimates of himself a Humility which largely tempered his bearing before God and man. Its visions and its vouchsafements nerved him to a Courage which came to exceed all the promise he had given in preceding periods of his journey, and which looked heroism itself when compared with his life in the city of his upbringing.

Now, even before the intense self-regard of the transitional stage of his career had slackened, this same Faith had been leading him to embrace other men too within his concern. But when that transitional stage had passed, the outgoing sympathies of his nature, broadened and quickened and enriched by his new world of thought and feeling, took free course and ample compass. His Faith developed the more generous activities of his being, and while it drew forth his fearless energy, drew forth also his affection, his considerateness, his charity, his TENDERNESS.

This group, then, of more delicate qualities, which is conveniently represented by the word we have chosen, is not perhaps allotted an inappropriate place when we introduce it just after the group which we headed by the word "Courage." On the one side of this previous group we have already set Humility; on the other side of it we now set Tenderness: it has affinity to them both. True Courage can well afford to be flanked by these, though they may seem at first sight to be out of kinship with it. We spoke of this in relation to Humility; but we can equally speak of it in relation to the qualities which we are now to consider. For the truest Courage is not a hard thing: it is not a stony column, even when it is most robust, but has succulent root-growths that are nourished deep down among springs of tender feeling. The real hero—such magnificent examples of manhood as poetry hints at, and as Christianity sets itself to produce—is not a man of iron strenuousness only, or of indomitable urgency alone. The strong intrepid manhood of him has something in it of the richness and touch which we associate with womanhood,—crashing through ramparts of hostility, or wrestling against the widespread stubbornness of things, with a heart in it that can love, and pity, and rescue, and relieve. The texture of such a heart is not indurated, though it may be toughened, by its valour: it is readier still to feel than it is to fight. On the other hand, if Courage needs tenderer qualities to attest its genuineness, the tenderer qualities need Courage to give them firmness of tone, and to furnish a vindication of themselves from any suspicion of feebleness. For a pulpy softness of character, however sympathetic it may be, lays little tax upon our respect, and its kindly emotion has but slender value to us compared with the feeling which wells out of a character that has in it the fibre of daring or endurance. In the Christian life, moreover, no less than in the common life of the world, this untempered tenderness of character is perilous, since there is no tenderness in the oppositions which array themselves against the highest interests of the Christian, and which challenge a holy untenderness in himself, if only that he may defend, in the name of his Lord, all that is dear to him for time and eternity.

But we must turn to Bunyan's record, that we may make out how far the representative Christian of the Allegory, who has hitherto sustained our inquiries with so considerable credit, shall answer our expectations in this particular.

When we look for the tenderer qualities in a man, we are entitled to seek first the circle of the family as a scene of their manifestation. If we fail to find them there, we need look no further. The man may have sentiment enough, but we shall scarcely charge him with having affection. Christian, however, does not thus put arrest upon our inquiry. He is a man whose *Domestic Affection* is evidently deep and tender and strong. The story is scarcely opened when we go with him into his home. His wife and children, struck with perplexity at his unaccountable concern, are lingering around him. (We owe this passage to the Second Edition.) His intercourse with them in the past may not have very largely prepared them for comprehending this new turn of things with him; but he shows no lack of tenderness, whether as a husband or as a father, when we first see him there among them. The exclamation with which he had at length begun to "break his mind" to them, though introducing a declaration of personal anxiety, reveals affection on the front of fear :—" O my dear wife, and you the children of my bowels, I, your dear friend, am in myself undone ! " When erelong they alter their mode of treating his " distemper " from kindness to roughness, and he is driven into the loneliness of his chamber, it is " to pray for and pity them " as well as " to condole his own misery."— But it is afterwards, when he is upon the journey which is daily increasing the distance between him and them, that we obtain the best evidence of his affection as the head of a household. For it is one of the most unfortunate features of the Allegory, that it must needs take the pilgrim away from the heart of domestic life, and exhibit him as cut off from all his home interests and home duties,—making home a painful recollection only, and his personal influence upon its beloved inmates an impossibility of the case. Nevertheless, Bunyan's skill does a little to mitigate the rigour of the exigency. As Christian goes onward, we are led to think of him as a man whose family have much hold of his heart, and probably no slight proportion of his prayers.[1]

It is thus with a fine touch of naturalness that Worldly-wiseman is represented as striking in upon him with the almost abrupt question—" Hast thou a wife and children ? " " Yes, but . . . methinks I am as if I had none." Not the less, the tempter is most truthfully reported as crowning the powerful inducements with which he plies him, and as carrying at last his reluctant will, by only a still more explicit appeal to the attachments of home :—" ' Thou mayest *send for thy wife and children to thee* in this village, where there are houses now standing empty, one of which thou mayest have at a reasonable rate.' . . . *Now* was Christian somewhat at a stand." (This whole incident we also owe to the Second Edition.)—It must have been with a pang that this man soon afterwards replied to a question

[1] Note G.

of Good-will at the Gate—" Yes, my wife and children saw me *at the first*, and called after me to turn again." It was far from his own desire that he should have "come alone." —His sense of the absence of his best-loved on earth, even if it might have weakened whensoever he was among the hazards and hardships of the way, would return with strength when he was dwelling among its sweeter circumstances. This is more distinctly seen in the House Beautiful, where the damsel Charity, true to her name, thus begins her catechism :—"' Have you a family ? . . . And why did you not bring them with you ?' *Then Christian wept*, and said, 'Oh ! how willingly would I have done it, but they were all of them utterly averse to my going on pilgrimage.' 'But you should have talked to them.' . . . 'So I did.' . . . 'And did you pray to God that He would bless your counsel to them ?' 'Yes, and that with *much affection ; for you must think that my wife and poor children are very dear to me*. . . . All was not sufficient to prevail on them to come with me ; . . . they left me to wander in this manner alone.'" (Remarkably enough, this conversation with Charity was also new to the Second Edition.) Then the Allegory seems to thin away, as it is apt to do in this Palace, and to let through something of the daylight of real domestic Christian life :—" I was very wary of giving them occasion, by any unseemly action, to make them averse to going on pilgrimage. . . . I think I may say, that if what they saw in me did hinder them, it was my great tenderness in sinning against God, or of doing any wrong to my neighbour." Plainly, if this be unimpaired allegory still, and therefore a description of his way of life for any length of time before he forsook his own fireside, we have little reason to accuse him of parental carelessness even in his period of indecision, and we are not left quite in the dark, as we supposed we were, respecting his deportment while yet he was a citizen of the doomed city.

More probably, however, it is one of those instances in which the demands of truth are too large for the limitations of the figure, and inconsistency is preferred to silence, where silence would amount to grave defect or to positive misrepresentation.

And this is the last reference we have to the pilgrim's household. Enriched as the story was by new material in this department after the First Edition, it is perhaps disappointing that we meet with no further evidence of his interest in them, and no assurance that his affection for them continues unabated as his march goes on to widen his distance from their vicinity. There is a subsequent occasion on which we should certainly have expected something of this : it is the one occasion when he falls in with a pilgrim who had actually left the city, and the very neighbourhood of his old abode, some little time at least after he himself had gone. The opportunity was all that could be wished ; yet Faithful has no question to answer as to the condition or the prospects of the family known by the name of Graceless. Much commendable concern is expressed about Pliable and how he fared, and about the " neighbours " who chose to abide in the city even after this second pilgrim set forth ; but there is not so much as a perceptible glance cast at the five who were so much more than " neighbours " to one of the pilgrims. Is Christian's family-affection dying out? Is the absorbing interest of the pilgrimage quenching his Tenderness for his household itself as being among those who account it a fantastic enterprise? It may relieve our perplexity if we remember, that on every occasion since he left them, the references to his wife and children have been made by others, and never spontaneously by himself. Such references touch him deeply the moment they are made, but it is not he who makes them ; and we are not surprised that Faithful, even as we already know him, has no information to volunteer upon this subject. What, then, shall we conclude, but that the interest of this husband and father is so deep in its Tenderness as to be reticent in its utterance, and that it may be increasing all the while that the evidence of it is disappearing,—known to God, and expressed to Him—as indeed, in figure, it has partly been hitherto—but less than half-known to men, and avoided as a theme of talk with even the most "faithful" of his fellows?

It is not the way of Christianity, then, to lift a man out of the exercise of the family-affections. Antipathies begin to shape themselves around him when he makes decision for a Christian life, and sympathies begin to sunder between him and his own kindred as he holds along the way which they refuse to tread with him. But the antipathies, on his own side, have little of harshness in them, and have so much of tender anxiety investing them as to subdue them out of the nature of antipathies. His anxiety is, that their sympathies may advance to the level of his own, and may be restored to mutual response with his upon that higher plane of living to which he himself has ascended. Those loved ones,—he loves them with only a new and rich accession of feeling, though they may now regard himself with more of curiosity than affection. They are "so near, and yet so far,"—his bodily life with their own still, while his spiritual life is on tracks of travel which are leading him away from theirs—indefinitely, infinitely far. But he lives for them yet : he lives for them doubly now. No worldly needs, no earthly comforts, no sinless happinesses, are less to him for their sakes; only, unworldly needs, and unearthly comforts, and holiest happinesses, are more to him, for their sakes and for his own. His Domestic Affection is deepened, and widened, and purified, but not one whit decayed.

"Without natural affection,"—that is one of the ultimate

and most disastrous reaches of unchristian civilisation.
It has been left to the religion of Christ to recover this
pearl for communities that had lost it under the religions
or irreligions by which they were bound. Christianity has
been the champion of family-affection wherever it has gone.
It has rescued womanhood from degradation, and childhood from cruelty, to an extent which is but inadequately
acknowledged and but partially known. And it is doing
so at this hour around all the lands of the earth. We cannot visit even such unchristian countries as are reputed to
be highest in the domestic virtues without being struck
with the lift which it is still in the power of Christianity to
give to their civilisation within this primary sphere of
human affairs. The Author of the family is the Author of
the Gospel; and its message, when it comes to a man,
comes to quicken him first indeed simply as a man, but
next as a husband, a father, a brother, a son—a definite
active unit in an earthly household.

But we must look for Tenderness in Bunyan's Christian
beyond the circle within which his family alone is enclosed.
This quality has need to appear throughout the wider area
of *Social Sentiment.* Is he a sociable man?—and how
does he bear himself when he is in contact with other
men, whether true or false? In seeking answers to these
questions, we are reminded that the form of the Allegory,
in this case also, somewhat restricts the field of evidence,
and leaves us to make the most of what figurative hints it
is able to afford us. Instead of conducting his new life in
a busy world, Christian is for great part of his new history
a lonely man, and for the rest of it has usually but one
comrade to represent the multifarious society which the
Christian finds around him unless he be cloistered in a
life of artificial isolation. Nevertheless, we can gather
something of the social temper of the pilgrim, and can
pretty well guess how he would have deported himself

among men had the Allegory permitted us to see him among them.

As a preliminary step, we can easily ascertain that Christian is not at least a man who shuns society. He conserves his freedom of selecting it, where he can,—and he has somewhat decided tastes in this matter of selection ; but he is always pleased to find himself in human company when it does not conflict with duty and principle.—There may be something of this appetite for companionship, as well as much of kindly feeling and of evangelical well-wishing, in his persuasive appeal to the two citizens who have come out of town after him—"Be content, good neighbours, and go *along with me.*"—And this need of society appears, long afterwards, when he and his one fellow-pilgrim are together in Doubting Castle : it was one of the bitter drops in their cup that there was not "any to ask how they did," and that they "were far from friends and acquaintance." We get this glimpse, it is to be noticed, at the expense of a slight rent in the veil of the Allegory ; for even in their free pilgrimage their "friends and acquaintance" are very notably few. But, within the strict limits of the Allegory, there is no part of Christian's journey, whether alone or accompanied, in which he does not make frank advances to any who appear upon the scene.—Most of all, on those memorable occasions when he is a guest,—in the House Beautiful, and among the Shep·herds, and in the embowered domain of the Gardener in Beulah,—his delight in the society of the good, at least, brims upon the page, and great part of the joy of the circumstances consists in the feast at which social affections are banqueting.—Heaven itself is attractive to him, as he avows in his conversation with Charity, because "there he shall dwell with such company as he likes best." So, when the River is at last crossed, and the refulgent City is near, and the "heavenly host" has come forth to make a zone of melodious brotherhood around the advance of the pilgrims, we read—" But, above all, the warm and joyful thoughts that they had about their own *dwelling there with such company*, and that for ever and ever—oh, by what tongue or pen can their glorious joy be expressed ? "

This mere love of society, however, even when it rises to this congeniality of company with the loftiest types of humankind, is rather a thing of desire and of fitness than a thing of duty. The ingredient of duty more manifestly enters when the man and his fellow-men are in actual intercourse. Then we can note whether the love of society is ready to pass into the practical form of social love. In the companionship which Bunyan gives to his pilgrim, scanty as it is, we are not without some scope for observation. His fellowship with Faithful and with Hopeful, in other respects so invaluable to him, is of great advantage as an exercise and training in the practice of friendship on the footing of godliness, the splendid destiny of which we have just been anticipating in the scene before the gate of the City. Does Christian in these circumstances, as a matter of purpose as well as instinct, display the qualities of a true and abiding friendship ?

Perhaps there is no feature in which Christian is stronger than in this. When he meets with one to whom he is bound in the bonds of true pilgrimage, his Friendship ripens at once into *Brotherliness*, and the Brotherliness keeps steadfast and tender to the last.—His profound comfort at hearing "the voice of a man " in the Second Valley,—as touching a passage as the " Pilgrim " contains, —gives promise of his capacity for brotherhood no less than his need of it; and his joy on getting sight of Faithful at length, though somewhat damped by the unstaying march of the man, grows, as he reaches him, into a sort of petulant gaiety which is unique in the record of his history. The kind offices of Faithful in Christian's immediate

distress, and the sober gratitude which these called forth,
put just that very rivet upon their brotherhood which the
two friends, with their diverse temperaments, at that
critical moment required. Then Christian's self-respectful
heartiness of feeling takes a start which it never afterwards
slackens. It soon appears that each is the better for the
other, and that Faithful has as much need of Christian as
Christian has of Faithful. Meanwhile, the Dreamer "sees
in his dream" that "they went very lovingly on together.
. . . And thus *Christian began : ' My honoured and well-
beloved brother, Faithful*, I am glad that I have overtaken
you, and that God has so tempered our spirits that we can
walk as companions.'" That note sounds throughout their
entire intercourse, until, with their brotherhood made
tenderer under their common affliction in the city of
Vanity, they parted for a still happier meeting in the
better City.

When Faithful had "come to his end," however,
"another rises out of his ashes to be a companion with
Christian in his pilgrimage." This new companionship
into which the pilgrim enters could not with historic truthfulness be only a duplicate of the old one; and it is not
this. Hopeful is of a different character and experience
from Faithful, and Christian holds a different relation to
him from that which he held to the companion he has
lost. The former friendship was one of equality; and it
was well it should be the first of the two in order of time,
since this is the relation which least tries the virtues of
friendship. The new friendship was one, for Christian, of
superiority—in experience, in character, and in years.
Christian comes out of Vanity with the reputation of a
confessor, and with what prerogative may be based upon
the circumstance that his new fellow-pilgrim has been in
great part moved into pilgrimage by witnessing the confession he made. This companionship, then, will test a

set of qualities which were scarcely touched by the last. It must be acknowledged that Christian bears the test with remarkable success. His superiority to Hopeful, which sustains itself on the whole throughout, is the superiority of an elder brother — seldom condescending, usually respectful; firm when need is, but considerate, courteous, and affectionate, imparting the benefit of all he is and knows, without any undue assertion of the advantage over him which he cannot but feel that he might wield. His intercourse with Hopeful is a lively commentary on the intensely Christian words—"In love of the brethren be tenderly affectioned one toward another; in honour preferring one another."

Let us come in upon them at one or two points as they go.—Demas has been safely passed, and the "old monument" of Lot's wife is before them. "Ah, my brother," exclaims Christian, "this is a seasonable sight. . . . Had we gone over, as he desired us, *and as thou wast inclined to do (my brother)*." . . . The parentheses are expressive, and give a lingering tenderness, with a touch of warning, to the words. (The incident does not appear till the Second Edition.)—The plight in which Christian, with unwonted misguidance, involves his companion and himself when they get over the stile, gives play to a frankness and cordiality of brotherly contrition which is very fine as coming from a man who is "older than" he; and even when Hopeful has most distinctly the advantage of him, in the captivity which follows, there is not a little of Brotherliness in the temper with which Christian accepts the exhortations of his friend.—The appalling spectacle of Turn-away, haled past them to his doom, suggests the story of Little-faith, and Hopeful is slow to come abreast of his companion's sympathy with the hapless pilgrim: Christian becomes more "tart" than is at all usual with him, and Hopeful feels it; but Christian confirms his case,

and adds—" Here, therefore, my brother, is thy mistake.
. . . But pass by that, and consider the matter under
debate, and *all shall be well betwixt thee and me,*"—an
indispensable condition of things which on the instant is
realised.—-Atheist is leering beside them, and Christian
asks Hopeful, "Is it true that this man hath said?"
Hopeful is alarmed. "My brother," says Christian, "I
did not put the question to thee . . . but to prove thee,
and to fetch from thee *a fruit of the honesty of thy heart.*"—
By-and-bye, Hopeful would sleep on the drowsy ground
they were now entering : " By no means," said his friend,
and he skilfully engages him in a personal narrative till
the long danger is over.—And in the waters of the River,
at last, when their pilgrimage companionship is closing in
the companionship of transition, the friendship is as complete as ever it had been, and his " good friend Hopeful "
is to Christian as an angel of upbearing.

That very narrative about Little-faith which threatened
to be the occasion of rupture between the two friends,
while it is full of much besides, is also full of evidence of
a fine Christian sympathy on the part of the narrator,
although the affair is only one of report, and not of
personal observation, with him. It is a monologue of
Christian Tenderness from the first word to the last—of
Tenderness with a faint colouring of Pity over it, and a
high Sensitiveness of spirit guarding it,—such Tenderness
as a noble-minded Christian feels for a Christian who is
weaker, and through his weakness is less fortunate, than
himself. Thus it was that Hopeful found his friend more
uncanny to be trifled with at that moment than at any
other in all their recorded intercourse. He had a brother
to defend who needed all his defence, and who demanded
far more consideration just then, absent as he was, than
Hopeful himself did.

There are social emotions, however, which can be but

partially stimulated while the contact is a contact between Christian brethren only. It is not these alone whom Christian meets. Unhappily, he cannot well meet with any but such as are on the way, and are in some sense pilgrims, even if they be sham ones. The only genuine pilgrims whom he finds are those of whom he makes companions. And counterfeit pilgrims are not eminently fitted to foster emotions of Tenderness. Nevertheless, here and there along the way, we get opportunities of seeing a little into the wider social heart of Christian; and, as was hinted in the section on his Humility, we find it very much what we should desire.

It lies close to this, that the Tenderness of Christian, when occasion offers, very readily takes the form of *Compassion.*—Standing beside the miserable occupant of the iron cage, he asks the Interpreter—"But is there *no hope* for such a man as this?" He has not heart—(so it stands in the First Edition)—to ask the man if there is: "Nay, pray sir, do *you.*" And immediately the teacher touched a chord in his own bosom—(the words are Christian's own after the First Edition)—when he said to the man—"Why, the Son of the Blessed is *very pitiful.*"—And the trembling dreamer of the judgment arouses the same sentiment in him: he says to Piety afterwards—"It made my *heart ache* as he was telling of it."—His interest in the case of Pliable, of whom he gets word from Faithful, is expressive of his general concern about those who were still in the city, and is only enlivened into a special concern by the disappointment which aggravates it:—"Well, at my first setting out, I had hopes of that man; but now I fear he will perish in the overthrow of the city."—And it is but a maturer phase of the same concern which we recognise in his mood at the monument, where his commiseration of the woman's fate is mingled with sad wonder at the infatuation of Demas and his dupes "within sight" of such a warning.—But the liveliest instance of Christian's Tenderness, in this aspect of it, is furnished in the regret with which he regards his failure to impress Ignorance with the truth, although his patience had been considerably tried in the task. Bunyan "saw in his dream, that they went on apace before, and Ignorance he came hobbling after. Then said Christian to his companion, '*It pities me much for this poor man:* it will certainly go ill with him at last.'" Then the conversation expands into a discussion of the case of the many who are like him, in which we overhear Christian exclaiming, "Alas, poor men that they are!"—and so exclaiming in a connection which precludes the suspicion that it is anything of a heartless self-complacency which is inspiring the words.

Such a heart-hollow complacency as this,—and the asserted abundance of it is one of the thoughtless slanders with which Christians are sometimes misjudged, —would be apt to break down when the virtue which came to be demanded was that of self-sacrificing *Charity*. Unselfishness, benevolence, forbearance, forgivingness, do not go well with a self-gratulating self-esteem. But in Christian we can detect no lack of these. He is as indulgent to all as is consistent with fidelity and truth. His "faithfulness" is not of the sort which poses uneasily upon petty points of belief, and limits all its Tenderness to the range of the movement which its precarious posture affords it. He is tender all through and all over: his severity only qualifies his Tenderness at the hardest, and only then when the lines of vital truth have been crossed, and he is bound to reckon, with the light he has, that spiritual danger is near. He is travelling his road in an age when tolerance was little understood, and when views of theological things were apt to be straitened; but there is little to disturb us of intolerance in this man notwithstanding, and he might be a pattern to many of us in the largeness of his doctrinal allowances. Nor is it possible to explain his largeness by anything of hazy indifferentism, which so often gives a delusive look of largeness to the theological sympathies of men. He suffers for his doctrines to the very front of death ;—and Charity is overflowing the irons that clank upon him, and is streaming upon the wretches that maltreat and torture him :—" Not rendering railing for railing," says his historian, " but contrariwise *blessing, and giving good words for bad, and kindness for injuries done.*" His Charity bears rough handling : there is sterling stuff in it. His Tenderness is strong and prevails. It is severe to endure as well as to instruct and to rebuke. It is even more sturdy in trial than it is in debate, and is not put down although all but life itself is crushed in the brutal controversy of chains and fagots. That is the only " breadth " which Christians need care much to cultivate—tender breadth of heart, welded together with unconquerable tenacity of faith in the essential living verities of God's revelation.

But we must not linger upon the social love and lovableness of the pilgrim, and upon all the shades of sentiment which these embraced. We have seen enough to prove that his love of God, which must needs be the predominant sentiment in the new life which his Faith had opened to him, did not impoverish, but only replenish, his love of men. The fountains of Tenderness which had begun to fill when he resolved for pilgrimage, and which had brimmed themselves at the Cross, welled forth upon his fellow-pilgrims and his fellow-men, and upon all that had fellow-being with him from the same wondrous Hand. Did, then, the one or the other of those loves—the predominant or the subordinate Tenderness—bring damage to his love of truth? Did the accession which had come to his emotional nature generate refracting vapours or befogging mists within his moral nature? Was he still, or was he more than ever, a man of Candour, of Single-mindedness, of Truthfulness, of SINCERITY?

God is truth, and God is light, and God is love: Christian loved Him, and loved the men that He loved—in some feeble way as He loved them. Even his first compassion for himself as a man, so lively when the occasion was strongest, bore some resemblance to the compassion of his God for him. It was a compassion begotten of truth, and was true. When that compassion mellowed down and expanded into grateful love, the truth was not sublimated out of it, but only expanded likewise. His was no "show of pilgrimage": it had the least of show, and the most of reality. He had no doublenesses, no conceal-ments, no make-believes, in that heart of his, and therefore none in his pilgrimage. The Sincerity of the man is one of the charms and refreshments of our study of him.

To recognise this feature of his character we have only to open the book at any stage of the story. There is scarcely a separable atom of the history in which it does not appear.—He never permits a misconception, a mis-understanding, of a kind falsely favourable to himself, to keep place for a moment as a possible nucleus of more.—Before he starts at all, we witness this clear-heartedness in the frank avowals of his condition which he makes to his family, and in that honest "No" to Evangelist about seeing the Wicket-gate.—He is only started when we hear him tendering the instructive acknowledgment to Pliable respecting the glories that stand at the end of the pilgrim-age—"I can better conceive of them in my mind than speak of them with my tongue."—They get into the slime of Despond, and Pliable demands in no good humour where they are now? "Truly," said Christian, "I do not know."—There is a simple veraciousness concerning the same misfortune in his talk with Help.—His whole interview with Worldly-wiseman is that of a perplexed but single-hearted man in the hands of a practised deceiver.—His demeanour with Evangelist just afterwards is one of touching guilelessness.—The Interpreter finds him the most truth-loving of men.—The porter at the Palace Beautiful listens to the most transparent of apologies for his lateness.—The damsel Discretion asks him "how it happened that he came out of his country this way?" "It was as God would have it."—In the verbal rencounter with Apollyon, the words of the man were as straight-going as any dart in the quiver of the fiend.—The account he gives to Faithful of the combat which succeeded has as little of self-glorying in it as truth will permit, and as much of recognition of Divine deliverance as truth demands.—He smiles at the play of his own fancy when he is unmasking Talkative to Faithful: "But I am ready to think," says Faithful, characteristically, "you do but jest, because you smiled." "God forbid," rejoins Christian, "that I should jest (although I smiled) in this matter, or that I should accuse any falsely." And Faithful comes erelong to certify how habitually his comrade blends Candour with Charity:—"Well, brother, I am bound to believe you, not only because you say you know him, but also because *like a Christian* you make your reports of men. For I cannot think you speak these things of ill-will, but because it is even so as you say."—And thus we might step on to the end of the journey with him. But we may only recall how, at a stage comparatively advanced, his bearing and his utterances constitute a sharp running contrast to the bearing and words and name of By-ends, who would almost appear to be conceived as the antithesis to the character of Christian himself.

This is one of the virtues in which Bunyan never suffers his Christian to fail—in word, or in thought, or in life. His pilgrim seems to have no notion or desire, at any moment, of appearing other than he is—least of all, of appearing better than he is. He is aware of no reason why he should. His King knows the best about him, as He knows the worst ; the matter may well take end there as far as assumption is concerned. The opinions of men about him must be formed upon a prudent presentation of the reality ; if that is insufficient to secure their esteem, he is fairly content, only he will endeavour to be better still—more worthy of the credit which he may not receive, and less worthy of the discredit which he may have to endure, but always regardful supremely of the mind of God concerning him.

It is in this connection that we can notice the simple Cheerfulness of Christian when things are going at all well with him, and when his energies are occupied without being strained. Whether alone or with a companion, he will let forth his feelings now and again in a snatch of homely song, extemporised, as beseems pilgrim-minstrelsy, out of the thread of the circumstances. This is a sort of employment which comes into the programme of none but an unclouded and guileless heart—a heart that is overflowing, and overflowing with the limpidness of a mountain spring. The poetry is poor, but the spirit is rich ; and the poverty of the one, along with the richness of the other, enhances the artless naturalness of the strains as evidence of clearness of heart. In these, and at intervals in his conversation also, there are traces of Humour, which is never broad, indeed, yet often appears to be suffering the repression which it perhaps too readily receives. Oftener still there are vivacious touches that hover on the very borders of humour. But of Wit, as we should anticipate, there is not much that need be looked for in the recorded sayings of the pilgrim whose earnest " progress " was one " from this world to that which is to come."

Not all sternness, then—not all self-interest, even of the

highest order—was the character of this pilgrim in whom Bunyan pourtrays the average Christian. He has feelings which answer to the call of every relationship; and foremost among these is the feeling which so tenderly owns the claims of domestic life. He seeks the temporal good, he longs for the eternal good, of those whom the ties of blood have brought nearest to him in providence, and carries his kindred as a precious burden upon his spirit. He has more love to spare for them now than when he had less to love. It is a sign of much other than sanctity when the inmates of a man's home have little interest for him, even though they may live regardless of the religion which he believes that he himself possesses. The whole circle of our relatives has a primary claim upon our prayers and our patience, and, above everything, upon our most true and attractive Christian demeanour. But the emphasis of the claim strikes most strongly upon the instance of the household, and most strongly of all upon those who hold in this a position of natural and honourable responsibility. If there were not a plenitude of other reasons why parents should set themselves to be earnestly Christian, there is reason enough in the holy power with which it inspires them, as those who are training, and for the most part unconsciously, the young characters which are developing around them, and reason enough in the atmosphere of tenderness and sincerity which it is so fitted to intensify about a home—an atmosphere which is kindly without anything of laxity, and sunny without anything of unwholesomeness.

The "household of God," however,—Christian has his place and his duties in this also; and he accepts them with willingness and warmth. Into this circle of kinship he takes with him nothing of the responsibility of fatherhood, but he does take with him much of the responsibility, as well as the joy, of brotherhood. There is a domestic reality in this relationship which is apprehended and felt in proportion to the amount of faith-vision which a man brings to bear upon it. Every one who truly enters upon spiritual pilgrimage, it is evident, as truly becomes a unit of a great family as if he were born into it; which in a sense he is. But it is not the theory itself that is often declined: it is the practical through-going of the theory. Doubtless some heed must be given to social proprieties —perhaps even to conventional restraints. But let the feeling only exist in any measure that is proportionate to the spiritual fact,—not blunted by the domination of merely outward views of things, nor terrorised by the tyranny of worldly sentiment around it,—and brotherliness between Christians whom providence has brought into each other's way, in the same neighbourhood or in the same congregation, shall not seldom find opportunities and methods of expression which too frequently are never sought. It is not the perils of social impropriety that will account, on Christian principles, for all the frigidity—for all the unconcerned superiority on the one hand, or all the over-sensitive suspiciousness on the other—which run their course from year to year between undoubted Christians who are moving onward side by side to the same home. To a man whose outlook is one of Christian faith, the measurements of high and low are not all of them measurements of social position, or even of personal culture. Religious association has a right to take some stand upon its own system of estimates; and within that system—on the footing of Church-fellowship and social worship—men must, in the nature of the case, be apt to change places, so that the last becomes first, and the low becomes high. And the high here is the highest among all that is human where the human touches the Divine.

If it were to be asserted, that, in a partially-Christianised society like our own, Christians suffer more, and more acutely, at the hands of fellow-Christians than at the hands of the ungodly, it would be hard to disprove the assertion. The difficulty of annihilating the merest hint of such a thing is very significant. It means lovelessness, which again means worldly-heartedness ; and this does not mean Christianity, except at its poorest. If we had more of the love which is the operative sum-total of Christianity, we should have more of an every-day and well-wearing Tenderness, and therefore more of mutual helpfulness, and of happy confidence in Christians as Christians. Our secular freemasonries—the unsubstantial mimicries of truly Christian brotherhood—have sometimes threatened to overmatch us on our own ground. Intelligent heathens are bewildered with many things about our Christianity as it is lived under their eyes, but they are nearly swamped in their reckonings by the lack of brotherly temper we too often display. We might imagine the pilgrim of Bunyan getting into the way of a fellow-pilgrim, and acting towards him very much as he acts towards the merest pretenders to pilgrimage,— and perhaps a good deal less tenderly than he acts towards pretenders with some dash of distinction in them : we might imagine it ; but it would go some way to spoil the story for us, and to ruin all interest in the hero for every sagacious reader. We shall not bear likeness to this man in what we thus approve, unless we nourish the sense of family-kinship, and expand it as we can to the measures of a household that is dimensioned for the affection of an infinite Fatherhood. And it may perhaps quicken us to this if we meditate on the tender unswervingness with which the eye of the Divine Parent passes over every barrier of appearances, and crosses every line of human conventionality, that He may cast His great fatherly cherishings around each son or daughter whom He has redeemed to so unimaginable magnificences of being, and that He may conduct each one of them home to the hearth where the profoundest fellowships are gathering themselves for an eternal reign.

But the Christian carries his affections over a still wider field than this. If the love which his Christianity engenders were a parsimonious thing, it might well be content with exercising itself only within the sphere in which the domestic relationships of eternity are begun. But this love is not a too dainty or too selective thing. It is philanthropy. Its Tenderness has in it a holy ambitiousness of sweep. The love of the eternal family and the love of the race are the same love at work in dissimilar regions : the one shall seldom but be in proportion to the other. It is, then, no rival claim which the general world has upon our regard, whether in sentiment or in action. The Christian is never more like himself than when he is feeling and doing what good he can in every direction around him. None of the interests of men will count for nothing in his estimation, if only for the reason that the world and humankind belong to his Divine-human King. Christianity, above all systems, does honour to men as men, and approaches them as such with the most comprehensive and thorough friendliness. It need not fear to grasp the hand of mankind in the sincere fulness of its own heart, for that heart is tenderly true to their most abiding weal. So the earnest Christian man goes forth to foster the good which he finds in human society, and to eliminate the evil—to lighten the temporal ills of human life, and to take counsel and action for the uplifting of its moral and spiritual condition on the unfailing principles of his Christian faith. For he cannot but be acting the Christian all through. It is not for him to feel as if any toiling for mankind on the terms of a mere Christless "humanity" will suffice to meet the case of men. It is not for him even to seem to assent to the widespread falsehood, that culture, wealth, material greatness, artistic refinement, or even social good-will, are enough for mankind without the radical readjustments which the Gospel operates, and the solid starting-points which the Gospel alone affords for an infinitude of human elevation.

Nor in carrying forward these convictions does the Christian man need to flinch, if only he be sincere to the very depths of his being. Christian insincerity is Christian helplessness. It never in any age was more so than in ours; and, in truth, it is one hopeful thing about the age, that it will give only the least of heed to hollowness, however well disguised. But this spiritual untruthfulness is more than weakness; it is peril: it is the rotten timber which would sink Christianity if Christianity were capable of sinking. Short of this, it may work harm which is incalculable. "Lead me in Thy trueness,"—this is a prayer which every pilgrim heart has need to urge till its answer floods out of him every atom of falseness, of slackness to truth, in word or thought or deed. Froude utters a statement which every one who carries the name of Christian might ponder on his knees, when he says, that "of all the evil spirits abroad at this hour in the world, insincerity is the most dangerous."[1] It is for the Christian to resolve, in the power of his Lord, that henceforth this dangerousness shall derive no strength from the life and the heart which are his own.

[1] "Short Studies—'Education.'"

VII.

CHRISTIAN: HIS INTELLIGENCE—HIS HARMONY OF CHARACTER—HIS GROWTH.

IT is the moral qualities of a man which make up what we usually think of as his character. Really, however, these form only a portion, though unquestionably the supreme portion, of the whole character of a man. When we have considered all the purely moral features of a Christian personality, and watched them on their way to perfection under their new guise of spirituality and godliness, we have somewhat still left to consider and to watch if we would know all of the man which Christianity has touched and consecrated. The man has an intellect as well as a conscience and a will and a heart; and this too has upon it the sunshine of the new life. Christianity is friendly to intellect, and to all the true play of its multifarious powers. It can subsist with wonderfully little of intellect; but it never quarrels with however much, if only that much be loyal to the truth it brings.

Does, then, this loyalty to Christian truth impose any unpropitious restraint upon the intellect? Does it tend to diminish intellectual force, or to intimidate the outgoing of mental energy? Does it check the thirst for knowledge? Does it retard INTELLIGENCE? It is a common-place to say that all truth is one, and that Christian truth cannot but be on terms of amity with all other truth. It is equally a common-place to say that the faculties which have knowledge for their object are no less God-given than the faculties which have love and duty for their aims. But this is only part of the fact of the case. Christianity appeals to the intellect from the first, and puts it under employment to the last. It comes to a man, in great part, under its aspect of truth, and abides with him, in great part, under its aspect of truth still ; and truth, merely as truth, and first of all, can only deal with the faculties of the mind. We can revert to that significant picture with which we began our consideration of Bunyan's pilgrim : it is the picture of a man with his mental faculties engaged upon the contents of a book—upon a treasury of facts, for the most part, with much of exhortation that is but moral reasoning from the facts. His very faith comes of his knowledge, and has a strand of Intelligence running through its strength. He succeeds ill when his mental perceptions are hustled, and succeeds well when he is collected enough to have his faculties of mind in proper working poise. Defective intellectual operation, as a thing not more in accordance with duty than with safety, had no small share in the mischances of the Slough and of the path to Morality. The getting and the holding of the sight of the Wicket-gate was in no little measure a thing of the intellect. He could not even become a Christian, therefore, without having his mental faculties quickened in the act. And he could not continue to be a cordial Christian without having this department of his nature invigorated by use and enriched by acquirement.

It is evident that Bunyan had no thought of representing his pilgrim as a man of dull or ill-disciplined understanding. In the earlier stage, it is true, and until the man is well on his way, it would almost appear as if the Dreamer scarcely did him justice in this particular. But there are two considerations which must give some pause to our criticism :— we must take account, first, of the exceptional anxiety which agitated him before he reached the Gate, and the

soul-subduing gratefulness which filled him after the Gate
was passed—both of them emotional states at high-water,
beneath which all prominence of intellectuality would not
unnaturally be submerged ; and we must take account,
secondly, of the progress in intellectual clearness and
vigour, especially with respect to the concernments of his
journey, which time and experience must be allowed to
bring him.   In any case, the total impression we receive
from his history is that of a man who is more than fairly
well-informed and discerning—a man, moreover, in whom
reason is more salient than passion, and feeling complies
with thought.   His very temptations are such as would
befall a man of active and aspiring mind—speculative, imaginative, ingenious, yet withal intense, and sensitive without being sensuous.   So his victories, when he wins them,
are usually the allegorical victories of a gracious logic over
a graceless sophistry.   The man has his intellect to reckon
with, as well as his intellect to work, in the moral and
spiritual toil of his pilgrimage.

We have only one clear hint of how the pilgrim stood
in regard to Scholarship, and the hint is favourable to him
as far as concerns this valuable instrumentality in the line
of Intelligence.   Hopeful and he are in front of the " old
monument," and are gazing upon it without reaching any
firm theory of what it may be.   " At last Hopeful espied,
written above, upon the head thereof, a writing in an unusual hand ; but he, being no scholar, called to Christian
(*for he was learned*) to see if he could pick out the meaning.   So he came, and after a little laying of the letters
together, he found the same to be this—' Remember Lot's
wife.'   So he read it to his fellow."   The document was
not a tedious one, but evidently the skill was in him that
might have unravelled much more, and which may have
been of large service to himself and others on occasions
which are not recorded.   Christian has at least two of the

"three R's" pretty well in hand—at a time, too, when education, at any rate south of the Tweed, was by no means a common luxury in the land.

But this is no more than equipment towards Intelligence. Has he actual Knowledge?—and is his Knowledge well assorted under the ordering of Reflection? His Conversation is the richest store of evidence we have for our answer. Conversation seldom represents all that there is in a man; but when it is genuine, and especially if it gets into liveliness as Christian's often does, it more faithfully represents his available mental possessions, as far as it ranges, than any other mode of expressing mind. Now, Christian talks well—sometimes excellently well. And, on the whole, he really talks, and does not harangue or declaim. In his talks with his true-hearted companions we have him at his best as a converser; and in these we see him not only a well-furnished but a thoughtful and open-minded man— cautious of assertion, ready in suggestion, feeling after principles, and working up to causes. Plainly, his acquaintance with his Bible is intimate, and his knowledge of its contents well assimilated into his thought and life, though his interpretations in minor instances may sometimes be dubious. In this intercourse of his with his friends, moreover, he displays much insight into human nature, and a considerable knowledge of the world. His discernment of character, even when the character is garbed under the fairest exterior of pretension, was usually clear and decisive, and appeared to distinct advantage in comparison with that of either of the companions who enjoyed his continuous fellowship. As we watch and hear him, we are apt to recall the words of Swedenborg, quoted with admiration by Emerson :—" To be able to discern that what is true is true, and that what is false is false—this is the mark and character of Intelligence " (*The Over-Soul*). Of course we do not often see his mind at work except

within the region of what is strictly spiritual: the conditions of the history do not well permit us. But we can
easily conceive of such a man as bringing a lightful
intellect to bear upon all passing things, and as moving
with judicious good-sense, and with the respect of even
unspiritual men, in the midst of the bustling world which
lies behind the Allegory,—looking at everything in the
light of heaven, but seeing it in that, and seeing it only
the more truthfully for the very reason that his vision is
thus comparatively purged of earthly vapours, and set free
from the distorting prejudices of self-love.

But the knowledge he has acquired, and the good-sense
he has educated, are also well shown in his contentions
with such pilgrims as he finds to be walking in error or
deception. In Controversy, though he is never acrid or
unfair, he is always nimble and strong. He discomfits his
adversary—not in any case, indeed, by fully convincing
him, yet in every case by making the truth too much for
the disputant to bear. The way in which he disposes of
the specious rubbish of By-ends and his crew is clean and
complete; nor can we but admire the warm logic and
compassionate inexorableness with which he pushes "poor
Ignorance" out of his false refuges, and leaves him face to
face with the one true source of welfare. We who are
impartially listening can yield our testimony to the victoriousness of his reasoning, even if we must regret the
defeat of his purpose. And his adversaries are sometimes
sturdy arguers—subtle, plausible, and shifty: yet he meets
and overcomes them with the well-handled weapons of
truth. Truth indeed; but even with this upon his side,
he might not have won the best of it, and certainly in
some instances would not, but for the Intelligence which
made him master of the truth.

Capable in controversy, however, as he is, he does not
betray any fondness for it on its own account. When he

may, he can be an intelligent listener. He could afford
to leave Talkative to Faithful, only interfering indirectly
when Faithful appealed to him under the spell of
the man's tongue; and he interfered then to some purpose, by making the shrewd suggestion that Faithful
should press the subject of "the *power* of religion"—a
suggestion which turned the glib creature into a helpless
accuser of himself. But he could not afford to leave
Ignorance to Hopeful; and even at a point where the
benighted man was like to grasp Hopeful into the argument, Christian struck in for his rescue, and settled the
disputation by the reasoned appeal to which we have
referred above. And it is to be noted, that Christian will
not come to argument upon any subject which is not of
the solidest importance. He is no less judicious in
abstaining from argument than he is cogent in sustaining it.

Indeed, the general Sound Judgment of the pilgrim
appears in many of the incidents of the story, although
there do occur conjunctures when it proves insufficient.
He has no trouble about Demas, save to rate him in some
of the sharpest words he is ever recorded as uttering : the
impostor even appears to be abashed by the clear inquiries
which Christian flings at him from the road before he has
scarcely unfolded his allurements. But then the very first
inquiry was this—and it would bear to be printed in gold
upon the page of every Christian's practical catechism :—
" *What thing so deserving as to turn us out of the way to
see it ?* "—Old Pope, long before, sat muttering at him : he
could not have done more wisely with that personage than
he did, when he " held his peace, and set a good face on
it."—The adroit masterfulness with which he managed
Hopeful on the Enchanted Ground—a passage in his
history which we have already found fruitful in marks of
character—affords admirable illustration of most of the

qualities we are here considering.—And we have not a more instructive phase of his sanctified common-sense than is presented, once for all, in his words to Hopeful after their first interview with Ignorance, and in Hopeful's prompt recognition of their wisdom :—"' What! shall we talk further with him, or outgo him at present, and *so leave him to think of what he hath heard already, and then stop again for him afterwards, and see if by degrees we can do any good to him?*' 'Let us pass him by, if you will (responds Hopeful), and talk to him anon, even as he is able to bear it.'" Christian speaks to "do good," and to do greater good he can be silent.

There is an aspect of religion—that is, of the religion of Christ—by which it may be regarded, not untruthfully, as absolute Good-Sense working its way in a man,—first impelling him into the new life, and next, and always, controlling him along that life towards its own fulfilment and fruition. In this respect, fully conceived, a sound Common-Sense is both rudder and gale : it wafts as well as steers. For, indeed, this Common-Sense, though we have naturally slipped on to it in the line of mere Intelligence, has more in it than is intellectual only. It is more than bare calculation ; it is more than simple reasoning ; it is more than sheer perception of what is profitable. All these are in it ; but it has them all in balance with motives of duty and impulses of feeling, and is at touch with the whole contents of one's nature, even with those which seem most remote from what is intellectual. It may be said, perhaps, to be a mental perception of the size, and weight, and momentum, that there are in things as they move in space which is pervaded by laws that are moral— a purposeful apprehension, therefore, of the total results which under these conditions shall make for rightness, propriety, order, seemliness, beauty ; and these pass beyond the concern of purely intellectual operation, and reach into the region the most comprehensive name of which is Love. Yet the basis of this complex quality is plainly in the intellect; and still, religion may well be represented as the one theory of life which puts Common-Sense into complete embodiment and unlimited exercise. The pilgrim himself seems to feel something of this, on the side of self-interest, when Apollyon is confronting him, and is endeavouring to beat down his spirit by thrusting upon him a charge of desertion of service:—"I was indeed born in your dominions," answers Christian with a touch of manful sarcasm; "but your service was hard, and your wages such as a man could not live on (for the wages of sin is death): therefore, when I was come to years, *I did as other considerate persons do*—look out if perhaps I might mend myself." Christian had caught something of the philosophy of his Book as to who are "wise" and who are "fools."

While, however, religion admits of being set in this aspect,—and while it may even be affirmed that Christians themselves, when they display lack of Common-Sense, though it be in their very religiousness, are really irreligious to the extent of that lack,—yet it would be inexcusable to overlook how indispensable in religion the supernatural element is, and how futile all merely natural faculty must be if left to work out its own decisions unaided. Christianity not only quickens what valid materials it finds in a man; it contributes what it does not find. It even brings knowledge which is absolutely new to us, and which belongs altogether to itself. This knowledge, too, is just the knowledge which transcends all other in its importance to a man as he is. Under the message of Christianity, an intellect has to touch facts, and to face phenomena, which it could never touch or face, or even adequately fancy, but in the presence of that message alone. So far is Christianity from circumscribing intellect, that it throws back the horizon-line of intellect indefinitely, and the new great zone of landscape radiates light enough to flood even the old landscape for the first time with true visibility. Christians ought to be the most intelligent of men; and in a sense they are. But in every sense, the Christian man, emphatically in these days of ours, had need to be careful and generous in his mental culture, if only to offer his own witness to the queenly regard which Christianity entertains for all that is true, and for all that sinlessly concerns our humankind. Yet, too, for his own sake—that is, for Christ's sake in himself—it comes to every Christian not only as right but as duty, to fit and furnish his intellectual nature up to the utmost limit of his opportunity. And it shall not prove obstructive to his finest intellectual training, if he make it even his chief intellectual care to know intelligently, and to hold with a wise liberty, the substance of his faith; because, for this, it will avail him most to keep his intellect closely conversant with the sublime record of revelation, and to maintain himself in the attitude towards it of a learner who is stooping at the spring-head of Divine communication. In the direct line of this, it will also avail him much, he will find, to give himself to an earnest and appropriating attentiveness to the teachings of the pulpit; and there is every reason why he should supplement these, as far as he may, by making selection for himself from what is at least wholesome in the instructions of the religious press. It is a matter for lively congratulation that our age stands remarkable for its elucidation of the Sacred Writings, and for the ease with which almost any one can lay his hand upon copious and accurate illustration of the Book which is the fountain of the Christian faith. But while in that Book there are materials for the development, as well as for the engagement, of the highest Intelligence, it is not desirable that the Intelligence of any Christian, least of all in our day, should be derived from that supreme Book alone. Let books of science, of history, of art, come freely beneath its shadow: they shall find its shadow a kindly one.

Thus we complete our survey of the character which Bunyan has left on his canvas as the character of his hero —the character of the normal Christian man as he was led to conceive him. When we look back to collect the result, and to put together the parts again in the light of what fuller acquaintance with them our analysis may have brought us, we are sensible of a balance, of a HARMONY, in the character, which ought not to pass without obtaining our attention.

There are characters,—it is scarcely unsafe to say that there are Christian characters,—in which, "as Moses' serpent the Egyptian's swallowed," one quality "eats the rest." In such a case, much will depend upon what this one quality is. But even if that quality be of the highest, or be among those which are the least liable to become evil qualities by the very excess, this does not save the character from being one-sided, or from lacking the well-knit poise and lithe consistency which it is well that a character should possess. It is not any mathematical equality that is to be looked for among the various elements which compose a character—not an impossible communism which levels, whether up or down: it is not equality so much as equation—a balancing of values and powers according to the intrinsic import of each. Nor is it any tame uniformity that can be desired between one aggregate of character and another: even if such were conceivable, it would be an anomaly in the midst of the endless diversity which stands as the undeviating—we might almost say, paradoxically, the uniform—law of the universe. It is Harmony that is to be desired in each one—a Harmony which still preserves as much of distinguishableness as shall mark a definite individuality.

It is something of this which we note in the pilgrim as we have been studying him.   He is Christian and no one else, and he is Christian always ; but there is on the whole an evenness, a prevalent averaging, in his character, and in the conduct which translates it, that indeed is one of the most notable characteristics of him.   He is not " Faithful," he is not "Hopeful," he is not " Honest ": he is all of them in a modified measure ; he is " Christian." It may of course be considered that the principal pilgrim, by virtue of his place in the book, and as representing Christian life in general, must needs be invested with a more neutral character than any other pilgrim ; and there is force in the consideration.   But this pilgrim, so invested in his representative function, turns out to be more than a representative, and to appear, visibly, as not a little of an example, in respect of this comparatively neutral character of his.   This harmoniousness of character, it is true, scarcely tends to deepen our interest in him : indeed, it is due to Bunyan to remember, that this is an appreciable difficulty which he creates for himself in the management of his story, and that he overcomes it—most of all, no doubt, by such variety of incident outside of character as probability will allow, but also—by the borrowed interest of the characters, sometimes sharply distinctive, which are brought into relation with him.   If, however, it does not deepen our interest, it increases our respect, and commends itself to our imitation.   The rounded completeness satisfies us, even though the dimensions, in part or in whole, might conceivably be greater.

This pervading characteristic of balance will be perceived in the character of the pilgrim from whatever side we approach it.   One of the best-marked contrasts of type in the matter of character is the Contemplative as distinguished from the Active.   Christian is not conspicuously either, but is both in something of a due proportion.   His contemplation leads to action, is followed by action, re-plenishes for action. He was never so contemplative as when he was lingering in the Palace Beautiful; he was never so strenuously active as just after he left it. He is absorbed in contemplation at the Cross; immediately we read of him that he " gave three leaps for joy, and *went on* "—went on to gird himself, very soon, to the task of remonstrating with the three sleepers. In nearly all his conferences with others,—and those with his select companions are not seldom highly contemplative,—he is on his feet, constraining contemplation to minister to activity. —Or we may test him by the contrast of type which distinguishes the Theoretical from the Practical man. Christian had his theories, but they were working ones. He set no store by schemes if they would not fall into practice; and any scheme that profitably did so, he endeavoured to turn into livingness in his own personal life. He was unsparing with the mere theorisers who came across his path—not always because the theories were themselves erroneous, but because they stood bodi-less in the brain only. " The soul of religion is the practical part," says he to Faithful; and he could not accuse himself as he said it. When he has been learning new truth, or learning old truth with a new vividness, he is almost impatient to take it away with him into the experience and the duty of the pilgrimage.—Or, again, we may prove him by the two extremes of type which set the Intellectual over against the Emotional. We shall scarcely err, perhaps, if we regard the intellectual as relatively strong in him; but we have seen that the emotional in him is far from weak. He mingles the two in a manner that is advantageous to both. He thinks with feeling, and he feels with thought. There is often warmth in his arguments, and he never glows but he has solid fuel of reason for his heat. The energy of thought in him is stimulated by his emotion; but it is seldom that his emotion carries him beyond desirable bounds either in thinking or in acting. His wakeful Imagination—this is sometimes a help to him, and sometimes a hindrance, working as it does so near to the border-line which separates mind from heart; but he keeps it under rein, and evidently aims at compelling it into the place of a brilliant servitor to Reason and Duty.

Christian, then, will not bear to be classified under any extreme type of character, or even under any very decided one. We shall advance a step further in proof of the Harmony we are considering, if we are able to recognise in him an equal fulness of virtues which stand more or less opposite to each other: we should then have not only a balance in general, but a balancing in detail. Now, we have already been witness that there is much of this internal self-adjustment in the character of the pilgrim. We have beheld him as a sympathising friend, though he had won renown as a most dangerous foe. We have found in him a good capacity for doing, and we have marked in him a still better capacity for suffering. He is modest and humble, but he is boldly prompt in the defence of what is true and just, and is forward to face his duty whatever eyes are on him. He has the genial sunshine of charity in him, and the scorching flash of holy indignation. He has a hopeful buoyancy about him during most of his journey, but during all of it he is sobered by a wholesome fear. His love to God is not greater than his reverence for all that manifests the Divine. The future is vivid to him, but it does not impair his interest in the present, which is God's allotment for him now. There is contented calm about him, all the while that he is throbbing with spiritual ambition. He is strong in his own will, yet he is very leal in his loyalty to God's. He has a keen consciousness of the interests and responsibilities which gather around him as an individual man, but he cherishes a sense, scarcely less clear, of the close relation he bears to society, especially to that truest Society which is ripening on earth for an immortal history unto God by Jesus Christ. All round the subtle sphere of his character, as would seem, the diameter-points hang well in poise, seldom dipping so far as to greatly disturb the collective play of equilibrium.

It will need little more to confirm our apprehension of this Harmony in the character of Christian, if we further recall the just measure he maintains in respect of those qualities which by excess deteriorate into infirmity or error. We cannot have failed to take some note of this. He is eminently conscientious as we see him, but we do not find that he is given to fanciful or fastidious scruples. His courage does not pass on into recklessness, nor his valour into combativeness. He is firm, but we cannot say that he is ever obstinate. His confidence of faith does not push itself over into presumptuousness; his hope does not evaporate into visionary dreaming. His liberality stops short of looseness, and his liberty has nothing in it of license. He is always checking and counter-checking himself with all his spiritual onwardness; for he feels that excellence of character is not a matter of the urging of even good dispositions in him, one by one, as far as each will go, but is rather a delicate and firm-handed managing of them in the midst of a complexity of perilous possibilities. He comes ever better to know, as his great task goes forward and his experience gathers, that to be holy—to be whole, hale, healthy, inwardly happy—he must not only purge out of him what is positively evil, but must preserve what is in itself good from squandering itself into evil along the line of its own latitude. And it is as thus watching and toiling with himself that we see him to be infallibly in the way of achieving, under the good Spirit, that intricate harmoniousness which represents the ineffable

Equipoise of the Divine nature itself, on such a scale as that Eternal Harmony can be represented within the marvellous dewdrop of an individual soul.

In giving all due heed to this well-modulated play of parts in the character of the pilgrim, distinction must nevertheless be made between what demands our imitation and what may only demand our remark. We are not to be anxious to compress ourselves into the precise mould of this character, or of any other character whether allegorical or real. Not every human character is meant, not every individual nature is constructed, to play just the same ethical tune within itself,—though the laws of ethical music are as rigorous as the laws of artistic sounds. The Harmony for each man is a harmony which is set upon the key of his own individuality—a harmony which may present very perceptible points of contrast with that which is still harmony enough for his next neighbour. Moral excellence permits of a wide range of variety, and then is not only excellence, but is manifoldness of excellence. The noblest figures of Bible story are not more distinguished than they are distinct in respect of the characters they display. We have business enough on hand, in this loftiest of our employments, if we make sure that grace is correcting and adorning the type of character which nature has already predetermined for us, and is hallowing it to God, in its own uniqueness, as a living stone of the temple which is being built of human characters for eternity. For there is a wider and a fuller Harmony—a harmony of all individual harmonies—which is working on towards its own fulfilment, to the glory and delight of Eternal Love : it is the harmony of the whole kingdom of redeemed character in all ages —the harmonious moral completeness of the " Church, which is His body, the fulness of Him that filleth all in all."

In these later sentences we have been touching upon a

principle which shall now engage us for what remains of our consideration of Christian the pilgrim. It is the principle of Advancement. Bunyan's Allegory is a record of a " progress," and this is at least a *going forward*, whatever doubleness of meaning may be thought to be concealed in the word. The pilgrimage is a strictly onward one—onwards from a starting-point which, once for all, is left behind, and onwards towards a goal which is at all hazards to be reached. It is here that the essence of the Allegory lies.

For this very reason it may be well to work ourselves into some clearness as to the contents of this leading metaphorical idea in the book. There is a certain complication in the " progress." Christian is going through his *natural* life of days and weeks and years ; he is advancing, whether he will or not, right on to his grave, with a march that is measured by the clocks that are striking the hours all along his way, and are hasting to strike their last hour for him. In some degree parallel to this natural journey, however, his true journey is being conducted ; it is a journey of the *spirit* in him—a progress from experience to experience, which has the natural life for its outward element, but has a spiritual activity and a spiritual history for its essential texture. And here the Allegory meets us with its great underlying verity—that the life of a man is the life of the spirit which he is, and that his true biography is the biography of this; all else is circumstance and setting, occasion and opportunity—mere conditions of life and history. But, again, he is living a temporal life for God ; he is pursuing a journey of *good works* across the region of the world, in family and church and community—is making a progress through the task which has been given him in the world to do. That, too, is parallel with the pilgrimage of the natural life, and it touches closely the pilgrimage of the spiritual life. And yet, the precise line of Advancement which is now concerning us most—his Advancement in character—his Spiritual and Moral GROWTH —is not exactly any one of these. It is nearest of kin to the inner history, to the successive experience of his spirit; but there might be annals enough of these, while nothing of spiritual development was to be traced along the gathering pages.

A good old-fashioned word for the thing we have just particularised is "sanctification." The word, however, must be taken with all of its great meaning. Its foremost idea—that of purging out the unholy, the "profane," which lingers in the spirit—must not be the only idea we take. Along with this we must take the other idea, which is its complement—that of the rearing of the implanted holy, and the ripe establishing of the whole character on the principles of sacred consciousness—of love to God and imitation of the mind of Christ. It is a reaching on to attain the ideal of the "perfect man," as this has become possible "in Christ Jesus." It is the manhood getting back the lost harmony of its own mechanism, and, in progressive sympathy with this restoration, ever urging all its acquired harmoniousness into a richer and loftier melody of being and of life.

Now, it is this which is the core of the "progress" which finds its record in this book of pilgrimage. It is a progress to heaven, indeed: phenomenally, that is just the progress which it is; and the aspect of the matter which is thus represented is both real and momentous. But, after all, this is rather only the topography of the progress; the progress itself is in his heart, in his character—is borne along with him, and appears as a growing meetness for residence in that City upon which his aspirations are bending, and towards which the lapse of time and incident is bringing him. "The kingdom of God is within" him. True, as being under a government of things which has a prevailing regard to fitnesses and ultimate adjustments—as being loyal to a supreme Management, which cannot permit condition and place to present for very long the anomaly of severance—he is one who is taking the road of his destiny when he is nearing the heavenly City; and all the transactions which have controlled his character from the first, and all the emotions which declare its peculiar complexion to the last, have still the heavenly City for their source and home. Love to the King seeks its way to the presence of the King; and the King's own primal love—that, too, comprehends the presence with Himself of the man by whom that love has been accepted. Yet the central thing of all—the progress which is essential and absolute—is the advancement of the pilgrim in what the pilgrim *is;* and the very City is as much the metaphorical consummation of his personal perfection as it is the allegorical fulfilment of his hopes and his recompense.

It must be acknowledged that Bunyan has succeeded well in the general air of onward advance which he has thrown around his Allegory,—thus implementing the promise of its name. In this onwardness of movement it was needful that the character of the pilgrim himself should have a very appreciable share. The pilgrim and his progress must on the whole keep pace. It is a special mark of Bunyan's skill that they substantially do so, and that they do so with a naturalness of correspondency which betrays no strain. The Dreamer has quite a suite of progressive things to manage simultaneously:—he has the inward disposition of the pilgrim; he has his outward bearing among the happenings that occur with him, both the ordinary and the extraordinary; he has the colour, and form, and place, of the happenings themselves;—each of the three sets of things to exhibit as under an economy of ongoing, and each of the three to maintain in its mutual relation to the others. The progress in them all is as perceptible as the geographical progress itself is.

Within these lines of progress he has certainly some liberty left him as to the disposing of his incidents ; and he takes so much advantage of this right which the subject gives him, that some have felt as if the liberty were pushed to a *trans*posing of them : Bunyan knew his subject too well for this. But with respect to the general wisdom he displays in the ordering of incident, tested by the two-fold relation of incident—to the stage of the pilgrimage, and to the inherent characteristics of the pilgrim,—there can only be one opinion.—The place of the Interpreter's House is admirably well-advised. The Cross can come after this— to the relief of many a sincere Christian reader whose experience diverges here from some type of experience which has been too exclusively enforced ; but the Palace Beautiful comes only after the Cross ; and the tempestuous era of temptation may well come in, for the permanent clearing of the air, after the season of confirmation and riveting which was spent in that congenial abode.—And plainly, each of those epochs did a world for the development of the man : if we heard nothing of them, and only fell in with him in the successive intervals between them, we might almost read them into the history, very much as they precisely were, from the stamp of themselves which they have left upon his deportment and temper. They are at least noteworthy points in a period of remarkable advancement. We recall the tattered burden-bearer who is pursuing his troubled and precarious way across the space which divides the city from the Wicket-gate ; we now set our eye upon the accoutred champion who emerges, resolute and grateful, from the Valley of the Shadow, and attaches himself, with an unforced air of intelligent manliness, to the strong-willed companion he has found : we are struck with a contrast which is a contrast of progress, and of a progress which is deeper than the milestones can mark for us. And this contrast has both its boundaries lying within that stage of his journey in which he enjoyed nothing of the advantages of a constant human companionship.

We cannot well forget, that the contrast which this earlier stage affords us is sharpened very notably in as far as it includes the condition of the pilgrim previous to his true entrance upon the pilgrimage. It is worthy of remark, however, that the transition which is accomplished at the Wicket-gate does not, in Bunyan's hands, effect any very sudden or complete transformation of the man's ways such as many would have probably represented. The simple earnest urgency of him was there gathered up into a well-defined channel, and the old city was cut off from his paths henceforth, and the hopes of the brighter City began to work upon him with unembarrassed strength : his prospects were immensely certified, and the main purpose of his life was settled into concentration : his condition was virtually repaired. But we do not detect, in the substance of his inner character, any change that is very abrupt, or any advance that is more distinct than is produced by his stay with the Interpreter, or by his sojourn with the damsels of the Palace ; and we do not seem to observe an advance even so great as that which accelerates itself from the spot where the Cross is seen. The advance of character, as such, is slow as we see it here : it is a Growth—not indeed at a fixed rate, but still very gradual,—a thing of chemical, and not of mechanical, progress. It is the sight of the Cross which, subjectively to himself, consummates his "conversion"—sends him forth, that is, full of Christian consciousness and purpose. The deeds in the Valley, whether for the temptable material out of which their necessity arose, or for the latent courage of which they were the expression, or for the vigorous development of character which they undoubtedly wrought, would have been impossible but for the experience he enjoyed in the presence of the Cross and of the Three Shining Ones who there attended him. This is the most cardinal point in the history of the character of the pilgrim.

Onwards from this first great instalment of the journey, the personal directness of Christian's experience is broken by the companionship through which it so largely becomes a thing that is equally shared by himself and another. We can still think of him, however, as the principal figure, and of the happenings as falling out chiefly for his sake. That stage of the journey which he spent with Faithful is a calmly fertilising time for his character, after the storminess which preceded it, and before the inclemency which followed it. The roots of his character were being quietly fed, in an atmosphere that was bracing without being tumultuous; and its general fibre meanwhile was gaining robustness by evangelical effort and by defence of the truth. That period was needed for the splendid passive work which was awaiting him at the city of Vanity—the work amid which the period was closed. Here therefore we can report progress again. And, doubtless, the difference between the confessor in the grasp of those worldly fanatics, and the ragged man of the burden whom Evangelist is directing—nay, between this confessor and the man who is trembling past the tethered lions in the dusk, or even the man who is "vaingloriously smiling" in front of Faithful after the Valleys are passed,—this difference is striking enough when it is made clear by bringing together the points which space the interval. Yet we are conscious of no surprise, when we have kept company with him along the interval, that he deports himself then as we see him do. His character has been growing beside us—has been imperceptibly rising, as if by gradient of incline, with the ascending way to the City of the King. And when this nearer city stands inevitable in the path, he enters it on a high level of character—sober, strong, steadfast, able to have his noblest qualities in sway over his meaner ones, and to crown his heroism itself with golden fruits of meekness and benevolence. The active valour of the First Valley, and the more passive wariness of the Second, are now transcended by a waiting and suffering endurance of human devilry which tells us not a little of progress that has been, and speaks assuringly of progress that still shall be.

The remaining portion of the journey, in which Hopeful was his fellow-traveller, contains chapters which a less sagacious dreamer than Bunyan might not have located here. There is more of blameworthy mischance during this later period than during either of the previous ones. It is the period, doubtless, in which the River of God flows through the sunny meadows, and the pilgrim can go to rest beneath the fragrant shadow of the fruit-laden boughs, and can feast his senses day and night in the stillness that sleeps among the ever-blooming lilies.[1] It is the period, too, in which the Delectable Mountains are climbed to their calm summits, and the very City itself begins to take its place faintly in the far landscape. It is the period, above all, in which Beulah becomes a land of his habitation, and there is more of holy settlement with him than has ever before found its way into the lot of the pilgrim. Beulah, moreover, represents a progress—progress in the very valid form of maturing—as compared even with the crushed victoriousness of the epoch which transpired in Vanity. But the River and its meadows have just ahead of them the By-path, and the Meadow which that has made memorable; and these are darkened by the oncoming shadow of the Castle of Doubting : the Delectable Mountains themselves have the Flatterer and his net, away in the plain just beneath the glance of their genial peaks. There is in all this a slackening of tension,

---

[1] See Longfellow's version of Dante, "Purgatorio," notes to canto vii., line 70.

and a lack of heedfulness, which are not indeed consistent
with the highest attainments of Christian character, but
which are abundantly natural after noteworthy achievements have taken their position in the past, and foretast-
ings of coming fruition are like to allure the heart's interest
away from present duty and danger towards future rest
and reward. It is like the time when the orchard-tree is
setting its blossom into fruit: it may miscarry a little in
frosty nights and under unkindly winds; but it has vitality
enough in it, and productiveness enough, to carry into the
autumn days a load of fruitage that shall verify the good
hopes of the orchardman.

It is noticeable here that the period of Faithful's companionship has no mishaps in it. We cannot withhold
from Faithful himself some credit for this: it is hard
to think of Faithful, in this last stage of his journey, as
falling into any plight which his own weakness had brought
to pass. But the presence of Faithful need not be regarded
as wholly accounting for this immunity. It cannot be
doubted that there are periods when Christians are specially
kept, or are specially endowed with self-keeping; and
these periods could nowhere more fittingly occur than
between an ordeal of conflict and an ordeal of suffering.
We seem, indeed, to be sensible of underground roots of
connection passing through this period of peace, and
stretching secret links across it between the experiences of
the period which went before and those of the period
which came after, every root and link carrying tidings of
advancement still: Doubting Castle is the counterpart of
Vanity, as Vanity was the perfection of the warfare in the
Valleys. This era of the Giant no doubt means reaction,
when fidelity has become relaxed under a temporary
softening away of the edge of self-denial, and the soul gets
down upon itself to find—may it be once for all!—what it
just is that self can yield it:—in the hopeful, doubt; in

the despondent, melancholy ; in the thoughtful, perplexity wandering on the confines of despair. But with a well-recovered faith in the promises—why, then one more foe is laid in the dust, and the true pilgrim can step upon him to reach on to higher things, better able henceforth " to teach others also." The Flatterer—he plays the wiliest trick upon the pilgrim that ever was played, as it is the last : he ought not to have fallen into the snare—at that stage, and with the warning he had : but it is precisely at an advanced stage, and with such a history running up to a revelation of the Celestial City, that this seducer must come, and then with the look of an angel who might have hailed from the City itself, so extraordinary are his spirituality, his purity, his liberty—the decoys for nothing else but a genuine spirituality which is off its guard. Demas, too, cannot anywhere so properly appear as in this section of the road ; for avarice is a vice that flowers its infirmity towards the end of the season, although, as we are relieved to find, it is a vice which is by no means a vice of Christian's. The silver-mines have a pretty late place in the pilgrimage ; but if they had been assigned a later place, they and their showman should only have met with the warmer a scorn from the ripening unworldliness of this hero of the King's highway.

In one of his finest poetical conceptions, that of Beulah —a country of tranquil fulness of spiritual life, where the soul has battled its way to peace, and begged its way to plenty, and travelled its way to the spiritual neighbour-hood of the eternal land—Bunyan has constrained his Allegory to halt that he might the more richly picture the truth of his subject. Some reach Beulah early : here and there we find

> " A happy soul, that all the way
> To heaven hath a summer's day,"

even spiritually. But Christian was not such a soul. He

did abide in Beulah, however, for a while, making acquaintance with the happy residents, and meeting some who were residents of a happier region still. For heaven and earth are mingling here, that the transition may not be a violent one whensoever the pilgrim passes away into the heavenly places in person. Progress still, then, in this country where no pilgrimage is,—progress of character, assimilation in heart and will to the people of the City which almost dazzles with its lustrous proximity. It is no actionless community which peoples this place, for it is astir with a holy animation ; and in the background even of Beulah we must fill-in a present world of many and motley interests. But contemplation has grown to adopt activity as its handmaid ; and to the eye of the pilgrim, set free from pondering the path of his feet, the celestial light touches all things into hallowedness, while it evermore opens forth his own spirit like a flower to let itself in. The picture is a picture of character, of far-advanced personal sanctification, much more than of anything else. And here the progress may be rapid, with all the appearance it wears of a progress that has come to its limit. The character has still a far way to go to reach the perfection which the King has appointed for his yet homeless one. He too, however, has erelong to arise and go forward. A little more of waiting and working, of busy ripening in that wondrous sunshine, then the River will be crossed, and Beulah itself out-travelled. Visible advance again—not across the River only, but for no little way after the River has been left behind and forgotten. Long after his companions on the Beulah shore have lost sight of him, we see him still, and still he is moving upwards and on. So near the City is, the very City ; yet so distant. But in that disencumbered vesture,—if it be vesture at all he could scarcely tell us,—he is not any longer on pilgrimage. These holy, happy brethren—they are not pilgrims. This sunlight of music—it is not the land through which he has fought and fared. This glorious mountain—it is no Hill Difficulty, with fears in the path, and with a way stretching down beyond it through unknown jeopardies. He is now within the pure "native air" of his home-country, and it is thrilling his being with health such as he never knew or imagined. His character—it is throbbing at last into the full harmony which has never yet come to him but in broken feebleness. The gate unfolds—it closes,—and we are without—the good Dreamer and we—stricken with a longing to follow him, above all, thither.—The Dreamer has followed him, and many a reader who in imagination has lingered with him at the closed gate. We cannot, till our journey too is accomplished, and our task too is done. On that day, if we are not false to the grace of the King, we too shall ascend the mountain of the City, and shall take our own place "among them."

In our chequered climate, where a whole panorama of change may pass before our eyes between a sunrise and a sundown, we now and then witness a day which presents a fitting symbol of the Christian's course. When we first look out from our window, the heavens are gloomy, and the rain is driving pitilessly against the trickling glass. Before we are well astir, the clouds have parted, and glints of sunshine are shooting through rifts of blue. An hour more, and the clouds are closed in again, and the breeze has become chill, and the shadowed earth shivers in the wet wind. Another hour, and a patch of opening sky is seen on the horizon, and the breeze arouses itself to a gale, and the trees are shaken dry in the stir of the sunny air. Past noon, hail-showers are sailing black across the heavens, and sun and cloud compete for the mastery. But the wind quiets down ere long, and the cloud-masses begin to float at leisure, only half-hiding the sun as it bends towards the west. By sunset, the clear soft air is full of calm, and men come to their doorways, or pause on their road homewards, to look at the spectacle of the sun's going-down,—so glowing it is with unearthly colours, and so superbly mantled in the very clouds that threatened to quench it; and as they look, the glory sinks and shifts and fades, and the far stars come forth to sparkle their peacefulness upon the cloudless night. It is a natural parable of the Christian's way. He goes on amid vicissitudes of sky, though the sun is up; but without fail, the sky gets golden ere the night is in, and the night itself is a sparkling universe of peace.

But through all, and in review of all, the deepest interest which the changeful " progress " of the pilgrim claims from us is an interest in the progress of his personality—in the Growth of that which he himself is. This Christian, as being a Christian, does advance in the quality of his character, and also in the quantity of it—in both its purity and its power, its refinement and its massiveness. There are apparent fluctuations; sometimes he seems to have sunk back; weaknesses surprise us where we should have expected strength. But the character is really gaining in richness and symmetry through all things. His spiritual miscarriages themselves contribute liberally to this steady result. They tutor him, and he does not repeat them in their kind. For " a sound discretion," it has been said well, " is not so much indicated by never making a mistake as by never repeating it." In some matters of the soul, determined by the temperament which characterises it, experience would seem to be an indispensable method of tuition: in all matters of the soul it is an invaluable method. While it is true, by comparison, that

> " Experience is a dumb, dead thing ;
> The victory 's in believing,"—

yet " believing " seldom suffices without " experience," and experience has the intensifying of faith for one of its functions. We are naturally thinking now of experience which is more or less tinged with mistake or misdeed; but we must not confine our thought of it entirely to this. The actual range of a Christian's experience, as a means of development, is immense. It embraces much that the common world brings him; and all of this, of course, is only shadowed faintly in the allegorical history. It appears in as many forms and measures as the development which it so largely aids in producing. Even the field of experience which the soul furnishes for itself is important enough in its effects upon the character to supply the material of a romantic history, were it not too subtle to be vividly traced. Without and within, history is weaving itself about the personality of the Christian, and through it. And the history is one of progress, else it is a sad one. " In all the experiences of the saints," says Owen, " there is a universal oneness, and yet a beautiful variety." But the " oneness " must include Growth, if the name of " saint " is to be kept, or won : the " variety " rejects all beauty where stagnation or backgoing haunts the experience.

It may be taken as a maxim which has the whole genius of Christianity with it, that the absence of a desire and a purpose to grow—not indeed the absence of a sense of Growth—cuts off a man from any fair claim to be a Christian. Bunyan's pilgrim went back but once in all his pilgrimage, and he went back then because he would not affect an outward ongoing when he missed the inward testimony that he had any true right to proceed. There are wonderfully many among us whose onward happenings of soul are meagre, and whose inner history has little for any dreamer of spiritual pilgrimages to record. There is a great company on the road of religion to-day whose character is gaining nothing of advance in all their journeyings, and who would seek their way back to the

Wicket-gate if they were to become as honest-hearted as Christian. Not many deliberately design to deceive; yet their course, if we can call it so, is not less unworthy than it is hazardous. It is a mocking of magnificent reality; it is a squandering of the opportunity of splendid development in all that constitutes or ennobles manhood. Heaven is reached by the way of character which faith in Christ is building up into love to God. The portals of the City are waiting to open for the soul which is struggling onwards with itself that it may come into the likeness of the Man who alone is perfect. It is the destination which no power shall sever from the footsteps of any such one as this, whether his pilgrimage be heavy to him or light: it is

> " Triumph and joy to the strong,
> Strength to the weary and weak,"

if only they be equally true to the Will that is highest, and to the tidings which attest how wondrously that Will is a Will of grace and of uttermost salvation.

VIII.

I F we turn away from the express study of our principal
character with something of reluctance, and with a
lingering feeling that we have but inadequately fulfilled the
demands of the subject, it is heartening to remember, that
we are turning away to the study of a character who in
various respects is not far off from him. Our eye is
passing to one who was a fast friend of Christian's, and
who already is not quite a stranger to ourselves. From
Christian to Christian's first companion, the comrade whom
he loved and lost, the transition is as natural as we could
well desire.

Nor is Faithful a character who borrows all his importance, or all his interest for us, from his mere relationship
to his more illustrious friend. The figure to whom the
Dreamer has assigned this name is a stalwart and a striking
one. Perhaps the man, in the build and measure of him,
will at least stand comparison with Christian himself. He
moves upon his journey with an air of self-containing
strength, of well-controlled capability. There is a sturdy
self-reliance in him, so that it almost appears as if he
would as soon have held on his way alone as in any
human company. With his God above him, and his way
before him, he would have faced all things, in his lone
march, to the end, and have still been sufficient to himself.
But this was not best, and Bunyan does not permit
him. He becomes visible to us by encountering the man

of the story; and it must be owned that he accepts the method of his introduction to us with a good heart.

As with most of the characters of Bunyan, this man is happily epitomised in the name he bears. The contents of the word are rich. We can take it in its now almost obsolete force of faith-full, and can allow all subsequent meanings to fall in behind that. This pilgrim is conceived as having great faith in God and truth—as being remarkable for his trust in Christ, and his credence of Christian verity. We have the same use of the word in our version of Paul's discussion concerning the peculiar grace of the Hebrew patriarch—"So then they which be of faith are blessed with *faithful* Abraham"—(Gal. iii. 9); and we have it much later in the familiar lines of Isaac Watts' hymn—

> "That all the *faithful* might enjoy
> Eternal life above."

Yet the particular feature of faith which stands out clearest in the character of this pilgrim is its practical feature of steadfastness—of holding onward and holding out, unflinchingly, whatsoever betide — of strongly doing and suffering in the temper of obedient fidelity to the truth and the will of God. Here the trustingness and the trustiness reveal their identity of source. In one syllable, he is *true*. He is a man who is full of faith in the truth; and is also, and is thus, a man who is incorruptibly "faithful" (in the more modern sense) to God and men.

This name, then, somewhat pointedly reminds us, that we have now put forth into the wider region of differentiated Christian character, where we shall find men and women travelling the same road, and having very much else in common, but yet exhibiting, as compared with each other, certain ethical qualities in such predominance as to give a distinctive cast to their personality itself. And it confirms the position we have already assigned to Faith as a Christian virtue, that the first true pilgrim who appears on the scene, after the typical pilgrim himself, is one whose name implies, that the ruling characteristic of him is faith in God through Jesus Christ.

As soon as we begin to fix our eye upon this character, we are struck with the extent to which he departs from the normal type as it is presented to us in Christian. This departure appears, not even so much in the matter of disposition, as in the combination of disposition and history which makes up experience. Faithful is a somewhat exceptional pilgrim. It would almost seem as if Bunyan hastened to bring forward a lively demonstration that the ways of grace with a man are not to be thought of as confined to any typal form, however moderately conceived that form may be, but that the one essential mother-virtue of faith in Christ must have large working-room left for itself, as representing the twofold freedom of God and man.

It is quite in harmony with this, that Faithful should enter so exceptionally even into the structure of the story. When we see him first, he is already half-way upon his pilgrimage. We have a history of that half of the way which now lies behind him, but it comes in the fashion of a narrative from his own lips. Bunyan, with admirable skill, falls back upon the epic device of bringing up the new strand of the story to the present point of time by way of dialogue; and in this earliest interview of his second pilgrim with any listener in our hearing, the greater part of the conversation falls to the man himself as the central figure of the history to be thus unfolded. The earlier period of the pilgrim-life of Faithful, then, as has been the case in more recent instances, is put into our hands in the shape of AUTOBIOGRAPHY. The method serves every needful purpose in respect of the past, while it also throws a liveliness into the present, and keeps us attentive to the stranger till we seem to have overtaken all our arrears of acquaintanceship with him.

But it is the narrative itself, in the materials of it, which is so full of marks of divergence from the narrative belonging to the principal pilgrim, that it commands something of our special consideration. He "escaped the Slough," which somehow he "perceived" that Christian "fell into." No Worldly-wiseman troubled him, and we hear of no "burden" that he longed to get rid of. It is all but told us that he passed through the Wicket-gate, although we have no distinct account of his doing so. But is it to be assumed that he ever lingered at the Interpreter's House, when there is no hint that he did? Or is it certain that he had any such express manifestation of the Cross as we found to have been so influential an event in the journey of Christian? We have the clearest evidence that he did not halt at the Palace Beautiful : "it was about noon" on the day of Christian's leaving that hospitable roof, and "because he had so much of the day before him, he passed by the Porter and came down the hill." So he tells us, revealing an eager frugality of time, as a pilgrim, which is not to be overlooked by us. He had no armour therefore, and he needed none. There is a predictive as well as an ethical significance in the fact that "the lions" did not disturb him : he "thought they were asleep." For neither had he any of Christian's unearthly conflict in the Valleys, though he had temptations of his own which beset him there,—until he was present to the distant ear of the pilgrim whom he had already out-travelled, and was unconsciously wrapping the strengthening exhalations of his own spirit around the soul of his future companion, in the strain which floated from him on the still air of the dawn—"Though I walk through the Valley of the Shadow of Death, *I will fear no evil ;* for THOU art with me."

Even these negative circumstances in Faithful's history during the period which precedes our personal acquaintance with him, taken by themselves, yield us presumptive evidence of the sort of man that our actual observation is likely to find him. He is clearly a man of notable momentum. He is robust of will, strong of nerve ; and since, besides, he sees his ultimate mark more controllingly than he sees anything that lies between him and it, he goes very straightly and strenuously towards that mark. He is more largely developed on the moral side of him than on the intellectual side : perplexities which have their source in the intellect do not detain him—are scarcely intelligible to him. All the intellection he exercises is concentrated upon the cardinal and eventual verities ; and the exercise resolves itself into simple, living, unembarrassed apprehension. This, with the law that he is to himself, and the motive-power which is stored within him, renders extraneous aids of less indispensable value to him ; so that, while he recognises and honours them, he can make spiritual progress apart from their very conspicuous instrumentality. As we look back upon these negative features of his history, we seem to see a man who has a nature so receptive of the forces which the gospel brings, that the moment it succeeds in moving him under way for a Christian life, it is sufficient of itself to fill and propel him by the mere potency of its own great reasonableness. In his case, as indeed we might affirm it to be in most cases, receptivity of the gospel is to be identified with capacity and susceptibility for faith—with an unusual fulness and facility of those faculties which deal with the unseen, and which constitute the distinctively religious element in a man's nature. For nothing emerges in the narrative which would entitle us to ascribe the unhindered momentum of his ongoing to any extraordinary impulse imparted by the circumstances under which he set out. He "stayed till he could stay no longer:" that was all. After Christian left, "a great talk" arose that the city was shortly to "be burned down to the ground:" Faithful satisfied himself of the truth of the matter, and then was the only one who "*did firmly believe it.*" This "firm believing" of what he found to be truth—it was the continuous lever of all the onlifting energy which brought him to outstrip the pilgrim himself whose setting-out had led him to thoughts of following him.

There are, however, more positive circumstances which distinguish the history of Faithful from that of Christian, in this earlier and lonelier portion of their way. These do not diminish our sense of the difference between the two pilgrims. We find that this man whose garments were never smeared with the mire of Despond, and whom Worldly-wiseman never appears to have thought of waylaying, was nevertheless accosted, apparently before he reached the Gate, by "one whose name was Wanton, that had like to have done him a mischief." We find that this man who had no burden to be buried at the Cross, and who was cumbered with no such fellow-travellers as Formalist and Hypocrisy, yet, at "the foot of the Hill called Difficulty," "met with a very aged man" who "said his name was Adam the First," and "found himself somewhat inclinable to go with the man": he rallied anon, but as he turned for his journey he "felt him take hold of his flesh, and give him such a deadly twitch back, that he thought he had pulled part of him after himself." And the sequel of that interview followed, when, while he was toiling up the hill, he "looked behind him, and saw one coming after him swift as the wind": it was "Moses," with whom "it was but a word and a blow,—thrice smiting him to the ground like one dead, and affirming in his heartlessness—

"*I* know not how to show *mercy*." This personage, whom Faithful had met before, "when he dwelt securely at home," "had doubtless made an end of him, but that One came by and bid him forbear." "I did not know Him at first," continues the autobiographer; "but as He went by, I perceived the holes in His hands and in His side. Then I concluded that He was *our Lord*." It was Faithful's peculiar vision of the Cross, and his peculiar deliverance from the rigours of purely legal demands upon him through the work and person of the Crucified One. It was Sinai and the Cross meeting together—a conjunction of emergency, of rapid crisis beginning and ending on the very path of his pilgrimage, which is in full accordance with the straight-going temper of this pilgrim. Again, we find that this man who had passed the Palace, and saw nothing of Apollyon, "met with one Discontent" in that Valley of Humility—a person "who would willingly have persuaded him to go back with him again," on the ground that "the Valley was altogether without honour." Nor was he yet through this place of lowliness when he "met with Shame," whose "bold-faced" persistency about the "pitiful, low, sneaking business" which religion was, and the "unmanly thing" which a tender conscience was, and the obscure and ignorant "fools" that all religious people were, so put him to it that at first he was at a loss for reply: indeed, so stout was this encounter in its kind, that when at length the "bold villain" was "shaken off," the liberated pilgrim so relaxed his accustomed mood, that he "began to sing." And he "had sunshine all the rest of the way" through both the Valleys.

The light, then, is growing as we listen to the ingenuous story of Christian's companion. He too is temptable, and has passed through the fire in his time. He too, in his manner, has felt the strength of sin—its strength rather than its weight. He too has had to fight; and though his

foes have been less spiritual, his weapons have not been
less so. It is not the invisible world that has harassed
him, either by doubts or by dismay : his faith is too steady
in its strong clearness for this. It is the visible world that
has furnished his foes. He is a man of passions which
draw him earthward while he is a man of faith which
draws him heavenward. The invisible evil world approaches him dressed in the seductive visibilities of sense,
and makes assault upon him through present-world motives
which may allure or deter him. The fulness of his
animal nature, which lends such a swing of onward force
to his progress under the sway of faith,—until this has
been refined in the furnaces of trial, it shall offer an
unhappy compensation for the motive vigour it brings him,
by presenting manifold points of too congenial contact
with the lower spheres of things. He is a man whom
nature has largely fitted for the enjoyment of this passing
world : his discipline must be, that he may learn to enjoy
it only so far, and in such fashion, as is consistent with his
new life, and even with that uninterrupted onwardness in
it to which his spiritual earnestness is urging him. His
inherent energy, kept hold of by his faith, must come
under the sure controllings of obedience, and under the
gentle hallowings of love—all of it conserved, thus, and
all of it consecrated.

But we shall fail to do justice to the character of this
man if we think only of the driving-power with which he is
endowed, or the general strength of pulse that is in him.
He is not coarsely energetic : he is not a man who
tramples his way through what he supposes to be duty,
and wears about him a capable air in the midst of much
rough travelling, simply because his encasements are thick,
and his soul is impervious to the inconveniences of feeling. He is a man of sensibility. With that sensuous and
sociable nature of his, he is keenly appreciative of the

sacrifices he is making when he commits himself to a life of faith, and for ever renounces the world as the sphere in which to pursue his satisfaction and happiness. He meets and conquers the allurement offered by the baser pleasures of the world before his feet have touched the threshold of godliness; and by-and-bye he clears his way from the more general seductiveness of Adam's onset, with his " many delights," and his " all the dainties of the world," and his three marriageable daughters who have no lack of charm for this pilgrim. But in the Valley—where the supreme stress of temptation seems to await the true-hearted wayfarers according to the mode which is best adapted to their nature—the attack is made upon his higher sensibilities, and shapes itself to turn his flank by a determined movement of false confederacy with the high spirit that is in him, and his dread of appearing despicable in the estimation of men. Discontent fails to pierce the steady ranks: it does not overpower the man that he will break with his old friends " Pride, Arrogancy, Self-conceit, Worldly-glory, with others," if he go on to " wade through this Valley." Next, however, Shame consummates the system of assault, and clings on to him as if he would never let him go. It is this which is Apollyon,—it is this which is the issuings of hell's mouth, with its hauntings and whisperings and bad insistencies,—to the pilgrim who is holding on his way in front of Christian. His regard to the world he has left, even now when it is so far behind him, is still quick and tenacious. It is hard for him to brook a clean severance from the joy of having its good opinion. It costs him a struggle to incur so much as the semblance of lapsing in accredited manliness of spirit, or dignity of conduct, or estimableness of career. The shaft of the world's ridicule strikes through him like a pain, and estrangement from the respectability and sociality of the majority of men has for him the force of exile or bereave-

ment.   He must call to the front the whole phalanx of his
faith and his reason and his inflexibility of will, and must
summon his best reserve-guard at last to decide the fate of
the day, ere he can shatter the enemy's dogged lines, and
be left with the victory.   There is a magnificent magnet-
power, no doubt, that is drawing him onward, and his
nature, as regenerated, answers strongly to the power ; but
there are also clusters of less worthy magnet-powers drawing him backwards, and to these there is much in him still
that is acutely sensitive.   And just at this crisis, most of
all, the opposing forces are so balanced, that there is a
wavering swing of dubiousness for one critical moment, till
the better force gathers up its strength, and the man moves
away, weary but triumphant, under the holy ondrawing
which shall never again be greatly counterpoised until his
journey is done.

If we have interpreted the incidents of Faithful's earlier
history with any accuracy, we may now be in better case
for observing him intelligently in his capacity of companion to Christian.   When the two pilgrims meet, Christian
has overtaken an old neighbour whom in former days he
had reason to esteem, and whom he is ready now both to
esteem and to love.   This old neighbour and new fellow-
traveller, despite what knowledge he may have had of him
under the old conditions, is a man whom Christian shall
need a good deal of his sagacious charity, under the new
conditions, rightly to understand.   With himself, what was
unfriendly to pilgrimage was not a thing of objective back-
drawing, but of subjective challenging of his forward prospects ; and he won his clear way when he rid his own
mind into a certainty of his title, and confirmed to himself
the claim which his King had upon him, and the claim
which he had upon his King.   With this new companion of
his, the seen world and the unseen—almost, we might say,

the material and the spiritual—are not only sharply contrasted realities, but most real opposing strengths ; and his own consciousness is to him their most vital battle-ground. He feels as if his choice between faith and sense, between " this world " and " that which is to come," must be so decisive and exclusive, that this world and all its pertainings had need to be altogether suspected and shunned. There is discernible in his type of Christian life a slightest savour of pietism as well as of asceticism. At least just yet ; but now the tension is still on him of those hard struggles of his in which the regards of this world were the very material of the hostility which he had much ado to vanquish. The pietistic element will scarcely last ; for he has something of judgment, and his deeper Christian history is not yet old : we may date it from the vision of his passing Lord as he lay beneath the stunnings of Moses. But the ascetic element will longer keep its place. Perhaps Christian may somewhat help him, in respect of both, to expand his one-sidedness into a more rounded strength ; and the victories he has won may leave him more free to unbend the almost over-strained rigidity of his demeanour, as a pilgrim who still has relations to each of the two worlds, although the Allegory is rather powerless to reveal it.

The manner of the meeting of the two pilgrims is almost amusingly characteristic. Christian gets sight of Faithful a little distance ahead, and lustily calls, volunteering his company. Faithful looks behind him, but holds forward without response. Christian calls again, and urges him to " stay till he come up to him." " *No,*" says Faithful bluntly ; " I am upon my life, and the avenger of blood is behind me." Christian retraced his steps once : Faithful never did ; and he will not even stay them for an offered friendship. This incident should certainly appear to be overdrawn if we did not keep in view the character and present temper of the man. He can better postpone

companionship than lose way in his journey; and there is
the shadow of unhappy associations upon everything that
would again interfere with his ongoing, especially from
behind.   He is under thoughts of harm from that direction :
let all that would reach him reach *on* to him at the least,
and be scrutinized within the unstaying momentum of the
march, which is even now setting itself for the free course
that is opening out before it under the new-risen sun.
Christian accepts the conditions,—and is soon lying helpless
before him, with his " vainglorious smile " a little abruptly
quenched.   The on-hasting man must stay, and stoop, to
uplift him ; and the pilgrim whom he has out-marched
must submit to his succouring : a touch of consequent
tenderness in Faithful, and of thankfulness in Christian,
turns the interest of each upon the other ; and when they
have recovered from the necessities of the incident, they
find that it has already shaken them on upon a footing of
begun friendship.   Of course we shall expect Faithful to
appear somewhat over-grave still, some may say " dour,"
in comparison with the sunnier frankness of Christian.
Christian's " my honoured and well-beloved brother Faithful " is reciprocated by Faithful's " dear friend " ; but he
avers, in his first words, that he thought to have had
Christian's company " quite from our town," and that he
" was forced to come thus much of the way alone ; "—a
hopeful declaration in view of their meeting now, when
each had gathered so largely of that profounder experience
which after all must be gathered in solitude, and not in
any human company.   And as intercourse warms, Faithful's gravity lightens, as we may see in his terms of address :
" dear friend " blossoms into " good brother " five pages
on, and ten pages further has flowered into " *my* brother,"
—a touch of nature, and of grace besides, which we need
not miss.

Plainly, however, this fellow-travelling, which is the

particular representation of Christian friendship and fellowship that is most practicable in the Allegory, can only partially compass the whole truth of the case. The outward experience of the comrades, by this representation, becomes of necessity very much the same experience; and even their inward experience must be controlled into considerable identity by the limitations of their unseparating relationship. As a picture of actual Christian life this can be only in a measure true. Yet in its measure it has truth in it; and the missing complement of the truth—the essential solitariness of all deeper spiritual experience—has been already given us, by the one method which the Allegory allows, in accumulated detachment from that which it complements. Both pilgrims have been long alone, and we have seen them settling the deep issues of their personal spiritual well-being with none near them but their trial and their God. If Emerson is right,—" The condition which high friendship demands is ability to do without it,"—then each of these friends had fulfilled " the condition," by way of once for all, before they met as pilgrim-comrades. And even after they meet, it is still in the power of the author to sustain not a little of their individuality, by permitting us to overhear them as they utter their own sentiments in their own manner while they keep advancing along their common path. Nor are we seldom reminded of Emerson's yet larger qualification, when in fancy we are going at their side—" The essence of friendship is entireness, a total magnanimity and trust."

Strong-willed *Urgency*—perhaps this is the phrase which best fits our thought of Faithful as we first overtake him at the mouth of the Valley,—" in this so pleasant a path," as Christian is immediately calling it. Such a first impression would be correct in the main; but we shall do well to watch, as our acquaintance with him extends, for the appearing of some things which may lie behind this, and

some which may be dormant on either side of it. Or there
may be an element of effort mingling with spontaneous
strength in this stiff yet urgent will-power of his ; the effort
may slacken without harm, and the strength may relent in
its manner with nothing but advantage to its substance.
But still our first impression can only be modified, or
perhaps enriched ; it is not destined to be removed. We
can almost see him there at Christian's side, and almost
think we can note the keen onward eye, the firm mouth,
the head strongly set upon his full shoulders, the steady
tread which has something of a military accent in it, the
well-girded bearing which is touched with peremptoriness,
the self-containing silence when there is not real speaking-
work to do ;—all of it contrasted, not a little, with the more
easy glance, and the slighter carriage, and the gentler
onwardness, of his companion. It is not Christian, but a
man with a sharper ring in his voice, who casts his eye
quickly sidewards, and sets it upon a figure which has
somehow come to be almost abreast of them while the
story of the past was being told : "*Friend, whither away?
Are you going to the heavenly country? . . . Come on, then.*"
Every syllable of this is a cipher of the man. He is less
rigorous with this new pilgrim now than he was with
Christian ; but still there is abruptness breaking through a
crust of reserve, and resoluteness striking out into Urgency,
—not much of considerateness when the strain is on him,
and seeing straight rather than deep, with more of masterful decisiveness than of masterly discrimination,—disposed
to sweep into the stream of his own march whomsoever
appears to have the paramount good sense to be shaping
his course for the one true goal of existence.

This incident emerges, we might say, from the " centre,"
or at worst, from the "left centre," of what is characteristic
of Faithful. More plainly leaning to the left, while it yet
has relations with the centre, is a certain air of *Hardness,*

of righteousness lording it over love, into which his almost impatient clearness of movement leads him.—Christian is lingering gloomily over the case of Pliable. "These are my fears too," says Faithful briefly ; "but *who can hinder that which will be?*"—a sentiment which looks in the direction of a fatalistic unconcern that is scarcely amiable. —Again, when the superior intelligence of Christian has opened the eyes of Faithful to the hollowness of this Talkative as a candidate for " the heavenly country," the same obdurate temper stiffens into action : " Well, I was not so fond of his company at first ; but I am *sick* of it now. *What shall we do to be rid of him?*"—whereas Christian tones his shrewd advice by allusion to a tenderer possibility : " *Except* God shall touch his heart and turn it."— And is there not a flush of still the same mood in the words with which he dismisses the man and his fate, after his powerful interview with him is concluded?—" I have dealt plainly with him, and *so am clear of his blood if he perisheth.*"—We could not change the name of Faithful to " Charitable " so easily as we could change the name of Christian to this.

On the " extreme left," if we may still express it so, this despatch of manner, paradoxically enough, scatters itself into *Hesitancy.* When he does not see his way with sufficient clearness to arouse his will,—going, as that does, in straight lines however short, and not at home in curves however true to moral mechanics,—there is an awkward collapse, or a helpless dallying, in his demeanour.—From the paragraph which contains his own account of his rencounter with Adam the First (for there is need to go back upon his earlier history here), we gather these words in their order :—" I asked," " I asked him then," " I further asked him," " then I asked," " then I asked,"—until Christian himself gets impatient of the parley, and naturally interjects—" Well, and what *conclusion* came the old man and you to at last?"—And so, less blameably, with Shame: "Say? I could not tell what to say—at first. Yea, he put me so to it that my blood came up in my face." His sensibility was against him in such instances, as well as the unsanctified elements of his personality, when suspension of will let him down upon these unsustained. Nor would it be fair to forget that there is no further trace of Hesitancy in him throughout the period of our personal observation of his pilgrimage.

Indeed, from first to last we notice that when once his will has got its bearings,—and latterly it never loses its sure aim,—he displays a *Clear-headed Thoroughness* which is very admirable. This we may assign to the "right centre," although it has a way of following close upon the last characteristic in respect of time. There is a force of reaction in it when it does so. We see this in the clear echo of his replies to his tempters after he has gathered up himself; when, for instance, he retaliates upon Discontent that "as to this Valley, he has *quite misrepresented the thing.*" We detect a shade of it too, perhaps, in the pretty discernible toothiness with which he sets to work upon Talkative, who it must be admitted is the fairest of subjects for his "faithfulness." That work is well and earnestly done—relentless we almost feel, but carrying every atom of the enemy's position before it, from the picquet-ground to the very key of the citadel. It is good to hear him pushing the reluctant forces of Unreality in front of the inclement solidity of his well-managed logic: "Nay, hold, let us consider of *one at once;*" "I am only for *setting things right;*" "Well, if *you* will not, will you give *me* leave to do it?" Within the range of his intelligence his mental vigour is remarkable. There is no character who puts things more forcibly when his knowledge, and most of all his experimental knowledge, makes him sure of his ground. His vision will sometimes outrun his knowledge,—as perhaps in the instance of that noteworthy interpretation of his about "chewing the cud," and "dividing the hoof," while he is smarting under the temporary success with him of Talkative's deception: Christian adds warily—"You have spoken, *for aught I know*, the true gospel sense of these texts," but contents himself with very happily applying the more familiar figure of Paul.[1] Yet there are sentences of Faithful's which have the pithiness of aphorism about them; as these:—"At the day of doom we shall not be doomed to death or life according to the hectoring spirits of the world, but according to the wisdom and law of the Highest." "A man may cry out against sin, of policy; but he cannot abhor it but by virtue of a godly antipathy against it. I have heard many cry out against sin in the pulpit, who yet can abide it well enough in the heart, house, and conversation."[2] "A man may know like an angel, and yet be no Christian. . . . Indeed, to *know* is a thing that pleaseth talkers and boasters; but to *do* is that which pleaseth God Not that the heart can be good without knowledge, for without that the heart is naught. There is therefore knowledge and knowledge—knowledge that resteth in the bare speculation of things, and knowledge that is accompanied with the grace of faith and love, which puts a man upon doing even the will of God from the heart." The words are fresh enough to have been spoken to-day.

In a character like Faithful's, we shall look not only for clearness of head, but for clearness of heart—for much transparency of *Candour*. For this we shall not by any means look in vain, although the adducible instances of it are not numerous. This quality, in a strong character like his, lies very close to Meekness, Humility, Teachableness; and there is an increasing atmospheric presence of these about him from the hour in which he first appears to

---

[1] See "Grace Abounding," par. 71.   [2] Note H.

us. Ere he has told Christian that he got clear of Wanton by "shutting his eyes" and "going his way," he frankly maintains a doubt, against the better expectation of his companion, as to whether he "did wholly escape her or no." Indeed, throughout his story, he is earning our regard by the unfailing internal evidence which the narrative affords us that he is withholding nothing, and colouring nothing, in the interests of his own credit rather than of truth. If this most Christian characteristic did not in the least fade out of him as he matured, it may perhaps be recognised as becoming still more perceptibly tempered with a manly lowliness of mind. It is not long till we have signs of this. When Christian has been somewhat at pains to bring him round to truer ideas in the matter of Talkative, the sturdy man, who was a little sullen at first to lower his flag, now pulls it sheer on board, admits himself chargeable with error both of fact and principle, and adds, with something of the simplicity of a child who promises not to repeat his misdemeanour—"Hereafter I shall better observe this distinction." Probably Adam the First spoke one true word when he accosted him with the compliment—"Thou lookest like an *honest* fellow,"—a true word, however much of old or new meaning we may attribute to the adjective.

If we give a place beyond the "right centre" to this lowly Transparency in the character of Faithful, we must set on the "extreme right" a deep-lying *Fervour* that is in him, and such emotions as are akin to grateful joyousness. We should have been like to leave these out of the reckoning, in our estimate of this character, but for an incident which starts in upon the story as if to secure us against so serious an injustice. It is the sudden appearing of Evangelist upon the pilgrims' path. "My good friend Evangelist," Christian is saying, as if he would appropriate him. "' Ay, and *my* good friend *too*,' said Faithful ; 'for it was he who set me in the way to the Gate.'" Christian greets the venerable man with his hearty "Welcome, welcome." "'*And a thousand welcomes,*' said good Faithful: '*thy company, O sweet Evangelist, how desirable is it to us poor pilgrims!*'" In the dewy light of this revealing passage of Faithful's history, we can read into his whole story something more of tenderness than we find on the surface, and can remember how easily we can allow a certain brusque air of manner to keep us oblivious of the sensibility which we know that it conceals. For this superficial sternness is often but the defence which a man employs against the threatened indecorum of his too great feeling. In the instance we have just quoted, the fountains of emotion are surprised into a sudden upspringing, and the wonted severity gives way before it. Not that the severity is other than real, but that the emotion beneath it is real too, and its reality apt to be forgotten. It were well, moreover, we should allow for Faithful's development in respect of those virtues which at first may have been more deficient in him. His hastening days had need to be days of rapid maturing. And it is comfortable for us to have the light of this incident with us as we go on at his side through the gloom which is already mantling upon the horizon of his history.

With a forecast of this gathering tempest that is clearer than his own, let us find our way back to the core of all that is ever working within this man. Let us lean our thoughts about him, as he himself leans everything, upon his *Faith*—his name-virtue, which lies behind, and above and around, all that Strong Urgency which stands in the mid-front of his character. We cannot but see, that his Strength is yielded to God, and that his Urgency is a going on to God. The will of God is his law; the love of God is his life; the home of God is his home. "*What God says is best, indeed is best*"; so he "thinks" when he is fortifying his soul against Shame; and so he more than thinks to the last, and more than thinks in the face of all that may otherwise appear. "Those things that *he disdained*, in those things did *I see most glory :*" thus, with his new vision of "things," did he fling off this last of his early tempters; and it was the system of vision, the theory of appreciation, which controlled him still throughout the days of the end. "*According to the strength or weakness of his faith in his Saviour*, so is his joy and peace, so is his love to holiness, so are his desires to know Him more, and also to serve him in this world :" thus he speaks to Talkative, wasting upon him the innermost breath of his own experience, but, with unconscious authority, giving to ourselves the concise statement of a principle which his own life had illustrated hitherto, and was yet to illuminate in the hours that were coming on. Faith, with this man, was already more than a match for sense, and ere long should become its victor, even to annihilation. "And *this* is the victory that hath *overcome the world*—even our FAITH."

This, then, is he for whom that city of Vanity, now spreading its gaudy splendours along the plain beneath him, is to be the term of his pilgrimage. For it is the most exceptional thing of all about this pilgrim, that his history is a tragedy, and his death a martyrdom. Meanwhile, that way of his,—and his whole-hearted choice of it at the first, with all its consequences, has just been freshened to him by the opportune reappearing of his early guide in this capacity of a prophet,—that way, very evidently, goes on through this city; therefore he will go on through this city also. There is no perplexity: fidelity can have no difficulty but with itself; and even with itself it has little. He is warned, but he is not daunted: his courage begins to draw upon its deep resources as his successive footsteps bring him nearer to the bustling town. Strictly regarded, it is not the way that goes through the city, but rather the city that has obtruded itself upon the way. The way is the essential thing, the ever-rightful thing; the city is an accidental and a wrongful matter— an ancient after-thought. It is a second City of Destruction —more different in geography than in government or destiny—heaved here across their path, and therefore filled for them with more positive unfriendliness and more pointed opposition. It is the figure by which the Allegory would recall to us, that it is only the heart of Faithful, all the while, that has left "the world": he has to be going through it still; and its seductions, flung off him as they have been, can recoil upon him in the new form of brute force—more manifestly murderous, though now they are powerless to reach the soul. "Vanity" is but the world in its exclusively secular aspect; and its "lusty fair" is but the world-kingdom, the counterfeit of the kingdom of God, dressed in the intensity of its godless activity. Hence in truth, as the historian himself declares, "he that will go to *the City*, and yet not go through this town, must needs go out of the world." Less literally,—they who enter "this town" may not perhaps manage to "go through" it, but may "go out of the world" in the arduous endeavour, and may "go to the City" by "the nearest way."

The tragic element in the faithful encountering of worldly power and of worldly meretriciousness, in their fanatical combination,—it is not an element with which most of us are in these days very practically familiar; nor happily have British readers of the "Pilgrim," since at least the very earliest years of its existence, been able to find in the fate of Faithful anything other than a remnant of an almost unimaginable state of things which belongs for ever to the past. The *Pilgrimage of Man*, of which we have already spoken, has not one martyr only, but many;

and this feature is one which has its part in giving to the book its air of antiquated unpracticalness. Yet it is right to bethink us, that there have been readers of the "Pilgrim" in other lands to whom this passage had a vivid practical interest—men and women who, as they read of "these two honest persons" braving the singularity of their apparel and speech and holy indifference, felt every phrase to be yet alive for themselves, and as they stood in imagination beside the faggots which were fired by the menials of Beelzebub, were sensibly touched by the glare of a present-day possibility. They might not be careful to disentangle these cowls and crosses from the anti-Christian insignia which symbolise to themselves the same maddened world-spirit which Bunyan is here describing so promiscuously; nor might they readily imagine, that a fair-minded Christian author could be almost justified in slumping the lordliest mass of so-called Christianity itself within the heterogeneous hubbub of earth-born hatred of Christianity. But the hatred of Christianity they recognise, for its features abide; and the City of Destruction is ever meeting them again, under the new aspect of the virulence of those who deal in things which are but of human invention, and at the best are spiritually valueless.

We know how it fared with Faithful when he became a stranger wishing to follow his way through the midst of that crazed community. The conduct of the two pilgrims is so closely united in the narrative, that during the greater part of the proceedings we have no materials for the separate study of the deportment of Faithful; but it is worthy of note, as itself significant, that now his deportment is so little to be distinguished from that of Christian, as Christian's is so little to be distinguished from his. Faithful's strength has become richer, and Christian's richness has become stronger. Yet, even apart from the general place in the story which belongs to each of the two pilgrims, we carry with us a probability as to which one of the two is the more likely one to " suffer," if we may use the word, with Bunyan, in the terribly technical sense which was forced into familiarity upon the lips of our forefathers. In carrying with us this probability, we do not cast any reflection upon Christian on the one hand, nor upon Faithful on the other. It was in the nature of the men,—each of them, differently, brave and true. Let matters once come to a head, and a " trial " be instituted " in order to their condemnation :" then the latent probability shall begin to shape itself into certainty. Let there be a ruffian on the bench, and a pack of unprincipled men in the jury-box, and a reserve of lying witnesses slouching at hand ; and let an indictment be read which usurps the prerogatives of government, and distorts the conduct of the strangers into riot and treason : " *then Faithful* began to answer." And his little speech has already the crackle of the faggots in it, —closing thus : " And as to the king you talk of, since he is Beelzebub, the enemy of *our Lord, I defy him and all his angels.*" From his subsequent defence, after the grim farce of witness-bearing has been acted, we can cull such characteristic phrases as " Word of God," " Divine faith," " Divine revelation," " human faith ;" and again the stake is visible in the last bold words—" I say . . . that the prince of this town, with all the rabblement his attendants, by this gentleman named, *are more fit for being in hell than in this town and country ; and so the Lord have mercy upon me.*" It was inevitable : " the preferment " was his,—not snatched for himself, yet, half consciously and most willingly, secured for himself by his simply acting like him-self throughout.[1] " Scourged,"—" buffeted,"—" lanced with knives,"—" stoned,"—" pricked with swords,"—" last of all,"—" burned :" " thus came Faithful to his end." And to that beginning towards which the waiting " chariot and a

[1] Note I.

couple of horses" immediately bore him through the clouds with sound of trumpet.

That wheeled embassage from the City,—it has rapt from us a man for whom our warm respect, already budded into regard, would, by-and-bye, we imagine, have blossomed into love. For Christian, it has changed him into a stimulating memory of a manly brother who has "mounted up" from his side "with wings as eagles," while he himself has to "walk" on without him "and not faint,"—cheered still by the certainty of having him for his friend again, as Pollok's "ancient bard" would have told him while he sang within the bowers of the City—

> " All are friends in heaven ; all *faithful friends;*
> And many friendships, in the days of time
> Begun, are lasting here, and growing still."

For ourselves, a brave acquaintance has soon become again that floating voice which he was when we were about to meet him first—a voice that is saying with still stronger steadiness of accent, and will now be saying to the end of the ages—" *Though I walk through the valley of the shadow of death, I will fear no evil; for* THOU *art with me.*"

This metropolis of worldliness, from which Faithful found so short a way home, is by no means to be reckoned among the ruined cities of history. It has changed—even more greatly than it had done in the interval between the days of Christian's journey and the days of Christiana's, when a little company of genuine pilgrims (as is possible by a modification of the Allegory in the direction of real life) could afford to have their dwellings in it. Judicial murders are now unknown there. Pilgrims can pretty safely pass through—if they will. But the place is now, to speak truth, so very habitable, and so lively a place to spend at least a holiday in, that you will meet men and women in the garb of pilgrims as often as in any other garb, or with mingled bits of the pilgrim costume, if only by way of picturesqueness. The suburbs have immensely grown, and multitudes who like to be reckoned pilgrims have their residences and their trade-connections there. Persecution is restricted to an occasional jibe at their dress, or an occasional smile at their anomalous ways. But the old spirit slumbers in the community. Let a resolute pilgrim only work his way through the streets, with the old dress, well travel-stained, on his back, and the old dialect, undiluted, on his lips, and the old disdain of the wares in his eye; then the old mockery is abroad, and the old untruthful dislike, and the old murderousness of heart. For Beelzebub is still " the great one of the Fair." His city may have swelled on his hands to an empire; railways may pour thousands into its stations, superseding pilgrimage; telegraph-centres may flash messages to it from the ends of the earth; post-office tables may groan beneath its correspondence with two hemispheres; cars may glide along its roadways; the posters of daily newspapers may placard its walls; and even church-spires, with trade-marks in place of weathervanes, and flags of the Fair fluttering at their buttresses, may tower high above the tumult,—until Bunyan would scarcely know " the town " he knew so well two hundred years ago. But the heaven-lit eye of the Dreamer would not be quite filled with admiration. " What unhallowed mixture is this? " he might be apt to ask—" what jumble is here of pilgrimage and traffic, of a polished Beelzebub and a holy Christ? Hand me that gilded Bible !" Thou simple-minded Dreamer, thou art somewhat behind the age. Thou hast slept long. All is modernised now. There is an accepted version of the New Testament in use in the city—one that is much revised, and that bears the royal stamp of the learned ruler who quoted Scripture in a quiet lane of the city once, long ago, for the instruction of a Man in whom he had interest ! Let us read :—" Love

ye the world, and the things that are in the world!" . . .
" Ye are of the world, even as I am of the world!" . . .
" Be ye conformed to this world, and be ye not transformed
by the renewing of your minds!" The very minimum of
alteration is made ; all the old rhythm preserved !—Smitten
with strange dismay, the Dreamer would seem to himself to
have awaked to behold that his Dream is a dream indeed ;
and we might leave him breathing the great old petition
out of his heart, as if he were in the midst of a tinselled
heathenism—" THY kingdom come—Thine ! For it hath
not come yet, Lord, even in our blessed Britain."

It is true that here we must not permit even the good
Dreamer, or his admirable Allegory, to convey to our
minds any other than a perfectly just conception of the
case. The town of Vanity we feel, though it was needed
to represent an aspect or an element of the Pilgrimage, is
somewhat of a burden upon the Allegory. It has a good
deal of the incongruity of an allegory within the Allegory :
indeed it is wellnigh the whole matter reproduced under
the figure of a community still, instead of a pilgrimage
from one community to another. It is the City of Destruction developed into a commercial seat of government, and
restored as a city where Christians and Faithfuls, and
Hopefuls with them, at least in all times of less violence
than those upon which they themselves chanced to
fall, do not of necessity secede and depart when they turn
to adopt the new principles of living, but have it in option
—strictly speaking, have it for their lot—to remain, and
to face the hazards and discomforts of their remaining.
It is the dominant idea of the Allegory disenchanted into
a truthful but prosaic figure which he could not have
worked with any success as the ruling figure of his book.
The difficulty he is thus endeavouring to meet is the old
difficulty with which we have already found him manfully
contending—the difficulty which comes of the circumstance,

that the Allegory of the pilgrims "takes them out of the world." He brings up the world here on their way; but now it behoves him to make it a world which has too exclusive a concentration of tragedy and mad folly. This was scarcely the world even as he knew it then, and is still less the world as we know it now. The world as he knew it was the Pilgrimage and Vanity Fair continuously combined, and this he really strives to depict it in the general cast of the Allegory. The world, as we know it, is the Pilgrimage continuously combined with a modified Vanity Fair such as the succeeding party of travellers found it. On the whole, despite the confusing residence of pilgrims in the town at that later date—of pilgrims as distinct from hosts, —it may be said that in this respect the Second Part is fairer to fact, if not truer to art, than the First Part is able to be, with its necessity of giving a definite place to the more tragic side of Christian things. Only—Bunyan wrote them both, and the two are in some sense one.

This town of Vanity, then, we must take the liberty of expanding and attenuating to touch the entire way of the Pilgrimage. In real Christian life we find it so. The two kingdoms, the two communities, commingle and conflict wherever a Christian man exists, if he steadfastly answers to the vocation of a Christian man. They may be side by side in the same family, in the same place of business, in the same workshop, in the same congregation ; and in every instance Vanity Fair is more or less virtually rehearsed. Faithful had to "leave the world" twice :—before he met Evangelist first, and after he met him again. Externally regarded, he ended where he began. This must be interpreted to signify, that we never leave the world at all, except (and not quite even except) we hide ourselves from our duty. Vanity and its Fair are our discipline, though they may not be our death : they are the appointed gymnasium of our training for the City. They are the whole system of the kingdom we have renounced, in as far as that kingdom is something outside of us, and especially something which works through the wills of fellow-men under the instigation of evil spirits, whether as guile or as force, as allurement or as suffering. In no capacity, whether public or private, can we altogether rid ourselves of its contacts and resistances. In truth, much of the outward force of the entire temporal economy—in nature, in providence, in society—is under at least its secondary domination. The world is in many ways, and in mysterious ways, a strong world—a world that demands a store of gracious strength to bear up against it, or to match it. Under so fell a pressure of outward atmosphere, there is call for fulness of inward atmosphere, if yielding or collapse is to be kept off from our experience. It were wise to warn ourselves, that the heart of all unbelief around us is a heart of opposition to the root and branch of our Christian vitality. We shall often let this vitality suffer unless we ourselves are ready to suffer, to deny ourselves, to hold our own at the cost of pain—our own best, which is God's and Christ's. And we must hold up and hold on, too, amid the bristling enmities and thick-coming cajoleries, with as little of weak impatience and unholy wrath, of world-like temper and smallness of spirit, as God's grace can empower us to show. Christ would have us to be magnanimous in the world's hands as this Faithful was; and for that we need, most of all, just the faith which was his. There is nothing which more impresses the unbelieving with the sublime sacredness of that which they are withstanding in us, than the firm yet patient and large-hearted endurance of all which they are pleased to lay upon us as those who claim a citizenship in heaven—an endurance which faith at once supports and sweetens. At every turn, it is still this which is "the victory" that gives us the conquest of "the world."

While, however, it is imperative upon the Christian to guard his spiritual fidelity in the presence of the world amid which he is meanwhile a dweller, it is not needful he should forget that he is no alien on this earth of God's, although in great measure, as things are, he must regard himself as a stranger on it. He has a right to the world that now is, and to all the good it may yield him. How much of what is best among the things which unchristian men grasp and fondle as so specially their own, and despise the Christian while they grasp and fondle, are things which wear a borrowed light, or have a borrowed existence, from the very Christianity to which the Christian man is only striving to be wholly true! He, above all men, is pre-eminently entitled to live in the world, and to bend the world to his service, as a servant of the Lord whose world it doubly is. The Christian may do unconscious wrong to his calling, and to his Lord, by his individual surrender of the rightfulness of the whole position of Christianity and of Christ in a world which is so confidently claimed by the system of things that is only tolerated in it under the Divine motives of patience and of grace. Tolerated thus, however : therefore he himself ought to react upon the world as from a platform of superiority,—though he must rather feel this superiority, and draw strength from it, than assert or parade it. He ought to lay himself out to win conquests from the false kingdom as he lives on in the name of the truer dominion. Meanwhile, he ought to make it clear, that he as a Christian man is not a whit behind the unchristian man in the appreciation of all that is excellent, and in the accomplishment of whatsoever it becomes a man to accomplish. He may well go further still, and may claim—not much by word, but effectively by deed—that all which is in itself good, in art or literature or social refinement, falls by right within the appropriating control of Christianity, and comes to its true dignity only then when it is auxiliary to the kingdom of God and Christ.

Complicated, then, all this Christian living is, and arduous; yet noble beyond all else that this present world can show. Holy capability is demanded by it, and development of eternal strength—strength which survives all things, and goes on unimpaired into the Unseen of which " our Lord" is the undisputed Master. This again is of faith. It needs all the strenuousness, all the wise urgency, that through this faith we can ever find. We may appropriate the truth which pulses through words like the following, if only we refuse to let out of reckoning for a moment this living faith in a living Christ :—

> " The energy of life may be
> Kept in after the grave, but not begun ;
> And he who flagged not in the earthly strife,
> From strength to strength advancing—only he,
> His soul well-knit, and all his battles won,
> Mounts, and that hardly, to eternal life." [1]

Faithful might have set his name to the lines; but he would have breathed the name of " his Saviour " while he traced his own.

[1] Matthew Arnold—" Immortality."

IX.

THE man whose character must next engage our study is one who stands no further off from Christian than the man whose strong brief career we have been trying to interpret. Hopeful was the successor of Faithful as a fellow-pilgrim to Christian, and in several respects was more than a successor. Hopeful was longer his companion, and bore part with him in a far greater number and variety of experiences. Hopeful, moreover, we can afford to say, was of a more companionable nature than Faithful; so that in his second comrade, apart from his inferiority in years and achievements, Christian had a man with whom he could enjoy a closer, if at the same time a less dignified, friendship.

Yet, a successor to Faithful; and one, besides, whom Faithful was chief in providing as a pilgrim-friend to the friend he was soon to leave : so it afterwards appears, upon Hopeful's own testimony. By an inconsistency which again makes room for a fine touch of truthful interest, Faithful was Evangelist to Hopeful in the transition stage of his spiritual history while both were dwelling as old friends in the city of the Fair. We shall have occasion to recur to this. Meanwhile it is to be noted that the total effect of the action of the authorities of Vanity, under the merry approval of their prince, so far as it comes within the narrative, was this and no more :—that in giving way to their natural instincts in the managing of their realm, and in seeking to abolish pilgrimage by burning half-murdered pilgrims on their streets, they had accomplished the promotion of one pilgrim, and the creation of another—of "many others," as this new pilgrim himself would tell us. The "lord of the Fair" had almost need to reform his methods, if matters are not to go to ruin with him. And we may trust him that he will.

The name of this second companion, and the nature which so unobtrusively sustains the name, suggests the conjecture that the "three graces" were in the mind of Bunyan when he selected the words by which his three principal pilgrims are known. Christian represents Charity, yet in no way so distinctive as to show a greater predominance of that grace than shall fairly represent the whole living unity of Christian character, which no other grace could equally do. Charity is chief; Faith and Hope are next, and are both accompanied by Charity. Charity is beholden to them both, but tempers them both into a more full-formed Christianity. Faith, the efficient grace, comes sooner to its own maturity; Charity needs the longest course to bring it to its ingathering. Hope, too, comes of Faith, and can almost take its place; but Charity holds with each of them to the last.—Hopeful, then, is the complement to the round conception of Christian character and life which Bunyan would embody in the pilgrims of his First Part—itself originally intended to be in a measure complete. The character is quite a new one, as unlike to Christian as to Faithful, and comes before us clothed in an antecedent history which departs pretty widely from the history of either. The mother-virtue, in its liberty, takes to itself yet another form of ethical and biographical manifestation, and through that form asserts its still essential identity.

It must not, however, be overlooked, that the phenomenal difference of history between Hopeful and the other two pilgrims, so markedly great, is considerably greater than the real difference of it. Regarded according to the outward structure of the allegorical story, Hopeful never accomplishes more than half a pilgrimage,—has been picked up on the way, without ever having undergone the indispensable initial and initiating experiences on which so much emphasis has already been so properly laid throughout the earlier portion of the narrative. But it is not of course in reality what it thus appears to be in figure. Divergence in experience, free as it is, has its impassable limits; and while Bunyan, in his generous sagacity, may have no objection to set even the Wicket-gate itself a little in the shade, as being an item of spiritual topography which in some individual pilgrimages is not easy to locate or to define, yet no departure from the ordinary type of experience can comprehend an immediate start of any pilgrim-novice abreast of one who has toiled his way through such training and teaching and conflict and testimony as this Christian has done. We must relax the bands of the story, and must sympathise with the difficulties of the Author's task. We must permit him to give us a new pilgrim, and to give the old pilgrim a new companion, by such arrangements as are fairly open to him. And in the circumstances, he has conducted the matter with a skill which goes far to silence complaint.

We must revert to the composite capacity of that town of Vanity, as in some sense a City of Destruction, and in some sense the whole world-theatre of human living, Christian as well as unchristian. In the one aspect, it is a place which a young Christian shall quit; in the other aspect, it is a place within which all the initial experiences of Christian living may transpire, from the reality of the Wicket-gate onward through every reality which such a pilgrim as Christian has ever encountered. The difficulty of time we must simply wink at. It is in this light that we must listen to the autobiography which Christian elicits from Hopeful as they are faring together over the Enchanted Ground. Long postponed as the narrative is, it is the account which corresponds to that of Faithful just after the two pilgrims have met at the mouth of the Valleys. It is the chapter of pilgrimage, hitherto almost a blank to us, which fills up the story to the date of our acquaintance with the pilgrim whose first pilgrim-history it reveals. Faithful's account, however, while exceptional enough as judged by Christian's experience, was still allegorical at least, and pretty consistently so. Hopeful's account, on the other hand, quietly drops off from it all vesture of allegory, as far as the account itself is concerned, and gives us nothing else than a section of religious biography such as we might read in a volume of real life. The Author serves several purposes by this bold frankness of handling. He cuts the knot of whatever embarrassment threatens him from the complications which belong to the figure of the town of Vanity. He leaves upon us a truer impression of Hopeful's character as the narrator of the history. Most of all, he finds to his hand an opportunity of describing the more momentous stages of Christian experience as divested of the veil of figure, and as throwing back a flood of interpreting light upon the figurative narratives of these stages which have already interested the reader, and may now be made more distinctly to instruct him. The art with which this is done is worthy of great praise. Not only is the narrative kept in store till our interest in Hopeful is well deepened, and not only does it carry all the advantages of an epic completion of our knowledge of Hopeful's Christian history, but its unromantic reality and rather unusual copiousness are relieved, and the attention of the reader held fast, by the risk of perilous slumberousness against which the very narrative is contending from step to step. The prompt, almost hurried, leading-questions of Christian keep us as much awake as they keep Hopeful himself; and the whole story, admirably told as it is in these allegorical circumstances, is heard by us to the last word.

This early history, as we have it from his own lips, we may venture to set into its chronological place, that its suggestive materials may at once come into service for our more special purpose. The peculiarity of that history is citizenship in Vanity. He "continued a great while"— we shall scarcely err if we say, all his life hitherto — "in the delight of those things which were seen and sold at *our* Fair." "At last, by hearing and considering of things that are Divine"—heard from Christian, and also from Faithful, whose "faith and good living" were the occasion of his dying—he perceived that all this delight lay under the frown of Heaven. He, however, "endeavoured to shut his eyes against the light:" he did not know that these convictions were "the work of God upon him;" "sin was yet very sweet to his flesh;" he could not think of parting with his companions; and the hours of these serious thoughts were "heart-affrighting hours." But it needed little to "bring his sins to mind again:" the sight of a good man on the street, a word from the Bible, a headache, a sick neighbour, the toll of the death-bell, the thought of his own dying, the sudden death of others, the overwhelming reflection that he himself "must quickly come to judgment,"—any one of these would do it. (He is moving uneasily with his burden towards the outskirts of the City of Destruction.) He felt he must set about to "mend his life." (He is shaping his course for Morality.) "But at last his trouble came tumbling on him again, and that over the neck of all his reformations." (He is come beneath the brow of Sinai.) Whereupon he reasoned well: "'Tis but folly to think of heaven by the law." He "further thought thus :—If a man runs a hundred pounds into the shopkeeper's debt, and after that shall pay for all that he shall fetch ; yet, if his old debt stands still in the book uncrossed, the shopkeeper may sue him for it, and cast him into prison till he shall pay the debt." Besides, he "still saw sin, new sin," in his best endeavourings. He had fallen upon no sure way to be rid of his burden or his peril. The turning-point was reached when he "broke his mind to Faithful."

The witness Pick-thank, if we may believe him, had known Faithful "of a long time." Hopeful at least had done so, and to better purpose. This Evangelist meets him after the road by Sinai has been tried, and while no slime of Despond has yet beclogged his footsteps. Faithful told him, characteristically enough, that nothing would be safe with him "unless he could obtain the righteousness of a man who had never sinned." Hopeful "was forced to be of his opinion :" although "the words at first sounded strangely," he came to have "full conviction about it." But this did not yet end the difficulties. He "made his objections against *his* believing, for that he thought He was not willing to save *him*." Faithful "bid him go to Him and see." (The Wicket-gate is now before him ; but spatterings of Despond are blinding his eye, and filming it with a false humility.) "Presumption" —"what must he do when he comes ?"—"how "—"what to say :"—a great ingenuity of difficulty, which was partly diffidence, and largely the unwillingness of spiritual unbelief. But he did make his way to this Man—to God, —addressing him "over and over and over" in such earnest words as Faithful had taught him. "Not at the first," "nor at the sixth time neither," did the answer come. "Therefore thought he with himself, if I leave off I die, and I can *but die* at the throne of grace." He "continued praying until the Father showed him the Son"—

not to "the bodily eyes," but to "the eyes of his under-standing." "Suddenly, as he thought, he saw the Lord Jesus look down from heaven upon him, and saying, ' Believe on the Lord Jesus Christ, and thou shalt be saved.'" Between the Lord and him there were questions and replies; in the course of which he saw that "believing and coming was all one;" and it settled in upon him that "the Son did and suffered all, not for Himself, but for him that will accept it for his salvation, and be thankful. And now was his heart full of joy, his eyes full of tears, and his affections running over with love to the name, people, and ways of Jesus Christ."—He is through the Wicket-gate and at the Cross. And a good deal is covered by the twin statement, that he was "greatly ashamed of the vile-ness of his former life," and "confounded with the sense of his own ignorance;" while very much also is involved in another sentence, less remarkable for its good taste than for its passionate loyalty: " He thought that if now he had a thousand gallons of blood in his body, he could spill it all for the sake of the Lord Jesus."

Even in the absence of other knowledge, we might con-jecture that here we have a man in whom Christian shall find a trusty and congenial friend. He seems to unite in his character and experience not a little of what is severally distinctive in Christian and in Faithful. He has something of Faithful's natural attachment to "the world and the things that are in the world"; so also he has something of Christian's natural fertility of mind, and intractableness of spirit, as sources of religious difficulty. He first has a struggle with the world, and next has a struggle with him-self, ere he comes clear upon the way of the new life. The twofold hindrance imports some delay into his period of change; but when once the crisis is reached, there appears to be a greater conclusiveness and completeness in the experience than we observe in the instance of either of the other pilgrims. His Faith blossoms at once into vigorous Hope, and his Humility passes into its steady major key of Gratitude. He incurs less of subsequent conflict, and needs less of subsequent discipline, than the heroes of the Valley-region did. He has not their strength; nor is he modelled, perhaps, upon the scale of their dimensions: nautically speaking, he has not their draught of water, nor the dangers and exigencies that attend it. But he is not a feeble man. What he may lack in force he almost makes up in buoyancy; what he may want in power he almost compensates by the high average of strength which he displays in compact proportion to his measure. He has less mass of will than Christian, and much less momentum of will than Faithful; yet his genial nature can gather itself to effort, and he can hold his ground with a prudent perseverance while the pressure of duty or of danger is on him. There is much of symmetry in his character, reminding us of Christian,—although the lines tend—gracefully, and in truth somewhat firmly— towards the converging point of hopefulness, whether concerning things in time or concerning things in eternity.

When now we permit this background-light to blend itself with the history which is transacted upon the open stage of the story, we shall be able to gather some clearer conception of the character with which Bunyan has endowed this third pilgrim of his. The ruling characteristic which is assigned by his name,—this we may expect to sustain a persistent prominence throughout. But perhaps we may find it needful, for the sake of distinctness, to break it up into elements more simple than itself. Within the one general idea that is covered by the word " Hopeful," there may lie at least three particular ideas which we shall not do ill to separate. The pilgrim may suggest his name by a natural hopefulness of temperament; or he may support it by a gracious hopefulness of spirit among the experiences of the soul; or he may vindicate it by a fulness of the grace of Christian hope as having regard to the unseen verities of an eternal condition. Probably there is evidence that he does more or less of all the three.

The supernatural hold which Christianity takes of a character through its religious faculty, although liable to much modification by the sovereign Divine disposal of the circumstances of the change, is usually fitted to the natural contour of the character, and most frequently leaves its proportions substantially undisturbed. It vitalises and consecrates the character as it stands: it sets its claim upon every separate feature of it which is not radically beyond assimilation into a perfect manhood,—animating the old typical form with its own new life. *Natural Hopefulness* is a feature of character which is both distinguishable and interesting; nor is there a characteristic of the unchristianised nature which lies more open to the prompt appropriation of supernatural Christian influence. Only now is this feature of character utilised in proper accordance with the original design of nature itself; hitherto it has been almost wholly misappropriated and abused, stunted and degraded. In the unchristian state of the man, indeed, it is scarcely favourable to a religious life, and in some respects is peculiarly obstructive to it; but the moment it is lifted from its old worldly littlenesses, and is transfigured by the beams which then inspire its activities out of the unseen and eternal, it becomes an ally only less invaluable than a natural faith itself.

The mere glimpse which the history can give us of the unchristian period of Hopeful's life, somewhat uninviting as it is, affords but scanty materials for verifying our conjecture of the Natural Hopefulness of his disposition. But if we are not able to recognise it clearly on its original site, we may perhaps find traces of it in its transition, and in its subsequent subordination to the higher hopefulness of his new career. May we not regard that story of his change as a story of the conversion of his Hopefulness ? He had been hoping more from the things of the Fair than they were at all competent to yield him. He had been hoping that all would come right with him, somehow, some time, notwithstanding that his present abandonment to vanity and vice did not on the whole feel promising. The vivid presentation of spiritual truth to his mind, probably no less seasonable than it was impressive, struck at the heart of all this fallacious hoping. But first his Hopefulness only shifted ground : he hoped that he might manage the matter to his own hand ; and he clung to this hope until it was wrung from his grasp. Natural Hopefulness was now severed from the sphere of his spiritual concerns, and for a season was in a position of detached prostration—a painful period in his history. The right-hand power of his nature would seem to himself to have forsaken him. But grace then began to touch this Hopefulness, and to draw it to its feet in the name of a new principle, that it might work within the sphere of the spiritual under a complete alteration of will. Its operation was at first sufficiently faint and awkward. The hopeful man seemed simply the most hopeless of men. Yet the incipient effort of his Hopefulness, as set to work upon the footing of the new principle, is visible in the settled resignedness with which he lays himself down, as one may say, across the silent threshold of that way of duty and safety which he so dimly perceived. He is waiting new substantiality which shall fit and fill his renewing Hopefulness. When that glorious new thing at length appears, and slowly unfolds its excellence to his reason and his heart, the whole capacity of Hopefulness in him is flooded with satisfaction ; and a Person—living and loving, Divinely capable and humanly sympathetic—forms the transcendent centre of all that new world which comes in upon him as henceforth the true object of all his powers of hoping.

" This Hopeful also told Christian that there were *many more* of the men of the Fair that would *take their time* and follow after." "Truly I pitied the man [Temporary], and was not altogether without hope of him." In words like these we may detect the ring of the natural disposition, still working legitimately, within the sphere of outward things, although now upon the highest possible level of them. He is hopeful concerning others in regard to their future—that is, he is hopeful that they will come to adopt the only course in which he has found true hope for himself. He takes a bright view of things and of men within the limits of truth. The history of his own true hoping,—hope deferred to the verge of heart-sickness and of flat self-abandonment, then verified in a measure and a manner which exceeded all his conceptions,—did not tend to diminish his Hopefulness concerning all other men in their relation to the kingdom of God, nor concerning the kingdom of God in relation to other men, merely as matters belonging to the world-history around him. His Natural Hopefulness, in its social outlook, had less restraint upon it now than ever it had before, although now it was better defined and more truthfully bounded, and although now, in its personal activity for himself, it had expanded to embrace reaches of solid gloriousness which were undreamt-of till he saw the Lord Jesus as his own redeeming Friend.

This constitutional Hopefulness, then, itself an unquestionable gift, only appears in its sterling value when it appears as sanctified into a grace of the regenerated nature. The *Spiritual Hopefulness* of this man is written into the texture of all his history, and here and there shines out with striking lustrousness as the darkness of the story deepens. Bunyan is certainly thinking of more than of Natural Hopefulness when he employs the words with which he introduces him:—"There was one whose name was Hopeful (being *so made* by the beholding of Christian and Faithful in their words and behaviour in their sufferings at the Fair), who joined himself unto him." This "joining" was at once the result of Spiritual Hopefulness, then, and the beginning of its abundant proof.

This was the most practically valuable form of Hopeful's predominant characteristic, and the form in which it most constantly gave itself to action. To ascertain, however, the real measure of its strength, we must approach it at those periods where it is subjected to exceptional strain. We at once bethink us again of the Dungeon and the River—a scene midway in his history, and a scene at its close; in both of which he appears in strong contrast to Christian, and so deports himself, even absolutely considered, that his behaviour in these circumstances alone would have more than earned him his name.

The brutal Giant had twice opened the door of their dungeon—on the first day, to leave them battered and bleeding on the floor; on the second day, to turn the lock upon their meditations on his mock-merciful counsel that they should destroy themselves at their own leisure, since it was hard to see but they were prisoners for life. Christian leans towards the Giant's method of relief. Hopeful is by no means disposed to accept him for a counsellor: his chief anxiety easily moves off from his own situation to settle itself upon the mood of mind in which he finds his companion; and his care concentrates itself upon the brotherly task of seeking to buoy him up with a little of his own Hopefulness. The calm reasonableness and patient skill with which he conducts this endeavour are very remarkable. Death, he admits, would be far more welcome even to himself than "to abide *for ever*" in that horrible captivity: "but yet, *let us consider*," says he cheerily; "besides," "moreover":—arguing down, with a logic that gathers its premises out of the unbarred domain of hope, this weak proclivity of Christian's towards the fatal sin. Passing from the crime, he brightens on in his triumph of hope over misery: "*and let us consider again, that all the law is not in the hand of Giant Despair;*" "*others,*" he rather believes, "have *escaped.*" "*Who knows*" but God, who has not let go His rule of things while they lie there helpless, may bring death to the Giant himself?—*or*, that he may some day, stupid as he is, forget to lock their door?—*or*, that he may be seized with one of his fits when their door is open, and they are able to flee? "And *if ever* that should come to pass again," as it had done the day before, *he* at least is clear about snatching a manly advantage of the opportunity. "But, however, let them but *endure a while;* the *time may come* that may give them a happy release."

Hopeful and Christian, outwardly regarded, are here in precisely the same case. Each, having left the straight path of God's will, has come under the shadow of Despair, and each is aching under the pains which its dark dominion has brought him. But beyond this, comparison ceases. Christian bows beneath the tyrant's sway, and harbours an inverted faith in the finality of their condition: he is prostrate under the oppression of the dismal one, and the flame of his old hope is flickering in the miasma of the gloom. Hopeful trims his lamp, and asserts the old radiance in the heart of the darkness, as at once a reminiscence of the past and a token of the future. He firmly declines to let down upon him the sovereignty of this clumsy usurper. He holds up his head, racked with cudgellings that are lawless, and chill with the damps of a night that is unnatural, and dares to indulge the thought that he is still by birthright a son of light and freedom, and ventures to look forth for the coming of complete liberation, which he shall take care to hasten as he can. Through

that dark door he is gazing forward to their faring forth
again under God's wide heaven, as a thing that must
somehow come to pass.   They were not made—they were
not accepted into pilgrimage — for just this species of
existence.   Hopeful, strictly speaking, is not in the grasp
of Despair at all; for Hope is piercing his mere circumstances on every side.   He may be strictly enough described
as in the Castle of Doubting; but even his doubts have
beams of light shooting through them, and he is watching
how the doubts shall scatter by-and-bye into broad daylight and sunshine.   He does not see light clearly as
matters have meanwhile fallen out with him ; but he sees
that he shall see it erelong : it is hardly for him to say
when, or how.   Hopeful, it is true, enjoys some advantage
in not having taken the initiative in the waywardness
which has brought them both to this ; and to him the
whole experience has less the complexion of sin, and more
the complexion of calamity.   But the true secret is in himself—in his character—in the buoyancy which his bright
outlook gives him, and again in the bright outlook which
his buoyancy confirms.   His faith simply refuses to subside upon its dank roots, and still waves its flowers in the
rayless breezes of the night, abiding the sunrise.

"Towards evening" of the same day on which the
monster proffered his hideous counsel, the dungeon-door
opened again.   His "grievous rage" at finding them still
alive,—though "alive was all,"—left them "trembling
greatly" under the threat that "it should be worse with
them than if they had never been born."   The Dreamer
"thinks" that Christian swooned ; and on his recovery, he
"again seemed for doing it."   Hopeful arouses himself
that he may once more arouse his friend.   He confronts
him with his heroic past, and seems as if he were plying
him with his own identity :—"My brother, rememberest
thou not how valiant thou hast been heretofore?   Apollyon

could not crush thee, nor did all that thou didst see or
hear or feel in the Valley of the Shadow of Death. What
hardship, terror, and amazement *hast thou already* GONE
THROUGH!—and art thou now nothing but fears!" He
touches modestly upon his own companionship with him
in all his present trouble—"a far weaker man by nature,"
and yet unsubdued. He crowns the argument by a spirited
reference to Vanity Fair; and he rivets his reasoning by
the plea, that as Christians they must "avoid the shame"
of being found in such a plight of disconsolateness ;—for the
moment forgetful, it would seem, that their condition is
without witnesses, yet letting the light fall upon a spot
of the subject which is of the greatest practical concern.

And here we may pause to take estimate of the amount
of inherent Hopefulness which this man possesses. The
friend in whom he acknowledges a senior, a superior, and
in some sense a guide, is taking the gloomiest view of the
circumstances of them both : his experience, his valour, his
wisdom, all gave weight to the hopelessness with which
this man beside him is looking at their prospects. Did he
himself possess only an ordinary fund of Hopefulness, the
hopelessness of Christian would bear it down, and each
would but aggravate the despondency of the other. But
the Hopefulness of the younger man is sufficient to stand
its ground steadily against this hopelessness of the older
man, and still to do so after the new accession of reasons
for despair which the Giant has just left with them. This
is much, but there is more. The junior friend has such
abundance of Hopefulness, that he can even interest himself in the distress of the senior friend, and can manage to
sustain him with something of the energy of that cheerfulness of prospect with which he himself is sustained ; and
he can still do this while the darkness of things continues
to thicken. And there is more still. This man of Hopefulness is able to pass away beyond himself and his condi-

tion, and to forget himself and it. absorbed with solicitude about his friend, and about the honour of God, and about the dignity of the Christian vocation before the onlooking world, and can command a free movement of his thoughts in generous recollection and cordial survey, around the bent head of the man upon whom he has so much depended, and whom he would now rally to a becoming courage and patience.   He has to carry the staff of companionship on which he was wont to lean in brighter days, and has to carry it in days of darkness that seem only to be deepening; yet he is erect and scarcely dismayed.   The gale that used to waft him on has shifted to a head-wind, and the head-wind has blown to a storm, and the storm has settled into the ponderousness of a second cargo; yet he is not, more than ever, in a sinking condition, but only " casts anchors out of the stern, and wishes for the day."

And the day came—came strangely.   The day had been all the while with them—hidden from their eye, but at every moment ready for their hand.   It was dark enough before the dawn.   They were spending the Saturday night in prayer—to which they may have been specially urged by the sight of the skulls of murdered victims in the Castle-yard among whom it was their early destination to be numbered,—when, on the Lord's-Day morning, the light broke in the mind of Christian—the light of liberty. That " passionate speech " of his must have struck Hope-ful like a shaft of light from an unexpected quarter of the sky—a morning sun-gleam out of the west.   " A key in my bosom that will open any lock in Doubting Castle !" " *Pluck it out* of thy bosom," the man of Hopefulness will now say ; " *and try :*" he is in all readiness for the emer-gency.   And " Promise" proves itself equal to the whole occasion.   A little while of energetic employment as free men, and they were singing together on the king's own way, which Despair's gigantic footsteps never yet have pressed.

The scene at the River is the counterpart of this in the Giant's castle, in respect both of Hopeful and of Christian. " Be of good cheer, my brother : *I feel the bottom, and it is good.*" We could guess who the two "brothers" were, and where. At one point, Hopeful " had *much ado* to keep his brother's head above water," but he does not seem to have failed. He " did also endeavour to comfort him, saying, Brother, *I see the gate*, and men standing by to receive us." It is all for *him*, Christian replies : *he* " has been Hopeful ever since he knew him." " And so have *you*," promptly answers the man of Hope. And he adds words of great wisdom :—" These troubles and distresses that you go through in these waters are no sign that God hath forsaken you, but are sent to try you, *whether you will call to mind that which heretofore you have received of His goodness, and live upon Him in your distresses.*" Is Hopeful delivering up his secret in his last words? Not his last : the very last utterance of his voice had need to be just this —" *Be of good cheer :* JESUS CHRIST maketh thee whole."

These two crucial chapters in the history of the pilgrims are sufficiently illustrative of the persistently hopeful tone which one of them was able to preserve among the varying fortunes of his spiritual experience. It is almost forced upon us that it is only the accident of his association with Christian which brings such a man for a moment within the dreary domain of despondency or doubt. Had he been alone, we fancy, he never should have looked upon the face of Despair, or been barred out of reach of the happy sunlight. Even by the terms of the story, he never does take so dark a view of his spiritual affairs as is quite in keeping with his allegorical condition : he is superior to his circumstances in a degree which we perceive to be anomalous ; and great part of the glad interest we take in him consists in the sympathy we have with the protest of his spiritual consciousness against the temporary disorder of his spiritual history. Yet we must not too greatly minimise the depth of shadow which lay upon the spirit even of Hopeful during this sad period. If a man by any means moves out of the way of self-denying adherence to the Divine will, he must not marvel if his sense of his gracious relationship to the movements of that will becomes obscured, and all clear vision of Divine favour towards himself is for a while eclipsed. No amount of Hopefulness can suffice to fortify a man against this operation of cause and effect within the spiritual region. But his Hopefulness shall do much for him notwithstanding. It shall keep him true to the future under all the pressure of the present—a present which in the whole heart of it is abnormal and false, in bad harmony with the cause which has produced it. It shall guide his eye back upon the legible past, and make all that past a middle term in a syllogism which throws its sunny conclusion forward into the illegible future, touching the very mist with light across the dark episode of the present. Despair, despondency, are arrested into patience—a firm-hearted waiting which is not without a tincture of reverent curiosity, sombred always by a humble sense of having deserved all the painful gloom which has fallen upon the spirit: When shall the good Lord restore me to light and liberty?—how? His will be done, now and henceforth! For it is not His will, I know, to abandon me to this.—And the light and liberty never but returned,—revealing the solid truthfulness upon which all the subdued brightness of the hoping reposed.

And it is not substantially different as to the last earthly experience of all. The shadow which is apt to creep across the spirit at this crisis is that of the sin of the whole earthly past, as a past of imperfection and unworthiness: the future which has to be lighted up, in great measure out of that very past, is the future of another and an eternal world—so little known, that it is not easy to reason onwards to it through the premises of what we have ever felt or seen. But that past of ours has two elements in it—a human and a Divine : if we keep our eye upon the human element, we can only carry darkness forward from it into the untrodden future ; if, however, we fix our gaze upon the Divine element, upon the goodness and faithfulness of God's gracious providence with us,—from this we can carry forward nothing but light, and the light of the very world which is awaiting our spirits. It is that which is the same on both sides of the dividing river : the river only flows through, it does not bound, the territory of God's grace in Christ. This is the source of Hopeful's lightfulness of heart in the River : he regarded the Divine and eternal element of the known, and, from that, sprung his arch of Hope across the stream to the unknown ; while Christian let his heart become heavy as lead for a season, by his losing sight of the Divine under the obtrusion of the human, from which no arch could reach further on than the River itself and its shivering depths. " I see HIM again," he cries ; straightway the dark human past retires before the effulgence of the Divine all-present. Then—Christian becomes Hopeful too, and will never be hopeless again as long as he has being.

In thus endeavouring to measure what we have called the Spiritual Hopefulness of this pilgrim, it was almost inevitable that we should already touch, perhaps at more than one point, the third factor which we distinguished as entering into the general idea of the name—that of definite *Christian Hope.* The direct object of this is the unseen and eternal, made real to the consciousness by faith. It anticipates what faith apprehends. It brings near in time what faith brings near in space. It is rooted in the same soil with faith ; but it is somewhat more, and somewhat other, than faith. " Faithful " and " Hopeful " may be just as different as they are in the story : faith may be vigorous in proportion to hope, as with Faithful; or hope may be vigorous in proportion to faith, as with Hopeful. Or shall we again regard hope as but the blossom of faith? —then, faith may be sturdy in stem and branch, yet be scanty of bloom; or it may be more slender in branch and stem, yet break forth all over into flower. Whatever was faith in Hopeful appeared to flourish into hope with him. Time shrunk into littleness as interval between eternal conditions and temporal ones, so that they seemed in a manner to mingle together in his present consciousness as almost coincident conceptions. This Hope of his grew luxuriant as his faith grew strong: the Hope passes more easily into joy; which is like the fresh sunlight flashing upon the flower,—kindling its colours and wooing forth its odours, otherwise comparatively latent. Hope, as a Christian grace, pervades the course of Hopeful like a summer atmosphere: you cannot point to it, yet you never miss it. But it is towards the end, and after the days spent on the Mountains of the Shepherds, that he breaks forth in the face of Atheist with the words,—a manifesto of his creed feeling its way to music as a hymn of his heart,—" Now do I *rejoice in hope* of the glory of God!"

When we look beyond this predominant feature, this threefold name-feature, of the character of Hopeful, perhaps the quality which occupies the place of next importance is the prevailing air of *Simplicity*, of childlikeness, which we can observe about him. There is a youthfulness in his character apart from his years. This lies near to his Hopefulness. Hope is characteristic of youth; and Hopefulness of character is to be looked for along with youthfulness of character. It is not necessarily a matter of immaturity; it can survive all ripening, and then may only shed around the ripeness an altogether legitimate beauty. It may be said to be deeper in the character than

Hopefulness itself, and even to lend a good deal to Hopefulness in the way of cause. It is permissive, if not even productive, of that buoyancy which Hopeful so remarkably preserves. He looks at things without any of the subtle entanglements which are begotten of ingenious reflectiveness—candidly, simply, on the clear merits of them, and with a decided affinity to their brighter side, since the essential complexion of them he has once for all ascertained to be brightness, at least for him. He has no disposition to let in upon them a darkness which needs to be generated from without—even if it be from that *without* of theirs which is his own *within*. His Simplicity therefore works at any rate together with his Hopefulness, and agrees with it well.

But this childlike cast of his character operates in divers directions, and in variously modified forms. The very first recorded words of his have a guileless frankness in them :—" Ask him," says he to Christian, who has turned aside from By-ends for a moment to confide his suspicion that this pilgrim is identical with a certain " veriest knave " not quite unknown to him ; " ask him : methinks he should not be ashamed of his name." Much further on, when his journey has been half accomplished, his whole attitude in the notable conversation about Little-faith finds its key in the same Simplicity of character, hampered here by what we may describe as a corresponding simplicity of experience. He is incapable of sympathising heartily with Little-faith, and is equally incapable of affecting that he does. Relations get a little ruffled between the two companions over the matter. " *But, Christian,*" he interjects, employing a mode of address which has a delicate stroke of Bunyan's art in it ; and we have a " but " beginning no fewer than five of Hopeful's little speeches, and a " well but " beginning the last, before he comes round to say, with a sympathy which yet sounds somewhat boyish to the ear of Christian—

" I would it had *been* Great-grace, for their sakes."   There
is something of the same transparent stintedness of comprehension, but working now within his own history towards
his personal peril, in his readiness to succumb during their
march through the drowsy plains :—" Let us lie down here
and take *one nap. . . . Why*, my brother? . . . We may
be refreshed if we take a nap."   We can try to imagine
these words to be spoken by Faithful anywhere, if we
would feel the significance of them as words of Hopeful's ;
yet on his lips we do not feel them to be at all incongruous.   So the question, a little abruptly thrust in upon their
conference—" Are we *now almost got past* the Enchanted
Ground ? "   He is not in the least " weary of this discourse," but would "*know where they are.*"   There is always
lurking about him a simple-hearted disengagedness which
admits of curiosity, and puts on an aspect of easy impatience,—all of it youthful.   Such a man stands in need of a
guide ; and when occasion occurs, he will hasten to acknowledge it.   " Hitherto," he says to Christian in this
very connection—" Hitherto hath thy company been my
mercy ;"—although the dismal episode of By-path Meadow,
as the territory of the Castle, held its dark place in the
past, relieved only by the discovery of the " key of
promise."   And perhaps we can recognise the same disposition, as well as the same need, in the earlier incident of
Demas and his mine : " Let us go *see ;*" with its unfailing
sequel—" I am sorry that I was so foolish,"—and further
on, beneath the weird monument which had its own connection with the mine—" But what a mercy is it that
neither thou—*but especially* I, am not made *myself* this
example ! "   A sentence this, in which the very awkward-
ness of construction is more expressive than any choice of
words could have been.

But if we look longer in this direction, with its hints of
insufficiency of character underlying all its frank lovable-

ness, we shall be in danger of thinking more meanly of
Hopeful than he deserves.   He is strong in the advantages
which his type of character permits.   He has the better of
Christian in *Quickness of parts.*   He is keen of observation.
It was he who " espied " the writing on the monument,
though he could not read it; and again it was he who
" spied " the awful paper on the back of the apostate,
whom he characteristically turned to " look after."   He
sometimes displays an instinct of rightness which has much
the effect of acquired wisdom.   At the stile he pauses
with the pregnant query—" But how if this path should
lead us out of the way? "   For, as he afterwards explained,
he himself " was afraid on't *at the very first.*"   There is
little of false Hopefulness about him now.   Under the
recollection of his own experience, he cordially admits that
" fear tends much to men's good ;" and it was this which
had schooled an intuitive prudence into his Hopefulness
when he stood in the presence of right and wrong, though
that prudence was oftener than once overpowered by
stronger forces.—Under the same guiding of experience he
hits the mark shrewdly with Ignorance, when, in a way
which distinctly recalls Christian's own counsel to Faithful
concerning Talkative about " the power of religion," he
whispers to his friend—" Ask him if ever he had *Christ
revealed to him from heaven.*"[1]—His disquisition on the
causes of backsliding, suggested by the case of Temporary,
is done wisely and well.—He has not the intricate intelligence of Christian, nor has he the mental energy of Faithful; but he has probably more liveliness of parts than
either, and he is gaining in gravity of intellectual resources
as his mind and heart keep true to the nurturings of grace
and providence.

It only remains that we remind ourselves how much all

---

[1] " O friends, cry to God to *reveal Jesus Christ unto you.*"—" Grace
Abounding," par 125.

the other qualities of Hopeful were mingled and dignified with *Charity*—with brotherliness and compassion.—
Towards Christian himself, his warm considerateness, his
respectful tenderness, are so constant, that we are apt to
overlook how sometimes they rise into a very beauty of
fraternal conduct. Hear him in the night-storm on the
Meadow, into the miseries of which he had been misled
against his truer judgment :—" *Be comforted, my brother,
for I forgive thee ; and believe too that this shall be for our
good :*" it is " Charity hoping all things."—We need only
refer again to the conversations in the dungeon—conversations in which Faith, Hope, and Charity, seem to be
intertwined into reasoning, producing a logic of triple
strength and triple delicacy ; or to his whole behaviour in
the River, where an almost heroic self-obliviousness leaves
him free to exhibit how surpassingly tender he can be in
his timely helpfulness, though treating an infirmity which
he can hardly comprehend.—We shall expect to find that
such a man was scarcely less lively in his compassion
towards the unbelieving. He tells Christian that he
"pitied " Temporary, however his apostasy may have
vexed him. And there is a touch of gracious naturalness in his desire that they should wait till Ignorance
overtook them again—just after his own story of how
Christ became his, and how ashamed he then felt about
his own " ignorance."—Nor is all this rendered comparatively valueless as being the mere lovingness of a nature
that has no independence in it. He can be self-assertive
when occasion fairly demands. In one sentence of his
during the disquieting discussion about Little-faith, we can
mark the transition from the one mood to the other :—" I
acknowledge it ; but yet your severe reflection *had almost
made me angry.*" The first burst of his feeling in the
Meadow, when they find that all begins to go wrong, is
this—"O that *I* had kept on my way !" Then, when

they have aroused themselves to endeavour to repair their blunder by retracing their steps—"But, good brother, let *me* go before. . . . No, you shall *not* go first." On the Delectable Mountains, we notice, he ventures once to address the Shepherds on his own account, impressed with the sight of the by-way to perdition: it is a circumstance which is more significant than it appears, since it not only suggests his habitual unobtrusiveness, but indicates a growing reliance upon his own individuality. Christian, as is natural, overshadows him a little, in a kindly way, throughout the whole of his journey; so that it is not so easy to note his development as otherwise it would be. But he does manifestly mature; and we do not marvel that he " also has a fit or two " of home-sickness when Christian is prostrated with that sweet disorder, while both are lingering in the lightsome borderland.

The survey we have taken of this character must constrain us to admit, that it is not only a character of singular attractiveness, but is also one of unusual completeness. If it be inferior in capacity to the goodly characters we have already studied, it is superior to them in graceful fulness of form. There is a roundness and regularity of curve in the nature of the man ; and grace only gives it new adornment, while it expands its content and redoubles its strength —not once for all, but rather by more or less perceptible increments of development. His sunny attractiveness has relation to this roundedness,—as if the sunlight were thus able to fall upon every point of him. There are no shadows, because no sinuosities or shrinking hollows: not any part of him comes in the light of any other part. For neither is this sunniness lost when the religion of Christ begins to rule him ; it is only taken up and enriched. His is the character of sanctified geniality among the three characters of this First Part. It is a character which is conscious of the poetry no less than of the earnestness of life, and is well open to it. Christian, indeed, is not wanting in this; he has much more of it than his noble friend Faithful. But Hopeful has distinctly more, and has it in more constancy; for it more thoroughly pervades the framework of his constitution. We are able to recall, that the portion of the way on which Faithful was the companion of Christian, not quite a trifling fraction of the whole pilgrimage, contained no restful spot, and no moment of harmless relaxedness. Christian, while he was alone, had his guest-houses, and even his bower and water-springs; when he was with Faithful, he seems to have had nothing but his strenuous march. Is it only the accident of the route which brings it to pass, that when he is in the company of Hopeful he meets so much of loveliness on the King's highway—the "delicate plain" of Ease, the charming mead of the River of God, the delight-some Mountains, the ravishing country-side which confronted the City? We are ready to wonder whether Faithful would have felt no waste of time among these; but the eye of Hopeful will be quick for such outward agreements with his inward spirit. Faithful represents the tragedy of Christian life—righteous testimony and stern sacrifice, with reward to come; Hopeful represents the comedy of Christian life—holy sympathy and bright obedience, with something of reward on the way. It was but prologue, however, with both.

It is true that it does not wholly lie in a man's character which of these sides of Christian life he shall exhibit, but in his character and in providence together. Probably, however, it lies more in character than we are commonly in the way of supposing. Bunyan fits the circumstances in large measure to the character,—here and there starting in our minds a question, which it would scarcely profit us to discuss, how far particular incidents depict internal states or moods of the pilgrim, and how far they stand for external happenings in providence. This at least is undoubted,—that the mood, the more especially if it belong to the fixed cast of the character, shall make the same outward happening a very different experience to different Christian men. Hopeful, if we have regard to the inner experience of the man, had a considerably different history from Christian there at his side. This also is equally undoubted,—that a large proportion of our experiences—those of the outward lot as well as those of the inner history, though these keep touching each other at many points—are brought about by our own proclivities of feeling and will, as expressions of our own character. We may be sure that Bunyan would have given Hopeful a somewhat different set of incidents on the road if Christian's company had not restrained him, and would have done so in strict fidelity to his subject. In amending our character, then, it would seem, we are going some way to amend our experience itself: we are amending it at its human fountain-head.

Does not our acquaintance with Hopeful suggest, that one way to amend the character of most of us, and to enrich it indefinitely, is to train it into having an open side to the sunlight of things—the sunlight which floods the eternal heaven of our hopes, but which also lies abundantly about upon the passing scene of our work and warfare? All sunlight is ours. There does not fall upon the world a truly gladsome ray which we may not let in upon our own spirits—if we have already let in a willing sonship to the ever-blessed One. A cheerful deportment befits a Christian, and speaks of spiritual soundness. A hopeful buoyancy of soul is one of " the best gifts " which it behoves him to " covet earnestly." He may well guard himself against a hopefulness which comes of mere lack of thought ; but he may well pray and strive towards a hopefulness that

is steadfastly founded upon truth, and firmly compacted
with earnestness.   Sadness will not fail to visit us; fear
will not always refrain from haunting us ; regret will never
altogether melt away into sunlight : but the dark fringe
of hopelessness ought by no means to touch a Christian
heart as long as God's grace endures.   It is unworthy,
since God *is* faithful still ; it is disloyal, since there is entrusted to us the privilege of maintaining the honour of
the king and the kingdom in the midst of a disaffected or
rebellious world.   We have need to blend the character of
Hopeful with that of Christian : we have a right to be
Hopeful-Christians,—absorbing all pure sunbeams though
they may be only reflected, believing always the better
before the worse, cultivating such an optimism of spirit as
the glad Evangel of Jesus Christ sustains.   The healthy
Christian is able, with the loftiest meaning, to speak as the
First Brother in *Comus* did to the Second, and as " Brother
Hopeful " might have spoken at any time to " Brother
Christian " :

> " Yet, when an equal poise of hope and fear
>   Does arbitrate the event, *my nature is*
>   *That I incline to hope* rather than fear,
>   And gladly banish squint suspicion."

In the most of human concerns it is wisdom : in all
Divine concerns it is happy duty besides.

X.

CHRISTIANA : HER SPIRITUAL CHARACTER.

OUR plan now conducts us into that continuation of the pilgrim-story which constitutes the Second Part. This new attempt of Bunyan's, with all its hazards and disadvantages, wears upon it very few of the marks of exhaustion or deterioration which are apt to distinguish such attempts. We must reckon his success the more praiseworthy, that in this particular task of his, he had little choice but to accept a difficulty which was somewhat peculiar to it: he had the old ground to fill with a new history. The continuation, in the main outline of it, must needs be a repetition. Yet the new history does borrow something of interest from the old, and the interest of familiarity replenishes in part the diminished interest of freshness. It derives interest too from the circumstance, that while the continuation is a repetition, it is also in great measure a completion :

> " What Christian left lock'd up, and went his way,
>   Sweet Christiana opens with her key."

But Bunyan was not the man to confine his reliance to these merely external sources of interest, as long as an internal and richer source was ready to his hand—the perennial interest which belongs to character. The number and variety of the new figures which live and move upon the old road,—this reanimates all the familiarity, and works it in with the texture of a fabric which has many of the qualities of a new material. The unflagging productiveness of Bunyan's fancy in this department, informed as it is by his accurate fulness of knowledge, appears in a remarkable light when this second book comes before us, brimming with a choice abundance which seems oblivious of all decline. Indeed, as we contemplate the sparkling copiousness of this outflow of genius in the later work, instead of feeling as if we gazed into an overdrawn or diluted fountain, we are almost ready to aver that the generous entertainer has "kept the good wine until now."

The versified preface (quoted above), which he adopts as his "way of sending forth his Second Part," affords some hints of how the First Part had fared in the interval of years since its publication. He has indeed some solid reasons to offer against the hesitation which he is imagining this new adventurer to feel as it emerges into the light of public criticism. Its predecessor has been counterfeited and stolen from. It "has travelled sea and land," and never been "slighted." In France, in Flanders, in Holland, it is "esteemed." "Highlanders and wild Irish can agree" in making its familiar acquaintance. In New England it is "under such advance" "as to be trimmed, new-clothed, and decked with gems." "Nearer home" it is welcomed in "city and country": "brave gallants," "young ladies," "the very children," "they that have never seen him" (the Pilgrim), and they "who did not love him at the first,"—all are warm in their admiration. The testimony is important even on its historical side. On its biographical side, it suggests a striking difference between the states of mind, the felt motives and responsibilities, under which the two Parts were written. On its literary side, it reveals an instance of acceptance almost immediate and altogether great; and it leads us to surmise, that possibly the new work may be found to exhibit some reflex evidence of that wide and multifarious circle of readers at the conscious centre of which, as we may say, it was composed. Do we trace anything of this in the greater breadth and geniality of treatment, the yet homelier freedom of style, the more every-day attractiveness of incidents and characters, which are more than recognisable in this Part? Even if we do, no shadow need be allowed to fall for an instant upon Bunyan's motive. He had no thought of accommodating his subject to the great world by lowering its dignity or relaxing its truth. He may have reflected, with reason, that in his First Part he had filled the canvas with a Christian life which was exceptionally lofty, and that truth itself prompted a little reduction of scale for such a multitude of common readers ;—at least, that now, with the more severe and elevated picture before the world, the interest of truth would be even better served if he were to content himself with a delineation more level to ordinary experience and capacity. For the Second Part is a completion of the First in more than in its chrono-logical continuance : it is a completion of it in its ethical outstretch and in its spiritual inclusiveness. But if the good Dreamer, more discernibly than ever in his new work, " becomes all things to all men," it is easy to affirm from what we already know of him, that he does so with the still earnest purpose that he " may gain some "—not to praise himself, but to live for his Lord. The " some " have been incalculably many, and his most Christian purpose is yet to this hour being splendidly achieved.[1]

The manner in which he shall take up the narrative anew,—abiding by the old device of dreaming, yet avoid-ing tameness, and fitting himself to the altered circum-stances of things,—it would have puzzled us to forecast. But his fertility of invention solves the difficulty with all apparent naturalness. " Multiplicity of business," it appears, had greatly kept him back from his " wonted

[1] Note J.

travels into those parts whence he [the pilgrim] went ;" " but having had some concern that way of late," he " went down again thitherward." " Now, having taken up my lodging," he says, " in a wood about a mile off the place," —probably indicating his St Cuthbert cottage in relation to Bedford Jail,—"as I slept I dreamed again. And *as I was in my dream*, behold an aged gentleman *came by where I lay* "—an estimable member of the pilgrim-brotherhood, Mr Sagacity, who happened to be full of all the information which the Dreamer desired to learn. Within the dream—" *methought* I got up and went with him "—the two go forward together long enough to bring the narrative well through what is intermediate and preliminary, and to bring it on to the point of visible pilgrimage. When Christiana's group, under the old gentleman's description, are seen to be approaching the Wicket-gate, then the obliging narrator, who had "given him an account of the whole matter" from the beginning, " *left me*," he records, " *to dream out my dream myself.* Wherefore, methought *I saw* Christiana and mercy, and the boys, go all of them up to the gate." In the second sentence of the First Part he had written—" I dreamed, and behold *I saw* a man." . . . Thus he reaches the old allegorical standpoint again in all safety.[1]

As we now take our new departure with him, we bethink us, that there is more of newness in the story than a fresh beginning only : there is the novelty of female pilgrims and their pilgrimage, till now scarcely brought within the whole horizon of the Allegory. The women of the First Part are not pilgrims at all, or they are not pilgrims upon the ordinary footing of pilgrimage : the women of the Second Part, in a number of instances, are pilgrims indeed. By this alone, the skill of the Allegorist is subjected to a new test, in respect both to incident and

<hr>

[1] Note K.

to character; and by the wonderful degree of success with which he sustains the test, he has supplied a contribution to the full delineation of practical Christianity which of itself would have laid something like a necessity upon him to give to the world such a complementary sequel as this Second Part proves to be. There is not much either of wisdom or of truth in accentuating too sharply the difference between women and men within the religious sphere; yet, to speak generally, the difference is appreciable enough, as it is natural enough and admirable enough, within that sphere also; and by no means is the difference, on the whole, to the disadvantage of women. Bunyan knew it all precisely well. He could have permitted his earlier pilgrims to stand, as they might in an absolute way have truthfully stood, representative of mankind without further distinction; for he was too robust in his good sense to be painfully scrupulous about " his " and " her " in his teaching. But we should then have missed a life-like adaptation of the whole subject to the details of truthfulness, and should have had, besides, a whole phase of Bunyan's power still lurking undisplayed within the massive folds of the more general treatment. For his genius meets the occasion fully. His women are no other than women : their speech, their action, their experience, are the speech and action and experience of women,—all the while that they maintain that type of excellence and dignity which befits their womanhood. In truth, his delineations of female character are not to be readily matched within the range of our literature.

If now we turn to the more special study before us—to Christiana, the wife and widow of him whom we followed so long,—we shall find this delicacy of adaptation meeting us on the threshold. The introductory narrative of Sagacity, which conveys to the mind so beguiling an impression of independent and disinterested testimony,—this bears many marks of the new order of matters which the new journey is bringing us. The desolate woman mourns her departed husband,—chides herself for her harsh ways with him,—feels kindlier towards him than she had been wont to do,—relents towards his religion,—lets that religion come in to mingle with her natural feelings and regrets,—translates her wifely faults into human sins, and her whole past attitude of spirit into one of guilt and lostness. Her conscience is reached through the avenues of her affection, and Divine truth comes to her by the way of human love. It is still Divine truth that comes, and it comes divinely. Yet it does not so come as to drive her from her fireside into the fields; nor does any human Evangelist meet her, either abroad or at home. It finds her in her womanly sphere: it hovers about her in her night dreams; it visits her amidst the quiet seclusion of her hearth. Divine Comfort Itself, in the person of Secret, the holy messenger, stands before her consciousness, and, with his touching letter from the King, instructs her from his own lips in all that concerns her setting-out. So, too, it is still at home that her worldly-hearted neighbours set upon her—the womanly Obstinates of her history,—and still at her fireside that she wins the companionship of her youthful friend, the more constant Pliable of her happier story. There is a decent arrangement of all things before she quits her door, and she quits it with each of her four children at her side. It is the setting-out of one who is woman, and wife, and mother.

Another feature of the new pilgrimage may here occur to us :—it is manifest that now we are done with the loneliness of wayfaring. Hopeful, who is a link in several respects between the two portions of the " Pilgrim," is a link also in this. It is the progress of a company that we have now to follow—a company that nowise diminishes,

but goes from strength to strength ere it appears before
God, one by one, in the City. The strong and solemn
aspect of religious life in its individual solitariness scarcely
reappears on this pilgrimage. There is solitude of march
going forward, it is true, behind the scenes of the history;
only, the moment it emerges, its solitude is dispersed.
Honest, Valiant-for-Truth, Stand-fast, are surprised in their
long solitude, and, in the act, are snatched out of it into a
very caravan of sociable ongoing. Indeed, it is the social
side of Christian life, the side of Christian friendship and
intercourse, the side which leans towards the wide "communion of saints," that this Second Part illustrates as its
specialty; and in this too it is something of a complement
to the First.

Of this gathering company Christiana is from first to
last the heroine; nor can it be gainsaid that she very
becomingly occupies her position of distinction. It is
needful, however, that we should withdraw her in imagination from the collectiveness of the group, as far as this is
practicable, in order that we may the better acquaint ourselves with her as an individual Christian woman. And it
may lend a clearness to our inquiry if we even venture on
the liberty of analysing the totality of her character a little,
and of regarding it successively in its Spiritual, in its Intellectual, and in its Domestic aspects.

We soon make out to perceive, that the SPIRITUAL
character of Christiana is one of some womanly strength
and depth. She possesses not a few of the features of her
husband's spiritual character, rendered into womanliness.
Had the proprieties or the necessities of the Allegory permitted her to travel any good part of the way alone, the
resemblance would doubtless have better appeared. She
is little embarrassed, indeed, with that inborn faculty for
spiritual self-entanglement which he never fully fought

down ; and she looks with more of steady good cheer upon
her own spiritual prospects, as well as upon all things else
whether present or to come. But she has much of his
conscientious thoroughness of spirit, much of his firmness
of faith, much of his lowly-hearted trueness, and no small
proportion of his persistent earnestness of moral nature
and spiritual purpose. As being a woman, her spirituality
has still more of emotion in it than his, but not so much
more of sentiment as to imperil the dignified common-
sense of her womanhood. Her will is as fixed as his in
its main intentions, but it will not be expected to be so
strenuous as his, nor so full, in its executive activity.

Christiana too, then, has a sensitive moral nature, and
gives the primary control to *Conscience ;*—at least she has
come to this, like her husband, when we first see her with
any clearness. The upbraiding recollections that " came
into her mind by swarms " when bereavement had dissolved
the barriers of unreflecting prejudice,—these " also clogged
her conscience, and did *load* her with *guilt.*" " Sons," she
then said to her listening fatherless children, " we are all
undone. I have *sinned away* your father." The letter
which attested the personal and kindly interest of the
King, heartily accepted by her as in good faith, soothed
this powerful force into more than a peaceful ally, and set
her spiritual nature in motion, very resolvedly, towards a
pilgrim-life, as the one solution of the problem of moral
disquietude. " I am convinced," she afterwards affirmed
to the Interpreter at the door of his House, "that no way is
right but this." It was Conscience still approving what it
had impelled her at the first to decide. This singleness of
moral aim, this final adjustment of the moral will to the
will of the Supreme One in an all-friendly Saviour, held its
ground increasingly in her to the end. Her moral sense
appears delicate of touch, and her moral purpose has an
air of indomitable settledness, whether we see her in happy

converse with the Lord of the Gate, or observe her spurn-
ing with her virtuous feet the sneaking ruffians who had
such agility in leaping the Devil's wall, or hear her covering
herself with blame when she recognises that she has erred
in conduct or in judgment. But it is not till she arrives
at about "the place where Christian's burden fell off his
back," and she perceives the "deed" as well as the "word"
of reconciliation, that a clear sky begins to overarch her
Conscience, under the cloud-dispelling discourse of Great-
heart : then the sunshine quickens while it gladdens it, and
leaves upon it a luminous tenderness which she never
loses. All her emotion in that hour, overflowing as it is,
has a firm basis in the preception of the Facts by which
all had been made for ever morally right with her, and
in presence of which the whole strength of Conscience
went in the way of her safety and thankfulness and joy.
There would have been no ray of glad emotion for Christiana, it is plain, in the absence of a foundation of moral
rectitude which she simply knew that nothing in time or
eternity could shake. In her case, happily, the subsequent
presence of Conscience is traceable far less by its re-asser-
tion of right as against committed wrong, than by the
element of stability and depth which it imparts to her
spiritual peace, and by her almost instinctive preference
for that obedience to the King which is the only vital form
of morality beneath the sun.

Closely related to all her moral feeling, but especially to
its appeasement upon the terms of grace, was her *Faith* in
revelation, and in the unseen Saviour-King whom it most
of all revealed. The dawnings of her Faith are to be
discerned even before it comes to fix itself upon what
brings anything of solid comfort to her spirit. The unseen
takes on something of reality to her from the moment that
her husband has passed within its realm. Imagination
and affection follow him thither. In spirit she goes after

him : her heart draws her thoughts away from the world ; and her thoughts prepare a path for her believings, as they return upon herself and her own condition compared with him and his. The dream had incipient elements of Faith in it, and it provided tender materials for more. The letter appealed to her Faith in the direct line of its evangelical exercise ; and her Faith responded to the appeal with a quiet promptitude that meant a final and cordial acceptance of pilgrimage as the future form of mortal existence for her. "The dream and the letter together," she will by-and-bye tell the Interpreter, "so wrought upon my mind, that they forced me to this way." So Abram was "forced" from his land and kindred—"by faith." The simple confidence she reposes upon the heavenly document reminds us of Christian's own confidence in his "book :" "What now will ye say to this?" she asks her neighbours, with some triumph, when she has "plucked out her letter and read it." "*For the truth hath said,*"—these words of hers to Mercy were henceforth a guiding motto of her way. When Great-heart expounds the plan of grace more fully, in the hallowed region of Christian's release, her Faith keeps pace with her understanding ; and it is this Faith, by its firm grasp and piercing reach, which makes her heart "ten times more lightsome now," though it "was lightful and joyous before." So it remains, with little apparent interruption or diminution, to the very close of the pilgrimage. "'I wish you a fair day when you set out for Mount Zion,'" says Honest to her when the Royal summons has arrived, "'and shall be glad to see that you go over the river dry shod.' But she answered,"—and the answer has the truest and brightest of Faith in its accents, so finely womanly,—"'Come wet, come dry, I long to be gone ; for however the weather is on my journey, *I shall have time enough, when I come there, to sit down and rest me and dry me.*'" And this magnanimous unconcern—this meek, quiet-hearted heroism of a Faith to which the future and the unseen are all but known, and are altogether homely,—this abides unruffled through all her farewells, and is still to be recognised in that friendly beckoning of adieu with which she assures those who have "followed her to the river side," that even yet, and now for ever, all is peace.

A Faith so well-rooted as this can scarcely consist with a false self-esteem. Confidence in self has no competency for bringing to pass in a human soul any such elevated steadfastness of assurance as this woman sustained through life and death. Humility and Candour—a *Lowly-hearted Trueness*, as we are led in her case to express it—must be a virtue by which such a Faith is working all the while. We are witness to this at every step of her way. It is to be noted in her deportment and her speech before she leaves the roof under which the old life has been lived. It is a pathetic feature of her behaviour at the Wicket-gate :—"Then Christiana made her *low obeisance*, and said, *Let not our Lord be offended* with his hand-maidens for that we have knocked at his princely gate. . . . We are come . . . to be, if it shall please you, graciously admitted by this gate into the way that leads to the celestial city."—We may touch almost any of the points of pilgrimage at which she received more special favours, and we shall hear an echo of the same note of outspoken humility, now enriched with thankfulness, and always interesting from its womanly tendency to minuteness of detail. It takes a peculiar distinctness in the instance of her parting with the mere Porter at the Palace Beautiful, whose very subordinateness of position invites a greater freedom of lowly utterance and grateful action :—"Sir, I am much obliged to you for all the kindness that you have showed me. . . . I know not how to gratify your kindness. . . . So they thanked the Porter, and departed."

—This same humbleness, which accords so full appreciation to favours bestowed by others, exhibits itself no less clearly in her distrust of her own capability of maintaining her Christian career unaided. Her reply to the Interpreter, when he likened her to the son in the parable who "afterward repented and went "—" *God make it* a true saying upon me "—was no detached word of the moment, but signified the settled posture of her spirit.—Under this same true-hearted lowliness of hers, she cannot practise any disingenuous concealment of her faults and imperfections. "I am therefore *much to blame*," she affirms, when she has reflected upon the untoward incident of the two villains who stole advantage of their unprotected state though "so near the King's palace." The Interpreter is exhibiting the symbol of the lonely spider in the spacious apartment, and she apprehends so much of the meaning that the Instructor "looks pleasantly upon her, and says, 'Thou hast said the truth.'" But when he explains more fully, Christiana will keep no credit which is not her due: "I *thought something* of this, but I could not *imagine it all.*" By-and-bye, the Interpreter is encouraging her to rehearse her experiences: her open-heartedness struggles with her womanly modesty, and overcomes, when she says —"*Yea, I may tell my Lord*, though I would not have everybody know it ; "—and she mentions how they were "so sorely assaulted" by "the two."—She is not slow to make honest avowal when her own strength is near its limits : her remark on the slope of Difficulty may be taken as typical of many another, when, panting out the syllables, she confesses—"I dare say—this—*is*—a breathing hill." —At the close of the conversation between Honest and Great-heart concerning Fearing, long after this, she throws a gleam of light upon her whole pilgrimage, and lets us see beneath the surface from end to end of it, when she makes this declaration :—"This relation of Mr Fearing has done me good. I thought nobody had been like me; but I see there was *some semblance* betwixt this good man and I; only we differed in two things: his troubles were so great, they brake out; but mine I kept within. His, also, lay so hard upon him, they made him that he could not knock at the houses provided for entertainment; but my trouble was always such as made me knock the louder." A noteworthy difference, each of them: she was not paralysed with fear for the future, yet was somewhat oppressed with a present self-abasement, which, however, was at once discreet and urgently practical. It is evident that the picturesque transaction which closes their stay at the Interpreter's House would not have its slightest share of personal significance in the case of Christiana herself:—"Then said the Interpreter again to the damsel that waited upon these women, 'Go into the vestry and fetch out garments for these people;' so she went and fetched out white raiment, and laid it down before him; so he commanded them to put it on. 'It was fine linen, white and clean.' When the women were thus adorned, they seemed to be a terror one to the other; for that *they could not see that glory each one on herself which they could see in each other.* Now therefore they began to esteem each other better than themselves. 'For you are fairer than I am,' said one; and, 'You are more comely than I am,' said another." We need not forget, that we owe this admirable picture of reciprocal humility to the advent into the story of those female pilgrims whose grace it so fittingly illustrates.

If we be in danger of imagining that there was much of feebleness in a character in which there was so much of self-depreciation, we have only to guide our eye along the story again. We shall find that this lowly-minded woman was a woman of deep and onward *Earnestness.* Her character was like a goodly stream: it might appear to be only sunk deep between overhanging banks, which softened the sunlight over it, and pent up the murmur of its waters; but it had depth of its own after you reached its lowly surface. And it had a current in its depths—not loud, yet strong, almost swift, and unabating. That current had set in very soon after we come to know her: since then it may have had its sweeps and turnings, or its hours of slackening on the levels; but it never has ceased its onflow, and never has altered its absolute course.

We have but to look in at that old home of hers when she is under the visitation of the buzzing women from the nearest doors. " If you come *in God's name*, come in,"— this was the salutation which amazed them the morning after "the letter" had been received; and, "behold, they found the good woman a-preparing to be gone." "O neighbour, knew you but as much as I do, I doubt not but that *you would go with me*,"—so she turns the argument upon the speaker of the two, Mrs Timorous. This lady waxes voluble in her dissuasions. Christiana only rises in her resolvedness : " Tempt me not, my neighbour. I have now a price put into my hands to get gain, and *I should be a fool of the greatest size if I should have no heart to strike in with the opportunity*. And for that you tell me of all these troubles that I am like to meet with in the way, they are so far from being to me a discouragement, that they show me I am in the right. . . . Wherefore, since you come *not* to my house in God's name, as I said, *I pray you to be gone*, and not disquiet me further." Mrs Timorous goes to spread the news; but "by this time Christiana was *got on* her way."—To Mercy the sum of her counsel as they step onwards is this—"*Only, go along with me.*" The Wicket-gate, which is reached by steady victories of holy persistency, is the scene of much quiet enthusiasm of purpose. Then, having left it, her earnest rectitude is aroused to a storm when she exclaims—" We will *die rather upon the spot* than suffer ourselves to be brought into such snares as shall hazard our wellbeing hereafter." And this Earnestness holds its way through all the experiences of the Interpreter's House and the Palace Beautiful, giving purpose and profit to all her intercourse with her hosts. It throws a practical reality over all the instruction she enjoys, and lends an air of thoroughness to her listening. Hear her with Great-heart on that occasion of his most precious teaching :—" What will He have for Himself " — of righteousness, if He give it away to unrighteous men and women? " *Pray, make that appear.*" " But are the other righteousnesses of no use to us? " At last—" This is brave,"—adding, " Good Mercy, let us *labour to keep this in mind ;* and, my children, do you remember it also."— There is a great deal of genuine public spirit, of the type which is appropriate to womanhood, in the part she takes at the approach to the Palace Beautiful. " Now, to say truth," records the Dreamer, " by reason of the fierceness of the lions, and of the grim carriage of him that did back them, this way had of late lain much unoccupied, and was almost all grown over with grass. Then said Christiana, ' Though the highways have been unoccupied heretofore, and though the travellers have been made in time past to walk through by-paths, *it must not be so now I am risen*— now I am risen a mother in Israel.' " The three pestilent sleepers, now hanged, " shall never be bewailed by " her. —In that dreariest of regions which the Enchanted Ground has now become, we must still think of Christiana as the central figure of that group of most constant pilgrims. Earnestness here settles to endurance that looks wellnigh cheerful if we think of the dismal circumstances,—" mist and darkness fallen upon them all," who were " forced to *feel for one another by words*"—" but sorry going for the best of them all, but how much worse for the women and children, who both of feet and heart were but tender ! Yet . . . they made a pretty good shift to wag along."

Then the seductive "arbour," so cozy a contrast to the "wearisome" way of "dirt and slabbiness" and entangling bushes, without "so much as one inn." "Yet, for aught I could perceive," affirms the historian, "they continually gave so good heed to the advice of their guide, and he did so faithfully tell them of dangers when they were at them, that usually when they were nearest to them, they did most pluck up their spirits, and hearten one another to deny the flesh." Then the "other arbour," with its two deplorable occupants: "The pilgrims desired, with trembling, to *go forward.*" There could be no livelier picture of moral and spiritual constancy,—and the dark, dirty, sloppy footing, with the thickets plucking at the more slender drapery, constrain us to think most of womanly constancy, as we are doubtless meant to do;—for still "they were not off *by much*, of the Enchanted Ground "—" one of the last refuges that the enemy to pilgrims has,"—" only, now they could see one another better" until they came to the good land of Beulah.

In examining thus far the Spiritual character of Christiana, we have had only incidental regard to the element of *Emotion* in it. We expect this element to be an abundant one, and our expectation is verified by the history. But we shall not expect, after what we have already seen, that we have in this woman a personation of mere feeling and affection, vapoured over with a summer-haze of sentiment. None the less, Emotion in her, as is altogether seemly, appears full and active, sweeping the whole scale of feeling and affection,—mobile, strong, and ready to propel to its own hand unless it be guided and employed by steadier forces. We have even already found that such forces are not wanting to her; hence much of the womanly excellence, the rich balance of character, which she undoubtedly displays.

The change which revolutionized her inner life,—touching first, as we have seen, her emotional nature,—gave to that nature a quickening and expansion which were hitherto unknown to it. The mere " natural affection " which she so well discriminates afterwards,—this was gradually taken hold of by grace, and transformed in great measure into spiritual affection. All her feeling became henceforth more or less spiritualised, and was reserved for the objects and concerns of a pilgrim-life under the commands of the King. It was the upwelling of a new spring of Emotion which came to pass when, with the King's letter in her hand, she was "quite overcome." It was the touch of an unwonted tenderness which was on her when, that day, she was so apt to " fall a-weeping." The feeling which swayed and tided within her until she was secure in the House of the Gate, was a feeling which marked a higher flood than the old life had ever seen. And from the moment that the gate was closed behind her, and still more fully from the moment that her youthful companion too was safely folded, her mere tenderness of emotion became enriched by the more vivid mingling of Joy and Gratitude and Love. Nor was it an enrichment only : it was a turn, we may say, of the tide itself; inasmuch as Fear—culminating when " they were greatly tumbled up and down " on account of " the mastiff" which worried at them from within the portal—had hitherto been playing its most prevalent part, and was now cast into the background, to assume in future the function of instructive reminiscence. Its legitimate function this ; but with a nature like hers, and with a pilgrimage beset with so many dangers, we shall not wonder that now and again—as at the approach to the Palace, somewhat needlessly, and elsewhere with more reason—this passive function was considerably exceeded, and for a moment her spirit was touched with apprehension, or was shaken with dread.

But the emotional history of Christiana is on the whole a history of warmth and brightness. Her experience in the house at the Gate, which now appears as a palace of comforts—the Lord's " many good words to them, whereby they were greatly *gladded* " ;[1] " the top of the Gate," from which the Cross was descried; the " summer arbour below," where the two women could freely indulge in their gratulations ; the farewell feasting and washing of feet, ere the Lord " set them in the way of His steps " ; their having " the weather very comfortable to them " upon the new road, as they travelled forth singing,—all tells of a sunniness of Emotion within, even more than of any sunniness without.   The auspicious promise of such a beginning was not falsified by the course.   The long and happy sojourns in the frequent houses of hospitality,—these were periods of great exuberance of Emotion.   Was Christiana not listening to her own heart when the group were being convoyed by the ladies of the Palace, and " were come to the brow of the hill," where Piety returned for " a scheme of all those things that thou hast seen at our house " ? " While she was gone, Christiana thought she heard in a grove, a little way off, on the right hand, a most curious, melodious note, with words much like these—[the close of the 23rd Psalm]—

> ' Through all my life Thy favour is
>   So frankly show'd to me,
> That in Thy house for evermore
>   My dwelling-place shall be.'

And listening still, she thought she heard another answer it, saying—[the close of the 100th Psalm]—

[1] We have this word in the Scotch metrical version of the 46th Psalm :—

> " A river is whose streams do *glad*
>   The city of our God."

And Robert Browning, we notice, adopts the word.

> ' For why? The Lord our God is good ;
> His mercy is for ever sure :
> IIis truth at all times firmly stood,
> And shall from age to age endure.' "

"Our country birds," explains Prudence quietly: but Christian, we know, when he was here, ,heard none of them. "They sing these notes *but seldom, except it be at the spring, when the flowers appear, and the sun shines warm ;* and then you may hear them all day long."—A dispensation of music has fallen upon the whole vicinity. They get down the hill " pretty well," and now the Valley of Humiliation, of so sombre memory, regains all the good reputation which Christian lost to it, and which Faithful, it would appear, only partially won. It " is of *itself* as fruitful a place as any the crow flies over ;" " it is the best and most useful piece of ground in all these parts " —" fat ground, and, as we can see, consisting much in meadows," " delightful " the more because it is " *summer-time :*" " many labouring men have got good estates in it." The testimony is unimpeachable ; for it is Great-heart's. As the travellers advance along their verdant way, they come up to a shepherd-boy among " his father's sheep "— " very mean" in apparel, but " very fresh and well-favoured " in look ; " and as he sat by himself, he *sang*." " They hearkened, and he said—

> ' IIe that is down need fear no fall,' "

—twelve of Bunyan's best and best-known lines. The entire place is lovely with pastoral peace, and hallowed with sacred traditions : to Christiana and her company it is a place of nothing but tranquil happiness.—In the other valley " they had daylight " at least with them, besides the holy gallantry of their protector, who in himself is a whole escort of guidance. So, when they enter Vanity itself, in that darkening eventide, it proves to be to them a city of

rest and of refreshing sociality. Nor can we omit to note,
that the brilliant series of victories which they achieve over
hateful and dangerous enemies, however obnoxious it may
be to fastidious criticism, is ever and anon bringing in upon
the hearts of the travellers a new accession of grateful gladness which is not self-regardful alone. Of this joy the
women of the group had the liveliest share. We find it
easy to blend our own Emotion with the mirth of the
company when the head of no other than Despair is
brought in from the demolished Castle, and Christiana
" played them a lesson " on the viol while Mercy managed
the lute, and Ready-to-Halt " would dance," taking poor
Much-afraid with the one hand, and holding by a crutch
with the other, and thus " footing it well." In truth, it
says something for the healthiness of Bunyan's own type
of piety, " Puritanic " as it was, that he did not grudge to
light up his page with a scene so alive with all the fitting
circumstances of festive Emotion.

If we look, as we had need to do, for some manifestation
in Christiana of the kindly feelings of social life, we shall
not miss much that we should desire to see. She is
neighbourly and sisterly, unselfish and pitiful, promptly
and cordially sympathetic. " Bowels becometh pilgrims,"
she says concisely to Mercy at the starting, when the girl
is regretting her lingering relatives ; and she lived in full
accord with the saying. Her demeanour towards Mercy
herself in this earlier stage was very motherly in its wise
tenderness : the maiden undertook the journey solely
" upon her invitation," and Christiana " was glad at her
heart " to find the girl at her side. Nor did her services
exhaust themselves in this momentous preliminary :—
" When Christiana had gotten admittance for herself and
her boys, *then she began to make intercession for Mercy,*"
who still " did stand without." Nor did even this make
an end of her kindness :—" It shall still be as I said it

should when at first we came from home; *thou shalt be sharer in all the good I have,"*—so she speaks at the famous Arbour on the Hill; and she never failed to act a generous fulfilment of her words. Indeed, there was none of all the company, and few of those whom she came to know on the way, but felt the radiance of her sober good-will, and the seasonable unobtrusiveness of her beneficence ;—as when she flung aside her viol to appease the starving condition of Despondency, ere she went about to prepare him a more solid meal. She never declines the responsibilities of her position, and never snatches the honour it might fairly bring. She is as thoughtful of others as she is heedful of herself—a presence of capable tender-heartedness and of retiring readiness to help, who is never so fearless as when a clear occasion arises for her kindly offices. We can mark no decay of her self-denying interest in the welfare of others onwards to the days of the end, when " she bequeathed to the poor that little she had," and when she granted to each of the company a farewell interview with her ; for these interviews, one by one, and as a connected picture of touching Christian reality, seem to sum up and illuminate her whole career as an inestimable pilgrim-friend.

These farewell scenes themselves, however, only remind us that still the loftiest affection of her finely-affectioned nature was consecrated to the King Himself—the Divine Saviour, whose transcendent loveableness and adorable excellence she had been apprehending more and more vividly from stage to stage, and from experience to experience. A long time had passed since that morning in her old home when she made her appeal to the heavenly messenger—so beautifully natural, though so little considered —" Sir, will you carry me and my children with you, that we also may go and *worship this King?"* Yet " the last words that she was heard to say here " were but the maturity of this early desire :—" I come, Lord, *to be with Thee, and bless Thee.*"　Her temper of heart in the hour of her quitting Beulah and its brotherhood—it was but the riper rendering of her temper of heart when she was interrupted by the neighbours in the midst of her preparations to quit Destruction and its disloyalties ; and she might say only more fervently now, just as she said then—" The Prince of the place has also *sent for me.*"　Between this hour and that lay her pilgrim-life, with all its hardships and jeopardies and patient labours—ay, and all its reverent trustings, and thankfulnesses, and joys.　During the long interval, she had seldom dropt out of her consciousness that she was the King's, and was on her way, by the King's road, to the King.　That day on which Great-heart made warning reference to " the warmth of her affections " was doubtless a red-letter-day in the chronicles of her Emotion on earth : while, however, the sudden glow might subside, the temperature would never seem to have fallen low again, but to have rather increased in the height of its steadier average, though no flush so noteworthy as this might return.　Her words on that occasion so overflow with her character, that we feel as if we must recall them :—" Methinks it makes my heart bleed," she says, " to think that He should bleed for me.　Oh, Thou loving One !　Oh, Thou blessed One !　Thou deservest to have me ; Thou hast bought me ; Thou deservest to have me all ; Thou hast paid for me ten thousand times more than I am worth. No marvel that this made the water stand in my husband's eyes, and that it made him trudge so nimbly on : I am persuaded he wished me with him ; but, vile wretch that I was, I let him come all alone.　Oh, Mercy, that thy mother and father were here ; yea, and Mrs Timorous also ; nay, I wish now with all my heart, that here was Madame Wanton too.　Surely, surely, their hearts would be affected ; nor could the fear of the one, nor the powerful lusts of the other, prevail with them to go home again, and to refuse to become good pilgrims." The fleet ease of movement, and the free comprehensiveness of range, which are natural to her elevated intensity of feeling, are here depicted with remarkable truthfulness and power.

It is scarcely possible that spiritual Emotion like Christiana's should stand long apart from holy meditation. In this employment, the heart presses the mind into its helpful service. It lies close to prayer, though it is not the same with it : indeed, the difference between them is important, and is sometimes overlooked. The practical distinction between communion of spirit with the Divine, on the one hand, and definite prayer on the other,—between prayerfulness, we might even say, and specific petition,—is well illustrated in the first half of Christiana's journey. She had been in very peaceful fellowship with the Lord of the Gate for no brief space, it would seem, yet, having omitted to make a clear request for a protector on the way, she fell into the plight of the assault : even the Reliever could only rescue and return ; nor could she obtain a constant protector until she was leaving the Interpreter's House. From that hostelry, Great-heart, unrequested, was sent with them, but grieved them by resolutely bidding them adieu at the threshold of the Palace Beautiful. He explained that he had there completed all of his Lord's present commands : "When He bid me come thus far with you, then you should have *begged me of Him* to have gone quite through with you, and he would have granted your request." And now he took just such a request back with him, and by-and-bye brought them joy by his return with a favourable answer. All the while, communion with the unseen, and with God, is close and unbroken. It is only next morning that we hear her giving testimony which is more profoundly conclusive of this than she would think of :—"We need not, when a-bed, lie *awake* to talk with God. He can visit us while we sleep, and cause us then to hear His voice. Our heart ofttimes wakes when we sleep ; and God can speak to that, either by words, by proverbs, by signs and similitudes, as well as if one was awake." There is little of such experience as this, however, without much of the temper to which Mrs Adams gives utterance in her familiar lines—

> " Though like a wanderer,
> 　　The sun gone down,
> Darkness be over me,
> 　　My rest a stone,
> Yet in my dreams I'd be
> Nearer, my God, to Thee,
> 　　Nearer to Thee.'

And the lifelong desire grows on with its fulfilment, till the soul is dwelling where the sun never sinks, and sleep itself must begin to slip from the allegory of the soul's advance. We read concerning Christiana's company in Beulah,—bold figure breaking quite through the bonds of material conditions,—" A little while soon refreshed them here ; for the bells did so ring, and the trumpets continually sounded so melodiously, that *they could not sleep ;* and yet they received as much refreshing as if they had slept their sleep ever so soundly. Here also all the noise of them that walked in the streets, was, ' more pilgrims are come to town.' And another would answer, saying, ' And so many went over the water, and were let in at the golden gates, to-day.' . . . Then the pilgrims got up and walked to and fro ; but how were their ears now filled with heavenly noises, and their eyes delighted with celestial visions !" —Christiana cannot now have far to go till she be altogether " with Christ, which is far better " still—in degree of Emotion, though scarcely in kind of it—than even that which is pictured in the nourishing wakefulness and the voiceful sunshine of the luscious land of waiting.

The only remaining department of Christiana's character which claims our attention is that which finds its centre in the *Will*. Her Emotion, her Earnestness, her Lowly Candour, her Faith, her very Conscience,—none of them could ignore the firm presence of Will in the personality they adorned ; and Will reciprocated their respect. Indeed, the working unity of all character has been compelling us to imply the co-operation of Will at almost every step of our survey. It has been stiffening each moral characteristic, and each with every other, into a workable compactness and an orderly consistency of movement. Her Will was not naturally weak. It held its position, strongly if not well, when she permitted her husband to take his journey, and to travel away from her, in spirit if not in person, into regions whither she stoutly declined to follow. Here it may be said to degenerate into obstinacy—into Will without Reason,—the sort of Will which cynics delight to ascribe to her sex as its pre-eminent strength of weakness, and yet the very sort of Will which has just its unhappiest manifestation in this spiritual unreason of fixedness, of stubborn refusal to travel, for which the sex is not by comparison remarkable. But obstinacy seems absolutely to dissolve out of existence with her when she has let in the light upon her spirit. This Will of hers, and all of it, she freely laid at the feet of the Lord of pilgrims, and it did not diminish by this strong deed of surrender and gift. Rather, all gentle reasonableness had now begun to blend with its growing strength. It found only then the righting and regulation, the primal bias and bent, which it needed to set it in the way of perfection. Henceforward, taking its pulse from the Will that is supreme, it moved with an unjarring justness of harmony which would be marvellous to us if we did not make account of the supernatural sufficiency of the causes. Long before she came to Beulah, her Will appeared to work as true as if it were

already free of all derangement from within, and superior
to all disturbance from without. This could only be comparative, doubtless ; but even if it signify little more than
the external faultlessness of her life, it indicates a ripeness
around the whole character which ought not to escape our
regard. From no point of view can we better apprehend
the spiritual maturity of the woman—a maturity which is
relatively recognisable from the first—than from this point
of view of her Will, as the efficient factor in her action.
And still, no dull or flaccid ripeness,—if that be very conceivable,—but one that was as lively, and effective, and
steadfast, as it was true.

It is a conjunction with Will that developes several forms
of virtue in Christiana, which we have not yet articulately
noticed. It kept step with Conscience in her, and became
Rectitude. It had a covenant with Faith, and passed into
Patience. It companied with Lowly-Heartedness, and
appeared as Submission. It struck hands with Earnestness,
and grew into Courage. It had open friendship with
Emotion, and settled into Obedience. This last conjunction might be easily expanded to comprehend all,—the
lifelong amity between the two most potent forces of her
being, and for its product an obedience that was tender
and strong and complete—complete in as far as it was
obedientness of general spirit and purpose. For her
Will was never a waif upon the tide of her feeling,—
although the set of that tide was so increasingly safe, that
her Will might almost have been entrusted to its current.
Keeping her woman's hand on the helm of duty, and trim-
ming her sail to the heavenly breezes which were always
more or less fair to the course, she took advantage of the
current when she could, and crossed or stemmed it when
she must,—until at length, as she neared the celestial
shore, she might slacken her grasp of the helm, since current and breeze more steadily combined to waft the bark

along the latitude which answered the indications of chart and compass. And erelong, in that radiant home-bay of Beulah, tide and wind seem alike swift, and both are fair for the resplendent haven : therefore her Will, which more than aught else is her very self, has little to do but to glide on beneath the sunlight of the Will of the King.

Such is something of the Spiritual character which Bunyan unfolds as that of the Christian matron of his Allegory. The delineation is singularly free from all extravagance, and abounds with a truthfulness which commends it to us as a mirror of womanly Christian character. If it be notably scanty in the representation of positive faults, or even of weaknesses, other than such as blamelessly belong to womanhood, it is little chargeable, on the other hand, with the representation of transcendent feats of spiritual achievement. It has about it the air of an ideal which is not merely credible, but is entirely imitable. Yet it is an ideal which wins our respect and regard, if not even our admiration. And it is nothing other than godly womanhood as Bunyan found it in his Bible,—this, fashioned into lovingness by his own genius, and apparelled according to the Western modes around him. It is a vivid translation of the Scriptures within that theme, and its attractiveness has something of the value of a Christian evidence. We turn to our Bible, and we find proverb, and precept, and example—with less copiousness, perhaps, than the lofty humanity of the Bible itself has trained us to reckon to be fully due to the subject, yet with no reluctance of pen—setting forth the component virtues of an excellent womanhood, and most usually in this phase of matronhood which is now before us. Modesty (even " shamefastness "), sobriety, gravity, discreet silence, faithfulness in all things, unobtrusive influence, subordinate power, free-hearted endurance, the diligent following of every good work, a meek and quiet spirit ;—these are New Testament marks which we can recognise to be exactly reproduced in the picturesque rendering of the spiritual character of Christiana. Further marks we may come to recognise when we proceed to the other aspects of her character. Christiana is a New Testament figure of the 17th century in England—such a figure as would have fittingly filled a place among the women who followed the King when He was sojourning in person about the valleys of His own highway,—

"Last at His cross, and earliest at His grave."

And there have been women in real life—many of them, too, in life which was as obscure as it was real—who could have taken their place upon the canvas as creditably as she, and would as certainly have earned enrolment on the record of disinterested and brave devotion to the rejected Saviour of mankind.

Christianity has done much—tenfold more than many ever imagine—to emancipate the outward lot of woman, and to uplift her to the position which the God of Christianity designed and fitted her to fill. But Christianity has not done more in the past for the external lot of womanhood than it is ready to do in the present for the internal character of womanhood. Apart from the thought of immortal safety or peril, of essential lostness or restoration, the acceptance of Christianity by the womanly nature is the acceptance of a moral adornment which nothing else can bestow, and the setting-in of a spiritual excellence which nothing else can even imitate. The womanly heart is peculiarly adapted, one may say, for the reception of the religion of Christ, and the religion of Christ is magnificently adapted to the womanly heart. Some of its finest triumphs, its most lovely demonstrations of what it can do

for human nature even on earth, have been, and to the end
of time shall be, among the ranks of womanhood. The
faith of woman, the tenderness of woman, the brave
endurance and steadfast loyalty of woman,—they are due
to Christ. And when they are made a humble offering to
Him, He transfigures the offering into a surpassing inheritance for her who offered it—"incorruptible, and undefiled,
and that fadeth not away."

XI.

CHRISTIANA: HER INTELLECTUAL AND DOMESTIC
CHARACTER.

FEW religious works ever left the loom with so few
sectarian house-marks woven into them as this work
of Bunyan's. It does indeed carry the broad Christian
pattern from end to end, and here and there it asserts that
pattern according to the principles which found revived
expression in the Reformation; beyond this, its distinc-
tiveness is one of complexion rather than of mark. Of
course, Bunyan's book must take the general hue of
Bunyan's mind if it is to be at all a genuine book of his.
It is in accordance with this that his normal characters are
varieties of the most earnest type of Christianity with which
he was acquainted. Christian is a Puritan Englishman
of well-mingled character, holding a mean between its
sterner severity, as represented by Faithful, and its slenderer humanness, as embodied in Hopeful. Each of the
figures is a conception of Biblical manliness, yet of that
manliness according to the three leading modes of its
reflection in actual Puritan life. Thus it is, also, amid the
freer multifariousness of the Second Part. Christiana,
whose spiritual qualities we have been endeavouring to
gather, impersonation as she is of New Testament
womanliness, still impersonates that womanliness after the
manner of a Puritan Englishwoman of comprehensive
Christian character and well-blended Christian life. She
represents New Testament Christianity as the best women

of Bunyan's own school of opinion and taste represented it—a representation, it may be affirmed, which was as bravely honest, and on the whole as winningly true, as recent Christian ages have seen.

The manliness, the womanliness, which Bunyan thus delineates, have very much of religiousness in them, but very little of fanaticism. The men and women are possessed by enthusiasm in its better acceptation, and are all but untouched by it in its worse. Even the women have knowledge with their zeal, and are thoughtful, prudent, charitable. The pictures which history and poetry afford us of the women of the best Puritan stock as they were wont to be known in New England, and the living daughters of those women as we meet them in New England still,—these support the veracity of Bunyan's portraiture in this true dream of his. It is a womanhood not only of unostentatious purity and unparaded affection, but of kindly capability and of sober-minded intelligence. Not that we can deem every woman who bore the name of Puritan to have attained to this praise; but it is fair we should appeal from the caricature which generalises upon instances exceptionally unworthy, and should hold before us the worthier instances which honest-hearted men like Bunyan pourtray for us as the genuine representations of this type of Christian life.

This typical matron of the Allegory, then, is really a woman of respectable INTELLECTUAL character. That character shares as little in marvellous qualities, indeed, as we found her Spiritual character to do, and prevails upon our credence by the very moderation of its truthfulness. Yet we have evidently before us a womanhood of active and open intelligence—quick to receive, tenacious to retain, nimble to penetrate with the unreasoning intuition of womankind. No doubt this intelligence, as we see it,

is almost exclusively engaged within the region of religious
truth and life : her mental stores and her mental capability,
both of them asserting their vitality by growth, are limited
by the conditions of the story to what bears more or less
directly upon immortal interests.　But intelligence can
scarcely be the less actual that it deals with the highest
things ; nor does it thereby disprove its capacity for dealing with lower things, but will rather be giving hints, as
Christiana's does, that all the while there is no lack of a
capable interest in many things which lie outside the
immediate sphere of spiritual concerns.

When we begin to look more closely at the character of
Christiana on its Intellectual side, we are struck with the
general *Good Sense* which she displays.　There is no quality
in man or woman which bespeaks the sound intellect with
more distinctness than this most comprehensive of human
endowments.　Itself not so much a faculty as an evenness
of balance among all the other faculties, it is liable to
escape our full appreciation while it plays its quiet part
along the practical level of things.　But it is an invaluable
quality, as it is a significant one—most of all in woman.
The very excellences of the womanly nature are such as to
endanger the development of Good Sense, and yet are
such as to demand the presence of Good Sense to sustain
them in the true rank of excellences.　There has been
many a womanly character, rich in affection, and strong in
loyalty, and keen in perception, which nevertheless had its
dignity squandered and its influence neutralised by a virtual
absence of this quality which is so apt to be accounted
commonplace.　Not least within the sphere of religious
life has the lack of this quality in woman to be frequently
deplored, impossible as it is to compensate for its deficiency by the abundance of any other gift of mind or
heart.　It is doubtless in great part an inborn talent ; and
the assertion may even be hazarded, that it answers less

readily to cultivation than any other talent of the human economy. Still there is much in Christian belief which is congenial to it, as there is much in Christian duty which urges its exercise and development. It was a characteristic of Christiana, more or less clearly, from the first; but it seemed to make perceptible increase in tact and maturity from the day that she set it free by giving herself to a life of ongoing towards the heavenly City.

If we would verify her claim to the credit of possessing this gift in generous measure, we have only to have regard to the demeanour of the woman—in speech and in silence, in act and in refraining from action—all along her course. She speaks just at the moment when it is well to speak, and then says pretty much what it was well to say. There is a just sufficiency and fitness in her doings and devisings, whether for those above her own rank or for those beneath it. Her opinions were well controlled, wonderfully clean of prejudice, and based upon what she reckoned to be true facts or valid principles. Sentiment she would by no means allow to take the place of reason, though she did not forbid it to soften the hardness and to drape the angles of mere reason into something that was reason and more. Emotion impelled her intellect without flooding it. Her faith, which transacted with unseen facts, she would not suffer to be overborne by fancy or feeling. Her charity she strove to protect from dislikes; her duty she struggled to rid from the entanglements of weak likings. She scrutinized her predispositions; and let the light in upon her preconceptions, and put to rights her undesigned misjudgings,—till we might believe, at her journey's end, that she had dropt from her mind by the way whatsoever it may once have held of things unfair, or injudicious, or unjust.

Another quality which meets us broadly in the Intellectual character of Christiana, and one which claims scarcely less of our respect, is her *Love of Knowledge*, as distinguished from curiosity. Fresh light and new truth are treasures to her. She welcomes all true knowledge when it comes in her way, and goes forth to meet it when it lingers near. She is in circumstances of delight among the lessons of the Interpreter, and the Palace has much of its charm for her in the instruction she gains beneath its roof. Her "conductor" she values not least as an intellectual guide and teacher. At no point in her course has she the least notion, that in respect of knowledge she has attained to sufficiency. In the best sense she is " ever learning," for she is ever coming to a fuller " knowledge of the truth." "This is brave," she says, with keen admiration, when a great verity has broken clear upon her from the lips of Great-heart. But a lively desire for the exposition of the truth had preceded this expression of satisfaction :—" Wherefore, if you please, let us hear you discourse thereof." " Pray make that appear." It was precisely the same spirit she had shown before she left the residence of Great-heart, when she besought the Interpreter, after the homely emblem of the hen and chickens had been explained —" And, Sir, pray let us see some more." Not a moment of the precious season of opportunity is to be lost :—" So, when they were come again into the house, because supper was not yet ready, Christiana again desired that the Interpreter would either show or tell of some more things that are profitable." At the Palace too, when the hostesses are " showing her something on which she may meditate when she is upon her way," her whole heart is in the work. The Dreamer is mindful to record that she " held up her hands and wondered " as the matter of Eve's apple was opened to her—" food or poison, she knew not which ; " and he recalls that she " looked, and looked, to see the angels go up," when Jacob's ladder was before her gaze. And thus it was to the last—as open of mind as she was open of heart. Her Love of Knowledge closes its earthly exercise upon its own true keynote, but now touched with a solemn peacefulness :—" Then she bid him [Great-heart] that he should give advice how all things should be prepared for her journey "—the last brief fragment of the pilgrimage. And she took her way with all the knowledge that was needful to guide the steps of her faith into the land of vision.

If anything of all this be curiosity, it is such curiosity as commands our unreserved commendation. It is curiosity sanctified, and controlled into its most legitimate employment—the employment for which it was bestowed. Christiana maintains her inquiringness upon a lofty level, and keeps its activities a-working towards the very worthiest of things. We may be able to discern in it an instinct for minute particulars, such as Christian's own desire for knowledge, or even Hopeful's, would not have disclosed : that too, however, is womanly, and is simply an admirable qualification of womanhood wherever it retains its proper function, and wherever it refuses to degenerate into the petty gossiping inquisitiveness which it becomes when curiosity takes the rein, among the thousand undignified concernments which swarm around us in our common life.

This Love of Knowledge, if it does not also imply, yet very certainly ensures, that measure of *Intelligence* which consists in the possession of knowledge. In this sense of the word, Christiana appears as an intelligent woman, and as one who is increasingly so. While she is without a guide, her Intelligence nourishes itself upon her experience, which is usually at once assimilated into permanent information. While she enjoys the advantage of guiding company, as it is her lot at length perpetually to do, her Intelligence feeds itself still more richly from the highly intelligent atmosphere which surrounds her, and she breathes abiding Intelligence into her own spirit at every breath. Her action is a more full and fair exponent of her knowledge than her speech is; indeed, her utterance of her thoughts, especially in the latter portion of the story, is somewhat observably scanty. Her speech has always been devoted rather to the gaining of Intelligence which she does not possess, than to the unfolding of the Intelligence she possesses: in the degree, therefore, in which her mind becomes stored with materials of thought, she will probably become more silently reflective; and if, meanwhile, her pilgrim-company goes on to increase, and men of various experience join it who are well competent to converse on many themes, she will be growingly content to bear the part of a listener. Had this attitude not sufficiently served to promote her Intelligence as well as to affirm her modesty, she would not so steadily have employed it. But we have only to listen to her when she finds occasion to break the silence, that we may note how her knowledge is advancing in fulness and clearness, and within how well-ordered a mind it is kept fresh and living.

To all this it stands partly as cause, and partly as effect, that Christiana was intelligent in the deeper sense of possessing *Powers of Mind* which must be accounted exceptionally good. These powers, too, were so well poised, whether by nature or by discipline, that we can scarcely think of one without having to think of others in which that one obtains its complement or its check. If we find Imagination by no means weak in her, we see it chastened by a clear perception of sober Reality. If she was quick of Apprehension, she had a Memory which retained and recalled what she apprehended. If she had a keen faculty for Detail, she could still discern well between the important and the trivial, and could put her mind around scattered facts to feel the principles that were in them. If we cannot deny to her some poetic sensibility, some love of the beautiful, some sense of art, and a measure of womanly accomplishment, yet we cannot but observe, that she took the pleasure and the good of these as one who reckoned them to be after all but the embellishments of a life which must keep its foot planted upon the solidities of fact, howsoever intrinsically prosaic those may happen to be.

Bunyan himself, in one of his confidential "asides" for the information of the reader, credits her with quickness of mind—("for she was a woman quick of apprehension ")—while she is under instruction in the college of the Interpreter. But his own record enables us to credit her with more than a quick Receptiveness of mind: she shows a mental Readiness, which is a gift of greater compass; and she exhibits Presence of Mind, which is a gift more considerable still. She had a mental Self-Possession which permitted her quickness of Apprehension to pass into quickness of Comprehension and of Comparison, and gave her the right thought at the right moment: she had a Practicalness and a Decisiveness of mind, moreover, which could gather up all these in a crisis of emergency, and put her upon doing the right deed at the right moment. This feature of character, in which intellectual qualities are no doubt touched close by moral and by physical ones, is more rare than our life of surprises manifestly needs it should be; and it is of great price when it is found, whether in man or woman. We fear it must abide among the gifts which are rather born than developed; indeed, it has so near affinities to genius, that it may bear to be called the genius of common life. Yet it is certainly in some degree susceptible of culture. Perhaps we can make out traces of its development in Christiana: whether or not this be so, it ought to find a kindly nurture for itself in the composure and harmony and peace, the settled unity and alert earnestness, which it is the aim of Christianity to bring; and it ought to find for itself as invigorating a gymnastic upon the arena of the inner history, and among the activities of Christian well-doing, as it can find among the contingencies of the market or the senate, of the ocean or the field. And earnest Christian living, as a thing of culture for such gifts, adapts its power with especial appropriateness to the womanly nature.

Bunyan's Christian matron, then, had brains, and used them. There was mind in her as she gathered herself to go after her husband; and she went after him with her intellect on its feet, no less than her feeling and her will. Her piety had fellowship with intelligence, and each grew with the other's growth. As far as the scope of the story can permit us to judge, she went on towards the City of her desire with a mind open to all that was true, and in quick sympathy with all that was worthy. If she was not a woman very brilliant in mental gifts, or very rich in mental acquirements, it is not because her pilgrimage is at all out of keeping with these, or because these would not have still further adorned both herself and it. She comes before us upon a good representative level of intelligence, and no higher; but she is enriching her mind by inquiry and by thought,—she is lifting up her intellectual level,— as long as we see her. Bunyan's ideal is pitched just about the mean which will neither disparage intellect on the one hand, nor exalt it unduly on the other, as an element of womanly pilgrimage. Her intelligence might have been lower, and she might still have been a good pilgrim: her intelligence might have been higher, and she might yet have been no better a pilgrim; but it would not have been her intelligence that thus hindered her excellence as a Christiana—a traveller towards her heavenly City and her heavenly King. Faith is first, and Will, and Heart; but close behind them, for womanhood as much as

for manhood, there come Knowledge and Thought and all
Wealth of Mind, to be sought and esteemed as only holding a subordinate place because of the supreme rank ot
those moral possessions which they help and adorn. Christian womanhood may develop the type of Christiana to any
degree of intellectual affluence which opportunity makes
possible ; but the type will be lost in the moment that
intellectuality claims rank above spirituality, or takes a
position independent of earnest Christian life, or displays
itself as something which subsists in any measure upon
human admiration. The instincts are profound, and they
are true, which regard these departures from the reserve
of genuine wisdom as more grievous deformities in the
womanly character than they are even in the manly one.

From all this we have not far to pass that we may reach
the DOMESTIC character of Christiana. If it were not the
features of a womanly character that we were endeavouring
to unveil, it would be more possible than it is, upon the
mere principles of fitness and truth, to stay our inquiry
before it had crossed the threshold of the Domestic sphere.
This is a sphere which a man enters and quits,—"going
out and coming in," like a rightful visitant ; but this is the
sphere in which a woman abides, like a queen within the
realm which owes its whole condition to her sway. It is
true at least of a matron and a mother, that her home is
her domain, where she has not only the fittest field, but
the fullest play, for all the gifts of her mind and all the
graces of her spirit. There may be interests and engage-
ments for her beyond the circumference of the household,
but these must get only the overflow of her time and
energy. That is the order of things with her as a denizen
of this world, and in fullest view of the next ;—husband
and household first, and whatever else thereafter.

The Domestic ways of Christiana are evidently worthy of

her as a wife and mother who is conforming all her ways
to the will of the One whose ideal of wifehood and motherhood is the ideal of Him who ordained it in the love of
His infinite heart.   The story seems fain to bear its best
witness to this.   But we know how little of direct evidence
it is able to yield us.   We hear scarcely anything of her
till she is a widow; and almost as soon as we hear anything of her to purpose, she has turned her back upon her
home.   That the typical Christian matron should be without a Christian home,—this is perhaps the most serious of
all the exigencies which the Allegory has to suffer at the
hands of its own inherent structure.

It would scarcely reward us to speculate about the
Domestic behaviour of this wife of Christian's during the
period of her husband's wayfaring and his allegorical
absence from her.   She was not Christiana then.   Yet it
is to be noted, that we are introduced to her before she is
fully entitled to the name, and seem to get sight of the re-
treating skirts at least of that life which is so soon to belong
to the forsaken past.   When the veil is thus lifted again
from the household of Christian, the prevailing sentiment
in the breast of the central figure of the household is lively
regard for her husband.   It is her wifely affection which
becomes to her the conducting medium of the grace of
pilgrimage.   That affection must have been already deep
and strong, though now it was to become deeper and
stronger.   He had been in a great measure unaccountable
to her, and his ways had been irksome to her (if we may
speak outside of the Allegory); but she had loved him still,
and had respected him where she could not understand
him.   Humanly speaking, it was that natural loyalty of
love which made her all that she afterwards became.   She
was true to the light she had, and better light was given.
Her misguided harshnesses themselves had affection behind
them; therefore these have now become the goads by

which memory urges her forward to go after her husband, that she may be with him—yea, and with his Lord—for ever.

We are left to judge what Christiana would have been as a *Wife*, then, by what we find her as a widow. We know her as the wife of one who has gone on before her out of sight. And here we have to mark how finely the Allegory lends itself to the certainty, that he is only out of sight because of his farther advance—that she has lost view of him because he has out-distanced her. He is yonder—further on ; and she is making up to overtake him, because now his journeying has ceased. There is thus an air of merely provisional separation—of a kind of terrestrial and temporary severance—which hardly amounts to widowhood, and which keeps up in her the wifely sentiment, as if she were conserving it for their meeting again. There is really less of severance now than there was before he passed away.[1] This makes it less unnatural for us to think of her as a Wife, although we know her only as a widow.

The Wifely Tenderness of Christiana, as the story stands, must partly declare itself in regrets. Under this form it declares itself as fully as we could desire. We think how, when we see her first, there is " coming into her mind, by swarms, all her unkind, unnatural, and ungodly carriages to her dear friend ; " how she is " much broken by calling to remembrance " his distress before he set forth for the City ; how she fears that " her unbecoming behaviour towards her husband " is " one cause that she saw him no more ; " how " there was not anything that Christian either said to her or did before her, all the while that his burden did hang on his back, but it returned upon her like a flash of lightning, and rent the caul of her heart in sunder "—" specially that bitter outcry of his." And we recall how she " saw

[1] See Martineau's " Endeavours after a Christian Life," vol. ii. p. 269.

Christian ", in the City as she slept, and heard the harps and voices which made immortal music around him. This Tenderness lasts, and soon brightens into other sentiments than regret. When they reach the Interpreter's House, it is already "some years ago" since Christian travelled that way, but she is finding a fragrance in every recognisable trace of his presence. They are in the neighbourhood of the Cross: "But, Sir," she appeals to Great-heart, "was not this it that made my good Christian's burden fall from off his shoulder, and that made him give three leaps for joy?" And during the same memorable conversation, in words already quoted—"No marvel that this made the water stand in my husband's eyes, and that it made him trudge so nimbly on! I am persuaded he wished me with him; but, vile wretch that I was, I let him come all alone." Regret is not dead, but sleeps. (In this minute acquaintance with Christian's pilgrim-history, as perhaps also in the words above—"*All the while* that his burden did hang on his back,"—have we not Christiana speaking somewhat as one whom her husband had not absolutely left when he became Christian?) They come to the Palace Beautiful, and it is all the more beautiful because "he" had been so happy a sojourner there: nor can we forget how frankly she proffers the request as they retire on the first evening —"But let us, if we may be so bold as to choose, be in that chamber which was my husband's when he was here;" nor how she mused on that couch where he once lay, wondering that ever she had come to "think of seeing his face with comfort, and of worshipping the Lord the King with him; and yet now—*I believe I shall.*"

If that petition about the chamber may wear to some a whimsical look which is perhaps over-womanly, we need not be led to conceive of Christiana's wifely affection as being the mere doting fondness which has no respect in it, and has no sense of duty that gives it dignity. She has in her the spirit that honours a husband, and obeys him, on the foundation of deep-going principle. She is gladly content to be but half-seen under the shadow which he casts, and is concerned to make the shadow as large as may be. Before she has yet set out, she is keenly repenting that she had "foolishly imagined" his "troubles" to have sprung of "foolish fancy" or "melancholy humours;" and she is almost grateful, for the vindication it brings to *him*, that now it is taking hold of her "that they sprang from another cause—to wit, for that the light of light was given him." In the dream in which she saw her husband in glory, and heard the tuneful voices—"No man living could tell what they said, *but Christian and his companions.*" She is explaining the situation to Mrs Timorous : " Besides, I am now *as he* was then,"—taking comfort and courage, and just a little of wifely pride, in the coincidence of her own resolutions and convictions with those that had been his. Her words to the Lord of the Gate were doubtless touched with the same desire to magnify her husband, whose precedence she would think of as not a precedence of time alone : "We are come from whence *Christian* did come, and on the same errand as *he.*"

It is in this connection that we may best recall the demonstrations of welcome which greeted her at many successive points of her journey. These, while they whispered to her of the concern about her welfare which Christian's sad anxiety for her had awakened along the way, were a recurring banquet to her heart for the evidence they gave of the honour in which he himself had been held, and was held still. It put a thrill into her own journeying, that it was often so like a memorial triumph, and that her own silent presence did more to strike the strings to her husband's praise than all her words could ever have accomplished. When they had come to the door of the Interpreter's House, there was "a great talk" going forward within: she herself was the theme—the wife of Christian. "Can you think who is at the door?"—this was the question which Innocent flung in upon the talking company, who "leaped for joy;" and when the new guests had been admitted, "one smiled, and another smiled, and they all smiled, for joy that Christiana had become a pilgrim." At the Palace Beautiful it was only a variation of this. "The wife of Christian!" Humble-mind "went and told it. But O what noise for gladness was there within!" exclaims the sympathetic chronicler. Four times in two lines occur the welcoming words, "Come in;" and once is added, "Thou wife of that good man;" while, even in the night, the air was wafting joyous music. At a later stage, Honest has just been added to their company: "My name I suppose you have heard of," says Christiana quietly; "good Christian was my husband;" and "the old gentleman"—"he skipped, he smiled." Then they were guests of Mnason in the city of Vanity: "But who, quoth he, do you think this is? . . . the wife of Christian, that famous pilgrim." By-and-bye they are listening to Valiant-for-Truth: how it would stir the heart of Christiana to hear him as he affirmed, that "what caused him to come on pilgrimage" was his being told "about what Christian had done!"—and with what modest pride she would mark his delighted astonishment—"Why, is this *Christian's wife?*" Therefore it is most fitting that in the closing words of her history the historian should link her name with the name which had gone with her through every stage of the way:—"So she went and called, and entered in at the gate with all the ceremonies of joy that *her husband Christian* had done before her."

From the widow which thus she was, we think we may guess the wife she would have been—as Christiana. And had she been all that we can suppose she would have been, she would have found herself, and would have expected to find herself, as happy as heaven meant her to be, in a world where disorder and imperfection will never fail to mingle something of unhappiness in the happiest lot. Only, in view of the commonest facts of life, it is mere justice to remember, how mightily it would have supported Christiana in sustaining her high wifehood, that all the while her husband was such a husband as Christian would have been.

Had the form of the story afforded him opportunity, it is probable that Bunyan would not have shrunk from giving proof of Christiana's efficiency as one who *Administered a Household.* If she had anything of this, she was what the Apostle calls a "keeper (worker, R.V.) at home," and never was absent from her own hearth except for a better reason than she had for being present. Can we detect this characteristic at all in the fact, that she abides by her household during the disquietude of the opening chapter of her history as Christiana?—that heavenly messengers bring their messages thither?—and that gossips must find their way to her own house, as if they did not expect to see her soon in theirs? And however excusable household disarrangement might be in the circumstances, the atmosphere of the narrative is surely one of household orderliness, and of management which is fighting no heartless battle with turbulent arrears that are never subdued. Her home would look as if a home might really be worth the while of a woman's earnest skill,—as if that might be Christiana's opinion, and as if the result proved the opinion valid. For when the woman becomes thoroughly Christian, the housewife is apt to become Christian too.

It may pretty well complete our estimate of the heroine of the Pilgrimage, if we regard her for a moment in the capacity of a *Mother.* For her pilgrim-company embraced her pilgrim-family: she was a pilgrim-mother, and a mother of pilgrims. Christiana's heart was not weighted with yearnings after any, very dear to her, that were lingering still in the hapless city; her children were keeping pace with her on her way to the City of her hope. If we see her as somewhat less than a Wife, we see her as somewhat more than a Mother, because we see her left in widowhood. Her motherhood expands to occupy the void, and to compass the responsibilities, which are created within her wifehood by her memorable bereavement. She takes her children to her heart with more sense of parental charge, and with more consciousness of motherly pride. She might speak as the daughter speaks in the "Wanderer of Switzerland":

> " Yes !—I am a mother still,
>   Though I feel a widow too ! "

We do not find her, indeed, in the most favourable circumstances for exhibiting even her motherly virtues, since she only appears among the settled surroundings of a home of her own for a brief day or two of departure from it. But if we have still to be content with hints and slender indications, these yet combine to give us no very indistinct impression of her maternal character.

The first feature of Christiana's Motherhood which offers itself to our notice—the first in importance no less than the first in time—is her concern for the spiritual welfare of her children. She is already in heart and purpose a Christian mother before she quits the shelter of that familiar roof; whereupon she sets it before herself, with the promptitude of a paramount aim, that she shall be the mother of a Christian household. She succeeds; and it is to be observed that she succeeds without the appearance of difficulty. Something of this easy celerity of success, it is true, must be assigned to the necessities of the story. She must be gone; and if the children are to go with her, their decision must be unanimous and immediate. Yet there is reason to believe that we should miss not a little of the intention of this incident, if we were to leave out of account several other considerations which have less to do with the allegorical form.

Conspicuous among these, and able to be reckoned as the most effective cause of this success, is the frank earnestness of her manner with her children about this enterprise of setting out. She makes it clear that her own mind is fixed upon going; she unfolds the reasons which have moved herself to this decision ; and she presses these same reasons as reasons why they also should go. Her own example, and her own companionship, are presented as powerful corroboration of these reasons—corroboration, however, and nothing more ;—as it is also with the still tenderer example of their father, hallowed as it is by its happy issue. The mighty motives for going, she makes plain, are motives of safety and of duty, largely personal to themselves, and lying between them and the King— their father's King, indeed, and now to be their mother's too. The measure in which the motives of natural affection and respect on the one hand, and of spiritual rightness on the other, are blended in this account of the Christian setting-out of a family (which imports in some degree the Christian nurture of a family) is very wise and skilful. The influence inherent in the parental relationship is the vantage-ground which nature and providence have furnished, and which grace approves and employs : by every true-hearted parent it will be honestly occupied, and hopefully, and will not be for a day of his life ignored. But the motives which this may provide,—strong as they must be always, and nearly the only motives available during the tenderest years,—he will feel to be too shallow in their grasp ; and he will judge, that from the earliest, the matter must be touching its own deeper foundations, and that ere he can hope for any trustworthy result, it must be resting itself solidly upon these. Hence, in the first of the two interviews with her children before the day of departure, ·Christiana at once strikes the note—" We are *all undone ;"* and, more explicitly still—" I have also *hindered you of life :"* then—she seeks to have them share in her regrets that their father had so little of their sympathy. And so, in the second interview, she interjects between her penitent declarations about their father and his death—" I have been also much affected with the thoughts of *mine own state and yours*,"—ere she arrives at the point of practical urgency—" *Come, my children*, let *us* pack up and begone to the gate that leads to the celestial country, that we may *see your father*, and be with him and his companions in peace, *according to the laws of that land.*"

But the facile success of Christiana in persuading her children to set forth with her, while it may be reckoned to find its chief cause in this earnest plying of lesser and greater motives, has still other recognisable causes behind it. Somehow the household was singularly ready to receive her exhortation to pilgrimage. Whence did this readiness come? May we not reason, in view of this quickness of filial response, that Christiana was a mother who commanded the affections and the wills of her children, and wielded a sway over them that was as tenderly strong as a mother's ought to be? For the religious influence of a parent over his children will bear a strict proportion to his general influence over them : if that be affectionately firm all round, it will only then be triumphant here. And in accounting for this readiness of the children, may not our thoughts go back, and go past Christiana, to reach Christian himself? Does it not constrain us to lift the veil from the Allegory, and to see this father still among his children all the while that the pilgrimage was being travelled,—moving them to kindly thoughts of pilgrimage, and awakening in them a sense of their need of pilgrimage, and exhibiting something of the blessedness of pilgrimage? So Christiana's task was the lighter when she came to woo them with her solitary voice to take the road of life with her,—lighter than she may have feared it might be,—because of him whom she was now so wishful to have them following. His brave example, and his fervent prayers, had made ready their hearts for the decisive leading which it was now her privilege to bring.

Christiana, then, was at last beginning to make amends for one item of "the evil she had formerly done," as that is described by Secret—"the keeping of these her babes in their ignorance." But we have to follow her upon the journey if we would assure ourselves of how well she held on in the line indicated in the counsel of this "visitor" ere he left her roof—"I advise that thou put this letter in thy bosom; that thou read therein to thyself, *and to thy children*, until you have got it by rote of heart." Henceforward it is one of her cares that her children shall learn the truth as she is able to teach it, and as they are able to bear it. Whatever comes as great truth to her own mind she is eager to have lodged in the minds of her charge. We have a glimpse of a habit of hers when we see her turning from Great-heart, who has just made luminous to her the cardinal doctrine of justification, and saying— "Good Mercy . . . and, *my children*, do you remember it also." And we have a bit of testimony from the other side when "the least" of the children themselves, sitting in the Arbour on the brow of the Hill, says in his reply to Great-heart's question as to pilgrimage—"I remember now *what my mother hath told me*, that the way to heaven is as up a ladder, and the way to hell is as down a hill." "Come," said Christiana, on the same spot, "will you eat a bit—a little to sweeten your mouths while you sit here to rest your legs?" It is a right considerate motherly inquiry, and not least so in its deeper meaning: in any meaning, it comes from Christiana with the easy quaintness which signifies that her providence and her generosity in this sort are habitual to her.—When they have reached the Palace, the evidence takes a form more direct; for Prudence deliberately sets herself to "see how Christiana had brought up her children." "You are to be commended for thus bringing up your children:" this was the report of the examiner when the religious intelligence of "the youngest" had been tested. "Thy mother hath taught thee well"—"She can learn you more:" these were the praises which successively followed.—Her eldest son becomes sick here in the Palace, and her youngest in the Valley of the Shadow: in the first case she obtains the assistance of the physician Skill, but the other case she herself treats with success. The spiritual meaning is plain; and the one case no less than the other is creditable to her maternal fidelity,—although, in the alarm occasioned by the first, she upbraids herself, with some slight ground of reason, as a "careless mother." "Pray, sir, make me up twelve boxes of them"—the pills with which the physician had cured her son: she should be armed for emergencies when she had amply provided herself with the most infallible medicine she knew.—By the time they have reached the River of the Meadow, she is a mother of children's children. She has not even then retired from the spiritual solicitudes of motherhood. "Now, to the care of THIS MAN," we read, not perhaps without a touch of emotion,— " Christiana admonished her four daughters to commit their little ones, that by these waters they might be housed, harboured, succoured, and nourished, and that none of them might be lacking in time to come." Christiana appreciates motherhood too well to step in between mothers and children, yet also too well to neglect her right to instruct her own daughters; and it is thus that she reaches both generations at once with her benignest influences.

True maternal care knows only one period at which it will consent to lay down its rights, or put off its toils, or depute to others its burdens : it is the hour when it has been summoned to unmoor itself from the shore of all mortal concernments. Christiana has at last taken into hand and heart the summoning invitation of the King. She is ready. The Good One has given her to sustain her motherhood long and happily, and she must be less missed now than once she would have been. She has been spared the severest, surely, of all the sad sunderings which mortality can see—the going away of a young mother from the midst of her little ones that are too young to weep, and Christian faith must work one of its most wondrous miracles ere the motherly heart can say, " Lord, it is well : I come." Yet Christiana is still the mother when the end is at hand—gratefully this, and trustfully, and thoughtfully :—" Then she called for her children, and gave them her blessing, and told them that she yet read with comfort the mark that was set in their foreheads, and was glad to see them with her there, and that they had kept their garments so white." But this does not utter the whole thought of the motherly heart. There are contingencies of pilgrimage for them still, though the story must needs bring them to Beulah—shadows which she will not cast upon their own minds just then, but which she will think of as she is bidding farewell to the trustiest of fellow-pilgrims :—" I would also *entreat you to have an eye to my children*, and if at any time you see them faint, *speak comfortably to them*." It is the last motherly word—on this side the river.

Only once, and that very early in the journey, does the story reveal any occasion for Christiana's motherly reproof. Her boys were getting at the fruit which overhung the wall of the evil orchard, and were beginning to eat it. "'Their mother did also chide them for so doing, but *still the boys went on.*" For an earnest mother, such a moment—such a period, let us say,—when sons are adventuring their own power of will under the enticings of sense, and she feels as if her foot were now upon the uttermost verge of her directive authority over them ;—such a period is often a period of anxiety so great as to cast the mother's heart back upon the gracious omnipotence of the heavenly Father in an agony of prayerful helplessness. But Christiana does not realise the full gravity of the situation. "'Well,' said she, 'my sons, *you transgress ;* for that fruit is *none of ours,*'"—a thoroughly sufficient reason for such remonstrance as she made. "But she did not know that they did belong to the enemy." The narrator feels as if he must account for the mildness of the reproof, and for the dash of weakness we might think we discerned in it : " I will warrant you if she had (known), she would have been ready to die for fear." And been ready, we will trust, to strike in, with the utmost forthputting of her motherly capability, for prevention. She is faithful, it would seem, up to her light ; and the mother's light in such matters has a hazard of not being either copious or clear. But we almost wish we had more satisfying testimony to the strong-hearted fidelity of this typical Christian mother in the presence of her children's wrong-doing. " But that passed," happily, " and they went on their way "—a way so little marked with further cause for motherly apprehension, that we may need to hold as understood a good deal of motherly restraint and direction which is not related.

For Christiana, as is evident from what we have already seen, was such a mother as it were well that many mothers would show themselves to be. It is plain that mere nature by no means suffices to furnish the qualities of a competent motherhood. Motherly affection, even when it is fullest and finest, is no more than the natural instinct which would convoy motherhood on its way into all the excellence which only reason and principle can bring to pass. When it abides unsupported and unregulated by steadier forces, there is no emotion which is able to display more surpassing moral weakness. And the weakness is haunted by calamity. Generally speaking, it is a mother's impress that a child wears most tenaciously upon him throughout his life. And a mother shall spoil the growth of young characters, which offer themselves as magnificent materials for a thoughtful and skilful nurture, simply by neglecting to gird herself with something of clear-hearted intention for the duty which her position brings to her hand from heaven. There will then be for her children no training that can bear the name, because there will be no such trusty self-denial as comes of a sense of high responsibility and of far-travelling consequences; there will be no firmness of hand, no genuine gentleness, no wisdom of guidance, no watchful intolerance of budding evil, no happy tending of incipient good, no meting of reproof by morality instead of by impatience, no just adaptation of treatment to the wonderful diversities of character,—none of the true motherly strength which so usually wins the answering strength of filial devotedness, and sees it ripen into a lifelong thanksgiving.

In its deficiency as to this department of social obligation, probably our own time is not worse on the whole than most times have been. The times of Bunyan had enough of this delinquency in maternal duty; and he has it in view while he goes on to paint for us its antithesis in the picture of Christiana, the good average mother of the class among whom the best mothers of his day were found. Our own time is only marked, perhaps, by its own fashion of parental inefficiency. But we may well take note, that improvement in this department distinctly fails to keep pace with improvement in other departments, and that domestic science—all round it, and as chiefly represented by motherly nurture—is not studied with anything of the enthusiasm which its relative importance would claim. We have not gone so far beyond the time of Bunyan in this as we have gone in locomotion, or manufacture, or geographica' communication, or political reform ; not even so far as in education and general intelligence. Indeed, the genial air of freedom which pervades the time—the relaxation o' civil and religious rigours which were wont to pass their pressure through the mass of society — has wrought its way into domestic life, with effects which are mingled with evil perhaps as much as with good. In thoughtless households it generates a lawlessness which scarcely a single parent in sterner days would have known how to endure : it is a well-spring of the worst individual-ism. And even in thoughtful households, where there is really some design to do the best, it is observable that the danger of reaction from the stringencies of former times is not a fanciful one. All must be pleasant for the children now : they must be scared with nothing earnest ; they must be shadowed by nothing solemn ; everything must be bright, attractive, easy. Self-Denial, Discipline, Truth, are not to be permitted to trouble them. The more excellent our own fathers and mothers were, the more they blundered in their domestic training. If all this has in it a seasoning of verity and good reason, it yet demands but little penetration to perceive, that in its ordinary manifes-tation it involves a lurking insufficiency of parental integ-rity. It is a wonder if there is not less of science in it, less of good philosophy, less of sterling religion, than some fond mothers and fathers imagine. What if there be in it a slight lack of Christian thoroughness, made up by a slight superabundance of sentimental humanism? It is remarkable how a strong healthiness of Christian feeling keeps everything in due balance and just admixture with us. This alone can keep the balance and admixture here. It will assimilate as much of the geniality of the time as shall be wholesome, but it will not abandon itself to think of children as if they were too tenderly dear to be treated as immortal beings, or too angelic to be braced from the outset for a life of stern reality and of strenuous evil. And it is most of all to the mothers, as the whole facts of the subject go forward every year to confirm, that society and the Church must look for this thought and this treatment. It is in their hands to move the world onward with more blessed advance than the entire catalogue of its inventions can achieve, and to lift forward the Church with a quieter potency of progress than the entire category of her more mechanical organisations can accomplish.

But Christiana must not longer detain us. It may have done us good to deepen our acquaintance with her—such good as comes from our intimacy with an admirable woman, mellowing before our eyes into an "aged matron." It is this that Gaius calls her while there is still a good part of the way to travel. She travels it all along—does she not?—with a sober cheeriness, a hallowed good humour, and withal an even good fortune, which make her company pleasant—more pleasant, if a good deal less stirring, than Christian's own: she has all her family safe with her, and her husband is more than safe before her, and the times are less relentless than his. But she travels it too with a heart that feels the great verities which touch the individual soul, and with a head that thinks the thoughts of truth, and a hand that is ready for every work which is pleasing to the King. She is carrying the cares of a household all the way, and she enters into its meanest and its noblest concerns with an unwearying mind that is bent upon them in the name of Christ. She lives what

Milton has already stooped upon his seraph-pinions
to sing :—

> " Nothing lovelier can be found
> In woman than to study household good : "

and what Lowell has more explicitly depicted : —

> " Yet she sets not her soul so steadily
>   Above, that she forgets her ties to earth,
>   But her whole thought would almost seem to be
>   How to make glad one lowly human hearth ;
>   For with a gentle courage she doth strive
>   In thought and word and feeling so to live
>   As to make earth next heaven."

And it is in this wise—not quarrelling with her lot since
the very hope of glory shines upon it, but seeking still to
make that lot of hers more rich with her own obedience,
and more bright with the holy brightness of her own spirit,
and better thronged with the trophies of her earnest well-
doing for others—that she goes steadily forward to fulfil
her earthly destiny.   And she is fulfilling all the while the
greatest purpose which the King's heart has conceived for
herself : she is becoming—at last, upon the further side of
the River, she has verily become—

> " Earth's noblest thing—a woman perfected."

XII

CHRISTIANA'S SONS.

AFTER all, we cannot feel as if we had quite parted with Christiana, when it is her boys that we would now think of as claiming a little of our more special attention. We know little of them except as living by her side —sons, and her sons (though she was fond of saying they were Christian's): when she comes into full view for us, so also do they; and when she disappears, then they too, at least for us, are gone.

It was well—it was true, and natural, and happy—that Bunyan should set a group of children into the midst of this idyl of Christian life which he calls his Second Part. There is place for them here: in truth, place is found for them; and it would not be easy to determine how far this Part was made what it is that it might "suffer the little ones," and how far this Part, being what it was designed to be, rendered the presence of the little ones a practicable feature of its congenial variousness. Amid the "awful earnestness" which has been ascribed to the First Part,— and agonistic minds perhaps too readily deem this to be the only aspect of religion which is worthy of interest,—the boys of Christiana would have been trampled out of the way in the eager tread of the march, or would have been whelmed in the tides of intensity which billowed there so often upon lonely bosoms. But in a pilgrimage where a woman takes the place of hero, and that woman their mother,—why then, if she manages to travel it, so too may

they, if they only keep close under her wing. And, somehow, there is place found even in the undreamed world of
Christian reality for the pilgrimage of mothers and children, although no true picture of that pilgrimage would be
likely to display very much of spiritual athleticism. Nay,
a mother with her children at her side,—is it not the
allegorical manner of setting forth what is the normal conception of religion itself as to how it shall work its way
towards the blessing of the world?

We need not grudge to Bunyan, then, the evident
pleasure it gave him to add to his allegorical responsibilities the care of the four sons of Christian and Christiana.
For the Allegory gains in more than in truthfulness by the
admission of them. They enrich it with a new element.
It gets more tenderness of touch, and must bring into itself
a fresh delicacy of handling, because of them. The simplicity of youth has to be worked along with the gravity of
pilgrimage, and the one must be made to temper the other
in the measure that is due. Besides, the whole idea of
progress reinforces itself by a new combination, when
spiritual advancement is keeping pace with the natural
development of childhood into youth, and of youth into
manhood. The body and the mind, in the period of most
rapid growth, are visibly symbolising the growth of spiritual
life which lies as the reality beneath the figure of pilgrimage. The pilgrim-progress which the Dreamer has thus to
carry on is more normally complete, and more phenomenally harmonious, than it can be in any other instance.

It is not, however, to be said, that Bunyan gives much
appearance of having deliberately selected this element,
either for the exercise of his art or the enrichment of his
Allegory. He seems rather to have let in the element as
it came to him, and at most to have welcomed it as one
that was right natural and true for his purpose. He by
no means elaborates his treatment here; he is not making

the children a finished study, but is simply conceding them their place, and freely permitting them to act and be acted upon according to their stage in life. Not that his descriptions of them, while in some degree incidental and accessory in comparison with that of the senior pilgrims, are not fairly true to nature all the while, or not tolerably distinct and realistic : they could not be other than this in the hands of Bunyan. We may not find it easy to individualise very sharply each son by himself, or very clearly to interpret his character as distinguished from his years : this would have been a sure sign that Bunyan had overworked the subject by treating them as persons instead of treating them as a growing family,—thus in great part declining the representation of the collective domestic unit which the circumstances mainly demanded. But they are really a family of children who are flesh and blood—good and loyal, yet not conspicuously more so than any children may be expected to be who are living in our everyday world, however their eye is being taught to steady itself upon the vision of a better one. He might safely have made more of his opportunity, perhaps, than he has done. Had he been more deliberately setting this feature of his Allegory before him as a study, we feel as if he would probably not have selected sons alone for his model household, but would have brought into it a daughter or two, and have hazarded the successful treatment of the more mingled household upon the tenderness of his own experience, together with the exquisiteness of his own sensibilities and his own instincts of art. The felicitous introduction of Mercy into the household, at first as a maiden neighbour, and afterwards as a daughter, may be regarded not only as a happy compensation for what we may consider a defect, but as indicating perhaps some sense of this defect in the mind of Bunyan himself. The three daughters who were acquired on the way—for Christiana does possess an equal number of sons and of daughters at length—can scarcely be said to come into visibility for us.

Indeed, it is chiefly in the period of boyhood that the sons themselves appear with any prominence,—as is quite in keeping with the design of the Author that they should represent family-life and family-training in the story. No doubt they represent these in a way that is exceptional. They are fatherless when we begin to have any intimacy with them. What age they may have been when they came literally as well as allegorically under the solitary care of their mother,—the uncertainty of chronology in the "Pilgrim" leaves us somewhat dubious as to this. We must not press the fact, that at least the older ones were able to take some part in the unpleasant deportment of the household towards their father when he set out: this involves the perplexing question of the time which Christian occupied in his own pilgrimage. The age which Bunyan appears to design for the boys is that which the artists have usually agreed to assume—the youngest about seven, and the oldest about thirteen, at the period of their leaving the city. The artists naturally feel less sure about the age of the youths at the advancing stages of the journey; for this depends upon lapses of time which there are but slender data for determining. Nor is it of much account. When the boys found themselves fatherless, they were old enough to discern something of what the condition signified; and the older of them would enter into some sympathetic appreciation of the motherly anxiety and responsibility which it was their own lot to create.

As some of ourselves can bear witness, there are few things which more severely test the filial integrity of a boy, or more exactly measure the value of the training he has already undergone, than this remarkable anomaly of providence by which he suddenly finds himself with no parent but a mother. He feels, that an era of comparative liberty has come to him, unsought—an indefinite futurity of freedom, of which he sees the opportunity better than the dignity, and the dignity better than the dangers. It is an appeal made prematurely to the incipient manhood that may be in him : honour, magnanimity, free loyalty, are urged into position with him before he has the wisdom to apprehend their full ethical significance. It is an augury of all that is best for him if his filial conscience becomes a wisdom to him, and he freely bows himself to the sacred authority of love. The widowed mother knows no merely earthly consolation which she will compare with this—to see her boy acknowledging in his young thoughts, that he too has found responsibilities, and that the chivalry of sonship must awaken in him if he is to meet the unaided devotion of motherhood with a manly unselfishness. The discipline of fatherlessness, when it is thus accepted, may prove no less educative of character than the discipline of the best paternal control ; and the lad who grows to look upon every father in the midst of a household with the strange feeling that he constitutes a domestic redundancy, may be himself ripening into the best of fathers and the most estimable of men.

The boys of Christiana appear to have accepted their new position in some such temper as this ; which must be defined to mean that the older of them did so. If the older two were in accord with their mother, she had little reason for anxiety. It lay with them to turn her proud task into one of hope, lit up with flashes of motherly joy. The first gladsome gleam shone out upon her when she appealed to them to accompany her in going after their father, and " they cried out to go." For it must be taken into well-marked account, that in the instance of these boys, the starting of a Christian career and of a fatherless history were very slightly separated in time. Enough of filial fidelity was found in them to draw them into pil-

grimage, and pilgrimage then riveted that fidelity for all
the future. Fidelity to conscience and God,—this wraps
up within it all other fidelities, and, to the child, almost
blends itself into one with fidelity to the parent who is
to him in the stead of God. The mother who has persuaded her boys to go with her in mind and heart as
a Christian,—in the act of furthering the will of God and
the weal of her children, she has most amply compassed
her own will and weal besides. On the whole, therefore,
from the date of our better acquaintance with them, their
behaviour met her wishes, and her motherly solicitude
was seldom greater than to give zest to her motherly
capability.

But it may not be without avail to look a little more
attentively into the character of Christiana's sons, even
though we may be apt to feel that the explicit materials for
a judgment are somewhat slender. We shall need to question the narrative as to noticeable qualities of theirs—
first, and principally, their collective and family qualities ;
thereafter, what of individual and personal qualities it may
be possible to discern.

When we turn our eyes upon the sons of Christiana in
their capacity of a FAMILY, we are at once attracted by the
spirit of *Respectful Obedience* which animates them—boys,
and fatherless, though they be. We should look for this
first, even if it did not arrest our notice, because it is the
corner-stone of all family order and excellence and happiness. And we should look carefully to see how far it was
a spirit, and how far it was only a form, of obedience.
This family of sons are plainly cherishing in themselves a
disposition of obedientness, which attests its depth of root
by the very appearance of unanxious ease which it frequently wears. Their deference to their mother as law-
giver of the house is in great measure a freewill-offering
which gets fragrance from the affectionate reverence which

lies out of sight behind it. This happy element of freeness, it is true, is not overtaxed by the governing power. The government is not imperial, but constitutional and popular—more articulately this as the education of the subject advances. They are a good deal in their mother's confidence : she makes law as intelligible to them, and obedience as intelligent for them, as their inexperience allows. This at once tests and rewards their obedience as concerns the present, and trains it for command as concerns the future. And the public opinion of the family, which is itself sedulously nurtured, is sufficient to protect this confidence from abuse, even if the governing wisdom were likely to permit it to amount to a temptation. So all rights on both sides are conserved, and all liberties on both sides are secured.

Obedience like this in any home is " twice blessed : it blesseth him that gives and him that takes." " Him that gives" it blesses more, because more radically and more enduringly. For, after all, the order and peace which it works into the mechanism of a household is but the passing good which it yields. Even the comparative welfare of the child to which it is so favourable during the years of subjection, is by no means its highest advantage. That in which it is altogether invaluable is the education of character which it constitutes. To grow up under law, anywise, is wholesome and bracing to the character, even if it be almost too despotic or too questionable to admit of a free-hearted obedience. But to be conscious of law as soon as there is consciousness of anything, and to realise erelong that it is a law of love, and that free submission to it is safe and righteous and grateful—a chain of gold around heart and will alike, which has to be snapt asunder if disobedience is to assert its thoughtless brute-power ;—this is a heritage of the most blessed discipline to which any mortal can be born. And the first calamity to character, perhaps the greatest, is the rupturing of such a chain by son or daughter, in any instance in which it has been cast around the young life. It is a perilous necessity of our history, that when thought and knowledge are least, the hazards for the future are greatest,— if sons and daughters, who from any cause are disposed to self-will, could only be convinced that so it is.

It is true to the nature of the case, that the sons of Christiana should show towards others something of the same respectful regard which it was their habit to show towards herself. If the sentiment was crystallised into character with them, it would not confine itself to the household, but would go with them wherever they went, and would appear in all their intercourse with men. We are not permitted to have any doubt concerning their possession of a social virtue so seemly and so attractive. Their deportment towards Great-heart, the self-possessed modesty of their demeanour in the hands of Prudence, the air of respectful considerateness which we feel to be about them in the presence alike of the strong and the weak pilgrims who gather into the company when they themselves have become heads of families,—their whole behaviour, by speech and by silence, in boyhood and in manhood,—all of it affirms the survival and the expansion of those qualities which grew up within them as free obedience to the mother at their side.

But this consentaneous upward look of the family towards their parent could scarcely fail to qualify the look which they cast around upon each other. We do not wonder to find, that there prevailed in this household a pleasant *Brotherly Concord* and a strong *Family Unity*. If these brothers ever fell out with each other, there is no record, and there is no appearance of the likelihood, of any such misfortune. They stood by each other, they encouraged each other, they helped each other, else their history conveys no just impression of their life. It is true that all their outward interests, as well as their inward ones, kept to the same lines throughout; and we are not led to think of this brotherhood as ever becoming divided by the material barriers of lands and seas, which even our modern railways and steamships, and mails and telegraphs, leave so formidable barriers still. But as far as their circumstances can display it, they manifest that domestic *esprit de corps* which has been known to outlive vicissitudes and separations, and even the formation of far-severed households, as long at least as any of the barks which began the voyage together are still out among the tempests of time. This family fidelity has been reckoned a narrow and a narrowing thing; and indeed it is susceptible of becoming both, and of exhibiting a "clannishness" with just the shortest radius of which that social littleness is capable. But it cannot be affirmed that any such smallness of range belongs by necessity to domestic unity, even when that is trustiest and most enduring. In its elementary stage at least, it operates rather as largeness and width than as littleness and straitness, since it consists in the opening forth of individual feeling to the dimensions of the household. It does seem as if this rudimentary largeness had only to be wisely educated, so that its proportion shall keep pace with its scale, and then the family-group might abide compact in its old loyalty at the centre of a circle which had any possible reach of circumference. May we not venture to think, that it is this which best fulfils the ideal of providential intention in the case, as that intention is interpreted by the sentiments of Christianity? A brother is not called upon to give to family what is meant for mankind: he is not then most truly loyal to brotherhood itself. But may we not account him less loyal still to brotherhood, if he give to mankind, or if he retain for self, what is meant for family? The family offers a natural solidarity which it might be wise to accept as a provided nucleus of mutual strength in view of a wider life, and which it may be wasteful to throw away too lightly even when that wider life itself has been entered.

In the instance of these sons of Christiana, however, it admits of explicit notice, that they appear before us as a family who kept together in *Christian Experience and Sympathy.* We will not conceal from ourselves, that the structure of the Allegory presents us with an amount of identity of experience which is scarcely true to life. We must be ready to admit, that this travelling in close company does not leave much scope for the adapting of sympathy to such circumstances in the experience of one as might be different from the existing circumstances of the others. The sympathy, for the most part, has to confine itself to a sympathy in regard to intention rather than experience, to principles rather than facts. In real life, the members of the family must usually be at various stages of advancement; and the transpiring experience of each, if not very diverse in respect of the outward life, may be very diverse indeed in respect of the life that is inward. Sympathy will thus demand more of imagination and recollection if it is to be lively, and will give more room for an ingenious versatility if it is to be effective and helpful. All this we must supply to the narrative, as being more true to the spirit of it than it is to the letter. We can imagine these brothers taking counsel with each other upon matters which concerned the pilgrimage. We can think of the older as keeping a brotherly eye upon the younger, and as offering warning or godspeed which was not declined. We can suppose them conversing about their common hopes, their common perils, their common obligations,—with boylike conciseness, no doubt, and with a little of boylike reserve, but with none the less of effect upon each other's mind and heart.

It is not easy for us to transfer this line of habit, even in thought, to the actual arena of family-life. It is hard for us Britons, now-a-days at least, even to imagine brothers of a real family making religious truth at any time a topic of frank converse, and harder still to imagine them unfolding to each other their religious experience. Not that boys have no religious experience; for there are few boys living under Christian influences but have experiences of the inward life which are very lively even if they be transient. But the boy-nature with us is almost invincibly reticent upon all that is spiritual; nor least so as between boys and boys, and most of all perhaps as between brother and brother in the same home. It is less difficult for sisters to be frank with each other about religious concerns, and a favourite sister will sooner get the innermost mind of even a brother than another brother will. Better all this, doubtless, than that the young should talk a fluent cant, or should trade in phrases of infinite meaning which to their minds are wellnigh meaningless, and on their lips are perilously near to being profane. Nevertheless, there is place for something that is better still. It is not well that the thoughts of highest concernment should in young bosoms lie buried from those of their own household, or should tremble towards utterance and still abide unuttered, or should more readily be disclosed to such as are outside the circle of the home, or, as must too frequently happen, should decay beneath the stifling of an unhappy silence. We do not forget that a sympathetic and watchful parent will always be the fittest to deal with the spiritual thoughts of the son or daughter, especially in the periods of spiritual crisis. But there is a warmth of sympathy between young hearts and intellects and consciences, and there is a power of mutual help between young wills, which not even the parent can replace by all his tenderness and wisdom. And surely there is nothing finer on earth than a frank and genuine interchange of spiritual sympathy, and of spiritual guidance too, between the younger members of a household whose hearts are moved by the same spirit, and who are feeling each his own individual way along the same high road of faith and hope and simple-hearted righteousness. It were not easy to doubt, that the most blessed of all the functions of brotherhood is missed if it never contributes, save by dumb example, to the fostering of spiritual life or to the dispelling of spiritual solicitude.

Christian faith and fellowship always imply some little measure of intelligence, even if it be restricted to a certain department of thought and fact; and what intelligence they imply, they are not ill-fitted to extend. The well-governed Christian household never gropes in the sunless mist of ignorance. We have therefore to note the *Mental Activity and Acquirement* of the lads of Christiana. They had been fortunate in inheriting some predisposition to these; but the matter is not left to good fortune alone. There is mental work on both sides—on the side of the parent and on the side of the children,—with the effect · that the boys are growing before us in knowledge and in whatever of intellectual competency is to be looked for from their years. Of course, even the intelligence is mainly religious, and almost their one science is theology. Yet it must be said, that in the case of the boys more observably than in the case of the men and women, Bunyan seems to take pains to enlarge the horizon of the intellectual landscape, so that it embraces not a little of general wisdom and of more secular information. Evidently the boys might pass a pretty creditable examination upon other themes than those in which Prudence found them so much at home. The circumstances of the pilgrimage, it is true,—though we cannot speak with confidence about the earlier life in the city,—leave no space for such a phenomenon as school-attendance—for the intellectual stimulus of the class-room, or the whetting contacts of the playground. Their education was a "home education," and their principal tutor was their mother. And, in truth, perhaps the most successful tutors the world has ever seen have been intelligent mothers who schooled themselves to still higher intelligence that they might be efficient as guides and philosophers, not less than as mothers, to their boys. But we need not be reading the Allegory too strictly even here. Our Christianas commonly see their boys to school if that be practicable, and it was never for them that "compulsory clauses" were framed. They let forth their sons, not without misgiving, but with brave hope for the best, to mingle with the young world which beats around the home, and to be buffeted into the healthy hardness of character which the world needs in the men who are by-and-bye to do its work or to mould its destinies. Yet, in thus letting them forth, they cannot afford to devolve all their own responsibilities upon teachers, whether they be secular or religious : they work to the hands of these, and supplement and support all the training which these are seeking to supply, so that by every means the young minds may be well equipt and furnished both for time and eternity.

"You must still hearken to your *mother*," said Prudence to the boys when her well-pleased inspection was concluded. "You must also diligently give ear to what good talk you shall hear from *others*. . . . Observe also, and that with carefulness, what *the heavens and the earth* do teach you ; but especially be much in the meditation of *that Book* that was the cause of your father's becoming a pilgrim." It was a quartette of not illiberal working-directions for prosecuting their spiritual welfare through the intellect. There is some appearance that the transactions here in the Palace, as formerly those in the Interpreter's House, were shaped in great measure with a view to the benefit of the boys, to whose time of life the character of both places was especially congruous. Their experience in the earlier place would represent such instruction of youth, beyond that of the family, as is more purely moral and religious; their experience in the later place would stand for all intelligent influences, beyond those of the family, which have Christian truth for their background, and Christian life for their motive. The instruction in both places is largely managed by illustration; at the earlier stage, as was suitable both to the class of themes and to the comparative inexperience of the learners, it was all but exclusively so. Perhaps it is only candid to allow, that in most of the pictures of truth which the Interpreter had in store for this humbler company, Bunyan somewhat taxes the patience of readers of robust mind, and puts in peril his reputation for dignity of fancy and manliness of imagination. Probably he does so with full intent. His literary credit is less under his care than these boys are;—not to speak of the women, to whom the Interpreter explains, with a touch of apology after the "Hen and Chickens" had been beheld,—"I chose, my darlings, to lead you into the room where such things are, because you are *women*, and they are easy for you." The words had more of tenderness in them than of compliment: "boys" would give a better reading than "women." In the subsequent scenes, if not also in this one, the apology would have been appropriate as made to the women on account of the boys. Bunyan's fancy is stooping to the level of the young people, and he does seem to fall into the danger of stooping too low. He exhibits the unerring instinct of the true educator, inasmuch as the teaching is by vision whether ocular or mental; but he scarcely exhibits the severe good taste of the true educator, inasmuch as what is seen does not illustrate truth quite so much as it degrades it. But in the Palace Beautiful there is less to annoy the cultured reader. The passage of questions and answers between Matthew and Prudence, recalling the string of racy proverbs by which the Interpreter sought to vary his teachings, is perhaps artificial enough even where it is not weak; and when we hear James, the youngest of the four, replying to Prudence that "God the Holy Ghost saves" him "by His illumination, by His renovation, and by His preservation," we feel as if the needful simplicity of illustration were not supported by a concurrent simplicity of diction, or as if the little fellow had been culling sentences from the folios of theological Latinists and committing them to memory as knowledge of his own. Yet this catechism which is woven together by Prudence and the boys is on the whole an admirable one. And in regard to the examples of actual instruction, we must bethink us of the picturesque homeliness at which Bunyan was aiming, and which must be not less pleasing, at least, to Christiana's boys than it must since have been to many of the readers of their history.

But, not perhaps unfortunately, Christiana would seem to have kept the intellectual wellbeing of her boys very much in her own quiet hands. We witness less of the processes than we do of the results. It is highly auspicious, that the lads are excellent listeners—appreciative, but mostly silent. By an occasional word dropt in conversation, we find their minds are at work; by an occasional incident of the story, we recognise that their intelligence is ripening. There is little trace of mental precocity in them while they are boys, or of intellectual pre-eminence when they have become men; but we have enough of evidence, scanty as it is, to assure us, that they looked about upon the world, and looked above it, with intelligent eyes, and were as little likely to be duped by the plausibilities of secular unwisdom as to be ensnared by the sophistries of religious caprice. They would hold their own opinions,

and would be entitled to hold them because they had made
them their own; but they would hold them in charity,
since they had gotten glimpses of how much could be said
for some opinions that were not their own.   Perhaps they
would be more tolerant than their time, and more liberal
than many who had less at stake beneath their liberality.
We imagine they would not be much of speakers, finding
it hard enough to keep the life eloquent, yet bidding godspeed to every man whom God and his own diligence had
made eloquent in word as well as in deed: they would be
workers rather, and thinkers, in their own modest way, yet
would work with the tongue too when that came in course
—not "speaking," but "saying a word" with good judgment and good effect, or even with blessed power,—
perhaps each of them devoted to a Sabbath-class if he had
been living in our altered times—probably a member of a
Christian association, where his conscientious thoughtfulness would be a rebuke to all brainless flippancy, and
would raise the standard of intelligence and of genuine
profiting for years to come;—not "speaking" at any time,
but happening to say many glowing words on many things,
it might be to brothers or friends around the winter-lamp,
or far into the mantling dusk of summer nights; or "being
helped" to drop bright words of strength beside some
weary sick-bed; or "doing his duty" by sinking a few
weighty sentences through the joints in the armour of some
godless soul.   Men these, who grow up to enrich the
Church and to admonish the world, while they only half
know it,—worshippers, listeners, workers, office-bearers,
for whom ministers are constrained to give God thanks by
name in their lonely prayers.[1]

[1] We can note that the awakening Dreamer, speaking as he does
from the border-ground between vision and reality, glides out of
allegory into fact in his concluding reference to the Sons. He "did
not stay where he was till they were gone over:" this is allegory.

We have only now to gather together the family characteristics of Christiana's Sons by taking note of the *Heartiness and Constancy* with which they pursued the course into which their mother had led them. All true pilgrimage is cordially personal, and all guidance for the pilgrim must be still the guiding of a free choice—a cordiality of choice which will at least be in the dawn from the earliest hour of ongoing. From the first, therefore, and increasingly thereafter, as judgment and experience grew, these boys made the pilgrimage freely and heartily their own. At no time were they drags upon the little caravan which was moving along the track to the holy City. They were something of a care for a while, but they were never anything of a burden. Even they, with their limited powers of endurance, were not borne or wheeled upon the journey which all alike must do on foot: they trudged forward under their own due share of the general willingness, though their steps had need to be many if they would maintain a pace which was easy to older travellers. But indeed the time was not long until they and the women were coming to a sympathetic equality with each other in respect of their strength of limb and of heart. In scaling the heights of Difficulty, Christiana "began to pant," and Mercy "must sit down," and "the *least* of the children began to cry:" as afterwards when an interval had brought still younger pilgrims into the old road, "the women and children being weakly, they were forced to go on as they could bear; by which means"—for the area of pilgrim-frailty had extended—"Mr Ready-to-halt and Mr Feeble-mind had more to sympathise with their condition;" and later still, upon the dark way of the Enchanted Ground, where "was but sorry going for the best of them,

But—"since he came away he heard one say they were yet *alive*, and so would be for the *increase of the church in that place where they were*, for a time :" this is other than allegory.

but how much worse for the women, who both of feet and of heart were but tender." Of heart; for the pilgrimage is not all an affair of muscle. At sight of the lions, "backed" by Grim, "the boys, that went before, were glad to cringe behind;" and as they passed the beasts, "the women trembled," and "the boys also looked as if they would die." But even the boys did pass the monsters nevertheless, as they had just passed the slain bully whose expiring roars "frighted the women." And Great-heart can call them his "brave children" when that night he bids them adieu. But the equality must begin to be lost, erelong, towards the other side. By the time the pilgrims have reached the domains of Doubting Castle, the women are women still, but the boys are men. Nor has their heart gone out of the business of pilgrimage now, with all their developed strength and gathered experience and compacted will. Great-heart appeals for volunteers to carry assault into the citadel of the Giant. Honest offers his services. "'And so will we too,' said Christiana's four sons," with unanimous promptitude. "And the four young men"—these made up two-thirds of the little ex-pedition which "left the women in the road," and went "to look for Giant Despair" with so much result; and their conduct on that occasion wins "great commenda-tions" by-and-bye from the Shepherds, who, in the midst of their giving of gifts to the women, bestow words of warm acknowledgment as the goodliest gifts for the acceptance of youthful valour. Thus they begin to push forth beyond the intenser circle of their own wellbeing into that of the public weal of the pilgrim-community. Nor could this be very well the close of their career of brave beneficence: it might be, that long after "those who waited for Christiana had carried her out of sight," and they had "returned to their place," and had dried their manly tears, other giants of wrong not far from Beulah would feel the stroke of their weapons, and other tongues would speak the praise which they so amply earned and so little sought.

The boys never listened to a finer strain of counsel than the parting words of the Porter at the Palace :—" Do you fly youthful lusts, and follow after godliness with them that are grave and wise; so shall you put gladness into your mother's heart, and obtain praise of all that are sober-minded." There is more flow of rhythm in the words than the good man would likely intend: he might have chanted them. The lads must have set them to the music of their own heavenward steps. For their life is one long rendering of the words, in every clause of them. They were untried then. We could scarcely speak as yet of their cordial steadfastness. The words were only words of hopeful exhortation. After, however, a good deal had come and gone, and they were now guests of Gaius, we cannot but have lively interest in giving ear to the testimony of the most competent witness in the world :—" The boys," says Great-heart, *"take all after their father*, and covet to tread in his steps; yea, if they do but see any place where the old pilgrim had lain, or any print of his foot, it ministereth joy to their hearts, and they covet to lie or tread in the same." Gaius is glad that Christian "has left behind him four such boys as these :" plainly, his own first impression of them is all in their favour. " Indeed, Sir," continues their guide, "they are likely lads; they seem to *choose heartily* their father's ways." We should almost trust that the lads were not within full hearing of these things, but we ourselves are glad to be. The unconstrained Constancy of the youthful pilgrims, as we see, is the resulting fabric of many mingling materials—loyalty to a departed father, obedient regard to a living mother, guidance of friends, thoughtful sway of conscience, reflective observation of men and things, earnest meditation of truth, —all of them overruled into enduring unity by supreme submission to the Gracious Will. But it is full of instruction to note (as indeed Bunyan bids us on the margin) how especially the influence of the parent who has completed his pilgrimage abides dominant in its strength with the children, under the fostering care of the parent whose pilgrimage is as yet their own. Great-heart is telling us, by way of family-history, one most real mode in which "the good man never dies"—nay, in which the death of the good man gives impulse, if not creation, to the multiplying of himself and his goodness in succeeding generations, perhaps to the end of time. It is grace working together with nature, and example working together with prayer, to draw forth the most blessed issues which this world can see. Gaius "hoped" that the sons of Christian would "come to their father's end." And, in truth, every living Christian parent, who is watching over the religious character of his children as if he watched the upspringing of " trees of life with fruits of gold," may find a strong stay for his hope in the certainty, that, even waiving any inflexible doctrine of Christian perseverance, there is no course, among all the courses that human life can enter or forsake, which is so inherently fitted to assert its permanent Constancy, as the course which a child has begun when he has yielded with Heartiness to the pious incentives of a Christian home.

If we have given somewhat prolonged attention to Christiana's sons in their collective capacity as a family, we are not so likely to commit the same indiscretion when we now come to sift them out from the narrative as INDIVIDUALS. We cannot hope that the process will yield us much fruit as to character, yet it may not be without its interest as to the texture of the Allegory.

It may be statistical overmuch, but it is interesting, to observe the precise proportion of attention which each of the Sons enjoys at the hands of Bunyan, who is after all the true father of them, and indeed bears himself towards them with something of a father's ways. It is the youngest, " the least," by name James, who appears most frequently before us—as many as eleven times. With equal natural-ness it is the eldest, Matthew by name, who has in this respect the second place, since he becomes individually visible to us nine times. Still preserving the paternal as well as the filial probability, the second son, Samuel, comes six times to view; and the third son, Joseph, five times. The result remains almost unaffected if we notice how often each comes before us with speech. To James we have to listen seven times, besides hearing him "read a chapter" in the house of Gaius; to Matthew, also seven times; to Samuel, five times; to Joseph, four times. It is James who is first known to us by name [1]—as early as the nearer slope of the Hill Difficulty: the others do not deploy into recognisable individuality until the catechising takes place in the Palace which crowns the Hill; whereas James has been four times under our eye ere this comes to pass, and on three of those occasions has broken silence. This analytical process at the one end of the story has its counterpart in a synthetical process at the other end of it, where they relapse again into invisible family collective-ness. Not one of them reappears individually in the story after his marriage : Matthew and James therefore retire first, and together; next, and together also, Samuel and Joseph follow. And we may not overlook the timely age at which each becomes a husband—so timely in the in-stance of James as to put a perceptible strain upon the chronology of the earlier periods. Bunyan was looking back, with grateful tenderness enough doubtless, upon his own mortal pilgrimage.

The spoken wisdom of the four, as we should expect to find, is mostly with James and Matthew. In the case of

[1] Note I..

James, of course, it is for the first while little more than hearsay—very naturally unnatural. He is much with his mother, by way of fondness,—as his eldest brother is a good deal with his mother also, but by way of responsibility. Matthew is fast getting to have something of his own to say that is wise ; James will by-and-bye have less to say than now, until he is able to replace the thoughts of others by thoughts of his own. Samuel and Joseph occupy the intermediate position, and occupy it with all literary and all moral fitness—however little the Author may have deliberately designed that they should.

" *The Least*" is perhaps the most engaging of the four, and, in his earlier days, is a genuine study of childhood. On the Hillside, after his crying is over, and they are resting in the Arbour, Great-heart throws a general question at the boys as to their opinion of pilgrimage now. It is "the least " who responds, admitting his recent strait, and thanking the guide for "lending him a hand in his need "—right courteously and well. And he must go on to deliver his mind : *he* " remembers what his mother has told him "— (plagiarism is not a thing of intention with him)—about the two ways. "But *I* had rather go up the ladder to life than down the hill to death." He repels Mercy's playful objection like a man (and it is time the historian were letting out his name for us) :—"The day is coming when, *in my opinion*, going down hill will be the hardest of all." When "his master" commends him and his answer, however, " Mercy smiled, but *the little boy did blush.*" This is admirable.—But the hour soon comes when their guiding friend must leave them. Christiana and Mercy each address him in their own characteristic way ; and "James, the youngest of the boys," again is spokesman for the brotherhood :—"Pray, Sir, be persuaded to go with us, and help us, because we are weak, and the way so dangerous as it is." There is now a little of sterling experience at the back of his words. Then we hear him under the catechising of Prudence, in which the questions and the answers alike are pretty much in accordance with his years. His answering is not at all so fresh and hearty as Joseph's, nor so spiritual as Samuel's, nor so intelligently practical as Matthew's; nor ought it in truthfulness to be. Amid the subsequent sight-seeing of the place, it is Jacob's *ladder* that rivets him, and he must speak and request, through his mother now—"Pray, bid them stay here a little longer, for this is a curious sight." And they did stay, while he gazed with his young mind upon the thought, that the Lord Himself was most really "the way to heaven."—When they were again on the road, it was his quick eye that first fell upon the pillar, on which they found a warning written around his father's name.—In the Valley of the Shadow he "began to be sick," "the cause whereof," in the Dreamer's own opinion, "was fear;" but soon,—for it was not constitutional,—under his mother's medicinal ministering, "the boy began to revive." Not unfittingly therefore, he takes part in the conversation with which the story concerning Mr Fearing is dismissed: " No fears no grace," said James, —speaking last, however, now-a-days. "Though there is not always grace where there is the fear of hell, yet, to be sure, there is no grace where there is no fear of God." And Great-heart closes approvingly upon "James's sentence," as the sidenote describes it,—though it does not quite box the compass on the subject of fear.—We next see him quietly taking the mechanical part in the Bible-reading which was held one morning in the house of Gaius; as whose son-in-law he passes back into the dim group of the family.

It is the lot of *Matthew* to attain some distinction in the Palace where he first appears with clearness. His acquitting of himself under examination is but the first of four passages in his individual history there, making specially memorable to him this era of more public commitment to a life of pilgrimage. His serious illness is a somewhat sharp experience. The forgotten fruit of "Beelzebub's orchard" was killing him. We might have guessed it was he who led that evil frolic, rendering it so difficult for his mother to get obedience : so, very plainly now, it was he who had been most free with the pernicious "green plums." Before he can be well again, he must be down with sore sickness, and must take the medicines which are proper for his case. It needs all the steadfast persuasiveness of his mother to prevail with him to receive the prescription of the physician. "I must have you take it :" it is a clear note of maternal sway that strikes his ear. But her appeal at last has passion in it : "If thou lovest thy mother, if thou lovest thy brothers, if thou *lovest Mercy*, if thou lovest thy life, take it." The mention of Mercy, and its place in the climax of ascending motives, is a delicate stroke, which the shrewd reader can keep in mind, as a defence against surprise, until he comes to the eventful abode of Gaius. It meant, however, a gathering complexity of influence, in which Christiana's power stood no longer alone and unrivalled. But "the boy was healed," and Christiana was satisfied.—Upon his recovery, his first questions to Prudence show that his mind is still dwelling upon the disease and its cure ; and they are the only very natural questions which he propounds.—He is more like his father's son when he addresses the fears of his mother and Mercy after they have heard of the "great robbery on the King's highway" just as they are quitting the dwelling-place of Prudence : "Mother"—(Mercy is not named)—"*fear nothing*, as long as Mr Great-heart is to go with us and be our conductor." And he is still more so when he speaks under the glow of this conductor's defeat of "Maul, a giant :" "When you have all thought what you please, I think God has been wonderful good unto us ; . . . for my part, *I see no reason why we should distrust our God any more*, since He has now, and in such a place as this, given us such testimony of His love as this."—His part in the conversation on fear is more subdued, and is greatly more personal than James's deliverance on the same topic: "Fear was one thing that made me think that I was far from having that within me that accompanies salvation; but if it was so with such a good man as he, why may it not also go well with me?" These two utterances blend together well, and reveal a character which is on fruitful tracks.—After "the match was concluded" under the encouraging management of Gaius, it is reasonable that Matthew should be more frankly friendly with his host; whereupon we hear him drawing forth the wisdom of the good man on two occasions ere the marriage is accomplished and we hear of him no more.

We miss the discursiveness of these two brothers when our eye follows *Samuel*. His mind is not so much at large: he is taken with details and incidents. A firm sense of locality holds him. It is he who is so clear and earnest about heaven and hell in his catechising. It is he, quite as readily, who recalls the "plashing" and eating of the fruit, when even his mother had let it fade out of recollection. And it is he who plies Great-heart with inquiries as to the scene of his father's conflict in the Valley: "Sir, *I perceive* that in this Valley my father and Apollyon had their battle; but *whereabout* was the fight? for *I perceive this Valley is large*." He "perceives" a great deal, and likes to think within well-marked limits. In the more fearful Valley, when they were loathesomely beset, a cheery young voice follows a regretful reminiscence of Mercy's: "'Oh, but,' said one of the boys, 'it is not so bad to *go through* here as to *abide here always;* and for aught I know, one reason why we must go this way to *the house prepared for us*, is that our home might be made the sweeter to us. . . . . Why, if ever I get out here again, I think I shall prize *light, and good way*, better than ever I did in all my life." The guide need not have told us that the voice was Samuel's. And there is a strong flavour of his character in the last words of his we hear, whispered to his mother in Gaius's dwelling: " Mother, this is a very good man's house; let us *stay here* a good while, and let my brother Matthew be married here to Mercy *before we go any further*."—It is " Grace " that becomes his own wife, in the house of her father Mnason: his earthly " home would be made the sweeter to" him for her companionship—at least when he came more abidingly to have a home, amid the comparative settlement of Beulah.

Joseph shares the disposition of Samuel rather than of the other two. He is perhaps the best average representative of boyhood, as that is hallowed by Christian principle, and toned by reflection if scarcely ruled by thoughtfulness. When his mother, among the many interests of the genial Palace, is almost forgetting to send off a request for their guide, he gracefully reminds her, and she thankfully accepts the gentle admonition. In the dismal Valley, while Christiana has her eye on some weird unshapely object which does nothing but loom and approach, the boy finds the indefiniteness irksome, and speaks like a younger Samuel: " Mother, what is it? . . . But, mother, what is it like?" " The boys," as they huddled onwards, had been chorusing the natural question—" Are we not yet at the end of this doleful place?" Afterwards it is Joseph who sharpens the question into this—" *Cannot we see* to the end of the Valley as yet?" It is but a boy's unwitting echo of Hopeful's boylike inquiry long ago—" Are we now *almost got past* the Enchanted Ground?" Joseph will likely become a considerate man, and it will not be troublesome for him to divide burdens with his " Martha " in her possible "carefulness about many things," whether they be temporal or eternal.

So, with more of their father in the nature of the one pair, and more of their mother in the nature of the other pair, the lads make good their progress towards a comely Christian manhood. They have served their purpose in the Allegory when they have reached on to this; and indeed, as grown men, we might not find their history a very arresting one. In them, childhood has gotten its place and its due in the commonwealth of Christian life, and the rumour of boyish ways is left about the King's high-road for all time coming. Do not these ways enliven the very reality of that road and its places of sojourn? We would not miss the eager faces that crowd around Mercy in the house of the Gate, when she is proposing to seek explanation concerning that "dog" which turned out to have "another owner:" "Ay, do; and persuade him to *hang him*,"—the immemorial juvenile solution of the problem of evil power,—"for we are afraid he will *bite* us when we go hence." We scarcely grudge to hear the swish and rustle of that "plashing" of the plum-tree branches—"as boys are apt to do." It is no best sign of ourselves if it does not please us to see the attendants at the Interpreter's House "looking upon the boys," and "stroking them over the faces with the hand;" or to watch the lads "standing amazed to see into what fashion they were brought" when they had been invested with the "white raiment." We like to hear the sagacious hospitality of Gaius ringing out the order—"Let the boys have *that*, that they may grow thereby;" and we may be able to endorse the verdict of Honest under the same roof— "For an old (man) and a young to set out both together, the young one has the advantage of the fairest discovery of a work of grace within him, though the old man's corruptions are naturally the weakest." And we feel the touch of truth upon the record, " that one of the children " (the children's children) *"laughed"* when Heedless and Too-bold mumbled their incongruous responses out of their deadly sleep,—however we may regret the allegorical necessity which puts it on the same page, that " the children began to be *sorely weary*, and cried out unto Him that loveth pilgrims to make their way more comfortable." Every young reader of all this can feel, that he himself may be a pilgrim, although nothing within him may be urging him to a paroxysm of rigid earnestness, but only a loyal Godward intent giving sway of steadfast gentleness to his young life, and leading it upward into brave patience and undaunted quiet welldoing. Nor need he greatly blame himself if he lack either the moral force or the intellectual perplexity, either the self-isolating energy of will or the egoistic uncertainty of belief, which so often combine to create the earnestness that feels impatient in the presence of an unstriving integrity towards all that is true, and righteous, and Divine.

XIII.

MERCY.

IN the group which wended away across the plain
towards the Wicket-gate, there was one figure which
merits more of our distinct interest than we have yet set
ourselves to give it. It is that of a girl passing into
womanhood—comely, modest, and bright. This is no
daughter of the pilgrim-household; she is but a maiden
neighbour, who has a mind to see her friend a little way
upon her remarkable journey. If we know her well, we
shall have our doubts that ever she will retrace her steps
to the city. We may even hope, that she may become a
companion of the little band as far as Beulah itself—
perhaps that she may one day be a daughter of the matron
whom she is thus drawn to see started well upon her way.

Mercy fills more than one place in the plan of the
Allegory. She is the maiden; she is the womanly companion; she is approximately the daughter. Without
greatly meaning it, she distinctly adorns each place she
fills. The Puritan young woman, in the most winning,
and probably the truest, personation of her in existence, is
before us here under the name of Mercy. She is unquestionably the most attractive of the group of which she
so "accidentally" becomes a unit—if we may somewhat
extend the application of the word she herself afterwards
employs. We feel little difficulty in accepting the warm
criticism of Montgomery when he speaks of her as "the
most lovely" of all the characters in the Second Part; or

when he proceeds to say—"Though of the utmost simplicity, it would be difficult, among the most finished
portraits of womanly excellence by our first poets, to
parallel this in delicacy and truthfulness of drawing and
colouring."[1]   Bunyan, by his character of Mercy, has laid
Christian maidenhood under as deep obligation as he has
laid Christian matronhood by his character of Christiana.

"The manner" of her "setting out" (as Bunyan speaks
on the title-page of his First Part) was different from that
of any other pilgrim within the records of the Pilgrimage.
The dissimilarity of experience which the Author introduces
into this matter of finding the way—a dissimilarity which
is always ruled more or less by type of character in the
forthgoing pilgrim—is sustained well in the instance of
Mercy.   It is Mercy and no one else who just in this
manner is beginning to go upon pilgrimage.   On that first
day, she comes before us with all her more distinctive
characteristics as clear upon her as ever we shall see them
afterwards, and with the charm of freshness on them
besides.   It may therefore open the way to a fuller
acquaintance with herself if we recall the circumstances
of her outset as a pilgrim.

"Come, neighbour Mercy."   The words are not Christiana's, nor are they an invitation to set out for the better
City.   They are the words of Mrs Timorous.   She is too
hastily taking for granted, as people are apt to do, that
her young neighbour, who has slipt into Christiana's house
and into the history unnamed, is of one mind with herself
as to leaving this widow of Christian "in her own hands,"
and quitting the dwelling of a woman that "scorned their
counsel and company."   The youthful visitor "was at a
stand, and could not *so readily comply* with her neighbour."
For this, it appears, there was "a two-fold reason."   She
"yearned over Christiana," and she "yearned over her

---

[1] Introductory Essay to Collins's Edition of the "Pilgrim."

own soul." Under pressure of the first emotion, "she said within herself, ' If my neighbour will needs be gone, I will go *a little way with her to help her.*'" Under pressure of the second, "she said within herself again, ' I will yet have *more* talk with this Christiana ; and if I find *truth and life* in what she shall say, *myself with my heart shall also go with her.*'" We can see, that " what Christiana had said had taken *some* hold upon her mind." Mrs Timorous does not have much claim to know all her thought :—" I think to walk, *this sunshine morning,* a little way with her, to help her on the way." But Mrs Timorous is shrewd enough to perceive, that Mercy "has a mind to go a-fooling too." And Mercy and the household set forth together. As they go, Christiana expresses her sense of Mercy's kindness. The friendly acknowledgment touches Mercy into a more friendly frankness, and she draws aside the veil of her innermost mind—gently, prudently, firmly. " Then said young Mercy (for she was but young), ' If I *thought* it would be *to purpose* to go with you, *I would never go near the town any more.*'" Christiana is not insensible to the significance of this revelation : she quietly encourages the girl to " go along with " her,—invites her as if in name of the King,—will hire her as her servant to incorporate her with the household, yet will treat her as her friend. Mercy, however, continues to be hampered by her uncertainty as to whether "*she also* shall be entertained." This absence of personalness in the matter—this silence between the King and her—this incidental, undistinguished, unbidden movement on her part,—it wears about it such a look of presumption and futility ! In Mercy's circumstances, and to Mercy's nature perhaps no less, this was almost inevitable, and was slow to be altogether overcome. It was unenlightened lowliness of heart : it was the least unamiable of all forms of unbelief. But nothing besides this embarrassed her. She " would make no stick at all, but would go, though the way were never so tedious," if she "had this hope but from one that could tell," for then she would be "helped by Him that can help." She had come away on the plea of "helping" Christiana: she is already scanning the horizon of possibility in search of the Highest Help for herself. And as being one who so well directs her own willing help, might we not guess, that she is on the way to find more help than ever she can render? Meanwhile, Christiana, who is rapidly assuming the place of human help-giver, manages to cut the knot of the present difficulty :—they will go on to the Wicket-gate together, and inquire there; if the news prove adverse, she will "pay her" and "be content" she should return. In that moment, as Christiana could scarcely but surmise, the city of doom has for ever lost Mercy for a citizen. "Then will I go thither," responds the earnest-hearted maiden, "and will take what shall follow; and the Lord grant that my lot may then fall, even as the King of heaven may have His heart upon me." We somewhat trust that it will.

This brave decision of Mercy's has so much of final settlement in it, even to her own consciousness, that Christiana finds her shedding tears at the thought of the relatives she is leaving behind her in their unhappy condition. Her friend consoles her wisely, and erelong she is singing a song of prayer for herself and them. The progress of her heart and purpose is as rapid as the progress of her footsteps. Anon we find her bearing herself like a true pilgrim. The Slough, through the faithless engineering of "labourers" who make pretence of working for the King, has been more marred than mended of recent years: Christiana hesitates; Mercy is for getting forward: "Come, let us *venture;* only, let us be *wary.*" But as they "think they hear" the reassuring words out of the invisible, she drops back upon the less cheerful of her two conflicting emotions: "*Had* I as good ground to hope for a loving reception at the Wicket-gate as you, I think *no Slough of Despond would discourage me.*" Despondency was not Mercy's "sore," however it might be Christiana's; but Mercy had her own bitterness, which Christiana could do little to sweeten. At last, amid the contrary tides of fear and urgency, they are holding their place at the Gate while it resounds with their knocking. "The dog" desists; the Gate opens—and is again closed. Christiana and her children are welcomed tenderly, and the dwelling rings with trumpet-notes of gladness. The happy din was not for Mercy. "All this while, poor Mercy did stand without, trembling and crying, for fear that she was rejected." It bore a terrible appearance of this. There was slight look of a "loving reception" for her, now that the moment of reception had come. Was it, that in her terror of that hateful "dog," she had missed her opportunity?—or was it, that in her sense of unworthiness and uninvitedness, she had lingered out of sight, and so had failed to press herself upon the attention of the gracious "Keeper of the Gate"? Doubtless it was her sense of her slender right which was the mastering hindrance with her, and which now appeared to have heightened mere hindrance into blank obstruction. Yet it is little in Mercy's mind to go back. She will nurse her hope, she will urge her faith, she will gather up her will, until she has drained the last drop of her energy, of which there may still be something in reserve. Christiana, when at length she has begun to speak a word for her within, is startled by a crash of knocking without: "It is my friend"— "much dejected in her mind," she had already explained, "for that she comes, *as she thinks*, without sending for." Outside the Gate, when now it was opened, Mercy was prostrate in a swoon. "He took her by the hand," and roused her to consciousness. "'Oh, Sir,' said she, 'I am faint; there is scarce life left in me.' Tell me wherefore thou art come.' 'I am come *for that unto which I was never invited,* as my friend Christiana was. Hers was *from the King,* and mine was only *from her.* Wherefore I fear I presume. . . . As my Lord sees, I *am* come. And if there be any grace or forgiveness of sins *to spare,* I beseech that I, thy poor handmaid, may be partaker thereof.'" And "he led her gently in." "And now was Christiana, and her boys, *and Mercy,* received of the Lord at the head of the way."

It is plain, that here we have a study as careful and truthful as it is touching. The practical value of a picture like this is beyond price. The case is not a quite unusual one wherever clear decision for a Christian career is asserting itself before the eyes of the undecided. There will sometimes be a heart among the onlookers which is very susceptible to a happy infection from this loftiness of resolve. But the flame then seems to be caught at second-hand,—as in a sense it is ; and it is out of this peculiarity that the difficulty which besets the most of seeking souls will tend in such cases to spring. God is not felt to be in it. The whole movement can easily appear as if it were no more than humanly originated, and no more than humanly propelled. For when the soul is first stirred, by whatever means, to evangelical earnestness, and things begin to be seen as if a new fountain of light were pouring new aspects upon old realities, even familiar common-places are distrusted : the constant gospel-attitude of God towards all men, and the constant element of Divine contact which mingles itself with every worthier aspiration of the soul,—these fail to be grasped with firmness enough to be applied to the present exigency of experience. And this insufficiency of perception is apt to be complicated by the too veritable feeling of individual unworthiness—a feeling which not only is likely to be natural to those whose type of character renders them most susceptible to religious example, but a feeling, a sense, which also is now certain to be vivified under the closer view of the overpowering verities that fill the spiritual and eternal sphere of things. So the soul—as would seem needlessly, yet doubtless with results of deep discipline and of indelible teaching—is tossed or tormented, until it finds itself wondering in the sunshine of the Divine smile, upon the actual pathway of hope and righteousness.

We have to note, then, that the inspiration of a heavenward desire comes to Mercy as it were casually, through the new purpose which has taken hold of Christiana. We do not indeed meet this sort of influence for the first time now. In the instance of all who have gone upon pilgrimage, ever since Christian himself took his way with such seeming originality of resolve, human example has brought its tributary to the confluence of motives. Faithful bethought him of the need of going, because his fellow-citizen had gone. Hopeful was constrained to make for a pilgrim-life, because of the behaviour and the counsel of his two pilgrim-friends. Christiana was stricken with the needfulness of pilgrimage when she pondered the life and death of the husband whose pilgrim-ways she had so heartlessly disesteemed ; and the boys gave their voice for the journey very much because their father had ended his, and because their mother was beginning hers. But in all these instances, though in varying degrees, there was lapse of time enough for the entering-in of thoughts and emotions which developed the matter into a very personal one with them, and the movement got to have the drivings of spiritual necessity behind it. It was scarcely so with Mercy. From first to last she was rather drawn than driven. Although she was not within the attractions of a common domestic interest with this household, she was as ready to take Christiana's view of things as Christiana's own children had been ; and she had far less time to have her feeling brought abreast of her action. The family were wellnigh on the move when she caught something of their pilgrim-spirit—enough to put herself into motion with them. She accompanied them only provisionally, and in a manner prematurely: the ripening of the pilgrim-thought went on as she herself went on. Was this like a mere facility of character in her?—or was it like a mere tenacity of neighbourly friendship? To imagine this were to misjudge her. There is neither the shallow gush of ongoing, nor is there the imminent flood of backgoing, which distinguish your men of the Pliable stamp: her purpose is quiet, far-looking, self-denying, steady—faint at first, but every moment gaining strength from sober thoughtfulness. Nor does attachment to persons prove to be anything deeper than a kindly plea by which even she herself is in part deceived; the profounder motive soon ascends into more visible supremacy, and is acknowledged to be supreme alike by herself and by her companion. She gets into pilgrimage almost by surprise; and going forward with a gathering conviction of the sheer privilege of pilgrimage, and a growing persuasion that she is right in adventuring it on her own personal choice, she gradually braces herself 'to the whole demand of her position, in the struggling hope that all this felt rightness of action may somehow be vindicated by success.

It is not now difficult for us to make out the leading lines in the character of Mercy. Her young nature is rich in qualities which win our interest wherever we find them; and the dew is on them yet, in "this sunshine morning" of her years. She must have been a favourite among her neighbours in that street of the city,—affectionate as she was, unassuming, considerate of others, self-forgetful, and reverent towards all that was good and great, without as yet ruffling the citizen prejudices, or challenging the citizen wisdom, by any assertion of spiritual severance. That assertion, however, stood ready to arrive if ever it had fair opportunity. As her goodness and good-will expanded, and the grave realities of life pressed closer in around her,—as the strengths of evil began to be gauged by a sensitive conscience, and the foundations of good in the heart were felt to be less secure than it was well they should be, and the faculty of affectionate reverence groped far out beyond the limits of its present experience,—it became less likely that she would spend all her days among the settlers whose manners must often have offended her unblunted sense of what was true and worthy. We can more than imagine, that when this youthful neighbour went in that morning to Christiana's house, she went thither with a slumbering consciousness, the dream-whispers of which she had some- times been able to hear, that the city and its life did not meet all her need, nor promise to fulfil her rightful destiny. We can foretell, that this morning call of hers is probably charged for her with happy fate, and is of ill omen for her citizenship. For that gentle nature of hers will not recoil from danger if only she sees the way of right, nor from derision if only she perceives the path by which she may go on to answer the demands of her higher being. And she finds her neighbour on foot for a better city. She listens to her as she tells of the messages and the messengers that have come to her from its King. She hears her announce, like one inspired, that she has been " sent for ; " and she sees the very light of the City in her eye, steadied by a calm resolvedness to travel all the road that may stretch between her door and that abode where her husband has it so gloriously well with him. It strikes deep chords in the heart of Mercy. Thus casually touched, the hidden springs of her nature, themselves not at all casual, begin to well up within her to meet this firmament of verity that is now over-arching her where she stands. She feels more of respectful regard for Christiana at this moment than ever she has felt. Might she also go? That far-off City, that life of self-renouncing effort and lofty loyalty, this company,—they are more to her, she feels, and they are more for her, than anything that retains her here. She will satisfy herself further, by conversation with Christiana, about the "truth and life" there may be in all this; for she means to proceed with thoroughness, though she must needs proceed with little delay; and—is there not some wrench always at the thought of leaving the old city? But she is going all the while—is parting from it once for all, and scarcely knows she is; and by-and-bye she will feel that the separation is accomplished, and that her dearest kindred and she are getting far asunder. That nature of Mercy's, so gently strong, is in the grasp of God's grace, which is so much gentler and stronger still; and its inborn religiousness is about to be consciously linked to the God who gave it, and to be consecrated to all grateful service and noble fulfillings, from henceforth and for ever.

So, without "Book," or "letter," or anything more evidently heavenly than the fixed mind of a neighbour, Mercy comes to find herself a pilgrim in quest of admission at the portal of the King's highway. She has no sharp sense of lostness. It is not the *safety* of being upon the King's road which much moves her, but its surpassing *desirableness.* Her instincts towards rightness, and her cravings after a greater strength of goodness, incline her to this way, because it has come to her that this is the way of Him who is infinitely right and graciously best. She is longing for help to be good, and she is apprehending that this help lies along the way which Christian has trodden and Christiana is resolved to tread. This is her predominant motive. She has her fears : they are not fears lest she should be overtaken by doom in the city ; they are fears lest she may not be received—"lovingly," as her heart would have it—at the gate of the way to the better City. If she is not received at that gate—we almost believe she will accept the sentence as for her a just one, and will face the doom of the city with a heart sad but firm, and at the hour of calamity will lift her voice, through tears rather than terrors, saying, as we shall hear her saying soon, "I acknowledge that Thou dost all things well." But among all the mysteries which darken human experience, there is no place for so tremendous a mystery as this. Let Mercy advance to her great adventure; let her follow her truest impulses, though it may be through the darkness: she will scarcely suffer loss by her righteous courage, and she may win all that her heart desires to gain. She will see Christiana, at least, entered safely upon the way into which she has been "invited"! Yet it is very noteworthy, how the thought of being left behind fades insensibly out of the narrative, until, at length, Mercy herself seems to be as much amazed as terrified when she is actually confronted with the possibility of rejection. Her brave enterprise of spirit has been stimulating her juster instincts—fostering new faith, let us say—concerning the heart and purpose of the Divine One; and her own heart has been letting itself down, more really than she quite knew, upon the likelihood of her acceptance. At that shut door therefore, with the hum of the city far behind her, and the mire of the Slough upon her feet, and music pealing above the growlings of the beast-adversary, she who has hitherto pressed on so valiantly, "uninvited," cannot, will not, tamely accept of this frowning of fate. For a while wistfully, and then with gathering energy of look, and at last with tearful agony of purpose, she gazes upon that dumb gateway of her hope. *She shall have an answer*, even as she is a living being to whom God has given a will. If she hears no more than this—then, rather than silently turn her steps away from the path of righteousness, she is ready even now to shiver that gate to splinters, that she may enter, and may speak face to face with this kindly Keeper of the Gate, and may hear, with her eye on his, what her fate must be. No disaster which this daring may bring her can ever be great beside the disaster of being turned away without sign or word. Only once she knocked; but into this once, there was con·centrated a summer's day of more scattered summoning. Was she too impatient?—was she oblivious of how reasonable it was that she should apply on her own behalf, and should feel that this privilege of pilgrimage had need to be a personal thing between herself and the Good One? It may be so. But she naturally feared, with the light she had, that she was never to be a heavenward companion of Christiana's, and she flung the uttermost of her strength upon the hazard of knowing the worst;—and straightway she knew the best that ever she had known.

Mercy, then, has more and other in her character than we might expect from her name. For we must assume that this name of hers is in some measure descriptive, although she is far from being a mere allegorical shadow in whom a Christian virtue is personified. We look for marks of mercifulness in her young womanhood, and we do not fail to find them. But we find marks of more : we alight upon evidence of that for which we have not perhaps been looking. We are made witness of womanly strength and courage—of resolute will, and through-going energy, as real as they still are womanly. But were we right if we were thinking of mercy as if it must be a rather feeble thing?—or of this maiden, wearing its name so winningly, as if she must disclose no signs of well-harboured power? If we were, Bunyan shall at once set us upon truer thoughts. He will allow no such misconception of the Christian girl whom he would have us to know. Ere that first pilgrim-day is done, he will have shown us, with a surpassing lightness of touch that seems to leave nearly all the picturing to her own gentle self, what force of development is in her, what moral resource, what fearless self-abandonment to the sway of the right and the good. Fearless?—yes; for she feared, and held forward with her fears, and at last transformed her fears themselves into a storm of siege that carried the fortress around which they had become massed as an array of resistance. She feared—lest all her fearless following of righteousness might be in vain, because she felt that in herself she had no claim to a dignity so great. Without self-complacency, then, as well as without fear—dubious, even to some appearance of feebleness, because she knew herself better than she knew her God, and loved righteousness better than she loved herself apart from righteousness. Clearly, it is not Good-Nature that we can call this maiden : she has little of passive contentment, and little of a disposition to leave herself and all else undisturbed. She has gotten high aims, and she can strongly make her way to reach them. Her goodness *of* nature, which even hitherto has been urging itself into overflow as good-will and compassion and lovingness, has now its deep energies stirred with desire to have itself based and built upon foundations of ever-during strength, and it will suffer no obstacle but Divine decree to give it long obstruction. Her tenderness of nature is not an actionless saturation, but a dynamic of activity—now heavenward above all things.

But we must seek to trace a few of the threads of this character of Mercy's, in which these two sorts of moral fibre are twisted together so cunningly. For this work we shall need to welcome whatever light may reach us out of her entire recorded history.

The quality in her which is first to be noted is her *Unselfishness*. She has a disposition to look forth, and to go forth, from herself and her own personal concerns ; she has an instinct to communicate herself, her powers, her possessions, to those whom Providence has brought around her. There is implied in this a certain measure of sociableness, but it is implied rather as a means than an end : the end, if we follow it far enough, is beneficence. This Unselfishness is in her nature,—making her womanly, in the finest feature of womanliness, even before the pilgrimthoughts have led her growing character into a loftier order of growth. It is in her nature still when pilgrimage is doing its best for her,—making her still more womanly, in the finest feature of Christian womanliness ; for Christianity will not undo what is naturally amiable and worthy, but will only give it heightening and hallowing and enduring development. We saw how much she was engaged with the thought of " helping " Christiana, at the moment when she herself was awakening to great need of help. This combines two things which may be distinguished— thoughtfulness for others, and activity for others. We find the thoughtfulness even where the activity cannot come into the case,—as when they reached the spot where Christian's three sleepers were now " hanged up in irons." " What are those three men ?—and for what are they hanged there ? " She is moved with concern about them ; but immediately her concern widens off from themselves to possible victims of the " sloth and folly " which they taught as well as practised :—" But could they *persuade any* to be of their opinion ? "—We must get back, however, to her activity, as the more solid testimony to her Unselfishness. Whensoever opportunity offers, she never misses to afford us this testimony. We get a glimpse of her in the Palace when the door of the sitting-room is swung open to let in Mr Brisk. " Her mind was, to be always busying of herself in doing ; for when she had nothing to do for herself, she would be making of hose and garments *for others*, and would bestow them upon them that had need." Brisk "found her never idle," and the phenomenon misled him more than it is likely to mislead ourselves. "What!" he is forced to exclaim — "always at it!" "Yes, either for myself *or for others.*" "What dost thou with them?" "Clothe the naked." These "ill conditions" persisted in "troubling" her long after Mr Brisk had vanished. In the house of Gaius, where she becomes the wife of a better man, her hands and her time are still full of occupation that transcends any needs of her own :—"While they stayed here, Mercy, *as her custom was*"—(the historian looks for it now)—"*would be* making coats and garments to give to the poor, by which she brought up a very good report upon the pilgrims;"—an unwitting benefactor even of the cause and the followers of pilgrimage. She is a mother when they are making their long stay with Mnason in the city of Vanity. Her opportunity here is ample enough for all the extra-mural beneficence that her domestic duties can now permit her to indulge in. Accordingly, "Mercy, as she was wont"— (by this time it has become a very familiar idiosyncrasy of their expanding little brotherhood)—"*laboured much for the poor;* wherefore their bellies and backs blessed her, and she was there an ornament to her profession,"—there, where there were so many observing eyes; but Mercy was thinking less about keen eyes than about ill-clad backs and needy stomachs, and the blessing which these gave her only heartened her to toil on in her self-forgetful industry. We are ready to wish that the good Porter at the Palace could be witness of how the prayerful prophecy of his parting words is being fulfilled—"Let Mercy live and not die, and *let not her works be few.*"

But it was not her mind and hand alone that were unselfish; her heart was also. Her interest in others, and her lending of herself to others, far from being a mere mechanical appetency, was first of all a movement of affection beyond herself—a breaking-free from self-love. Christiana, who knew her well, addresses her, just a little way out of the city, as "*Loving* Mercy." She is emotional, as becomes a woman whether young or old; but she is emotional in the strictest and best acceptation of the word, —is most ready to be "moved outward" from her tenderest self towards definite objects, if only they do not freeze the flow of her feeling. She likes to give the best she has, which is her personal kindly affection—her charity of heart, whether in the phase of love, or of sympathy, or of pity; and it is under the lead of this that her beneficence takes its way. Her affectionateness does not helplessly depend upon response; but it finds lively satisfaction in such response, and it usually wins it. She is loved because she is lovable, and she is lovable most of all because she is "loving." There is a discernible tenderness in the manner of those whom we see to be resting their eye upon her, even if it be for the first time. We do not wonder at the gentleness of the Keeper of the Gate. The Interpreter does not surprise us when he calls her "sweetheart," "a Ruth;" and we expect that the attendants will "carry it lovingly to Mercy." Gaius, full of experience and tact as he is, does not quite conceal the fatherly regard with which Mercy inspires him: when he calls Christiana and Mercy "a lovely couple," it is no reflection either upon his gravity or his veracity to surmise, that he is thinking rather perhaps of the maiden than of the matron. And Christiana herself, so long her hourly companion, while she is too prudent to drop a hint of fondness or of flattery, is manifestly living under the winsome spell of this young nature, which from stage to stage is striking the roots of its inborn lovingness into ever-deepening soil, and hanging forth its flowers in richer hue and fragrance. The somewhat harder nature of Christiana must have owed something to this tenderer nature which leant upon hers so long—not in weakness, but in love ; yet, among "her children" who "wept" for her when she took her last journey, none would weep with a sincerer thought of having received much and imparted little than that "loving Mercy" who had now so much more to love.

For this outwardness of her emotions and activities embraces more than is represented even by beneficence which is nourished by love. Her outward look will sometimes fall upon what is great or excellent ; her interest will sometimes be engaged by those who are more or better than she can deem herself to be. The outward going of her heart must now and again be an upward going, if it be capable of such a movement. And of such a movement, whether of thought or emotion or action, Mercy is very capable indeed. She is *Reverent*, in all the degrees of Reverence —in respect, esteem, admiration ; in homage, submission, self-renouncement, obedience ; in lowly-heartedness ; in gratitude. Her nature is a religious nature. She would be religious even if she were not a Christian ; she is very deeply and very beautifully religious since she is a Christian. Her lowly estimate of herself in her total personality, —we may think of this as the negative pole of her Reverence. However it has come, and however much of it be natural to her, it is this which is potent behind all her perplexity about going without invitation, and about the presumption of her advance at the side of an invited one. She has never let her thoughts dote much upon herself ; but now the pure light of the City, the glance of its King, which seem as if they had come into the air around her, guide her eye inward with a sense of defect that is touched with dismay : anon she looks forth again, and far, "as her wont is," and the Righteous Lord of the good land seems so adorable, and His way so blessed, that she—is anything less unlikely ?—may not be at all worthy to be invited, or worthy even to be received without the trouble of invitation ! She will get light upon this, but the light will not a whit diminish her Reverence in any one of its forms. It is very touching to see and hear her after she has got so far as the presence of the Interpreter :—" And what moved *thee* to come hither ? " asks the venerable man, turning, not untenderly, to Mercy. " Then Mercy blushed, and trembled, and for a while continued silent. . . . So she began, and said, ' Truly, Sir, my want of experience is that which makes me covet to be in silence, and that also that fills me with fears of coming short at last. *I cannot tell of visions and dreams* as my friend Christiana can ; nor know I what it is to mourn for my refusing of the counsel of those that were good relations :'" how slender a virtue she magnifies into merit for " her friend "! . . . " And I am come, with all the desire of my heart, *and will go, if I may, with Christiana, unto her husband, and his King.*" The pilgrim-commonwealth is to understand, that Mercy desires to be permitted to travel on in the way to Christian's King, if only as a suffered attendant of Christian's widow. Such a spirit will not be unready to say, in respect of every mysterious proceeding which is indubitably Divine—" I confess my ignorance ; I spake what I understood not ; I acknowledge that Thou dost all things well." How will she feel in the Valley of Humiliation? Her sensations in that region, with its strange barometric sympathy, constrain her to make herself for a moment her theme ; when we must bethink us, that she has no thought of self-praise :— " I think I am as well in this Valley as I have been *anywhere else in all our journey : the place, methinks, suits with my spirit.*" Nor can she be silent about herself when the case of Mr Fearing is before them :—" If *I* might also speak my heart, I must say that *something* of him has also dwelt in me ; for I have ever been more afraid of . . . the loss of a place in Paradise than I have been of the loss of other things :" she would " part with all the world to win it." And when blessings fall upon such a heart, it will be deeply moved with gratitude. "*I of all* have cause to leap for joy," she says in her fervour as she begins to realise that she is accepted within the Gate. When the Reliever has left them, and she corrects her innocent notion that they had "now been past all danger," we find her consoling Christiana for her "neglect" by urging that "their Lord had thereby taken occasion to make manifest the riches of His grace ; for He, as we see," she continues, "has followed us with *unasked kindness*, and has delivered us . . . *of His mere good pleasure.*" So, also, there is more of gratitude, and of conscious incapacity, than of fear, in her almost passionate words to Great-heart when he must go back : "O that we might have thy company to our journey's end ! " And long after, when she obtained a gift of the coveted mirror from Sincere the Shepherd, "she bowed her head and gave thanks," as unfeignedly as she would have done at the beginning of her way.

We cannot have gone thus far without perceiving that the nature we are analyzing is one which is unusually fine as to its texture. Mercy is a maiden, a woman, who enjoys all the pleasure, and suffers all the pain, of a keen *Sensibility*. The chords of her whole being, whether physical, or mental, or moral, are of delicate quality. In this respect also she is a woman of women. On the side of her physical constitution, we have early hint of it in that collapse of her strength at the Gate, and more subtle evidence of it in her observable exhilaration at the resting-place on the Hill Difficulty. We see it working from this side, along with her reverence, when we witness her blushings and tremblings and silence before the Interpreter, or when we mark the blushes with which her riper womanhood accepts the gift of "the great glass." We see it working from this side, along with her sense of the awful, when we find her "looking white" as she hearkens to the sounds from "the hole in the hill." We hear it, mingling with an apprehension which is more moral than physical, in her words concerning that " most cruel dog " which was "thereabout " when she was outside the Gate. We feel it to be at work, as a delicacy of instinct, in her relation to the young lads of the story : we hear her addressing herself, and very affably, to James, but never to any other of the youths, and only to him when he is comparatively a child;—not that she is under any prudish thraldom of self-restraint, or that we must interpret this silence with an unnatural literalness, but that, within the compact limits of the story, any represented interchange of words with them would convey an impression more or less at variance with the modest self-respect, and the maidenly regard to the privilege of her accepted companionship, which must have ruled her manner as a maiden-pilgrim of that company.   Yet, before she had got further than the Palace and Mr Brisk, she can let forth the secret, that she " might have had husbands afore now "—a fortune possible enough to many other maidens with attractions of person; but she "spake not of it to any "—a considerate modesty which is not so possible save to maidens like Mercy.   And we see the same Sensibility operating in the region of emotion, when she tells, with flushed cheek, of how her "heart burned" while Christiana spoke that morning in her house, and of how " heavy a heart " hers was as she came away from the city thinking of her unhappy friends : so, indeed, we see it operating thus, both as to "burning" and as to "heaviness," along the whole course of her beneficent and sympathetic life.—We have been recalling incidents in which it was pain rather than pleasure which Mercy's Sensibility brought her; we can recall incidents, happily, where the joy it brought her wellnigh verged round upon pain again. Her lively happiness at the Gate will occur to us.   At the Interpreter's House, where the light o   acious truth was let in upon her Sensibility, she "could not sleep for joy," but "lay blessing and praising God." In the Palace, where the comfortings and nurturings of intercourse with the good are thrilling her Sensibility to its centre, her experience on that first night is one of ecstasy, in which body and mind and spirit are all pitched to the highest strain of delight: it is "wonderful!—music . . music . . music" as long as she is awake; and when she is no longer awake, weary with her gladness, she "laughs in her sleep," it appears—"laughs heartily;" and she has a "sweet dream" to confess to her companion at the sunrise. This Sensibility, no doubt, will yet have to work within the shadow, even the shadow of itself,—as when they were groping on through the thickest of the dreary valley: "*Then* said Mercy to Christiana," touching keys of recollection which the others hardly possessed,—"There is not such pleasant being here as at the Gate, or at the Interpreter's, or at the house *where we lay last.*" No; but this Sensibility of Mercy's must have occasion yet, and many a time, and by-and-bye when the life-dream itself is past, to "laugh again."

It must be owned, that this fineness of nature, with its lively susceptibilities and aversions, is not without its perils. Charity and reverence will do much to preserve it in a "sweet reasonableness;" yet it needs more than this if the character is to be adequate: it must have tempering, and steadying, and strongly competent control. This Sensibility of Mercy's, we have seen, pervades her whole nature. In this pervasiveness, which might seem to threaten weakness, we may recognise the lurking promise of strength. It involves a delicacy of the moral sense, and it hints at a quickness of moral emotion. These look at least in the direction of strength that is of the highest. And among the moral characteristics of this maiden we are free to set our eye upon more than mere delicacy of moral fibre.

This sensitive character is fortified—more sufficiently than even the highest order of sensitiveness, simply of itself, could fortify it—by the group of qualities which we may gather under the name of her *Right-Heartedness.* The point at which this group touches her Sensibility is the point of Will. A strength and constancy of purpose, in great part natural to her, is the electric link through which all tempering, and steadying, and control, are flowing in upon her sensitiveness. This current allies itself most congenially with her moral nature. But we must look further within the group to make out the power which gives so unfailing direction to this current of will, and really sharpens it into ethical purpose. It is a loyalty to all that is true—a passion for all rightness—a supreme longing to be herself profoundly right. This is in her nature ; but, under the touch of grace, it is transfigured into a "yearning" after harmony with the eternally Righteous One. This again, in contact with her will, becomes a steadfast ordering of herself under that Will of His which is found to be so full at once of truth and grace ; and, in contact with her Unselfishness, passes into a public spirit to which her very Sensibility will sometimes lend the appearance of sternness. It is thus we can explain the energy of such words as those alongside of which Christiana's sound so mild, when they were invited to inspect the three hanged ones at a nearer distance : "No, no ; *let them hang, and their names rot, and their crimes live for ever against them. . . .*

> "Now, then, you three hang there, and be a sign
> To all that shall against *the truth* combine."

This backbone of resoluteness which gives stay and form to her character is so closely knit with all in her that makes for rightness, that it is impossible to define how far it is natural strength of will, and how far it is force of will under

the impulses of moral earnestness. The two were connected closely enough when, at the Gate, she "thought she
must either knock again *or die*,"—as, before, at the Slough
—"Come, let us *venture ;*" and as, afterwards, near the
Devil's garden, "Mercy also, as well as she *could*, did
what she *could* to shift them "—the peculiar Apollyon of
the defenceless women. There is the same blending of
righteousness and resolvedness in her words as the truth
dawns concerning Mr Brisk :—"*I purpose never* to have a
clog to my soul,"—even though it should offer itself in the
guise of a husband : "*that* I *purpose never* to admit of as
long as I live :" "I am for none of them all." (The words
which immediately follow these are—"*Now Matthew*, the
eldest son of Christiana, fell sick ;" and a page onwards
occurs the appeal—"If thou lovest Mercy." No chivalrous
reader will allow this literary circumstance to detract from
his estimate of the self-sacrifice of Mercy's resolutions.)
And indeed there is the same duplex force to be discerned
in the patient steadfastness with which she adheres to her
lifelong habit of doing good and working righteousness.

Perhaps we see most of the involuntary instinct of rightness which is in her when it is her ingenuous Truthfulness,
her simple Candour, that breaks into view. " I made
account we had now been past all danger, and that we
should *never see sorrow more*"—"Sir, I *see nothing*"—" I
am *glad* of my *dream*"—" Pray, if they invite us to stay
awhile, let us *willingly accept* the proffer "—" I must say,
that something of him has also dwelt in *me ;*"—all such
utterances, with their childlike simplicity, come from near
the source of all the most royal strength which Mercy ever
displayed. This Candour, it is noticeable, seldom takes
the form of confession of positive sin or error : she had
little of this which she could mourn with honesty, and she
will not confess what she does not feel. " Then said they
yet further unto him [at the Gate], ' We are sorry for our

sins, and beg of our Lord his pardon,—and further information what we must do;'"—Mercy's share in this regret,
although it must be permitted to stand for more than the
almost perfunctory record of it might mislead us into thinking, would not appear to have been at all overwhelming,
howsoever thoroughly hearty. Her moral regret is a thing
of quiet growth, and is a thing greatly more lived than
spoken. She rather reaches on to what is before than
lingers back upon what is behind. It is shortcoming
rather than transgression that grieves her; and she is
always candid enough, at least in thought and deed and
bearing, about the gravity of this.

So, all the outwardness with which we began our study
of Mercy's character, though never to be lost sight of in any
aspect of that character, has been leading us round to an
inwardness from which all the outwardness gets its quality
and measure. Her character is above all a moral character—this, intensified and heightened by a spirituality which
thrives through a hungering and thirsting after righteousness, and through the feasting which continues to fill it.
She aspires to be "pure in the heart," and she does begin
to "see God." Inwardness the deepest—outwardness the
loftiest. She has sought God in the way of seeking His
righteousness, and she finds both. That dream of hers in
the Palace—so far, and yet not so very far, on her way ;—
it were well to steady our eye perhaps on this, for it is the
crisis of promise which enwraps all fulfilment of this
method of hers. This dream within the Dream is in itself
striking and beautiful ; it is, moreover, brimming with
character. She was sitting, she thought, *"all alone in a
solitary place."* She was *"bemoaning the hardness of her
heart."* Many gathered around her,—mocking her, hust-
ling her. A winged one glided forward to her side :
" *Mercy*, what aileth thee? . . . Peace be to thee." He
wiped away her tears, and clad her in silver and gold—

adorned her, crowned her, and led her away, saying—
" *Mercy,* come after me." They arrived at a golden gate
—at a throne, from which One said to her, " *Welcome,
daughter."* " The place looked bright and twinkling, like
the stars ; *and I thought that I saw your husband there.*
So I awoke from my dream.—*But did I laugh ?* " This is
perfect,—setting retrospect and prospect in one compact
jewel of representation. But its best value lies in its significance as a gathering-up for Mercy of all arrears of spiritual
experience. She is abreast of Christiana now. " Dreams
and visions" have come even to her at last. The King
Himself has had regard to the " uninvited " one. She too
has been " sent for," while she was feeling " all alone " in
spirit amid her journeying companionship, and was penitent after her own manner,—" bemoaning the hardness of
her heart." Perhaps she " *did* laugh ; " for a beatitude was
once spoken which says —" Blessed are ye that weep
now " . . .

Her very considerable *Intellectual Qualities* took strict
order under the sway of what was moral, what was spiritual,
in her. Her Curiosity, which is easy to be noted, takes
usually a direction which is at least inferentially for the
ends of spiritual advancement. Her prayer of inquiry concerning that " filthy cur " at the Gate—(one can appreciate
her cordial phraseology in this connection) ; her request,
" Mother, if it might be, I would see the hole in the hill,"
and her " hearkening awhile " there ; the remarkable passage about her " longing " for " the great glass ; "—these
incidents, the last two being the final glimpses we have of
her, bear testimony to the spiritual subserviency of her
intelligence as much as to its liveliness. Her Observing-
ness is as womanly as her Curiosity is : " I *thought* he
gave you something,"—though her thought only transpired,
we reflect, when Christiana was telling what it was. Her
Sound Judgment is most phenomenally attested by her

whole behaviour at the period when she "had a visitor," attracted thither by her "fair countenance" and her busy hands. Her dream itself might stand for proof of some gift of Imagination; and there are little sallies of hers which bespeak a bright playfulness that is akin to Humour. And, with all her activity, she is Meditative, and has pleasure in retired contemplation. With our knowledge of her, we should certainly look for this; but it might be difficult to find evidence of it had we not her own words, which are almost as valid witness as actual happenings would be :—"I love to be in such places where there is no rattling with coaches, nor rumbling with wheels." (We can afford to let the allegory drop for a moment.) "Methinks, here," she continues, "one may without much molestation be thinking what he is, whence he came, what he has done, and to what the King has called him. Here one may think, and break at heart, and melt in one's spirit, until one's eyes become like the 'fish-pools of Heshbon.'" It was the Valley of Humility; but it is plain she was not out of character, even literally, when she dreamed of being "all alone in a solitary place."

What Mercy was as a companion we have had some occasion to see. What she was as a daughter, and still more what she was as a wife and a mother, we are very much left to surmise. Bunyan can entrust her to our best opinion as she retreats from our view within the envelopments which gather around her ripening life. When she is brought to dwell in that border-region of comparative abiding, where her Sensibility would be almost exposed to strain until it became mellowed with the soberings of matronhood, we think nevertheless that we know on which side she would be likely to take rank among "those 'devout women' who," as Matthew Arnold affirms, "in the history of religion have continually played a part in many respects so beautiful, but in some respects so mischievous."[1]   While the years went on, her home and her person would beam with ever richer illustration of the "beautiful" Christian grace whose name she bears, and she would grow into a truer picture of that grace as set forth by a Matthew of remoter date (Roydon) :

> " A *sweet attractive* kind of grace,
>   A full assurance given by *lookes;*
> Continuall comfort in a *face*
>   *The lineaments of Gospell bookes.*"

But it is as a Christian maiden that Mercy has place in the " Pilgrim," and as a Christian maiden that she has so surpassing value as a personation of character.   Not that every girl who aims at excellence will either reach it, or be designed to reach it, just after the lovely model which is before us here.   None the less is this picture fitted to bring both stimulus and guidance to every maiden whose better sympathies are not quite poisoned down by the atmosphere of frivolity and vanity, of selfish disingenuousness or petty worldliness of mind and heart, which she may too probably have been born to breathe.   She can scarcely but have healthier influences not far off from her—straight-going Christian choice, and lightful Christian example.   Let her permit these to touch her, to move her, to give direction to her life,—not distrusting them, nor fearing them, nor misjudging them ; for assuredly they represent all radiant rightness as it never has been represented in a world so smitten to the heart with wrongness as ours unquestionably is.   There is but one path to the sterling adjustment of our veriest selves—an adjustment that is full enough of hopefulness to be thorough, and thorough enough to be full of hopefulness : it is the path which Mercy took, and found to lead her to all that her deep nature ever craved. It does make some demand upon thoughtfulness, and it

---

[1] "Literature and Dogma," ch. ix.

does make much demand upon fixedness of will, to gird the soul thus into travelling trim, and go,—leaving those behind who elect to stay, and leaving those to deride who are too weak to follow. The effort may be great to a sensitive nature, thus to get once for all upon the eternal track. But it is so true a path for a fresh womanly life— it so begins to fulfil whatever of loveliest promise young womanhood can wear—that if effort be ever ungrudged when it seems likely to bring the graces of attractiveness or the prospects of wellbeing, this lealest of efforts can only be grudged by such as have not the best weal of their womanhood candidly and bravely at heart.

And this very Mercy of Bunyan's is still to be seen among us. Can we not call up her image in the person of some one we know, or have known? We see her tenderness, her self-obliviousness, her sunny good-will, her strong-hearted love of righteousness and purity and holy peace; and we feel that the world is the richer for her, her friends the better and the happier for possessing her. We may have seen her pass, whether imperceptibly or with more of observation, out of the region which is pictured by the hopeless city, where she had tried to be satisfied with what was agoing there, and on to the way towards the region which is pictured by the Supernal City, with her heart set and settled upon all highest fruitions of her inmost destiny. She was lovely always, but she was never near her best till then. She feels, and tells, that she is *right*, now that she is moving on in the highway of her finest impulses, under the governance of the King whose abode is filling the eye of her faith as the central abode of all righteous affection. She had been more tired than she knew—more weary at least than she confessed to herself—of repressing her spiritual instincts, and putting off her profoundest aspirations with Christless responses of mind and hand : she is now set free from all this bondage, and her very dissatisfactions have the air of boundless ambitions of holy liberty. She is Mercy yet—more this, more her very self, than before : she is tenderer, stronger, more full of sympathy, more inventive of help, more unwearied in helping, more wide in her vision of how far the horizon-line of human need extends. The schedule of poor-rates does not compass the history of her temporal benefactions, nor does her pew-rent stand in full of all claims as between her and the millions of the spiritually destitute at home and abroad. She wellnigh holds her whole self at the disposal of genuine need, whether of body or of spirit. Nor has she any thought that she is doing wonderful things ; she is only doing what her heart dictates, and what her King permits her, honours her, to do. But the Church itself is the better for her ; and it greatly needs—more needs, it may be, than relishes—the resolute righteousness which all her untiring good-will only sweetens. Whatsoever of charity may be in her, she has little heart for feckless compromise between the Church and the world, and would fain see the world blessed upon the plan of keeping the Church still purely and strenuously the Church—a power more than ever in contact with the world, and a power less than ever lost in it. Her beneficence, which is hardly to be called a timid thing, yet shrinks from participation in methods of promoting Church prosperity which embody the world's ways, and borrow the world's tricks, and give these an unhappy consecration alike for Church and world. She thinks she would not willingly have given herself to embellish a hired booth in Vanity Fair, or have equipt herself to beguile the citizens into parting with their gold, for the support of the hard-up pilgrim-brotherhood who were sojourning among them,—at least never again after she made sure that so many of her laborious " coats and garments " went for half their value into the hands of greedy devotees of Beelzebub, and that all the while her companions of the pilgrim-sisterhood were so apt to give the rein to many of the least Christian propensities, and many of the most selfish littlenesses, beside which the smuggled rafflings and lottery-lists did but slender damage to Christian rightness. She feels as if the Church were almost brought to a desperation of spiritlessness before her eyes, when she sees her stretching forth an empty palm to Mr Gripeman as he passes, or hanging about the door of Mr Hold-the-world, or bespeaking consideration from Mr By-ends, that it may be well with her, and she may not starve ! Our modern Mercy would give half her living to see the Church doing her beneficent work in the world with a holy nobility of spirit, which cannot stoop to take the world's crumbs with thankfulness, or cringe to deal smoothly with godlessness when it chances to be affluent in possession or in power. She cannot make the Church what she would like to see it ; but she will make the best she can of at least one member of it, and shall wish her influence to travel as widely as God shall approve. And she will hope—doubtless she will pray—that many with a more potent influence than hers shall arise in the Church, and shall thrill it with a purer strength, after she herself has gotten fulfilment of all which old Honest wished for Bunyan's Mercy, when he said—" Mercy is thy name ; by mercy shalt thou be sustained, and carried through all those difficulties that shall assault thee in the way, till thou shalt come thither where thou shalt look the Fountain of Mercy in the face with comfort." [1]

[1] Note M.

XIV.

HONEST.

IN aiming at a fairly copious representation of religious life, Bunyan could not afford to neglect the element of age. His Second Part therefore, with its purpose of wide inclusiveness, takes this element into full account. The First Part had almost overlooked it. Middle age prevails there, with only limited deviations from the implied prime of manhood. Ignorance, perhaps Talkative also, lean to the side of youthfulness, but they are not of the brotherhood. Even Hopeful seems only younger than Christian to the extent of the interval between Christian's setting-out and his own; and we never see Christian himself as a man of advanced years. It is different when we open the Second Part. Diversity in length of days is now a feature which is brought more explicitly into view. Christiana starts in middle life, but is filling the acknowledged place of an "aged matron" before we see her depart. Mercy sets out in maidenhood, and is lost to us at about the same period of life at which Christiana comes into view. The sons are in a gradation of boyhood, which we follow until it passes into the haze of an early manhood, with its furthest point reaching perhaps to the age of Hopeful, or of their own father, when we first found them. Great-heart, as far as we reckon age in him at all, restores and emphasises the mature manhood of the First Part; nor is it much otherwise with Valiant and Stand-fast, though they bear themselves as if rather on the nearer side than the further side

of their prime : indeed, in the versified Preface, Valiant is
spoken of as " a very youth." Gaius is ripe in years, and
Mnason is older still,—sheltering their hoary heads,
however, under roofs of settlement. But Honest—"old
Honest," "old Mr Honest," "the old gentleman,"—he it
is (avowedly enough, as becomes his name and character)
who is brought into our acquaintance as the venerable
pilgrim—as the "aged disciple" who is making his progress
a visible one along the way towards the City.

It was due to old age, and it was due to Christianity,
that Bunyan should invest Christian old age for us with a
body and soul, and should let us see, in all naturalness
and truthfulness, how it also would comport itself among
the affairs and the company of the Pilgrimage. The
Allegory is considerably the richer for this debt, since the
Dreamer has discharged it with all the heartiness of a
labour of love as well as of truth. He has given us no
character which is more firmly drawn than this ripe one
which so consistently sustains the name of " Honest."
There is none whose individuality is better marked, or is
more happily carried clear of every other from the first
moment to the last. Perhaps no figure has so much of
crisp livingness, or so much of a genial originality which
yet holds itself within the strict limits of likelihood. The
place which old Honest fills in this Second Part can only
be fully realised by imagining—what is difficult to imagine
—the Second Part without him. There is a bright breezi-
ness which enters the story when he enters it : a sunny
rustle passes over the company, like a rippling of summer
wind across a ripening cornfield ; and the blithe stir never
long subsides till the journey is ended.

The word which Bunyan selects for the name of this
pilgrim is a word which may bear a sentence of remark,
by way of breaking ground in the consideration of the
character which he has filled in under the name. When

people of his day used the word " honest," they were apt to put a richer meaning into it than we commonly put now.[1] There may therefore be some occasion for us to expand our modern conception of the degree of meaning which Bunyan would probably design in the name. Perhaps we are entitled to assume, that, to Bunyan's mind, the man who could worthily bear the name of " Honest " was a man whose character was of first-rate rank and quality—no mere commonplace man of respectable integrity, but a man whose integrity stood like a Greek column, and whose candour shone like snow in sunlight, among the average honesties of men. We may even permit ourselves to guess, that when the Dreamer saw in imagination a pilgrim-figure who answered his ideal of "honest," he saw a man in whom every natural medium of expression was finely perspicuous, whether it were the word of the life, or the deed of the hand, or the deportment and the very form of the person—all of them toned to a commanding gracefulness of symmetry, because they were harmonised to the one regnant quality of translucent uprightness.

When we have kept our eye a little upon this old pilgrim, we may be unwilling to quarrel with the fitness of his name, even if we regard the word as holding all the meaning that ever it held at its best. And it may be noted about this name, that it is more ethical and less exclusively spiritual, more human and less specially Christian, than almost any other name in the roll of pilgrims. That of " Great-heart " may match it in this respect, but he is exceptional as a pilgrim. Bunyan seems here to bethink him, that Christianity is morality raised to its highest power. He bethinks him again, that one of the choicest of the evil reports which unevangelical people bring up against men of Christian profession, and bring up without

[1] Note X.

variation or weariness from age to age, is the "hypocrisy" in them, the dishonest meanness, which, it is implied, presents so unfavourable a contrast to their own honest, unaffected, unpretentious living. At the heart of it, this is the challenge which unspiritual ethics throws to spiritual faith. The ripest of all the pilgrims, therefore, unwittingly takes up the challenge and answers it—answers it as it can best be answered, by living it out of countenance before the eyes of men, and in the absence of that prejudice which casts its fogs around every Christian character when it is only displayed in real life! Honest is great in that very virtue which worldly righteousness reckons to be so much its own and to be so little the Christian's ; and he is not a whit less clearly Christian than he is totally and admirably honest—the embodiment of Christian ethics on the side of transparent and incorruptible rectitude. To how many anti-Puritan sneers is old Honest the quiet Puritan reply !

This Honest, it is pleasing to find, is not only old in years, but is old also in pilgrimage. There is nothing to forbid the conjecture that he may have been afoot for the City before Christian himself was. "I am, as you see, an old man," he says, not long after he comes into the story, "*and have been a traveller in this road many a day.*" The greater part of the old man's pilgrim-history lies away behind the clear narrative,—not altogether to his own disadvantage, and plainly to the advantage of the narrative itself. The haze of uncertain distance into which his past pilgrimage extends, suggesting no more than faint outlines of fact to give direction to fancy, throws an air of almost mysterious interest around his presence in the actual history; while it may be that it veils some earlier incidents which might tend, not very justly, to depress the esteem inspired in us by our knowledge of him in his maturer days alone. And the narrative itself, by the late period at which

it receives him, not only gains in variety, but obviates
something of the tediousness of repetition. Yet the
glimpses we get into his past are not without freshness.
If we prefer to surmise that his setting-out was a movement
quite independent of Christian's, or perhaps even earlier
than his, the surmise will not be discountenanced by the
little which we come to know concerning that movement.
He did not hail from the City of Destruction, but from a
"town" that was "worse," as Great-heart affirms and
Honest himself agrees. "I came from the town of
Stupidity : it lieth about four degrees beyond the City of
Destruction. . . . We are more off from the sun, and so
are more cold and senseless ; but was a man in a mountain
of ice, yet if the Sun of Righteousness will arise upon him,
his frozen heart shall feel a thaw. *And thus it hath been
with me.*" Mr Fearing, we afterwards learn, was a native
of the same town ; " which lies four degrees to the *northward* of the City of Destruction," says Feeble-mind, who
himself came from a different region still. The geography
and climate of the evil world are somewhat opening out
before us, as is truthful they should.[1] It becomes probable, then, that Honest had personal knowledge of Mr
Fearing at an early date. "When he first began to think
of what would come to us hereafter, I," says the old man,
"was *with* him"—presumably for counsel and company,
and by way of Evangelist to this "troublesome" brother ;
for the Allegory must bear a little straining in some
direction at this point, and the direction we are left to
choose.

This is the sum of our knowledge concerning the origin
of Honest's pilgrim-life. What were his fortunes, up to
the date of his appearing, there is no record to tell. Our
curiosity is not indulged, save to the extent of plausible
inference, as to whether he found his way into the "road"

[1] Note O.

by the familiar Wicket-gate, or whether the Slough lay across his path, or even whether his journey led him into the mansions of the Interpreter and of the ladies of grace. ("He had been entertained there awhile," says Great-heart of Fearing at the Gate—"as *you know* how the manner is:" he is addressing Honest. "I had heard of you before, *by my Master*," he says on their first meeting. And Honest himself we find saying of Self-will—"I persuade myself he never came in at the Gate that stands at the head of the way.") He is in the common road now; and he himself is the evidence that he has come rightly and well, by whatever route he may have travelled. His fellow-townsman Mr Fearing, heard of as being both at the Slough and at the Gate, had his guide from the Interpreter's House to the River; but he evidently travelled as far as the Interpreter's without a companion, and certainly without Honest. Mr Feeble-mind also, as we gather, took the Gate in his way, with the Interpreter's and the Hill in their due course. So may Honest have done; but we look away into the haze, and have to guess that he did, and to fancy after what fashion he did it. This is a new thing in our study of the "Pilgrim." We were not made witnesses, indeed, even of Faithful's first pilgrim-days; yet we heard much of them, and heard it from his own lips. Hopeful, who was longer in coming upon the scene than Honest himself, was still led to disclose to us the whole history of his becoming a pilgrim. Even Feeble-mind, in the grateful moments of his deliverance, pours forth a rapid summary of how it had gone with him since he took to that way of life. But Honest makes scarcely a sign concerning his past history; indeed, some dubious hints of it, such as his apparent acquaintance with Gaius and his inn, only puzzle us the more. Nor does Great-heart, who knew something of it, give us any light. Plainly, old Honest was not brought forward to furnish any illustration for us of Christian life in its bud, but to unveil it before our gaze when in the flush of its fruitage.

Some demand was made upon Bunyan's ingenuity when he would bring into the midst of the story so long-travelled a pilgrim as this. No method by which he could manage the matter would be able to preserve the entire consistency of the Allegory; but it were difficult to imagine any device more happy in the circumstances than the one he has chosen. The pilgrim-company is aglow with the victory over Maul, following as it did upon their emergence from the Valley of Darkness. They had reached almost the precise spot where Christian overtook Faithful, and where the pleasantness of the road made a grateful contrast to the experience which had troubled the immediate past. They had their eye on an oak that stood ahead of them by the side of the way;—and here the road may have had something of the "room" which is ascribed to it when Talkative was accosted, at a point but a little further on. When they reached the tree, they found lying beneath its shade "*an old pilgrim fast asleep*,"—a pilgrim assuredly, as they could well judge by "his clothes, and his staff, and his girdle." When Great-heart awoke him, "the old gentleman, as he lift up his eyes, cried out, 'What's the matter? —who are you?—and what is your business here?'" Here were "none but friends." "Yet the old man gets up, and stands upon his guard, and will know of them what they were." Great-heart explains. "Then said *Mr Honest*, 'I cry you mercy [I beg your pardon]; I feared that you had been of the company of those that sometime ago did rob Little-faith of his money; but, now I look better about me, I perceive you are *honester* people." And what would he or could he have done if they had been the robbers? "Done! why, I would have fought as long as breath had been in me; and had I done so, I am sure you could never have given me the worst on it; for a Christian

can never be overcome unless he should yield of himself."
"Well said, *father Honest*" (Great-heart unfortunately
addresses him by name before he has inquired what his
name is)--"for by this I know that thou art a cock of the
right kind; for thou hast said the truth." "And by this,
also, *I* know that thou knowest what true pilgrimage is, for
all others do think we are the easiest overcome of any."
With the quick shrewdness of kinship, they are rapidly
finding out each other. His name and place? "*My name
I cannot*" . . . "'Your name is *Old Honesty*, is it not?'
So the old gentleman blushed, and said 'Not Honesty in
the abstract, but Honest is my name, and I wish that my
nature shall agree to what I am called.' . . . Then the old
gentleman saluted all the pilgrims," warmly addressing
each in turn; and he was one of them from that hour, as
if he had never been else.

We feel already as if this new pilgrim were not much of
a stranger to us, so fully has the device of his abrupt introduction answered its end. Old pilgrimage and new have
come together without a shock. The circumstance of his
being discovered asleep, and in a sleep so profound,
operates with the indefiniteness of the chronology to ease
the pressure which the long duration of his journeying
must lay upon the story. At the same time, his sound
slumber on the wayside is itself a mark of advanced age and
of failing bodily vigour; for in his case we must account
sleep to have nothing of its unhappy spiritual significance,
but only a physical and literal bearing,—as when afterwards he "nods" during the prolonged conference in the
lamp-lit room of Gaius. The felicitous reference to the
mishap of Little-faith—an event that took place "some
time ago," and yet is so fresh in the mind of the old man
that he imagines it may be repeated on the spot—further
abets the purpose of mingling the past and the present so
as to obliterate exactness of date. His momentary con-

fusion too, and the slow adjustment of his awaking faculties to the actual state of things, are not only eminently natural for a weary man who has a long life behind him, but also give admirable opportunity for flashing upon us true gleams of acquaintance with his character as a man who has a life before him yet, and a life to be lived henceforth alongside of the pilgrims we already know so well. Before we quit the shadow of the oak, we have gotten a good deal of light concerning the sort of man we have found. We think we see him : the good farmer of Grand-Pré reminds us of him, and the simile of the oak in the description is an acceptable coincidence :—

" Stalwart and stately in form was the man of seventy winters :
Hearty and hale was he, an oak that is covered with snow-flakes ;
White as the snow were his locks, and his cheeks as brown as the oak-
    leaves." [1]

He will be " hot " with his foes, and warm with his friends. He will be open-hearted in the midst of safety, and strong-hearted in the presence of peril. He will be " cleare and straight," as Herbert speaks, in all the doings and believings, the followings and shunnings, that belong to pilgrimage. He will be a man of genial trustiness—steadfast, but not hard—both worthy of trust and quickly winning it. And with all his veteran courage and well-seasoned resolvedness, he shall be as modest as a woman when his own excellencies look him in the face. Even Great-heart himself has found a worthy companion ; and every pilgrim, from Christiana to James, recognises an unlooked-for friend.

But now that the King of the way has brought this man out of his comparative solitude, and bestowed him on the company whose fortunes we are following, we have no

---

[1] " Evangeline," part I.

need to pause at probabilities as to the character which is his. He leaves us in no doubt as to what is in him. We cannot give heed to him long until we discern three sets of qualities playing into each other before us : they may be summed up by these three words—Singleness, Efficiency, Delicacy.

The SINGLENESS of this man leaves no part of his nature outside of its sway. He is single in heart, in will, in mind. There are no folds or doublings either in his make or in his manners. His life is a life of straight lines, with a distaste for curves. He has little skill in policy, and little capacity for expediency, even when these may be innocent and really advantageous. He was not constructed for diplomacy, and he has given himself no training in its arts. Judged by a standard of perfection, we may have to acknowledge some approach to defect in him at this point ; but we may forgive it when we find how surely we can count upon him, and how clearly we can follow him. And we may do more than forgive it when we take note of the unentangled movement and cordial simplicity which distinguish his whole deportment as a man and as a Christian.

The Singleness of *Heart*, the child-like guilelessness of him, which never gets degraded into an unmanly simpleness, is one of his most charming characteristics. He seems to have nothing within the whole region of his affections which has any slenderest affinity to untruthfulness or unreality. He has some impatience of all concealment : we can even imagine that he has to put pressure upon himself to keep the seal of secrecy unbroken concerning what it would be quite indiscreet to disclose ;—an insecure repository of insignificant mysteries, as all gossips must have found that nature of his to be. But it is not love of telling, it is not incontinence of what he knows which thus moves him ; it is the instinct he has to be thoroughly truthful, and the irksomeness to him of bearing a part in what has even the appearance of other than open truth.

This pervading truthfulness will give proof of itself in everything and always. It is seen first of all, perhaps chief of all, in his outward representation of his own inward character. He has faculty enough to dissemble cleverly if he pleases, and he has enough knowledge of men to play the pretender with success if he has the mind to do it ; but he dissembles none, and he pretends nothing. He would be thought to be just what he is ; therefore, just what he is—nothing finer, or more, or other,—that he appears. The profit of unreality he reckons nowise equal to the loss. If he would be better thought of, he recognises no way to this but by becoming better to his own consciousness, and then simply appearing to others what he has now become to himself. He cannot endure that he should profess other than is in him—more of good, or even less of evil, than he believes to be literally his. It is with manifest zest that he leaps back upon the theme of his antecedents, and dwells upon the circumstances which have most of discredit in them :—" My *name* I cannot ;—but—I came from the town of *Stupidity*. . . . How could you guess that I am such a man since I came from *such a place?*"—a place of numb insensibility and frozen hearts. Yet, but for his modesty, which itself is sincere enough after its own manner, he would frankly claim all that he finds in himself worthy of praise, no less than acknowledge all that he finds in himself worthy of blame,—only, an amiable suspicion of himself, which rests on too sufficient grounds of long experience, gives him a slow eye for his merits and a quick eye for his faults, while even conscious truthfulness has a battle to fight with his inevitable discomposure under the accents of applause. And this rigour of verity which he follows as to what he is, he equally follows

as to what he does.   His deeds, even in themselves, are
genuine expressions of his character—are only words of
truth more picturesque and solid than those of the tongue.
Still, those deeds, as they stand written upon the past, or
as they take their place upon the present, are liable to be
misread or misreported : of what is praiseworthy his friends
may make too much, his enemies may make too little, or
may quite misinterpret them in their malignity ; of what is
blameworthy his friends may make too little, his enemies
too much.   Over all this he mounts guard, in the interests
of reality.   But his contention in this relation is mostly
with his friends.   Doubtless it wounds him when his
doings are translated into slander of his good name, or
when his lealest motives are poisoned into material of
odium ; yet it wounds him more for the wrong which is
done to truth than for the injury which is inflicted upon
his own reputation.

But this Single-Heartedness, while it would tell most
directly upon his own character and conduct, could not
fail to do its part in presence of the character and conduct of others.   With all his good nature, he never uttered
a syllable of conscious flattery : it would have stumbled
upon his lips.   Nevertheless, as we shall have to notice
afterwards, he seldom could withstand an occasion of
interjecting a true word of generous recognition.   The
prejudice with which he judged his own merits was removed
when the merits of others were in question, and he seems
to have suffered no opposite prejudice to take its place.
At whatever time he saw his own best features of character
projected before him as characteristics of other men, then
it was that we might hear him paying laud to himself, with
a freedom which was at once true to his own consciousness
and true to the fact.   In the matter of faults he was
straightly impartial, even where his strong feeling of friendship might have warped him : he had a tender admiration

of Mr Fearing, but he stands to it that he was inordinately "troublesome." There is no pilgrim more trenchant in his criticism of such as live their lives in accordance with any of the Protean shapes of error and unbelief; but when he speaks the keenest, it is always a true criticism of untruth that we hear. Every shade of ungodliness is to him a shade of falseness; every doctrine which is out of harmony with revelation, as he believes it, is to him a doctrine of falsehood: and he confronts it all with trueness and with truth.

And his heart dealt with more about others than their conduct, or even their character; it dealt with themselves. There was no doubleness in his friendship, and there was no stealth in his enmity; nor in his indifference itself need we search for any trace of affectation. With fair regard to proprieties, he bore himself towards all no otherwise than as he felt towards them. Neither friend nor enemy was puzzled with ambiguity in his attitude, nor deceived by misleading ways: his feelings towards them stood before their eyes, for better or for worse—legible to all whom they happened to concern; nor perhaps without commentary of reasons. He loved when he could : then his love went straight like a ray of light; and it abode, as a perpetual sunbeam, unless it were broken or quenched by detected falsehood; which was singularly seldom an experience of his. If another honest heart came in his way, his own heart sprang out to greet it, even if it had little by which to commend itself besides its clear honesty. He was always looking for "honest" people, and he was more fortunate than Diogenes in finding them. A companionship of honest hearts was to him a continual feast; and he requited the luxury by a transparent loyalty in himself that was unswerving and incorruptible. The compact simplicity of his friendly motives offered no dangling cordage to the hand of any stray influence which might venture to pull them awry; and they held with a firmness which nothing, and no one, had much encouragement to tamper with, whether by fraud or by force. And, since his friendship was never colder than it seemed, he was the same friend among the unexpected demands of misfortune as he had been among the mutual benefits of more smiling times.

Thus unequivocal and lucid was the emotional life of this man. The fountains of his character were "cleare," and their issuings were "straight." The fountains of it; for his emotions were the more spontaneous inworkings and outgoings of his nature, wearing his Singleness of character where it was furthest beneath, and where it was deeper than his *Will*. But the Singleness by no means stayed short of the executive department of his nature. His management of himself as the possessor of a power to choose and to do, to suffer and avoid, to aim and endeavour, was a management with no "double-mindedness" in it, and none of the "wavering" which bemocks the manhood of every man who has a mind *and* a mind. He selected his mark of action in every instance, rid it right clean from all minglings with other marks, then struck on towards it, and held onwards till he reached it, or still held onwards because he was only approaching it in as far as he approached the close of his earthly way. Hence he knew vividly, at all times, just what he was about, and whither he was tending. Hence, too, he was always, in the whole being of him, going one way or another: there was no squandering of his energy, and no trifling with his self-respect, in the haltings of hesitancy, or the backings and fillings of shifting advantageousness, or the stand-still swingings of compromise. Hence, also, other men had a chance of knowing what his course in any instance was, or even what it was likely in any contingency to be; and they had a certainty of knowing what it was on the whole, as a course which traversed his life.

Plainly, such clear consistency in his moral ongoing could only arise from a clear unity in the principle of his self-guidance. His Will, then, which got impulse from his emotion, got supreme and sole regulation from his Conscience—that is, from the Divine Will mirrored and maintained within him. This unearthly principle was consistent throughout and always; therefore his life was consistent too. If he erred, it was in his judgment of what really was the Divine Will in the case: we have no hint of default ever tainting the purity of his intention. What was God's will?—that, when he believed he had found it, he made to be his own according to his strength; and that, without a jot of conscious abatement, he put it upon himself to carry through. It might be arduous; it might be painful; it might look impracticable. But it was the one thing for him; and he had not at least the humiliating irksomeness of a choosing and determining that was never over, because it was falsely begun. He took chart and compass into counsel with him ere he set his course; from that moment, all his steering was a silent contest with wind and current in the name of his right to keep it. Any that chose might look on, and whatever pleased them they might think; for they would know any day where to sight his bark: but they must beware how they sought to bend him from his track; for it was his, and God's.

The Singleness of this man's character, however, should not have been complete if it had not been shared to a good extent by his *Intellect* also. We cannot miss observing that it did. There is a remarkable directness and precision in the working of his mind, as far as conversation can reveal it to us. He saw single, and he saw clear. He had little patience with mist as an accompaniment of mental action: he preferred darkness itself to fog or smoke, and could perhaps too easily have dispensed with a haze of " atmosphere" which would only have fulfilled the par-

donable demands of poetry or art. Perception, conception, memory, imagination,—we can see them all answering to the same straight-forward love of reality and of
whatever most truly represented it. Language, in his
esteem, is a simple revealer: its utility, its very ornament,
begin and end with this function alone. And the vividness of his own utterances very well illustrates his opinion
of the purpose for which the gift of utterance was bestowed.
Whether it is recollection or description, reflection or
analysis, which he is setting before us by his words, we
recognise the same incisiveness of expression depicting the
same verity of mental view. There is little of hesitancy or
circumlocution, of half-seeing or approximate representation, in his talk. He is literally a man of " honest mind "
—a man who put up with no doublenesses even within
the region of his intellection ; and if he thinks freely and
frequently in metaphor and simile, or even in hyperbole
itself, he does so, most of all, because he feels how often
these are virtually truer than the most rigid exactnesses of
prosaic statement, or the severest amplitudes of philosophi-
cal phraseology.

A character like Honest's, whether it be ideal or actual,
always invites us to remark the undoubted connection
which subsists between trueness in the disposition and
trueness in the intellect. Honest's clearness of heart had
something to do with his clearness of head ; nor is it
scarcely less certain, that his clearness of head reacted
helpfully upon his clearness of heart. He commonly saw
true, because he always wished to see true. The small
success which sophistry had with him, even if he were unable to strip it bare by syllogism,—this, together with the
slight degree in which he permitted fallacy to enter into
his own reasonings, was largely due to his strong preference for truth, and to the wholly truthful temper which he
cherished throughout his being. If a man set his entire

nature to the note of veracity, his judgments as well as his utterances will become wonderfully veracious. Truth will come about him like a companion, when it would be shy of a man who is himself less true. He who deals in deceit is himself deceived. We do not know how a man's mind operates until we know his moral bent and bearing. We cannot guess how many of the fallacies which have hag-ridden the race were generated deeper than the brain. " The truth shall make you free "—as to all the workings also of the intellect—if it be allowed to take its rightful tenancy of the heart. On the other hand, it need not be held in question, that a moral nature has in several respects a better chance where it is supported by a mind which is naturally keen-sighted, and that sometimes a moral career may be affected unhappily by an inborn incapacity for seeing things sharply as they are. But this shall not last long as a source of harm where there is a lively desire to possess a sense of the reality of things ; for mental vision will respond to cultivation as readily, at least, as any other faculty will.

The happiest case, doubtless, is that of a man like Honest himself, who would appear to have been endowed by nature with a clearness of head which got nothing but development, after the adoption of the new life, from his fervent adherence to veracity and verity. All his clearness could have fallen upon nothing so congenial as this Christian life which now he so cordially lived. Under the riddings and adjustings of Divine dealing, clearness of heart set in as a mighty ally of his clearness of head ; and the man of clearness became a Christian of conspicuous clearness. It is good to notice how his sayings and his judgments almost seize the approval of those who hear them : their accuracy, their fairness, their transparency, strike the ear even of such competent listeners as Great-heart and Gaius ; and we are continually hearing his utterances hailed by such hearty words as "right," "true," "the truth." This did not come of his ripe experience alone. It came of a sympathy with truth which led him to see his way to its core, and which both constrained and enabled him to tell clearly—that is, truly—what it was he saw. He went after truth under one harmonious set of motives, which all converged upon the God of truth, as a God who revealed His eternal mind to all who brought faith with them into the sunshine of His revealings. Honest sees, feels, works, along the line of Divine manifestation; and as he goes, he becomes true to himself, and to God, and to all that is. To God supremely: the Singleness centred itself at this height. He held to *honesty towards God*—to frankness, ingenuousness, simplicity, justness, in all his intercourse and relations with the True One; and he carried that transcendent honesty to its issues. He kept himself to the giving of what was due to God—gave himself, therefore, to God in all that he was, which was really all that this very God had made him to be. To some he might appear needlessly generous in his bestowings upon an unseen Benefactor; but Honest was better informed than this. He knew—he saw—that when he was most abundant in his givings, he was still far short even of being just, and gathered up himself more singly than ever as a consecrated man for eternity. Hence most of all it was, that Christiana, when "she called for old Mr Honest," could "say of him" as he entered her presence for the last time,—entered it to speak to her, as well as she to him, which no other pilgrim did,—"Behold an Israelite indeed, in whom is no guile." And hence most of all it was, that Honest himself, when his own turn came, "left the world" with the tranquil words, "Grace reigns;" for "in his lifetime he had spoken to one Good-Conscience to meet him there, *the which he also did*, and so helped him over." It was a trusty trysting, and was kept: the Singleness of soul which Honest cherished so long,—it now came to his side, like a strong angel of light, to cherish himself through the closing act of his earthly obedience.

> " Therefore we can go die as sleep, and trust
> Half that we have
> Unto an *honest faithfull* grave;
> Making our pillows either down—or dust." [1]

If we had now traversed the whole character of Honest in as far as it merited our attention, we should still have before us an aged pilgrim from whom we could not withhold either our regard or our respect. But we have only made a good beginning in our appreciation of this man when we have learned to admire the Singleness which pervaded his nature. He might have had all this straightness without very much of strength. At several points, it is true, we have already found his simplicity lifting itself clear of all suspicion of weakness, and standing as a strong thing which had capable motives for itself. And indeed all honesty, if it be of so genuine and persistent a temper as his, must be reckoned to be eminently harmonious with a great degree of masterliness of character. It can therefore be no matter of surprise, but only of satisfaction, to find that Bunyan has deemed it truthful to fill into the picture of old Honest many marks of what we have called EFFICIENCY.

Perhaps we select the phrase which will best comprehend the *Moral* side of this capability of his, if we say that he is somewhat remarkably a Man of Spirit. There is nothing of tameness about his character. Old as he is, he never betrays a trace of spiritlessness. There is more of spring and freshness about his words and ways than there is about the most youthful of his fellow-pilgrims. He is prompt, willing, energetic, fervid, fearless—always in good heart, in good humour, steady beyond the tyranny of mood, and

---

[1] Herbert —" Death."

overflowing in his healthy abundance of spirits. The invaluable accession which he was to the pilgrim-company, unpromising as his hoary age may have made him appear, was largely due to this strong buoyancy of his nature, which his age seemed only to enrich, and not in the least to diminish.

Whether or not Honest had fought battles in his day, he must always have been in readiness to fight them. Not that there was much of the purely military in his disposition : he would never allow that he was anything of a warrior; and he was not—such as Great-heart or Valiant was. None the less, the general courage of the man was indomitable, and could cast itself into the military mould when urgent need arose. There is the earliest possible proof of this in the unpremeditated incident at the oak, where we see him standing on guard while only half-awake, ready on the instant to scatter his drowsiness in the clash of conflict, and, with utmost literalness, to " fight as long as there was breath in his body ; "—which is virtually the very courage of which Napoleon spoke so approvingly as the " two-o'clock-in-the-morning sort." It was easy for the armoured champion of the family of Christian to acknowledge in this man a pilgrim after his own heart—a man whose straight-going downrightness " *will* know of them what they were," and whose bravery will draw his weapons upon them whatsoever be the odds against him, and will count upon victory, if only they be foes of the King and him. There was an undertone of this dauntless valour beneath even his quietest words and least militant ways : it was the valour of a man who was profoundly peaceable ; yet, at any moment along his pilgrimage, the man or fiend who should presume upon his yielding a jot of principle in the interests of peace would encounter sharp evidence that he had reckoned ill.

A summons to bear his part in any enterprise of benevolent prowess could never come wrong to such a man. He was out in the expedition against Slay-good; nor would any of the "spears and staves" which bristled forth that day have been wielded more effectively in support of Great-heart, had there been need, than the weapons which were borne in the hands of Honest. He does not seem to have made one of the band who went out from the city of Vanity, and compelled the monster to "make a retreat:" that force consisted of pilgrim-minded citizens, who only took advantage of the leadership of Great-heart. But when the day arrived on which they "sat down and consulted," at the historical stile to Bypath-Meadow, whether the time had not now come for a bold march upon Doubting Castle, Honest was the first to hail the appeal of their leader with his "*I* will;" and when they crossed into the Meadow, with motives so different from those which led Christian and Hopeful into that region, there was not in Great-heart himself a steadier purpose to do daring work. Therefore, when they had gone thus "to look for Giant Despair," and had found him, and he had come forth upon them equipped with his gigantic harnessing of steel and fire and iron, and in his hand his infamous club, and they had beset him round, and Diffidence had acknowledged the extremity of the case by "coming up to help him," it was "old Honest," according to the history, who "cut her down at one blow." The deed was so worthy of some more soldierly pilgrim, that the inexcusable slip of Bunyan, who in the metrical Preface gives to Valiant the credit of having been brother-in-arms to Great-heart during that exploit, is not altogether unnatural. But it was long after the six heroes had "fought for their lives," and had brought Despair to the ground, and despatched him, and demolished his castle, and taken Despondency and his daughter into their brotherly keeping, that Valiant was found standing in the way with his drawn sword in his

Z

hand, and blood on his face,—having done, in sternest fact, precisely what Honest had been so stubbornly prepared to do when they found himself. What, then, shall we say of the metrical account of the matter which is imperishably "writ" by Great-heart's own hand upon the "marble stone" which he sets beneath the giant's head, "right over against the pillar which Christian erected"?—

> . . . "And Diffidence, his wife,
> *Brave Master Great-heart* has bereft of life."

Bunyan seems as little concerned for the modesty of the monument-maker as for the military credit of the old hero who is all the while an unchallenging spectator of the proceedings.

We have hinted,—and we scarcely need to enlarge upon the hint,—that not seldom a manly spiritedness, now and then rising to courage, must have stood behind the frank truthfulness for which Honest was so remarkable. There was a certain bravery pervading his very honesty under all its forms. In the mere sustaining of that pre-eminent virtue of his, there was sometimes a real risking of consequences, a genuine defiance of danger, which drew upon as much of latent heroism as would have won him honour in front of an armed foe. He never feared to take sides with the truth, and he never shrunk from giving it voice— not with the obtrusive bluster of a shallow heedlessness, indeed, but with the considerate reserve of a courage that had body enough in it to stay till it had need to summon itself to the doing of valid and valuable work. Such demands must have been made upon his manfulness more frequently in the days before we meet him; but even in the days when he is journeying under our eye in the company of none but appreciative friends, there are not wanting occasions when it needed courage to say all that he said, even though it would probably have cost him as much in self-reproach to have courted silence, or to have clipped anything away from the round entireness of the truth.

This moral capability of Honest's, when it went into conjunction with his unselfishness, passed into the phase of Public Spirit. His interest in men and things travelled a good way beyond himself, however it may have fixed its starting-point there. His heart and hand he held engaged for the good of his fellow-pilgrims, for the good of the whole brotherhood present and to come, and, at least indirectly, for the good of the wide world. His Singleness was an amplitude of Singleness, instinct all over with practical energy. He was catholic in the range of his sympathies, and he was not in haste to set barriers around the scope of his activity. That toil of breaking down the walls of Doubting Castle, and the hazard of making an end of the baleful pair who were so long its denizens, though it was an enterprise of no personal moment to Honest, and was scarcely a recreation for an aged pilgrim, yet entirely fell in with the temper of a man who held himself at the service of the general weal. The town of Vanity, with its tragic memories, represented many interests which touched the King-loving folks who dwelt in it; and Honest, though he would not himself have elected readily to make his residence there, manifests a lively concern in the condition of affairs within that anomalous community. The pilgrims are at Mnason's table on the evening of their arrival :—" *Mr Honest* asked his landlord if there were any store of good people in the town." A few such were summoned forthwith to meet them :—" Then *Mr Honest* (when they were all sat down) asked Mr Contrite and the rest in what position their town was at present. . . . ' But how are your neighbours for quietness?'"—an inquiry which may be thought to reveal some interest even in the " people " who were *not* " good." We recall what he said at the inn, by way of brief approval of the "innkeeper's" more voluble anxiety to see matrimonial alliances on foot in the family of Christiana: "It *is* a pity this family should fall and be extinct." To Honest the pilgrim-brotherhood was a commonwealth in whose prosperity the world should most truly prosper ; and it is one of the aims of his life to give ungrudgingly of word and deed and substance, if by any means he might leave the world better than he found it by leaving the Church of God in greater strength. If it had been much in men's thoughts in Honest's days to beleaguer the strongholds of foreign heathenism with the armaments of truth and grace, the veteran saint should have glowed with the enthusiasm of youth to bear his part in a cause so completely congenial to his spirit.

We should doubtless be right if we were to trace a good proportion of Honest's moral Efficiency to his deep trustfulness in God and in the victorious excellence of godliness. If these were worthy of his trust at all, they were worthy of his whole trust, and his honest heart must give itself thoroughly to them in a happy abandonment of itself to faith and hope. His buoyancy, his promptitude, his readiness to sacrifice personal comfort, his cheery patience, his rich resources of endurance,—all this, so inseparable from our thoughts of him in those latter days of his, had its roots in the heartiness with which he bestowed himself upon the most honest things he knew beneath the sky, for he felt they had their home in the regions of stability beyond it. They appealed to all that was strongest and finest in him, and he responded to the appeal with the whole force of his being. It was worth while to gird his healthy nature to a glad energy in the living of a life which was penetrated by such privileges, and illumined by such hopes ; therefore, whatever others might find it well to do, he must claim the right to set himself in God's sunshine, and to go forth and

forward with radiant clearness of heart, and with unfaltering confidence in that eternal goodness which had con-
descended so marvellously to invest the footsteps of men
with its "grace and glory" as they went on through "this
world to that which is to come."

But it is time we should notice how much the *Intellectual*
nature of Honest participates in the Efficiency of the man.
In respect of mind, this aged pilgrim stands in the first
rank among all the characters in either part of the Allegory.
It is well that it should be so. It is good that Bunyan
should so fully avail himself of the opportunity of conjoin-
ing unusual guilelessness with uncommon sagacity, and of
showing how naturally the two can dwell together in the
same Christian manhood. The mind of the most transparent man in the story is a mind at once strong and keen
and rich. Nature has been generous with him at the first,
and he has acknowledged the generosity by a culture and
equipment that give evidence of having been diligent and
varied. He has observed, read, remembered, thought, for
himself, and has done them all pretty widely and well.
The conversations, it is true, are seldom so exhaustive as
those in which Christian deploys his mental resources, nor
are they ever so strictly ordered as the lectures of Great-
heart to his listening and learning friends are sometimes
found to be; but his utterances are more shrewd than
those of the typical pilgrim, and more incisive than those
of the guide. There is a racy vigour about all he says,
which is so distinctive that at any time we might dispense
with the name of the speaker. But for the pervading
geniality which is never far off from humour, he would
often remind us of Faithful at his best.

It is not without significance, that the earliest evidence
we obtain of his mental acumen is in his talk with Great-
heart about their common friend Mr Fearing. While it is
causes and principles that are on hand, he is in the attitude

of inquiry : "But what should be the reason that such a good man should be all his days so much in the dark ?"— a condition strangely unlike his own ; yet it is he himself who is seeking beneath the phenomena for the causes of them. When, however, it is the character itself which is under consideration, Honest is at home, and displays a discrimination which is both keen and well-measured, both just and appreciative. Almost immediately thereafter, we have illustration of the same keenness in the instance of a character which he introduces by way of contrast, as would seem—that of Self-will ; and now it is practical opinions, occupying a middle place between character and principles, which are chiefly passing beneath his treatment. His account of them is sharp in its outlines, and firm in its fidelity. "You must understand me *rightly*," he says, when he perceives an exaggeration in Great-heart's apprehension of his words : "he did not say that *any* man might do this, but that *those that had the virtues of them that did such things* might also do the same." How fully he has followed the subtleties of this dangerous sinner is still more apparent when he reports him thus : "Why," he says, "to do this by way of opinion seems abundantly more honest than to do it and yet hold contrary to it in opinion." This sort of honesty the old man does not greatly esteem. "There are many of this man's *mind*," nevertheless, "that have not this man's *mouth*"—a dishonesty which has still less of his admiration, but which, it is plain, he can very clearly discern and very cleanly describe.

Even Honest, bright as he is in all circumstances, has his moments of more sparkling brightness, when the intellect shares the glow. That "very merry" evening, the first they spent at the inn, would appear to have been such a moment. It was "the old gentleman" who sprang the first "riddle" upon the company while they were "cracking" their more literal "nuts"—a riddle which carried

within it an ingenious compliment to their host, to whom
it was propounded :

> "A man there was, though some did count him mad ;
> The more he cast away, the more he had."

And Great-heart's more difficult one was readily "opened"
by "the old gentleman," as Bunyan persistently calls him
here.   Out of this their host raised the question—whether
the graces of a pilgrim who set out young, or those of a
pilgrim who set out in later life, would "shine the clearest,"
supposing they kept the way together.   Honest answers
the question with acute impartiality : "The young man's,
doubtless.   For that which heads it against the greatest
opposition, gives best demonstration that it is strongest,
especially when it also holds in pace with that that meets
not with half so much ; as, to be sure, old age does not.
Besides, I have observed, that old men have blessed themselves with this mistake—namely, taking the decays of
nature for a gracious conquest over corruptions, and so
have been apt to beguile themselves.   Indeed, old men
that are gracious are best able to give advice to those that
are young, because they have seen most of the emptiness
of things ; but yet, for an old man and a young to set out
both together, the young one has the advantage of the
fairest discovery of a work of grace within him, though the
old man's corruptions are naturally the weakest."   The
Dreamer seldom has to stretch himself so far in the direction of metaphysical thought as when he is reporting the
sayings of this venerable pilgrim.

This verdict of his reminds us, that no small part of the
wealth, as well as of the clearly-rid movement, of Honest's
mind was due to the fulness of an experience the materials
of which he had thoroughly digested and assimilated.   "I
have *taken notice* of many things " was evidently as true a
word as ever he spoke.   The passage in which he repeats

four times the refrain " I have seen some," and twice
appends the twin refrain " I have heard some," is not only
graphic and eloquent, and sadly true, as a peroration of
their talk about Fearing and Self-will, but it is admirably in
character from the lips of this old traveller on the King's
highway. We have already mentioned the frequent com-
mendations which his accuracy drew forth, especially from
Great-heart :—" Well said "—" I believe it, I believe it, for
I know the thing is truth "—" You have given a very right
character of him "—" You say right ;" and again, " You
say right ; "—echoed once by the hearty " It is right " of
Gaius. Something of this exactness of stroke may be put
to the credit of his prolonged acquaintance with men and
things, and to the tact which an intelligent everyday practice
has brought him. Thus, he hits the mark very deftly in
his first recorded word to Feeble-mind, to whose story he
has been listening :—" Then said old Mr Honest, ' Have
you not, some time ago, been acquainted with one Mr
Fearing, a pilgrim ?' ' Acquainted with him !—*yes.*'" So
also with Stand-fast about Madam Bubble, whose name
touches the chord of some by-stored recollection of his—
(it turns out that reading is on this occasion the form of
experience which helps him)—" Is she not" . . " *Right*,
you hit it." " Doth she not " . . " You fall *right upon* it
again." " Doth she not " . . . " It is *just so.*"

The faculties of this Honest we can therefore say, are
neither dull nor meagre. His intellectual competency,
scarcely less marked than his moral robustness, makes with
it a very capable nature in this aged traveller towards the
City of the King. As we follow him in his hale maturity,
we acknowledge it is not because he is shallow that he is
clear, nor because he is slender that he is so simple of
heart. He knows fully as well what he is about, on that
heavenward road, as any man who ever took another ; and
he has carried into that road as manly a temper and bear-

ing as was ever carried elsewhere by any one who thought himself too much of a man to enter it. And there have been many Honests—both before his day, and since.

It only remains that we complete our view of this old pilgrim's character by giving a moment's attention to the fineness of quality which adorns his strength, the DELICACY which adds so much attractiveness to the Efficiency of his nature.

The point at which this finer side of his nature has closest touch with the vigour and the simplicity which we have found in him, is the unequivocal *Warmth of his Feeling*. "I cry you mercy:" this hearty admission of mistake, signalling the start of a long companionship, is the earliest possible token that the valiant veteran had also some fervour of good feeling in him. We are not unprepared, by his frank cordiality with Great-heart, for the kiss of affectionate greeting which goes round the group, or the friendly asking of the names one after another, or the kindly inquiries as to how they had fared, or the joy at finding the widow of the man whose name "rings over all these parts of the world;"—all this, while the guide looked on "very much pleased, and smiled upon his companion." As here, so also throughout, this Warmth of Feeling has a special fragrance of brotherly-kindness and hearty good-will. He has a warm tenderness in store for pilgrims who are feeble, and a warm admiration in readiness for pilgrims who are strong. Mr Fearing, as we have seen, had unfailing interest for him, "most troublesome" as he was. Great-heart, it appears, had large experience of that pilgrim after this "great companion of his" had somehow fallen out of his company: "Well, then, pray let us hear a little of him," begs Honest, "and how he managed himself under your conduct." The guide satisfies his heart in this particular by vividly recounting the history of the pilgrim onward to the end—(a history in which Bunyan gets by-and-bye to mix up himself with the speaker, and mingles "I" and "we" and "Mr Great-heart" in a way that is somewhat confusing, though it may be regarded as testimony to the Dreamer's absorbing sympathy with the subject.)　"Then, it seems he was *well at last*," breaks in Honest, as if with moistened eye, when the story of the guide can reach no further.　He was "such a good man;" "he was very zealous;" and many things that others feared "he feared not at all."　Thus tenderly, and thus generously, he lingers over the memory of the man who had drawn so heavily upon his kindness; and the man had not even yet gone far from his thoughts when Feeble-mind brings the name once more to his lips.—There is less of tenderness, but not less of Warmth, at his first sight of Stand-fast: "But so soon as Mr Honest saw him, he said, 'I know this man. . . . He is *certainly a right good pilgrim.*'　'Ho, father Honest, are *you* there?'　'Ay, that I am, as sure as *you* are there.'"—Indeed, the old man loved in all circumstances to look upon the faces of those who were of the brotherhood: to this extent at least, his fervent sociableness suffered no decline as his years advanced.　"Whatever you want"—so Mnason spoke when they had entered beneath his roof—"do but say, and we will do what we can to get it for you."　"Our great want awhile since," replies Honest, "was harbour *and good company;* and now I hope we have both."　Anon he is asking the benignant host "if there were any store of good people in the town. . . . But *what shall we do to see some of them?*　For the sight of good men to those who are going on pilgrimage is like the appearing of the moon and the stars to them that are sailing upon the seas."[1]　The old man had in him something poetic, not only in feeling but in fancy.

[1] Note P.

This fine quality of his feeling is the link between his Warmth and his *Sensitiveness.* A nature so fine in tone will probably be fine also in the tissue. Perhaps so outspoken a man may be likely to suffer injustice in this particular. A brusque air may sometimes be worn by his words or deeds that must not mislead us; and when signs of delicate feeling unmistakably emerge, we have need to give them liberal recognition. In this connection his Unobtrusiveness, when we consider his frankness and his ripe experience, is very worthy of note. It is made up of humility and modesty. His modesty is like that of a maiden. We cannot forget his blushes in presence of his new friends—a guide, and a woman, and a few young folks: his "name he *cannot*" be telling; it means a lifelong compliment to him. But in the interests of accuracy he has to tell it at last. It is not by any means "Honesty in the abstract"—not so huge a flattery as this; "but Honest" is his current name,—if only it was certainly his nature also!—For a man so well-stored and so self-sufficing, his respectful dependence on Great-heart is not to be overlooked;—as when after they had left the farewell feast of Gaius, he says—"Pray, sir, now we are upon the road, tell us some profitable things of some that have gone on pilgrimage before us." For those pilgrims he has a reverent regard, and Great-heart is looked up to on account of his large acquaintance with their history. In an hour or two they are about the spot where Evangelist warned Christian and Faithful "of what should befall them at Vanity Fair." "Say you so?" He was deeply impressed: "I dare say it was a *hard chapter* that then he did read unto them." He seems doubtful whether he himself could have behaved worthily in the circumstances: the shrinking of his sensibilities gives him proof of how much bracing he should need for such a trial. But we will not doubt that he would have faced the trial steadily, and borne himself

through it bravely, if it had been his lot.—That evening,
Mnason is inquiring of them how it has gone with them :
" It happeneth to us as it happeneth to wayfaring men,"
he says, revealing the more sombre pensiveness that lay
below his blithesomeness of spirit, for he is speaking now
to a man of his own ripe years :—it is not all pleasant on
the way; they "have met with some notable rubs already."
" What rubs have you met withal ? "   At this point the
veteran spokesman of the party must give place : " Nay,
ask Mr Great-heart, our guide ; for *he* can give the best
account of *that.*"   And Honest becomes a generous listener
with Mnason himself.

We must not dwell longer upon the character of Bunyan's veteran pilgrim.   *Truth manfully lived according to
love ;*— thus we may now summarise the cheerful presence
which threw its helpfulness into the pilgrim-group ere it had
travelled half its way, and made it a brighter group every
hour afterwards.   Cheeriness was only the natural radiation of such a character, which had too much of light in
itself to be much under the dominion of shadow, and had
enough of generous force of its own to shed around it the
light which it held.   It is a character of wise light-heartedness (for the word " light " will press all its better meanings
upon us when Honest is near),—mingling the best features
of age with the best features of youth, and thus offering a
Christian fulfilment of the familiar sentiment of Cicero—
" As I approve of a youth who has something of the old
man in him, so I am no less pleased with an old man who
has something of the youth."   The character is not one of
commanding proportions, but quite as little is it a character
of mere respectable ordinariness.   It gets a piquancy from
a dash of something which can hardly be described as
eccentricity, yet has much of the proverbial effect of a
good eccentricity as a source of popularity and influence.

This happy unusualness he derives, in great part, from a fearless individuality in the acting-out of his obedience to God, and from an unborrowing appliance of his own disposition as he finds it to the fulfilling of a godly life. Hence it is that he wears so much of the flavour of a true originality all the while that he takes upon him no least air of oddity; for his very instinct of transparent thoroughness strikes its way past the poor suspensive one-sidedness that there is in all odd things. Spiritually, there is less of loftiness in him than of depth and breadth: he is a strong structure of bright Christian character—grounded steadfastly most of all, yet also pointing its 'summit unmistakably towards the highest regions. His spiritual strength lies in his simple unwavering Godwardness. There was no spiritual intricacy in him, whether good or evil. Complex Christian characters like that of Fearing are problems to him; unchristian characters of the type of By-ends he seems to have failed even to recognise as existent:—"By-ends," he asks innocently—"*what was he?*" We may answer, that he was as nearly as possible the antithesis of himself. Honest was the pilgrim-man whose conspicuous quality was his Godward genuineness—a genuineness so great, that it would have revealed every flaw in the Christian method of life if there had been a flaw to reveal. But so far from this, his transparent manifestness, as it settled under the sway of God's gospel, grew into translucent manifestation; because he was clear, he became luminous, and shone like a lamp among men. Happily we meet him sometimes still, for he is as immortal as Christianity itself is. We meet him never too often, whether he be old or young. When such a pilgrim "leaves the world," his own personal "honesty goes with him:" he cannot, he must not, "will" it away; for it is not to be transmitted through human hands, and it is as fitting an ornament in heaven as it is upon earth. But the true fountain of the "honesty" is full for each of us ; and blessed it is for ourselves, and for the cause which is the blessing of the world, when we draw so liberally thence, that even to a sunny old age we can tread the pilgrimage with the lowly royalty of God's children, and can face a captious ungodliness with the clear eye which looks forth from a lucid heart.

XV.

THE Second Part of the "Pilgrim" owes not a little of its well-sustained interest to the repeated accessions which are made to its company as they journey on. In freshening the flow of the narrative by the incoming of those new figures,—in broadening the variety of the group by a gradual and not too plenteous forgathering of pilgrims, —Bunyan is true at once to his subject and his art. With their one aim, their one destination, their one King, their one road, yet with differences in their pace and in their occasions of delay, what more likely than that pilgrims should fall-in with pilgrims, or that a banded group of pilgrims should grow as the distance lessens between itself and the City? Christians may well find out Christians, and keep with them when they do. And even as a matter of art, there is something fine in this picture of men and women hailing from different quarters, and moving forth without concert, or perhaps without any knowledge of each other's movement, yet by-and-bye coming to greet each other upon the road together, as those who are urging their steps towards the same spot of horizon, with their hearts loyal to the same Lord whose horizon, whose road, it is. Nor is the picture finer than the reality, or the reading of it than its actual experience.

There is plainly a limit to the diversity of ways in which these meetings may be represented in the Allegory as coming to pass,—though Bunyan, perhaps, has not taken quite so much range of liberty in the matter as was open to him to take. His method includes only two main forms, with but little diversity in the individual instances of each. Honest, Valiant, Stand-fast,—each of these is happened upon by the company on the track of pilgrimage, and is surprised in some characteristic attitude amid his fancied loneliness. Feeble-mind, Despondency and his daughter,—each of these is delivered by the warriors of the company, and welcomed as a happy spoil of conquest. And always it is the company that finds out the pilgrim, and not the pilgrim that finds out the company. The only case which ·might refuse to be thus classified is that of Ready-to-halt, who limps past the company when they have mustered at the door of Gaius to take their departure thence, and is installed a companion through the sympathetic recognition of Feeble-mind. Yet there is a great deal of character, with the peculiar diversity which that entails, in the particular circumstances which attend the discovery of each of those pilgrim-brethren. Honest is deep in unsuspecting slumber, but starts to action ready for the worst, and glad to hear the best—as soon as he has thoroughly assured himself that he can trust it to be this. Valiant is standing like a monument of single combat— weary too, but not with travel, and terribly awake,—his face trickling with blood, and his right hand closed fast upon the red-damp hilt of his weapon : he is in no mood to challenge friends, since for three hours till this moment he has been looking into the eyes of foes. Stand-fast is holloed back from the "run" with which he has resumed his journey over the Enchanted Ground, unwitting that he has been seen by the whole band upon his knees, with earnest face upturned but bloodless, and with prevailing hands uplifted but without sword—thankful for a different deliverance. Ready-to-halt is identified while he is jogging forward upon his unaccompanied way at his own laborious pace, and threatening, it would seem, to make up time by going past the inn where the company had so long lingered. Feeble-mind is found in the act of being rifled by the cannibal-giant—a recent capture, and as yet but slightly harmed; while Despondency and his daughter are discovered living among a litter of dead in Despair's dungeon, almost dead themselves with starvation. These are key-notes, one by one, struck true to the whole piece which each announces as beginning.

It is the fate of VALIANT in the story, that not only do we learn little of what his history has been before we see him,—though we really get far more of his than we got of Honest's,—but we have little history of his to observe even after he has come into sight. Where Little-faith was robbed, and Valiant was assailed, is not a great way from the River which borders the territory of the City. It is his last conflict that he has just fought when we break in upon him at the moment of victory. We could almost have wished to see him find good cause for unsheathing that " Jerusalem blade " of his again, by the side of the hero-guide who so "delighted in him " as " a man of his hands "—if only to witness how far he should have rivalled or eclipsed the generous warrior of the company. But his period of strife takes end with his period of solitude, as Christian's did before him. Doubtless he had need of the change, lest his pilgrim-life should become too one-sided, and should be lacking in the calmer and richer virtues which prosper best among the tranquillities of fellowship *in* the truth "*for*" which he had been so " valiant." For a pilgrim may be too exclusively military, and his pilgrimage may be too exclusively militant—at least for his own finest wellbeing. Only, when a man like Valiant comes at last into a course of quietude that he may sweeten the juices of his character under the still sunbeams, it must go for something that he brings a well-weathered heroism with him into the stormless light.

But here a question may arise as to the precise meaning which Bunyan would have us to attach to the word "truth" in this pilgrim's name. To a clear determination of this question the record does not greatly help us. It appears likely, however, having regard to the empty niche among character-types which Valiant should thereby fill, that while Bunyan would not have us to accept the word in a sharply restricted sense, yet he would have us to take it as looking mostly in the direction of truth as the embodied material of faith. He probably meant to retain dignity for the name by suggesting in it that the man was "valiant" on behalf of *all* that was true, while he left us to infer tha the special task which his valour usually found to its hand was that of a defence of "*the* truth"—the revealed truth of God : indeed, if we may trust the metrical Preface, it is " Master Valiant for *the* Truth " that is the full form of his name, which Bunyan takes from the Authorised Version of Jeremiah (ix. 3). "They are *not* valiant for *the* truth upon the earth,"—since he could scarcely be aware that the article is here an interpolation of the translators. At the same time, the history does not permit us to think of Valiant as a mere gladiator on the arena of orthodoxy, or as an eager champion of points and articles. It is for the vital heart of the truth that he draws his sword. It is moreover for immortal interests that he makes his stand, and not for the credit of a creed. If he be polemical, it is as for life and death ; if he be unbendingly orthodox, it is with an orthodoxy that has regard rather to moral and spiritual than to logical issues. Valiant fought only for that for which Faithful died and Christian suffered—his whole religion as a belief and a life. Nor must we too readily conclude that he loved fighting at all. It is in his nature to believe strongly, and to project his beliefs into vivid actuality before himself, as if he almost personified them ; it is in his nature, too, to defend stoutly what has thus become so real and moment-ous to his own consciousness. With these qualities in his nature, he would doubtless come to recognise many a call to arms which he could not brook to decline. So he may well have found one conflict involving another, and a life of warfare setting in upon him which inured the prowess of his first conflicts into a skilled unconquerableness that was too conspicuous to abide long unemployed.

Practically, however, as far as the story is concerned, any special limitation of the scope of Valiant's valour takes almost no importance. We do not see him as a defender of anything but his own spiritual wellbeing. We do not hear of him striking a blow for the deliverance of any one, but only of his own soul. Not any deed of knightly beneficence, not any strong stand for the welfare of the brotherhood, not any riddance of the way from foes that might have molested pilgrims to come, lights up the record of his career. "I believed," he says in the business-like summary he gives of his history—"and therefore came out, got into the way, fought *all* that set themselves against *me*, and, by believing, am come to this place." It is simply faith working by dauntlessness, in the interests of personal safety conceived as truth,—this, and no more, that we actually witness in the man. We are disposed to feel as if Bunyan desired us to fill up the silent chronicles of his course with visions of his prowess which should justly earn for him the title of a "defender of the faith :" if he did desire this, we are free to grudge him the silence as a deficiency in his work of delineation, when a brief hint or two would have pierced the mist of uncertainty with clear tokens of the man's distinctive calling. The slip in the Preface, the putting of Valiant into the exploit at Doubting Castle, does not much relieve the matter for us, even though it may give us a glimpse into Bunyan's own view of what was congenial to this character. As he stands in the narrative, it demands some imagination to recognise in him the allegorical counterpart of the "Luthers" and "Knoxes" of history, save in the element of that personal spiritual conflict which such men have so commonly waged in the background of their more public contentions for the truth.

Yet it is possible (may we say?) that Bunyan, in spite of the unhappy couplet in the Preface, has an open-eyed meaning in his silence about public motives and services in the career of Valiant. The defence of the truth in ourselves as a personal possession,—is not this the stem of all defence of the truth in the world as a human blessing? An unquailing courage in the promotion of our own soul's safety and life—is it not the same courage which guards the heart of the truth for peoples, or grasps back the lost jewel of the truth for generations?—and is it not that courage beginning where alone it ought to begin? Has it not been found, that every man who has defended or up-built the truth for his fellow-men, with any great or enduring success, has done it with so much of deep personal conviction in it all, that his whole conflict became almost a conflict on behalf of his own soul? And is it not incontestible that many a doughty champion of right belief, as he deemed it, has been but a troubler of the truth when he fought for things that floated to his hand out of history, and not for verities that welled themselves out of his burning heart? If every Christian were to be "valiant for the truth" in his own spirit,—having made sure that he has gotten it there in some purity,—we should have less need to rely upon the tactics and the heroes of apologetic warfare. Bunyan may signify such things as these, though perhaps with little deliberate purpose to signify them, when he veils the light from Valiant as a defender of anything further than the truth which is the life of his own soul.

But we must turn our eye more fully upon the character of the man : we may be able to make more of this than we can of his work. When we have beheld him for a little, perhaps the impression we first take of him is that of a man at high speed—a pilgrim with an almost impatient rapidity of movement, which is not the result of lightness but of decisive force. This rapidity, conceivably at least, we might adopt as the central feature of his character, and might account for his dominant characteristic by saying, that what to other men would be only hindrances, or only seducements, become to him antagonisms because of the momentum which is on him when he meets them,— that, with him, contact is collision whensoever the contact is obstructive. It cannot be mere haste, however, that is moving him, else he should oftener avoid and flee, and seldomer stand and fight. Indeed, this first impression is rather one of look than of character, and we must regard him more carefully. He is a man who gives the whole of himself to whatever has true claims upon him—gives the whole of himself to the whole of that thing. The considerable mass of character that is in him, we can see, has had reason to be set into entire full motion in the way of a pilgrim-course ; therefore the swing of his ongoing is great. This fast forwardness comes of a clear strong apprehension of what is behind and what is before him—an apprehension which works itself at once into impressive visibility, through the congenial thoroughness of his nature and the responsive vigour of his will. Moreover, whatsoever he shall find in front of him that threatens to be unfriendly to his progress—or, what is the same thing with a seasoning of loyalty in it, whatsoever he shall meet that would menace the sovereignty over him of the True One who has gotten his trust, or the sway over him of the Truth which has gotten his faith—must therefore be challenged and smitten back, if not demolished, ere he again takes his way. Falseness and Error are sharply real to him in proportion as the Truth is so, and that in which he has least faith starts into importance to him because of that in which he has most faith. He sees in every form of untruth an enemy to strike and wound—to settle with, once for all, at least as concerns himself; for it never enters his thoughts that compromise and softness, even tact and policy, have anything to do with the case. "*How* to lay on"—that is the only matter in which there is even a hint of anything other than crushing energy as the one demand of the circumstances. This particular untruth which is getting right across his path—it is a foe to God and him, and just absolutely *a foe* in the essential genius of it; well, the plain thing which has to be done with this—(his sword is already half-way out of its scabbard)—is to close with it, and at the least to send it crippled and disgraced from his path and his presence. For defeat almost as little occurs to his mind as compromise does, since the splendid sturdiness of the man, in the nature of him, is sanctified by his faith into a virtual impossibility of comprehending that he should ever bear away with him anything worse than the scars of victory.

Some light will be cast upon the character of this somewhat remarkable pilgrim if we turn to the account he gives of himself in answer to the kindly inquiries of Great-heart. It is scarcely more than a narrative of his setting-out; but the earliest period of a pilgrimage is never the least characteristic period it contains. He hailed from "Darkland"—a region which "lies upon the same coast with the City of Destruction." One Tell-true came thither, and "told it about what Christian had done." His "*forsaking of his wife and children;*" his "killing of a serpent that did come out *to resist him in his journey;*" his welcomes

at his " Lord's lodgings ; " his last great welcome with
" sound of trumpet " and bells of joy,—these are the incidents that lie upon the surface of this man's recollection
of what he heard about Christian from Tell-true. " That
man," says he with a lively memory of it still, " so told the
story of Christian and his travels, that my heart fell into a
burning haste to be gone after him, nor could father or
mother stay me. So I *got from them."* " *Yes, yes* "—he
came in at the Gate : that of course. (And here Great-
heart has a notable surprise for him :—" Christian's wife,"
and " also his four sons "—his own companions henceforth. " It gladdens him at heart," this happy discovery,
but mostly for the sake of Christian himself, the human
lodestar of his own pilgrimage. This feeling in him is
so strong, that he strikes off into a digression of inquiry
as to the recognition of friends in heaven, and is pleased
to find Great-heart prepared with an implied affirmative to
the question.) His father and mother, it appears, " used
all means imaginable to persuade him to stay at home : "
it was " an idle life," a " dangerous way," a delusive enterprise,—as they sought to demonstrate by numberless very
discouraging details. However, the appalling particulars
" seemed but as *so many nothings* to him : " " he still believed what Mr Tell-true had said, and *that carried him
beyond them all."* And following the biographic summary
which we have already quoted from him, the Dreamer
himself, unable to repress his own sympathetic enthusiasm
as he listens to this man, breaks out into the most stirringly
musical piece of verse in the whole " Pilgrim," and perhaps
the best stanzas that ever he penned :—

> " Who would true valour see,
>   Let him come hither ;
> One here will constant be,
>   Come wind, come weather :

There's no discouragement
Shall make him once relent
His first avowed intent
　　To be a pilgrim.

Whoso beset him round
　　With dismal stories,
Do but themselves confound—
　　His strength the more is:
No lion can him fright,
He'll with a giant fight,
But he will have a right
　　To be a pilgrim.

Hobgoblin nor foul fiend
　　Can daunt his spirit:
He knows he at the end
　　Shall life inherit.
Then, fancies, fly away:
He'll fear not what men say;
He'll labour night and day
　　To be a pilgrim."

In this account there are one or two points which invite our notice. The concern which led him to strike out for the new life did not arise within him by spontaneous thoughtfulness, nor by direct perusal of the Book, nor by special messages to himself from heaven, nor by the yearnings of bereaved natural affection. The human agency, moreover, which intervenes between him and the Divine pity was twofold—a living agency and a dead. A missionary of light, in the aspect of a teller of truth, came near to his ear amid the local darkness—a fellow-man with a message about another fellow-man. The truth reached him as a thing concreted into biography—vivified into the brave life of a stranger who had ventured and fought and won. It was a story that awoke profound responses within his own bosom. A story such as this—why might it not be repeated by himself?—what motives could urge Christian that ought not also to urge Valiant?—what success could reward Christian that Valiant himself might not humbly hope to earn? The resolution grows, fixes, becomes immovable in its strength, that he will follow this man. He "delights in him," as Great-heart afterwards delighted in himself. No doubt, the figure of Christian would erelong be wellnigh lost to the eye of Valiant in the atmosphere of solemn and glorious verity which would gather itself far around and above the person of that human traveller, and a Man infinitely greater than Christian would soon come to transcend the manly pilgrim in his regard; but it was the thought of that lonely figure, in his courage and his triumph, which won his thought and heart to all the rest.—And now a testing strain of temptation tightens its pull upon him. He has no wife or family to make his departure difficult, yet his hinderers are those of his own household. This man who is so readily actuated by human example,—he has to hold to his purpose against the parental wisdom and experience which have guided him throughout his life hitherto. No opposition on earth —not the opposition of demons—could have been so formidable to such a man as this elaborate and determined obstruction of his way by those to whom he owed so much more of merely human consideration than to an unknown person like Christian. His sword, even if he has gotten it, can serve him little here. But the will and heart that were always behind his sword can serve him, and the help which always came, by faith in God, to the strengthening of his will and heart.—For this matter has carried itself further than the chivalrous admiration of a man, or the romantic charm of danger and victory. Through these, as the outlying points at which attention and attraction entered, scattering the mass of his dark content, the matter has gone on to fasten upon the centres of his being, and to arouse a manly discontent which shall not on any terms abide restful as now he sees things actually to be. His sense of God, of duty, of the unseen and the future, is on its feet; and all human influence, except such as goes in the line of his new convictions, flutters around him like a spent breeze.— Of the two sorts of motives which hold sway with a pilgrim in the days of his setting-out—the repelling and the attracting—the attracting ones seem, with Valiant, to be considerably the stronger. Dark-land, indeed—he would have said it, and probably did say it over and over to his mother and father—is more dangerous than any other quarter to which he can betake himself under God's heaven; and this, no doubt, has power to loosen his attachments to the place and people of his birth. But the most powerful forces upon him are rather those which draw him away than those which drive him away. The active energy of his nature, his inborn love of daring enterprise, have found a life-long calling on which they can throw their whole strength, and can feel every hour that conscience and God are with them, and that magnificent recognition is before them. And when such a man thus finds at once the true destiny that he was almost missing, and the true loyalty that he had risk of sending from him while he had a living man's power of choice, it is not even the pressure of parental persuasion that will move him from his purpose. He will be " heartless " just as Christian was " heartless ; " and he will " forsake " them,—he will "get from them,"—though he should rack his heart-strings as he goes.

A man of enterprise, then—a man in whom the active powers are more conspicuous than the intellectual—a man of whom motives take a tenacious grasp, and whose very believing may be said to be action in its first stage of intensity—a man of soldierly nature, indomitably true to the best he knows,—this we can thus far make out Valiant to be. But we may gain further knowledge of him if we turn from listening to his reports of how he did in the past, and observe what is represented to us of his doings in the present. By far the most significant of these is the one combat in which we all but find him so fiercely engaged—"one against three," as he tells us ; for the three are out of view ere we reach him, and we must be indebted to his own reports in good measure still. We may note that he speaks of them as "thieves"—as a trio of villains who live by organised robbery. Theft, nevertheless, is not their object with Valiant. They do not want anything he possesses; they want himself,—or, his return to Dark-land,—or, his life "upon the place." The first and main of these alternatives is the audacious demand that he should become a fourth in their own gang—an impudent compliment to the valour that was to give them all to their heels by its single right hand. The second alternative is still a compliment to the same valour, by seeking to get rid of it from the path of pilgrims without further trouble—the next-best issue of their brazen-faced interference. The third alternative is one of intimidation, covering a secret hope of theirs, that if he should be intractable about the other proposals, this valour of his should prove just stubborn enough to work the revenge of their own disappointment by making an end of itself where they stood. His replies, one by one, to these alternatives is a triumph of cool constancy. He "had been a true man a long season, and it *could not be expected* that he *now* should cast in his lot with *thieves*." "The place from whence he came, had he *not found incommodity* there, he had *not* forsaken it at all ; but *finding* it altogether unsuitable to him, and very unprofitable for him, he *forsook it for this way :*" which is enough for them and him. His "life cost more dear far than that he should *lightly give it away.* Besides "—(the thought only stirs in him his manly sense of right)—"*you have nothing to do thus to put things to my choice ;* wherefore *at your peril be it* if you interfere." The self-repression, both of conviction and of courage, which throbs through the whole of these clear quiet words, betokens a large reserve of genuine heroism, and bodes the worst for the wellbeing of "Wild-head, Inconsiderate, and Pragmatic."

As to the fight itself there is quite a warrior's proverbial meagreness of descriptive detail. Engaged " for the space of about three hours "—" marks of valour " borne away by both sides—one side "just now gone" at last, perhaps because they heard the voices of a pilgrim company : that is the combatant's account of his combat, and it is not a war-correspondent's account of those three hours. Under cross-examination, the bleeding victor makes no marvel of the victory, inasmuch as he "has *the truth* on his side." He " *did* cry out "—not to reach the ear of pilgrims, how-ever, but the ear of his " King," whose " invisible help was sufficient for him :" (nevertheless, the seasonable approach of pilgrims may have been part of the King's answer of help). Great-heart finds further reason for his victory in the weapon he is clasping : it is the experience of a brother-warrior which suggests the request, " Let me see thy sword ;" " which is the Word of God," as we per-ceive when we look with the eyes of the brave men them-selves—a blade with which a man " may venture upon an angel," Valiant declares, if only he knows how " to *use* it." He " fought with most courage " when sword and hand " were joined together, as if a sword grew out of his arm," and when " the blood ran through his fingers " while he was doing what Great-heart speaks of as if it were " striving against *sin*." Valiant had earned " worthily " his cordial initiation into the fellowship of a better gang than that of the thieves ; " and so," as soon as the weary stranger had been refreshed, " they went on together."

Together ; yet it is not clear, from anything that is re-ported of him, that Valiant entered very fervently into his new conditions. Save when he breaks silence at the sight of Stand-fast, and questions him anxiously why he was upon his knees (for both the occupation and the attitude are interesting to the man who prays best when he is standing foot to foot with the foe), we hear nothing from his lips till we find him in the presence of Christiana receiving her farewells. But we must reckon that he was by no means a man of words. Our first meeting with him may in this respect deceive us. He was even voluble then, and ran on as if he were Talkative himself:—"I am a pilgrim, and am going to the celestial City. *Now*, as I was in my way," he proceeds, without a pause, "there were three men did beset me, and propounded unto me these three things." . . . And he keeps up the conversation with Great-heart vigorously for pages of the book: "*Now*, that which caused me to come on pilgrimage was this"—"Have you any *more* questions to ask?" But is it not so with many silent men, that when there comes pressure enough to set talk in motion with them, their speech is apt to become as continuous as their silence usually is, and the *vis inertiæ* of the tongue works now for going on? Valiant is under high tension—in less sturdy men we should call it excitement—when we see him first. After that forced rush of talk has spent itself, and we have gathered out of its flow whatever is essential about his history, we are fain to let him relapse into his average mood again, and are well satisfied to get a glimpse of him such as we get once when we see him in his true place of defender of the weaker pilgrims as they move on in the rear of the brotherly band. Allegorically, it is not by his lips, but by his sword, that Valiant does any service for the truth.

Perhaps it may throw some afterlight upon both the character and the calling of this man, if we look back for a moment at the character and manner of those assailants of his. The attack,—and we may regard this affair as typical of others in this particular,—was really made by the enemy, and was only resisted by the hero himself. It was a fight of defence, as little sought as it was shunned : "They drew upon me, *and I also drew upon them*." So too, while the fight was in its immediate aims a personal encounter between the one and the three, it was by implication a good deal more. Valiant was confronted by three redoubtable foes, not of himself only, but of "the truth," and of himself because he was a champion of "the truth." They were plotting against "the truth," and they were striking at "the truth," in all their operations upon Valiant. Their hostility, moreover, was moral rather than intellectual, and was highly dangerous as it swaggered around upon the confines of the pilgrims' path. "Wild-head :" what champion of God's truth does not meet him in every age, as he clatters out upon the sober-minded traveller to the City, and rings down his challenge of surrender and renouncement, since he will brook no reasonable inquiry about anything, and least of all about whether he himself may be right or wrong? "Inconsiderate :" where has the truth ever been making its way in a community, and this being of brainless impulse has not dashed out upon its stoutest adherents, thoughtless even of defeat? And "Pragmatic :" how seldom is this pretentious meddler to be missed by the man who bears the truth in a brave heart, and strikes for it with a brave hand? If these can scarcely be said to have much courage in them, they have at least enough of bold assurance—when all three are against one, as they much prefer to have it : they then fly at the largest game by choice, and take discomfiture without heartbreak; for they have little to lose, and they will take care they do not lose their lives. Therefore, gentle dealings are thrown away upon them, and compromise is damaging. It is fortunate if anywise, within the limits of honourable warfare, they can be driven from the path whereon earnest men are pursuing and promoting the truth of heaven—a path and people they hate, without reflection enough even to perceive, that their objection is more of the heart than it can well be of the head. Hence we are not to think of this victory as merely a matter of the spiritual safety of the man Valiant; nor need we think of it, on the other hand, as picturing only a polemical triumph. It rather pictures an active resistance to lawless folly in all its movements, as it thrusts itself into the way of a selected follower of law-abiding wisdom—a resistance in terms of Bible verity as it is believed by a strong-hearted man—a resistance so invincibly sustained, upon its base of Divine Wisdom and Power, that it brings the opposers at length to feel, almost to *think*, that their opposition is costing them more than it is like to yield them. A half-conscious benefactor after all, then—a defender of the faith—we may reckon this Valiant to be, as he swings his dripping sword for those three hours on behalf of his own life and his own truest liberty.

It supports this view of the conflict of Valiant as being largely a representative event, that we can trace so slight an affinity between his allegorical assailants and any points of his own real character. They and he are fighting men on different sides—that is all: therefore his particular pattern of temptation is sword to sword. We may not indeed be able to affirm, that there were no elements in the character of Valiant which might tempt him to err in the direction of wildness of head, or inconsiderateness, or pragmatic impertinence; nor can we well disprove that he might have been liable enough to become "one of them" if he had not been grasped by the truth for which Christian before him had hazarded so much. But there could hardly have been so great a store of these weaknesses remaining now as to give body to such a desperate and prolonged combat as that which covered him with his freshest wound-marks. Christian himself, whose conflicts were undoubtedly characteristic and personal, was done with them all long before he came to the stage at which this battle was fought. Valiant, perhaps, was not too strong in judgment; he was not a man of fine nature, nor was he much restrained by a self-conscious sensibility; he was not a man of any mind beyond common intelligence sanctified. But he had too great a mass of manhood in him, and that mass was too compactly knit by the equal pressure of truth, to make any temptation to lawless un-wisdom a temptation of very formidable strength for his own spirit.

If we knew even as much of Valiant as his fellow-pilgrims would come to know, we might find reason to set him into close comparison with the greatest of the characters we have already considered. We miss the record of that "*long season*" during which, as he does not shrink to say to the miscreants, he had been "a true man." We can only dimly imagine the facts which led Christiana to say, in her hour of departure, that he had "in all places showed himself true-hearted;" and we may well think highly of the man whom such a woman "entreated to have an eye to her children," although he was one of the last of the company who had come into her acquaintance. If she committed this trust to him because of the likelihood of his surviving the others, she miscalculated; for he received his summons "by the same post" with old Honest himself, who, but for his years, had many a claim upon this confidence. But it was like the wife of Christian to entrust the children of Christian to a man to whom the name of her husband was dearer than any name on this side the River; yet it is not upon this she grounds her confidence, but upon the character she knows to be in him. To her he must have been tender, with something of the tenderness of true warriorhood, for her husband's sake; and doubtless his whole intercourse with the family of Christian, both before and after the departure of

Christiana, would do much to draw forth all the finer elements of his strong nature. Not that he would confine all his tenderer fellowship to these: we feel the unlikelihood of this when we see how naturally Ready-to-Halt and Feeble-mind, no less than Christiana, turn to Valiant in the day of their departure, and devolve upon him the duties of a sole trustee, as if he had become the recognised executor of the brotherhood. It is plain, that the longer he dwelt among them, the more he grew to be the staff of the pilgrim-company. He would never have the richness of Christian's spirituality, nor the sunny youthfulness of Hopeful's, nor the bright clear-heartedness of Honest's, nor perhaps the passive strength of Faithful's; but with his own dauntless trueness some grains of all these might happily mingle ere he went his way to his King. "I am going to *my Father's,*" he almost surprises us by saying when the summons has found him: had he thoughts of the earthly father whom he had "got *from*" at the darker extremity of his pilgrimage, and in spirit had been bereaved-of all the way? But the ruling emotion emerges again, when he has made his three characteristic bequests, and is stepping steadily into the deeper places of the River; for death itself is only the last of his foes, and the word which his voice leaves to linger upon the air of the pilgrim-land is "victory." "And *all the trumpets sounded for* HIM" too "on the other side."

The historical considerations which prompt us to set STAND-FAST under the same heading with Valiant, obvious as they must be, are not the only considerations in the case. The last pilgrim who came into the company is in several respects the complement and the counterpart of Valiant. Like him, he is strong, courageous, true—not to be moved from his pilgrim purpose, and crying for "invisible help" in the solitariness of his struggle with confronting falseness. They both take after Faithful rather than after Christian and Hopeful: we do not hear that ever they gave way before any form of enemy. Valiant, in his own manner, is "standing" too, and is standing "fast" enough, when he first appears to us: "having done all" that the circumstances admit of, he "stands;" for he deems it no part of his duty to pursue the foe after he has beaten him from his path. So Stand-fast, though a man of a different mould, is found in the moment of victory, tenderly thankful that his enemy has at length abandoned him, hopeless of conquest. His enemy, however, rather than his foe. It is seduction that Stand-fast has to foil, and seduction as a thing pressing against the personal loyalty of his own individual spirit, without the appearance of any wider aim. His fight has been an internal one—more subtle, less for on-looking eyes to measure, less a matter to describe in terms of history, yet as real and arduous as any combat fierce with the clash of swords. Stand-fast is waylaid within the region of brain-conquering enchantment, where Valiant has little likelihood of meeting anything that will appeal to the temper of his sword, and where a vigilant march-through is all that his nature and function demand. Valiant might not have dealt so brilliantly with Madame Bubble as he dealt with the armed robbers, nor should Stand-fast have held his own so triumphantly before the three as he did before the one; only, the robbers would not have selected Stand-fast for a prize, nor would the witch have put off her time with an unworldly warrior like Valiant.

We do not long remain dependent upon the hearty testimony of Honest that Stand-fast "is certainly a right good pilgrim." It grows upon us, that perhaps this man, if only we had longer acquaintance of him, would be found no whit behind any character we have yet seen upon that hallowed road. We are almost constrained to surmise, what in itself is not improbable, that Bunyan consciously put forth his strength upon this last character of his ; nor need it greatly discourage this surmise that he omits the name of Stand-fast from his Preface.   If he did design to close his long series of portraits with one that would win our regard as fervently as so brief an acquaintance made possible, we should not be disposed to affirm that he has failed in his design.   Our heart warms to him at his very name.   For we are in no danger of putting into the name any but the loftiest meaning, after the exquisite method by which Bunyan introduces him to us.   The company, weary of foot and of spirit, were nearing the end of the tract of witchery.   A little ahead of them, becoming more and more audible as they advance, is "a *solemn noise* of one that is much concerned."   Immediately, "behold they see, *as they think*, a man upon his knees, with hands and eyes lift up, and speaking, *as they think*, earnestly to one that is above."   So absorbed is he that they can "draw nigh," though they are not "nigh" enough to make out his words.   "So they *went softly till he had done*.   When he had done, he got up, and," without observing anything of their presence, "began to *run* towards the Celestial City."   Great-heart does not need to send after him his question to Valiant, "*What* art thou?"—but only "So-ho, friend! let us have your company."   And the man stops to give it,—and to find "old Honest" at his side, and to break out into accents of greeting so cordial as to be something of a happy contrast to the "solemn noise" which he "blushes" to know was overheard at so close a distance. "Why, what did you think?" he asks.   "Think!" answers Honest cheerily : "what *should* I think.   I thought we had an honest man upon the road, and that *we should have his company* by-and-bye."   "If you thought not amiss, how happy am I," replies the good man ; "but if I be not as I should, I alone must bear it."   The shadow is fringing him yet; but perhaps it is scattered by the conviction which this tone of his only deepens in Honest, "that things are right betwixt the Prince of pilgrims and his soul."

It is Valiant that draws out of him the story of his distress. Honest breaks in upon the story when it has been formally begun. "But let me go on with my tale," pleads Stand-fast—even in smaller matters true to his name. As he was musing, then, upon the peculiar perils of the neighbourhood, "one in very pleasant attire, but old," appeared before him with offers of all she could give. To him, just then, the offers were especially alluring. He "repulsed her once or twice;" but she would not be bidden away, and still beamed with smiles. She renewed her offers; she would make him "great and happy," for it was this she did with men as "mistress of the world." "Her name?"—"that set him further from her;" but "Madame Bubble" held at him with her wiles. Then there was nothing for it but to get to his knees,—"as they saw him,"—and pray "to Him that had said He would help." As with Valiant, "just as *they* came up, the gentlewoman went her way." And he remained on his knees giving thanks; "for," he adds simply, "*I verily believe she intended no good, but rather sought to make stop of me in my journey.*" When Great-heart has made vivid revelation of her true character and aims, her conqueror is profoundly impressed:—"O *what a mercy* it is that I did resist!—for whither might she have drawn me?" This combination of simplicity with steadfastness—this unvaunting conquest upon motives so much less pointedly strong than a fuller knowledge would have furnished—throws a tender lustrousness for us, like a halo of rainbow, around his name.

Bunyan has made this incident, and the conversations which turn upon it, unusually radiant with revelation of character. The incident stands absolutely alone as history of Stand-fast up to the date of our meeting him, and almost alone to the very day of our parting with him again. Yet we seem to be even better satisfied about our knowledge of Stand-fast than about that of Valiant, whose earlier pilgrim-biography at least was so graphically outlined for us. And already we feel more drawn to the later pilgrim-companion than ever we have been to Valiant. We would not do that hero injustice; his qualities are different. His brilliant indomitableness earns our admiration, and commands our trust; Stand-fast wins nearly as much of both, and our lively sympathy besides. We have a positive affection for Stand-fast, and we think of his strength itself with a respectfulness which has a deal of tenderness in it. It is not so with Valiant, though Great-heart's military admiration of him was doubtless touched with brotherly regard. We miss in Valiant the delicacy of feeling, the genial responsiveness of nature, the well-springs of manly sensibility, that we find in Stand-fast. Valiant is little more than a man of battles, and withal of victories; Stand-fast is a man of rich roundness of character, all of it stiffened into a balanced steadfastness, which appeals to our whole humanity, as it pervades the whole of his. Stand-fast's spirituality is deeper, we imagine, as well as more personally intense; and we almost forget, that the intensity is all directed to upholding the integrity of his own pilgrim-course. We feel that he has harder work with himself than Valiant has, and that he has nothing of energy to spare beyond the difficult charge which his own heart is to him. Madame Bubble represents nearly all that can oppose itself to spiritual prosperity. She is "the world" with a liberal dash of "the flesh;" and in respect of both, she recognises materials in him that render him worthy of her hopeful attention. She is Vanity Fair embodied under a woman's attire, and got into ubiquitous locomotion along the length of the way—this, and Faithful's Wanton, in one.

He does not need to be assaulted by "the Devil" in person, as Christian was; nor would the Valley of Humiliation be to him a likely field of conflict at all. The adversary reaches him more effectively by proxy; for she is as much the deputy of the Devil as she is the "mistress of the world," though upon this she is more silent. And it is significant that she turns up to ply him with her solicitations on the inner margin of the ground which is the very last region of trial for pilgrims: the natural elements in the man must have been stubborn, we reckon, and deep in their roots. For we see that even now it is only with a struggle and a strong grasping of the aid of Heaven that he overcomes. He is a man more *in* the world than Valiant is, yet he will be as little *of* it as Valiant can be— as little to the last, though to the last he has qualities and susceptibilities in him which make a worldly life a much more powerful attraction to him than it ever could be to Valiant.

It is interesting to note the number and variety of circumstances in which Stand-fast appears as a special and exceptional pilgrim under the fond ingenuity of Bunyan. We have noticed the mere blank which his past history is to us: it is not so with any other pilgrim. We have seen how he was found upon his knees—an attitude which it is not unimportant to remember is a singularly rare one in the Allegory. It may have occurred to us, that he alone of all pilgrims encountered an active tempter on the drowsy ground which margined the frontier of the region of rest. And even when this region itself is reached, the touches of specialness in the instance of Stand-fast seem rather to multiply. Christiana was speaking her farewell words, and dispensing her farewell tokens: "*But*," it is said, "*she gave Mr Stand-fast a ring.*" Of Stand-fast's own summons it is recorded that "the post brought it him *open* in his hands." ("This Mr Stand-fast," interpolates Bunyan, with a kindly anxiety that he should be identified in connection with the characteristic incident by which he emerged into view, " was he that the rest of the company found *upon his knees* in the Enchanted Ground.") The summons bore, that " his Master *was not willing that he should be so far from Him any longer* "—a tone of explicit tenderness which is reserved for this pilgrim's summons alone ; nor is it entirely accounted for by another distinguishing circumstance—that he was the last of the company to be called away save only the children of Christiana, whom the story leaves in Beulah.   So, also, his message by Great-heart to his " family," the " wife and five small children " whom he left behind him when he took his way,—while it is remarkable as giving a late and unexpected glimpse into the good man's past, and pathetic enough as revealing a heart-burden which he had all along been carrying, is no less to be noted as a thing unparalleled in the annals of the Pilgrimage.   And equally unusual was his departure itself, which Bunyan so much more fully describes than he describes any other but that of Christiana : " Now there was *a great calm at that time* in the river "—so great a calm, within and without, that at a point about mid-channel, he " stood awhile, and talked " to the convoy of friends who watched him from the bank ; and it was while he was speaking from this unwonted spot, with a voice that must have had no little energy in it as well as composure, that " his countenance changed," and he was gone.

We cannot but wonder at the copiousness of imagination which is still able, in passing before us the last of so long a procession of living figures, to endue it with such freshness both of character and of incident.   Perhaps the pilgrim of whom Stand-fast most reminds us, however, is Christian himself.   In his conception of the last of his pilgrims, Bunyan seems to recall a consciousness of the first of them.   Yet it is by no means a repetition of the first with which he closes. The death of Stand-fast is almost as striking a contrast to the death of Christian as even Bunyan himself could well draw. "*Now*, methinks, *I stand easy:*" so spoke he whose habit it had been to "stand *fast*" while he was yet in the midst of the hazards of the way. They were among the first of the eloquent words he uttered from the same river-channel where Christian gasped out his syllables of hopelessness in the intervals when his drooping head was not down beneath the flood. This wide difference of experience suggests no little difference of character. But the resemblance between the two pilgrims in their domestic relations, and in the tender anxiety which those relations inspired, is very noteworthy as supporting the conjecture that the two were conjoined in the mind of Bunyan. When we hear the sender of the touching message proceeding thus—" Tell them also of Christian, and Christiana his wife, and how *she* and *her* children came after *her* husband,"—we feel that the earlier pilgrim and his household are hovering vividly around us again, because they have taken a parting grasp of the mind of the Dreamer. And when we listen still, and hear him say, as if with quavering voice—" I have little or nothing to send to my family, except it be *prayers and tears for them :* of which it will suffice if thou acquaint them, if peradventure they may prevail,"—we think we might be giving ear to Christian himself, or reading particulars of his parting days which had hitherto been withheld—withheld, perhaps, on account of their bold freedom as allegorical history. So the echo of Christian's footfall, which has reverberated through this Second Part from the beginning, only gathers force and articulateness as the history closes. And we cannot but notice, that the first pilgrim and the last, whom we judge to lie closest to the soul of Bunyan, are the two who come into nearest resemblance to himself, and not alone in respect of the family affections which occupied so much of his heart. But it is this domestic similarity which that heart guides him instinctively to select as the most visible feature of resemblance. This Second Part of the " Pilgrim," we cannot doubt, gets something of its hearty joyousness from the sustained sense of the fact, that it is in substance but the story of Christian's wife and children going after Christian. Surely Stand-fast was followed too by that family of his, whether the years were few or many since the Allegory and his duty compelled him to leave them behind him.

Since we made the acquaintance of the prime pilgrim himself, we have met with no one who so equally mingled the gentler and the sterner qualities of character as this man whose departure closes the record of pilgrimage. In the later pilgrim, these opposites are more sharply emphasized, and the fusion of the two is probably less pervading and complete, than in the earlier pilgrim. Stand-fast's character is the more piquant; Christian's is the more fully furnished, and the more variously blended—even to complexity and complication, of which the character of Stand-fast is almost wholly free. Every inch a man he is, —throbbing full of a brave loyalty of heart and conscience that holds down the evil in himself with a hero's hand, and impels him to strike onward with a hero's ardour of holy ambition in the way of the loftiest righteousness. Yet he has much in him, all the while, of the unaffected gentleness and quick sensibility of womanhood. His heroism casts an air of chastened power and companionable strength around the liquid depths of an emotional nature. It is such a man who is apt to be at once the idol and the worshipper of womanhood—a quiet star in social circles, both attracting and attracted as he moves among the dames and maidens who give to society its tone and ornament. Stand-fast had probably been no stranger to female society in his less earnest days; nor need he have been afterwards. Are we not getting some hint of all this when we see him encountered by that womanly form,— and when we hear his touch of description, "In very pleasant *attire*, but *old*,"—and when we mark the intuitive gallantry of the phrase, "The *gentlewoman* went her way," —and when we observe the distinct note he must have made of her appearance and manner when he can so promptly respond to the catechising of Honest on the subject? Are we not getting a tenderer hint of it when we see the matron of the company bestowing upon him so special and so significant a farewell token? But now, in these advanced pilgrim-days of his, whatever was naturally good in all this has been sanctified, and whatever was naturally evil has been forgiven and overcome. From the first of his new life, both the manly and the womanly in him have been for Christ, and his affection for this wondrous "Master" has drawn forth even unsuspected strength of steadfastness in the treading of those paths which He Himself has trodden. "Wherever I have seen the print of His shoe in the earth," he says by way of unboasting reminiscence, "*there I have coveted to set my foot too*." Coveted, and more and more succeeded. A strong sure-footedness this, well worthy to become the pattern of our own supreme ambition—so firm in purpose, so delicate in feeling, so holy in energy, so glorious in issue, it is. Stand-fast knew nothing of an easy Christian life : he deemed his Christian calling to appeal to every power that was in him—if not for resistance and endurance, then for activity and advance. It was from the personal side that he approached all his Christian arduousness, while Valiant approached it from the public side ; but he did approach it all, and grappled with it as a settled habit, into which he concentrated the watchful constancy of a character that was strong by nature, and stronger still by grace. And the summer-calm at his heart grew only the deeper for this as his strenuous days gathered behind him, until it became at his departure a tropical effulgence of peace, which sunned the solemnity of death itself into the tender gladness of a festal noontide that is thrilled with the music of bridal farewells.

XVI.

INFIRM PILGRIMS : FEEBLE-MIND—READY-TO-HALT—
DESPONDENCY AND HIS DAUGHTER.

THE " Pilgrim's Progress " is not a book which is set for
the praise of Christian life in the world, but for the
portrayal of it.   Christianity as it ought to be,—this,
although it is not forgotten, does not take precedence of
Christianity as it is.   We have almost no faultless ideals,
but have faulty men and women ever going on to better
things, and only passing at last into what appears to be
faultlessness entire and everlasting.

Bunyan, with his sagacious honesty, could not have
gone far in his delineation of actual Christian character
without doing more than merely touch-in occasional spots
of infirmity upon the conduct of his heroes and heroines :
he must bring before us persons whose whole bearing
wears the aspect of infirmity, and who are not heroes or
heroines at all.   It must be allowed that he has done this
part of his work amply and well.   In the six characters
who are clearly to be classified as true pilgrims of pervading infirmity, he has represented Christian weakness without needless hesitancy on the one hand, and without
unwise exposure on the other.   It would be rash to affirm
that he has exhausted all the conceivable types of Christian
feebleness, or to maintain that there is not a certain degree
of sameness in the moulds of infirmity in which those six
characters are cast ; yet he has not stinted himself of
choice within the range of that order of Christian weakness

to which he has confined his view. It is plain, moreover, that the characters he has selected are singularly fitted to attract our interest and awaken our sympathy, while they give the very smallest encouragement to our contempt. Indeed, there is scarcely a character among them who does not manage, notwithstanding his infirmity, to command something of our admiration, or whose very weakness itself is not so rooted together with strength that we have a frequent misgiving as to whether we are doing him justice by accounting him "infirm" at all.

It is to the Second Part that we naturally turn for the greater number of our Infirm Pilgrims. Little-faith, whom Christian champions so jealously when he tells the story of him to Hopeful, is the only one of the class who enters into the Part which is the chronicle of strong pilgrims; and he enters into it only by hearsay. Mr Fearing in the Second Part has a parallel place to Little-faith in the First; and even if Mr Fearing stood alone for his kindred in the later narrative, that narrative should still be richer than the earlier one in respect of this department of representation. But the Second Part, more true to its vocation than be content with this, permits us personally to see and hear as many as four of these interesting brethren of the road.

The first who comes to light is FEEBLE-MIND. He probably derives his name from 1st Thessalonians (v. 14) —"Comfort the feeble-minded;" where, however, the Revisers have had need to substitute—"Encourage the *faint-hearted.*" He takes rank with Despondency and his daughter, and with Little-faith, in having his feebleness associated with calamity. When the guests of Gaius find him, his plight is unhappy enough. The "flesh-eater" Slay-good was bending over him at the work of "rifling him," with an eye to the subsequent luxury of "picking his bones." The "servants" of the giant had "taken him in the way," and had brought him thus to their master in his cavern: so at least we read in the history. The account of the poor man himself is slightly different:— "*This giant* met with me, and bid me prepare for an encounter; but alas! feeble one that I was, I had more need of a cordial. So *he* came up and took me." The man's recollection of the events may be a little confused; but if he was confronted by "this giant" in person, we should scarcely have marvelled that the gigantic ruffian "took" him, even if he had been a pilgrim of stouter heart. However, the "rifling of his pockets," as he afterwards describes his mischance, was the worst that came to pass with him: Great-heart's sword put a full period there. And it is remarkable enough to be noted at once, that the man himself seems to have had nothing of the terror of death upon him when he was under the handling of the giant:—"I *conceited he should not kill me.* Also, when he had got me into his den, since I was not with him willingly, I *believed I should come out alive again;* for I have heard that not any pilgrim that is taken captive by violent hands, if he *keeps heart-whole towards his Master*, is, by the laws of Providence, to die by the hand of the enemy." This Feeble-mind, then, in his hour of extremity, gets prompt hold of a principle which meets his circumstances, and meets them with hope; and he grips that principle with so firm a hand, that he can decline to accept all the contrary likelihoods which appearances are arraying against it and him. This Feeble-mind too, we are able to infer, "keeps heart-whole towards his Master," even when things look worst with him in that Master's service. These are observable items, meanwhile, in the conduct of a pilgrim who, "feeble one that he was," considers that "a cordial" would have been more appropriate to his condition, when he was about to be captured, than an attitude of resistance on behalf of his liberty.

But it is well we should gather up the little handful of particulars which he gives us of his history. It is "from the town of Uncertain" that he has travelled—a town of less positive hostility to pilgrim ways, it would seem, than some that stand upon the map of the Allegory. The determining motive of his setting-out is in keeping with this : "Because death did usually once-a-day knock at my door," he says, "I thought I should never be well at home." Reasons for remaining, thus reduced to a minimum of force, left reasons for departing to have the fuller play upon him ; so that his setting-out has the air of a preference which he deliberately exercised, and little the look of a necessity which he could not decline. Nevertheless, his preference has clearly had all the pilgrim effect of a stronger and stormier resolve. He has gone on unswervingly ; and this is nearly all his story. At the Gate he was "entertained freely," and, without a word of reproach, was furnished and heartened for his way. At the Interpreter's he "received much kindness," and "one of his servants" carried him up the Hill. From pilgrims who overtook him in their more rapid march he has "found much relief," and gotten much good cheer, ere they passed on. Then came "Assault Lane" and the giant : all details of the interval between the Hill and this cavern are swallowed up in the magnitude of his latest experience—his only experience, we may presume, that has anything of historical emphasis in it.

These biographic hints, few as they are, arrange the affairs of the capture into something of perspective, and reveal its consistency with the antecedents of the man. There is the same limpness of executive will, with the same hopeful tension of innermost purpose. There is the same solitary and slow advance, which cannot, however, be arrested save by what overpowers him from without ; and there is only sharper evidence that he cannot be overpowered but by a violence which swoops down upon the weakness of what we may call his muscular will. There is the same dependence upon the casual help of stronger fellow-pilgrims—upon "relief," that here develops into a deliverance which comes scarcely short of a ransom of his life. And the unwonted gravity of this misfortune does no other than offer an occasion for the more striking intervention of that superhuman Power which has been mantling round him with its vigilant kindliness during every step of his road ; for is not the one calamity of his history the finest mercy of his history, since it is but the grim portal through which he emerges into that companionship of considerate pilgrims which henceforth makes cheering and guidance and defence to be his hourly possession?

We can now begin to guess the feelings with which the party of Gaius would regard this unlooked-for accession which the brotherhood had won for itself by its own right hand. If we give further attention to the words which they heard from him, we shall better understand how their feelings could not have been those of pity alone, but rather of tender respect. He is not a reticent man—not silent concerning himself, and least of all concerning his own infirmities. There is a touch of true art in the copious frankness with which his weakness is represented as making a topic of itself, and as almost pleading for recognition. " I am a sickly man, *as you see :*" these are his first words in the history. Again : "I am a man of *no strength at all of body, nor yet of mind.*" So also : " My *feeble body;*" " My *feeble mind ;*" " To go so softly *as I am forced to do;*" " *Feeble one* that I was, I had more need of a *cordial;*" " I am, *as you see*, escaped with life ;" " Though I am, *as you see*, but of a feeble mind." And afterwards : " He (Mr Fearing) was my uncle, my father's brother. He and I have been *much of a temper.* He was *a little shorter than I*, but yet we were *much of a complexion. . . .* What I have

read in him I have, for the most part, *found in myself.*"
This, it must be granted, would soon become a test of the
patience of a listener. But all this is interspersed with
words like these:—"But (I) would, if I could, *though* I
can but crawl, spend my life in the pilgrims' way."
" Robbed I *looked* to be, and robbed to be sure I *am;* but
. . . ; for the which I thank my King as author, and you
as means. Other brunts I also look for ; but *this* I have
resolved on, to wit, to *run* when I can, to *go* when I cannot
run, and to *creep* when I cannot go. *As to the main, I
thank Him that loves me, I am fixed. My way is before
me; my mind is beyond the river* that has no bridge,—
though I am" . . . Gaius seeks to impress upon him how
welcome he is to all the entertainment his house can
afford, and the poor man's heart is touched :—" This is
unexpected favour, and as the sun shining out of a very
dark cloud. Did Giant Slay-good intend me *this* favour
when he stopped me, and resolved to let me go no further?
Did he intend, that *after* he had rifled my pockets, I
should *go to Gaius mine host?* Yet so it is." The tidings
are brought that Not-right, who had for some days clung
to his company, but took to his heels at sight of Slay-good,
had been stricken dead by a thunder-bolt : the pith of his
remarks upon the event is this :—" But, it seems, *he escaped
to die, and I was took to live ;*" or, as his verse renders it,

" Hands crossed gives death to him, and life to me."

Such a man these pilgrims can by no means despise. They
do not dream but of his joining them for all time coming.
They have little reason to reckon him unworthy of their
company : he is one for whose sake they will by-and-bye
agree to slacken their own pace, and to " deny themselves
some things "—not, as we may now judge, from motives of
compassion alone.

Up to this point at which we have arrived in our

acquaintance with Feeble-mind, however, it is to be noticed that his feebleness, though manifest enough to give some reason for his name, is not quite so well defined for us as his strength itself is. It appears as little else than the general foil of the force that is in him, or the peculiar necessity of the case by which that force is summoned into display. We do " see," as he would have us see, a man who has all the aspect of an invalid—wan in look, decrepit in gait, of a pace that is tedious for most men even to look upon, his mere locomotion demanding all his energy and getting all his care, content to have no more than his feeble body and feeble mind for his company, and in most evil case if sturdy foes should happen to find him. But we need more detail of how his feebleness unfolds itself among the common conditions of pilgrimage, and of how it works out its own analysis in contact with other pilgrims, before we can easily translate it in terms of Christian character. His association with the brotherhood would offer scope enough for all this in the subsequent history, but that history gives him only scanty opportunity of self-revelation. Fortunately, however, before he starts on the journey as one of them, and when he is defending his reluctance to accompany them beyond the door of Gaius, he makes a little speech which goes some way to supply the lack we feel. We must hear it all :—" Alas ! " he begins, " I want a suitable companion. You are all lusty and strong ; but I, as you see, am weak. I choose, therefore, rather to come behind, lest, by reason of my many infirmities, I should be both a burden to myself and to you. I am, *as I said*, a man of a weak and feeble mind, and *shall be offended and made weak at that which others can bear. I shall like no laughing ; I shall like no gay attire ; I shall like no unprofitable questions.* Nay, I am so weak a man as to be *offended with that which others have liberty to do.* I do not yet *know all the truth.* I am a *very ignorant Christian man.* Sometimes, if I hear some *rejoice in the Lord, it troubles me,* because I cannot do so too. It is with me as with a weak man among the strong, or as with a sick man among the healthy, or as a lamp despised "—(he is quoting from Job xii. 5, and quoting very aptly as the patriarch is reported in the Authorised Version; but both "lamp" and simile have disappeared under the hands of the Revisers)— . . . "so that I know not what to do."

Some of these sentences pierce with real life those phenomenal statements about his feeble body, and go like wedges of cleavage into those somewhat dense generalities about his feeble mind. We begin to understand the man as well as to "see" him. He is a pilgrim, a Christian, who is hampered and bowed down with exaggerated *Concern for Himself.* He lives in a continual apprehension of suffering harm—with a phase of this which appears as an apprehension of working harm. Apprehension : we already know he is constitutionally "uncertain," and has the blood of Fearing in his veins. He was apprehensive at home; so he started to a life in which his apprehensions would have a background of hope "as to the main," and a foundation of rightness as to the whole multifarious body of them. But he is apprehensive still. He is not afraid for his getting to heaven, but he has it in him to be sorely afraid for himself all the way. "The main" is "fixed" enough—fixed as personal purpose, and fixed as personal assurance of safety : this great length of reliance on God he has reached. But that fixedness seems to absorb all his capability of certainty, and to use up all his slender stock of courage. He has nothing of either to spare beyond what is of life and death—beyond what is at once pre-eminent duty and supreme security. The strain which this puts upon him be cannot relax ; he feels as if he dare not. He cannot afford any freedom of thought, any play of sympathy, any stepping forth into open regions of holy venturesomeness. Harm might come to him—harm, at the least, in disturbing the concentration of himself upon the few great verities he is grasping. Therefore the Christian life is to him a matter of almost unrelenting gravity : it must needs have many inconveniences, many anxieties, many pains ; but it must have no secondary pleasures, no collateral pursuits, nothing sanctified for it out of the unhallowed world, no enriching of itself with the best of what is natural and innocent. Anyhow, Christian life as it stands with himself is not able to assimilate any of these. He is like a man who has no ear for the happy pleasantries around him, and no eye for the lovely things that are inviting his gaze—no heart to deem anything relevant, or even tolerable—because he himself is hard bestead with a task which the most of other men might manage with a margin of disengagedness, but which to him is a sustained extremity of effort touching the verge of danger. This painful seriousness is not a thing of principle with him : if he grew stronger, it would not grow into sternness ; it would simply disappear. It is an involuntary thing with him ; and he pleads and appeals and apologizes about it in the presence of stronger men, as if he were sensible it must fairly be reckoned a wrong thing unless he make clear the exceptional ground for it that there is in himself.

At the back of this self-regardful concern, then, there is a *Constitutional Sensitiveness* which has something morbid in it. He is too tender for common contacts, and every touch is to him like a blow. Purely spiritual handlings do not pain him—least of all, the exquisite dealings of his God with him for the settlement and sustenance of his spiritual hopes. But the mere loomings of God's providences, and the very neighbourhood of God's hardier children, make him wince and shrink. There is imagination in this, but there is also reality ; and imagination and reality conjoin to make it all, for himself, but one larger reality. Physically regarded, it is of the nature of hypochondria, either constitutional or become chronic ; and it tends towards the disease which physicians call "megalophany," whereby small things appear large, and large things prodigious. And, indeed, we shall leave out of our reckoning the deepest root of the anxious sensitiveness of such a man if we omit from our consideration his physical make and temperament. Grace has to deal with nothing so obstinate as these when they are adverse to robust Christianity. Often even grace itself seems capable of no more than a limited modification of weaknesses which are worked into the physical fibre of a man, and flow in his blood. Bunyan is touching shrewd truth when he rings the changes upon the "sickliness" of this man—the "weakness," the "feebleness," of his body—the daily knocking of "death" at his door from our earliest hearing of him,—whatever complexion of spiritual meaning he would have us to cast over these material circumstances. We have had already to do with pilgrims whose temporary infirmities might well be put to the account of temporary ailment of body; but with poor Feeble-mind the ailment, though not acute, is permanent. We shall not think of such a man with justice, or even with intelligence, unless we give due weight to the extent in which his character has been determined, and is held to its singularities through life, by the mere quality of the body with which he was born.

The *Conscientious Scrupulousness* which we find in the man is little else than the manifestation of this Sensitiveness within the region of moral feeling and action. His conscience shares it ; and microscopic carefulness rules throughout that royal faculty, putting it into tyrannic ways which are by no means a part of its primary intention. For conscience with him does not merely regulate ; it threatens, and watches, and worries, and turns life into a sea of troubles on which you are unhappy whether you are keeping above the water or lapsing beneath it. His conscience has not, properly speaking, a sense of touch, but only a sense of pain ; it does not so much discern, as resent. Its instinct is wholly with rightness, and here is one of the strongest strengths of the man ; but in its tenderness to the touch of things, it suspects and repels many a thing that is soundly right, and keeps off many a contact that would fain soothe it with the soft warmth of its congenial rightness, — suspects them, and keeps them off, merely because they do not approach with the pace and appearance which give the most commonplace assurance of their harmlessness. Will God in very truth, he asks himself, be glorified by human smiles ?—can laughter sort with saintship ?—is this a world where the unbending of bows and the slackening of strings can be done with impunity ?—is it fitting for any one to give way to joy of spirit on this arduous road to the great Unseen ?—is it worthy of a Christian to waste breath on any themes but such as are vital for the soul ?—can sauntering in the paths of science or art, of literature or music or politics, be other than hurtful to the spiritual life ? He would try not to judge others ; but for himself—certainly he will keep safety, whatever he may be thought to lose, if he answer, " No, *probably not.*" We shall not be keen to blame him ; but we shall be very ready to desire that he may come to enjoy a more healthy tone of conscience. In many ways he is impoverishing—is at present compelled to impoverish —even his moral life. For it is but few things that are really lawful to a moral sense like this, since so few things are " of faith " to it. The monotony of the round of allowed activity is itself oppressive, and the unrelieved reiteration of permitted experience is enough to sink ruts of jolting into the two or three over-used roadways of moral living. Nor is this mere exercise of defence an exercise at all sufficient for a powerful faculty like that which deals with right and wrong. Yet—better this than violence, which as the matter stands should only damage it with wounds, or encrust it with scars of insensibility; for the cure lies in the line of bringing organic robustness into the conscience itself, and not in the line of sending mechanical impingements upon the morbid refinements of its surface.

Perhaps we shall have named the last of the leading elements in this man's feebleness when we have named his *Lack of Light.* The poor man is as free of speech about this as about most of his other infirmities. We may demur to his declaration that he is "a very ignorant Christian man," but we may accept his plea that he "does not yet know all the truth." It is something that he knows his scantiness of knowledge: he might have been too ignorant even for this. But there is a peculiarity in these protestations of his ignorance which deserves our attention. They are made by way of reason for his following behind, or, at the least, as a reason for the reasons which he offers in declining to go with the company. But would not the companionship of these men and women—would not fellowship with his enlightened deliverer—be the likeliest remedy which the whole pilgrimage could supply for a deficiency he so dolefully deplores? Poor shrinking pilgrim, it is "a *suitable* companion" he desiderates;—not any number of companions who may dispel his darkness, but a companion, though he may chance to be as dark as himself, who will sympathise with his whole weakness, and step on at his own pace. His plea of ignorance, then, is not so clear a plea as it may seem, and is open to suspicions of over-statement. It is not his want of information about the truth that is giving him uneasiness; it is his want of practical ability to fulfil and enjoy the truth as these pilgrims can. He is speaking somewhat from the point of view from which his listeners will regard him. He does not "know" as truth a great deal that they live, and live as if it were truth which they clearly "knew." It is not knowledge, because it is not certainty, to him : it is all dubious ; and he would much prefer to keep out of the company of those to whom it is all firmness and freedom.

It is only the more obvious, then, that this pilgrim does lack light—light for his intellect indeed, but mostly light for his conscience, and light for his heart. He is not in the dark, but he is in perpetual twilight,—is glimmering on, with his foot waiting on his eye, and is having most of his light from the glow of eternal day upon the far horizon above the City. That to him is in every sense "the light of life." It is "suitable" to his eyesight, which is much more keen than strong. If that light ever does cast any shadows, they are faint, and mostly fall behind him. He will not make great effort to obtain sunshine: it might hurt his eyes; it might reveal troublesome things; it might render himself too visible. All the while, we are bethinking us how it would bronze that pallor out of his face, and brighten his eye, and give a surer tread to his foot, and help him to recognise what is friendly as much as what is unfriendly, and warm his joints into fleetness, and woo his heart into good cheer—if he could be brought to endure it. But if he could endure it, he would be Feeble-mind no more. So, from stage to stage, he "does not *yet* know *all* the truth"—as a thing applied to the theory and practice of Christian living according to Christian liberty : nevertheless, need we doubt that he knew more of "the truth" ere his journey was done, with so much of it travelled under the kindly eye of Great-heart, and amid the genial earnestness of his gathering company?

For, with Ready-to-halt of all men for a bosom-friend, he threw himself nobly into the numberless risks of going forward with the brotherhood ! This of itself was hopeful, and was the most momentous step he had taken since he crept away out of the town where " he and his father were born." " The laws of Providence "—the bye-laws of it, which have just as much of providence in them—had been leading the good man up to this, and been doing so in his own best interests. The appalling event at Assault Lane—the clash of weapons, the headless trunk of Slaygood, the tender rescue—the hospitable intercourse with the " strong " pilgrims at the inn—his sincere unwillingness to part with them, and to let them go forward with their pleadings resisted—the seasonable apparition of the honest face above the crutches ;—only a single slight movement of his own will was needed, and he was heartily stepping on as one of a very caravan of pilgrims who were somewhat renowned for their freedom from infirmity. The man was not very sure of providence, short of death itself ; yet this providence enfolded him with a quite special care. And providence was only working at one remove when he felt upon him the delicate considerateness of his new companions, and of all everywhere that were friendly to pilgrims. Gaius was right brotherly with him while they stayed, and when they departed he took leave " particularly of Mr Feeble-mind," and gave him "something to drink by the way." When the Shepherds have guided the company to their "palace door," where they " have comfort for the feeble as well as the strong," it is the Infirm Pilgrims they first welcome in, and " Mr Feeble-mind " first of all. When the band are getting into marching-order for traversing the perilous "forest" of the Enchanted Ground, " Feeble-mind, Mr Great-heart commanded, should come after *him*." We feel that all this is strictly in accordance with the principles of pilgrimage. True-hearted feebleness of Christian character casts a tender responsibility upon all the strength on which its shadow falls. The responsibility is first and most grandly owned by a gracious Heaven ; it is owned next by every capable Christian who has enough of the brotherly heart of a Christian in him. Outside of Christian friendship the world can furnish no study in social things that is more suggestive than the tender handlings of Feeble-minds by Great-hearts and Valiants and Honests and Christianas. It is so strikingly fine to see,—it so evidently brings into play what is deepest and noblest even in a Christian—it is so pleasurable for him who gives, and so grateful for him who takes,—that the pity and the wonder grow, that it is so comparatively rare in modern Christian society. For this companionship of weak Christians—it humanises, it even Christianises, the strong ones themselves, when they cheerfully accept their part, and gird themselves with self-denying patience to fulfil it. If it does sometimes try the best strength of a man, he may truly take the thought to his heart, that it is one of the most Christ-like tasks which a pilgrim can receive from the hand of his King.

We could wish for more decisive evidence than the history affords us, that Feeble-mind reaped improvement as well as advantage from his association with those most brotherly and sisterly fellow-pilgrims. He was not unimpressible, nor were they unimpressive ; surely he caught some infection of their courage and their freedom of heart. Do we see anything of the one in this record—"So they left the women in the road, and with them *Mr Feeble-mind*, and Mr Ready-to-halt with his crutches, to be *their guard* until they came back"? Do we see anything of the other in this further record—"Now when *Feeble-mind* and Ready-to-halt saw that it was the head of Giant Despair indeed, they were *very jocund and merry*"? Yet when he has been for some time in Beulah itself, Christiana must in faithfulness leave this in his ear as her last counsel :—"Only, I advise thee to *repent thee of thine aptness to fear and doubt of His goodness,* before He sends for thee; lest thou shouldest, when He comes, be forced to stand before Him for that fault with blushing." The reproof was gentle; for it came—rather, let us say, *but* it came—from the lips of a woman! He was not long in following her. His Master "had need" of him—even of him; and his warning was short, as was most "suitable" it should. His last will concerns his "feeble mind" alone; which now appears, with gleaming clearness, to be something other than himself: "THAT I will leave behind me, for that I have no need of *that* in the place whither I go. Nor is it worth bestowing upon the poorest pilgrim : wherefore, when I am gone, I desire that you, Mr Valiant, would *bury it in a dunghill.*" And "this" was "done." There is a touch of contemptuous revenge in his retrospect of the figure he has been bound to make as a pilgrim; and his second great repentance is achieved in the moment when every trace of his diffusive tenderness over his "feeble mind" is gone. He is aspiring to the ranks of the strong at last, and is stepping into those ranks as we listen. Is there a thought of this in the words—"He entered the river *as the rest*"? And is there not some evidence of it, even while he is yet visible, in his own words that we hear from the midst of the current, and after them no other—"*Hold out, faith and patience*"? At his brave bidding they seem to have held out well. When he had set his foot upon the other side, he would climb the radiant mountain with a strange lightness and liberty, and there would be awaiting him in the City "a new name."

It cannot be said that his old name, or at least his old nature, has disappeared from the domain of pilgrimage. Some of the truest of Christians are some of the feeblest—in the way in which Feeble-mind was feeble. Their weakness, no doubt, is greater in look than it is in reality : they are more or less feeble in everything, but they are not in every respect feeble. They are feeblest in what is most visible, especially to the onlooking world of those who are not of the pilgrim-brotherhood. They may possess, like Feeble-mind, no little intellectual pith, which puts a pointedness into their thought, and a raciness into their expression; they may display some tenacity of will; they may show no lack of affection; they may win the credit of fidelity to great principles; there may not be a hint of anything that is sensual in them, or worldly; and their sensitiveness may be seasoned with some grains of true sensibility. But men behold them, and their back is not straight, and their step is not firm, and they have no sound self-possession on their brow. They give the impression that Christian life, if only it be taken in hand with downright seriousness, is a spiritless business—a lifelong anxiety; a thing of greater strain than strength; a thing that only gets staying-power by using splints and bandages; a travelling of sick men to hospital in what they call heaven, where the gentler climate and the better medical skill may dispel all this wrinkled carefulness, and may put a healthy unconcern in the place of all this anxious fending of the soul. There is an air of contractedness about their views and conduct which forces the word " narrow," with more of justice than ought to be, to the lips of pitiless men. They are liable to a most unjust charge of " hypocrisy " at the mouths of the thoughtless. They are themselves apt to misconceive their more robust brethren, and to shake their heads about them when they might be clapping their hands. Their charity itself is weighted heavily. They make themselves a care, and sometimes a cross, to their ministers and their Christian associates—if they do not keep studiously aloof from these, and nurse their weaknesses in solitude, or in the select company of some " suitable " friend. Arguments may have little power to better these abnormal Christians; yet there are arguments fraught with spiritual motive that might well bestir them to make efforts after a freer Christian life. That they may breathe the atmosphere of these arguments, let them by all means encourage intercourse with such vigorous Christians as can be tender with their infirmities,—not concealing their infirmities from themselves, nor yet turning them into the irksome refrain of every conversation. A ministry with any sympathetic manliness in it will help them, if they see to doing it justice for themselves. Drinking of the "cordials" which are stored in the Book will strengthen them, and the tonic ones most. Prayer, if it be plied with steadiness of aim—praise too, if it be fetched from the wellsprings of personal gratitude—will beat like water-wearing upon the soft mass of their feebleness ; and the obedience of Christ, conducted in the elevated open of active service, will work weathering upon it and slow dissolution. It may give way less obstinately, and further too, than they are likely to anticipate. For both truth and charity command us to remember, that the *soul* of the Christian character of our Feeble-minds is fleet and strong ; it is only the *body* of it that is heavy with weakness. Their painful laboriousness, indeed, is often the travelling of a willing spirit under a load that is doubled round it, and their tardy momentum is frequently a wealth of force swallowed up of friction.

Between Feeble-mind and his friend READY-TO-HALT there is quite as much of contrast as there is of resemblance. Ready-to-halt is infirm, but he is scarcely to be called feeble. His infirmity is more local, and more mechanical—has lodged itself wholly in his limbs, and seems as if it held so insecure a lodgment even there, that we should hardly be surprised to find it some day losing hold altogether by just a little further gravitation downwards. For, although he enjoys but a slender share of the narrative, his appearances give him some right to be regarded as in many ways a very competent pilgrim.

While, therefore, our feeling about Feeble-mind was one of tender respect not unmixed with anxiety, our feeling about Ready-to-halt is rather one of respectful interest not unmixed with pleasure. The slightness of his infirmity not only precludes our uneasiness, but it permits the Author to introduce some good-humoured picturesqueness into this matter of pilgrim infirmity. This subject, which is a little depressing as it is seen in Feeble-mind, is both relieved and enlivened by the well-ordered emergence alongside of him of this brighter brother of his, and by the play of light-heartedness which we associate with the man of the crutches even when we are not hearing him. The moment he toils himself into view at the door of Gaius, we feel in mood to echo the hearty words of Feeble-mind himself— "Welcome, welcome, good Mr Ready-to-halt." Only, when he goes on to say, " I hope thee (thou) and I may be some help (to each other)," we are apt to consider that the new pilgrim has more likelihood of being "some help" to Feeble-mind, and to the zest of the story, than Feeble-mind has of being any help to him.

Bunyan brings our new friend upon the scene as if he were already no stranger—at least to the writer himself :— "Mr Ready-to-halt came by, with his crutches in his hand ; and he also was going on pilgrimage." The name is transferred from the 38th Psalm—"for *I* am ready to halt," —the words of a godly man in great distress. The halting of this pilgrim who has gotten the words for a name would seem to be at most but a relic of distress that is past : we see little of it now. The crutches, we learn from a side-note, are " promises ;" and he may well be keeping those beneath him still, because of the stay they have been to him when he was more sorely in need of them. " I shall be glad of thy company," he keenly responds to his feeble welcomer; "and, good Mr Feeble-mind, rather than we will part, since we are thus happily met, I will *lend thee one of my crutches.*" He does not so utterly depend upon them, just at present, but he can partially dispense with them in a brother's extremity. It is plain to see, also, from which side the more of help is to come, and, to speak truth, on which side we are to look for the greater disposition to help. There is a brotherly generosity in Ready-to-halt which we fail to find trace of in his friend, who never seems to get the length of cultivating this—perhaps because he cannot rid from it a look of unreality, at least to his own eyes. But here is a man who is fertile in resource of helpfulness to his still weaker brethren, and who can enjoy the satisfaction and the self-respect of being useful, even at a sacrifice to his own comfort, if not to his own progress;—at this sacrifice, as far as concerns the literal facts of the story. "If either myself *or* my crutches can do thee a pleasure, *we are both at thy command*, good Mr Feeble-mind:" with such boldness of benevolence, and without a shade of disappointment, he accepts the reply in which his offer is declined with thanks. Yet Feeble-mind is right in his disinclination "to halt before he is lame." Crutches did not meet the case of a pilgrim whose general feebleness would only be taxed the more by having the management of an implement added to the management of himself; yet, as a weapon—a weapon "suitable" to his valour and to the rank of enemy he could venture to deal with—it might, we think with him, be of service: "It may *help me against a dog.*"—Thus making out each other, and thus adjusting their plans and feelings for the journey, they went on with the advancing company.

The abrupt opportuneness with which Ready-to-halt drops into the group as it is resuming its way, and the happy air of recognising a known figure which the record casts around the lucky event,—these illusions are not disturbed by any hint as to his previous history. Feeble-mind's question of delighted surprise at the sight of him—" Man, how camest *thou* hither?"—stands absolutely without answer. What led him to take the road—what speed he had made—what misadventures he had met—what help and cheer and guidance he had gotten;—it is all of no account to us beside his pre-established fitness for being a companion to Feeble-mind; and all his foregoing experience seems as if it were only preliminary to the brotherly work which has now found him. Indeed, the cheerful devotion with which he throws himself upon that work, together with the general self-obliviousness of the man, leave us little sense of want in the absence of all information as to his antecedent biography. He has swung himself along every inch of the King's highway, from the Gate onwards—right faithfully, and with a right good heart: we have no uncertainty about this. And we should not wonder to discover that he had travelled at a brisk pace: for we gather the notion, that it is not lack of rapidity, but rather lack of ease, that is his failing. His going is toilsome, and the beads of sweat stand upon his face—sunny as his way will always be; and up Hills of Difficulty he may have to make baggage of his crutches, and to modify his method of advance into an energetic clambering, for which the peculiarities of the road must be held responsible. But withal he covers the ground with an amount of spirit that leaves the clock-hands and the sunsets further behind than many a man who can boast a more graceful gait. We do not think of him as one who has met with opposition or disaster. His crutches have been all his armour; for he is not a man, we imagine, who would be likely to be sought by enemies, as he is not a man who would be justified in seeking them. His King has seen to it that his feckless limbs have comprised the most of his troubles. And now, with half of his journey done, he is brought into the doing of good, and into the getting of good, in a way which bears heartening witness to the abiding mindfulness of Him whose eager pilgrim he is.

We twice find his name casually coupled with that of his comrade, and find nothing else of him, before we see him left as one of the two whose part in the overthrow of Despair was to keep "guard" near the fateful stile on the highway. In that capacity he would be of more account than Feeble-mind; yet Feeble-mind himself, we may hope, would be at his best, with his infirm friend as his only competitor in the task of defence. But perhaps, upon the most sanguine view of the situation on the roadside that day, we are entitled to reckon it fortunate that no watchful foe made good his opportunity,—however it may be, that even Feeble-mind might have found a courage in the new labour of shielding others which he could never find in the old labour of shielding himself. The difference of character between the two men starts into pleasant demonstration when the warriors reappear over the stile with both news and evidence of victory. We know they were alike "very jocund and merry," and so far the comrades were as one. So far only, for disposition will have its way. The joy of Feeble-mind might be already spent; and reaction from so unwonted an outburst of feeling, or misgivings about the propriety of the excitement into which he had been surprised, might be setting in upon him : Ready-to-halt is in no mood to let the occasion pass so tamely. The women are moved to answer the mirth with viol and lute, whereupon "Ready-to-halt *would dance.* So he took Despondency's daughter, named Much-afraid, by the hand, and to dancing they *went* in the road. True, he could not dance without *one* crutch in his hand ; but, I promise you, he *footed it well.*" The hearty gaiety of the scene, with Ready-to-halt as its unchallengeable hero, is not in the least out of character. We are not troubled with the faintest sense of incongruity, nor puzzled as if there were sprung upon us a revelation of somewhat on which we had not reckoned. The considerate gallantry which makes choice of the dejected girl to be his partner in celebrating her deliverance; the triumph of jubilant gratitude over conventional restraints; the tide of high spirit, consciously lit up with a gleam of humour, taking its own brave way without leave asked or given; the sacrifice of thanksgiving only seasoned by its dash of the ludicrous, because itself is so full and pure;—every one of them belongs to the man whom we heard last at the door of the inn. The uniqueness of the character now before us becomes clearer, however, in the light of this incident. We could not have borne it in Great-heart; it should have alarmed us in Faithful; we should have beheld it uneasily in Christian; we should scarcely have been satisfied with it even in Honest, and not at all in Valiant or in Standfast; it could only have suggested insanity in Feeble-mind. But we are charmed with it in Ready-to-halt, it is at once so like him and yet so odd in him,—to dance, of all things; and yet it is the one thing which we like most of all just then to see him do, till he pants in testimony that he has at length worked down the energy of his joy, and till he wipes his smiling forehead by the side of his comrade— even he only recovering again from the mirth which the sight has perforce been reviving in him.

The next that we hear of him—for he is not named with Feeble-mind and Despondency as marching under protection on the Enchanted Ground—is at the leave-taking of Christiana. "Then came in *that good man* Mr Ready-to-halt to see her"—(a phrase which betokens a distinct regard for this pilgrim on the part of the historian). "Thy travel hither hath been *with difficulty*," she says; "but that will make thy rest the sweeter." She has no counsel for him but to " watch and be ready,"—as if she knew that he himself was to be the next to depart.—The messenger comes to himself " in the name of Him whom he has *loved and followed, though* upon crutches." His lameness does not, in the retrospect, awaken those bitter feelings which the " feeble mind " awakened in his comrade. His last will has regard to his crutches, the symbols of his infirmity : he thinks of them tenderly, and bequeathes them " to *his son that should tread in his steps,* with a hundred warm wishes that he might prove better than himself had done." A somewhat enigmatic bequest, it is true, in respect of the heir. Had he at home a child, who was already his heir as far as concerned his own infirmity, and whom he had faith enough to believe would come after him when he had grown into fitness for independent pilgrimage ? It seems greatly more likely, and is quite in harmony with what we know of the man, that with a touch of his old humour, he is describing as a "son " of his any one of kindred lameness who may hereafter betake himself with it to the journey he is now ending, and that he is leaving to such a pilgrim the supports which he himself has found so helpful, and leaving with them every good wish that he too may find them a strength, till he comes, with more credit than the testator himself can boast, to the heavenly City. " He thanked Mr Great-heart for his conduct and kindness " ere he took his way. " Now I shall have no more need of these crutches," he said on the River's brink, " since yonder are chariots and horses for me to ride on." His last happy word crowned very many happy words from the same lips : it was, " Welcome, life ! "

These four scenes are so full of character that we have reason to be content with them as the sum of our knowledge of this interesting pilgrim. Perhaps there is no one towards whom we feel more kindly, or whom we should sooner choose to meet. If we cannot meet himself, pos-

sibly we may meet—possibly we have met—some one of his
" sons." He is a Christian who has a hard task with himself, but goes through with it—puts his hand to it with a
will, and succeeds. His battle is mostly with his own
frailty of faith, but he keeps waging and winning it. He
needs to be always in contact with God's faithfulness—to
be always feeling for it beneath him—to be always letting
down his weight upon it, and so stepping on. He cannot
live his Christian life without the present personal consciousness of God's pledged word to him ; he cannot make
advance in that life without grasping hold of that word
from hour to hour with his own firm hand. He has not
the faculty whereby to fuse the spirit of God's promises
once for all into his pilgrim limbs as inherent capability,
although in happy crises of his life he may seem to be
approaching this : he must use them as aids external to
himself; yet he compels them, even thus, to do him nearly
all the service which in any case they could. The very
continuity of effort, with its parallel continuity of conscious
success, does something of itself to sustain him in good
cheer, since every new step is in some sense a new victory.
But he is so bright most of all because of the general
excellence of his spiritual constitution ; which is kept in
good condition, doubtless, by the almost violent exercise
which his mere ongoing involves, yet has inborn elements
in it of healthiest courage and good-sense and good-will
—inborn by nature, and new-born by grace. Apart from
this inability to fund his trust in God as a practical power
in his Christian self-management, he is sound in heart and
conscience, in mind, and probably in body too. There is
nothing morbid about his whole being—no tenderness
for himself, no anxiety about himself, no lingering upon
the theme of himself; for self is still the pivot of all that is
morbid in religion. His service to God and men is limited
in kind, but scarcely in degree, and not at all in spirit.

His life as a Christian may be visibly laborious, at least to those who know him best; but he is a Christian who is a credit to the Christian cause, and is like a ray of stimulating example to every Christian brother who cannot plead the excuse of that infirmity which is his.

If Bunyan gives but little prominence to Ready-to-halt in the action and dialogue of the story, he gives still less to DESPONDENCY and MUCH-AFRAID. For many reasons this is well. It were not good to appeal too much to our compassion, which is almost the only sentiment that the cheerless couple are capable of awakening. And they have little about them that could be turned to use, either for our pleasure or our profit. There is, besides, a certain tenderness in passing thus lightly over them. We know they are still there, and still downcast amid all their safety as the company moves on: let them move on among its happier travellers without remark: they shall come to better days in the end.

The whole matter concerning them is well summarised in almost the first sentence of which they are the theme: —"They took Mr Despondency"—(there is a touch of delicacy in the prefix of honour which Bunyan so frequently employs in naming those unhappier pilgrims)—" and his daughter Much-afraid *into their protection;* for they were *honest people,* though they were prisoners in Doubting Castle." We have seen very "honest people" in that plight since we began to follow the fortunes of pilgrims. But, it may be, there is considerateness in the silence which rests upon the subject of how they got there, with Christian's pillar of warning still extant at the spot of danger. " Of pilgrims they found one Mr Despondency, almost starved to death, and one Much-afraid his daughter:" that is all the history of their experience of the direst calamity which the Pilgrimage comprehends.

Probably they were longer in this frightful durance than
the couple of the First Part ; certainly the manner of their
release was different, and significantly so. In the absence
of intervention from without, we cannot conjecture how
they could ever again have beheld the light of day. There
was something of the same providential care at work in
this instance as we found in the parallel case of Feeble-
mind. The movement of purpose in the stout hearts of
the pilgrim-party was but the reflection of a higher movement of purpose in the heart of the all-seeing King. And
if our satisfaction at those timely rescues is perhaps slightly
shaded by a dread lest some pilgrim should ever fall into
such hands and no deliverers be near, we must bethink us
of the resourceful vigilance of Him whose "honest people,"
all the while, they are.

Much-afraid, we may guess, was the "Hopeful" in the
dungeon to the "Christian" that her father was. The
trial, anyhow, has not told so heavily on her younger
nature. It is not she that is "almost starved to death."
She has still enough of energy to fall in with the mood of
the merry pilgrim of the crutches, and enough of spirit so
to conduct herself in the novel circumstances as to justify
the record, that "the girl was to be commended, for she
answered the music handsomely." But "as for Despondency, the music was not much to *him*; he was for *feeding*
rather than dancing, for that he *was* almost starved." The
urgency of his case arrests the musical fingers of Christiana
for more homely arts : he must needs have a stimulant on
the spot, until she can get ready for him some more solid
fare ; whereupon, "in a little time the old gentleman came
to himself, and *began to be finely revived.*" We are left in
doubt as to whether "the girl" partook of any refreshment
at all. But it is good to see, that even the old man has
his constitution so little shattered by his misfortune
as to recover so speedily and so well by the adminis-

tration of scarcely anything more medicinal than a hearty meal.

Would imprisonment in Doubting Castle, after all, strike very much of new disaster into the lot of a pilgrim like this? It would seem to do little more than sharpen his ordinary daily experience. Doubts, only more definite and acute, supervene upon a life of doubting. It is but the black night dropping down upon perpetual dusk. To Christian and Hopeful it was sheer calamity, mantling a daylight sky with the gloom of a misty starlight. True ; but night is worse than dusk, and the environment of blind walls, damp with exhalations of dead men's bones, is harder to bear than the breezy road, and the freedom of being unhappy on the recognised path to the City of happiness. It is one thing to be despondently making way in the Christian life, and it is another thing to feel as if all advance in what is at least the direction of hope may be cut off for ever. To wade in a slough of heartlessness from day to day, and all the days from the bad city to the better, is dreary enough ; but to have doubt shutting you in, and to think you hear the voices of pilgrims who are faring on amid the mere difficulties and dangers of the road—the road that does lose itself at last in the light of the King's face—while you sit peering through the silent unbreaking midnight, in terror lest the opening door should let in the light and Despair together ;—that is new calamity still to the heaviest heart that ever went the pilgrims' way.

It ought to have enlivened the glad gratitude of this father and daughter that they were not only set free from the Castle and its wedded tyrants, but that the Castle was in the dust, and its tyrants dead. We may therefore accept it as an indication of the low average of spiritual barometer in the father, that this hungering faintness in his own soul is the only feeling of his which finds its way to the surface of the narrative. Yet there was spiritual health in this faintness, since it was so evidently no other faintness than that of hunger. There was spiritual appetite in the old man when he so missed his meals. We know not for how long he had been shut off from spiritual nutriment, but it seems he was utterly shut off from this; and if his craving for that nutriment be now so ravenous, there is spiritual vitality in him which must have gratitude too for one of its elements, if only he were far enough "come to himself" to let it struggle into manifestation. The old and the weak, medical men tell us, must eat often, if not much : it is the arrest of periodic spiritual supplies which is the most telling feature in the case of a soul like Despondency's while it is immured in dark doubt. On the road he has low spirits, and digestion, and frequent food; in the dungeon he has low spirits, and digestion, and nothing of food—no means of recruiting his scanty spiritual energy from without, and he never has much power of recruiting it from within. God's sensible communications to his own soul, from which he could always contrive to distil for himself some extract of nutrient hope, were no longer with him ; wherefore he must pine, and knows not but he may perish. Christian would fain have died by his own hand to rid himself of his strange miseries ; Despondency feels those miseries less strange—and withal more mild, for he has not spirit enough to provoke the cudgel,—but is like to die, in spite of himself, of the one great misery of having nothing to put to his lips.

If the old man's health was not completely re-established before he left the neighbourhood of By-path Meadow, it would surely come to its best at the next stage, for it was the Delectable Mountains. But the history is more careful to note for us the special welcome which the feebler pilgrims received at those places of pleasantness than to describe the effect upon them of what they enjoyed there.

Was Despondency still despondent while he was gazing forth from those exhilarating mountain-tops?—did his eyes fall as low when he took the road again as they did before they were raised to descry the very City, so bright beyond that intervening sweep of sober landscape? We know not: we only see the father and daughter stepping timidly behind the two other infirm comrades as they file in at the "palace-door," and only hear the Shepherds quickening their dubious advance with the words "Come in, Mr Despondency, and Mrs Much-afraid his daughter." And next we see the father, and must infer the daughter also, "under the eye of Valiant," as they tread the Enchanted Ground. Then the two are standing together in the presence of Christiana to hear her farewell word—a word which has always something of a verdict in it: "You *ought with thankfulness for ever to remember your deliverance"*— so she begins. We are free to suspect that their "thankfulness" had never risen to the measure which so merciful an interposition demanded : Christiana seems to feel this, and to know, besides, that more of thankfulness would mean for them less of downcastness and less of dread. "Be ye *watchful,*" she continnes, "*and cast away fear ;* be *sober,* and *hope* to the end." A word of wisdom for them, if they got grace enough to root it in their lives. How wide an interval stretches between sobriety and heartlessness !—how great a gulf is fixed between watchfulness and fear !—and how apt are the drooping and the timorous to be off their guard, with all their self-concern !—as this father and daughter must have been when they fell a prey that day to the prowling giant.

But "when days many of them had passed away" since Feeble-mind had gone across the bridgeless stream, " Mr Despondency" himself "was sent for." As with Feeble-mind, his term of notice was brief: "by the next *Lord's-Day*" the "trembling man," as the messenger addressed him, was "to be ready with his King to shout for joy at his deliverance from all his doubtings,"—the supreme deliverance, of which the earlier was only the symbol, and awoke little in him of joyous utterance. (We recall, that Christian's deliverance from Doubting took place on a "Lord's-Day.") And now, for the first time in the history, the old man finds his voice. He speaks for his daughter as well as for himself, since she had "said, when she heard what was done, that *she would go with her father.*" This man of a single speech yet manages at last to speak so well, that we must report him fully:—"Myself and my daughter," he says,—"*you know* what we have been, and how troublesomely we have behaved ourselves *in every company.* My will and my daughter's is, that our desponds and slavish fears *be by no man ever received, from the day of our departure, for ever*"—(there is an emphasis of redundancy)—"for I know that after my death"—(the singular is to be observed)—"they will *offer* themselves to others. For, *to be plain with you, they are ghosts,* the which we entertained when we *first began* to be pilgrims, and could never shake them off after; and they will *walk about and seek entertainment* of the pilgrims; but, *for our sakes, shut ye the doors upon them.*" He is only "coming to himself" really now. And, indeed, this profounder self of his, now rallying its manhood around the thought that those infesting "ghosts" were under notice to quit, is a self which we are able to regard with some admiration. In his tone there is not the revengeful contempt which Feeble-mind indulged, nor is there the unregretting gratitude which inspired the last will of Ready-to-halt, when now the spell is broken in the near view of "the next Lord's-Day;" but there is a frank tenderness of self-reproach, and a gentle decisiveness of conviction that he and his daughter have been held down unrighteously by shadowy tyrants, and a liveliness of disinterested concern lest those same ghostly vermin should gain quarter in the breast of any other pilgrim, which must have touched chords of earnest forgiveness in the hearts of his brethren, and which does a good deal to raise the mark of our own feeling concerning him from the beginning onwards. His only other words perpetuate the happy effect of these : he is glancing back into the past that he may gaze forward the more triumphantly into the future :—"farewell, night ; welcome, day." At his side, the daughter who danced in celebration of the lesser deliverance, now sings as she enters into the greater,—going, with Lord's-Day worship on her lips, into the "day most calm, most bright" which mortal eye cannot see ; but when at length we thus hear her uttering her heart once for all, her tuneful accents have so mingled themselves with things unearthly, that they fall unintelligible upon the ears of the lingering listeners.

Thus, for the second time, two comrades in pilgrimage are comrades also in the River, and two companions among the trials of Doubting Castle are companions too in the last trial of all. We felt the difficulty which pressed upon the allegorical narrative when we found Christian and Hopeful meeting death side by side ; that difficulty does not press upon the narrative more lightly now when it comes before us again. The first pilgrims made no lengthened stay in Beulah, and the River seems as if it were but the last stage of their long journey together : these later pilgrims, one after another, leave a vicinity of comparative residence, going singly and alone from the side of the dearest comrades, and never without the delivered summons of the King ; yet Much-afraid, on the authority of her own desire, and on the strength of the summons brought so specially to her father alone, takes her way with him "out of the world," as Bunyan elsewhere expresses it, and the pilgrim-convoy to the bank is for two instead of one. It is brave of the girl—presumably a woman now,—even if we must believe, that the thought of being left without him was more formidable to her than the thought of death ; for she had to resolve as she did in the face of much that might have daunted her. And the two-fold event does give striking emphasis to the passion of attachment which this feeble daughter cherishes towards her feeble father, and does furnish a touching illustration of how a weak womanhood is apt to be found a very strong womanhood after all if you test it on the side of affection. Still, the incident cannot be rid from a certain unhappy look of high-handedness, with a positive shadow of voluntary death,—however it may occur to second thoughts, that this most daughterly Christian woman, from the strength of her affection and the weakness of her individuality, may have died under the news of her father's early departure, and thus by intensity of sympathy have departed, as it were unsummoned, with him.

But they departed well ; and, as we look where we saw them last, and see them no more, and know that they are mounting the invisible heights with royalty in their footsteps and glad courage in their bosoms, our pleasure for their sakes has in it a sense of wondering relief, and we turn away to give thanks for that grace which makes sure of guiding even the true-hearted Despondencies and Much-afraids into glory.

XVII.

IT is not by courtesy alone that these two names take a place upon our list of True Pilgrims, although that place is naturally the last. They are pilgrims, and are true and good ones. The historian of pilgrimage, partly in consideration of the sort of pilgrims they are, and partly for the reason that he holds himself free to go beyond the actual movement of the story for types of Christian character, simply alters his method of history in telling us of these men, and sets us to listen to a narrative within the narrative when he would bring us into acquaintance with them. This indirect method of history, however, is employed with infirm pilgrims only; and the fact has probably some significance. It suggests, that Bunyan had more in view than merely to lighten his narrative by a new manner of representation: he could have done this as effectively with capable pilgrims as with infirm ones. He seems to have felt, that those feebler pilgrims somewhat taxed the living narrative, and must be brought into it sparingly; yet he seems to have felt, none the less, that it was important he should enrich his book with more examples of infirm pilgrimage than he could venture to introduce by direct history. Hence we have the stories concerning Little-faith and Fearing without the men who bear those familiar names. Indeed, in his dealing with the several pilgrims of this class whom we have already considered, he appears to have been successively approaching such a withdrawment, until, in the instance of Despondency and his daughter, he leaves them out of the dialogue of the story, and we only see them, and see them but little. It is just a step further not to see them at all. Not to hear them, at least till they are passing out of sight, is not very different from only hearing *of* them.

Yet it sounds almost untrue to say, that we do not see these two men,—so well has Bunyan succeeded in picturing them by the lips of men whom we do see and know. He has entrusted their portraits to his two ablest limners; the one he has given to Christian, and the other to Great-heart. Little-faith and Fearing, therefore, are as well known, and perhaps as vividly apprehended, as any of the characters who live and speak before us. It is plain that there are few who have taken a firmer hold of the popular mind. Bunyan's faculty does not fail him when he turns to his indirect method: he gains in compactness of treatment and in flexibility of narration, while he loses nothing in naturalness, and scarcely anything in livingness itself.

In the case of LITTLE-FAITH, we must not undervalue the advantage earned for broad truthfulness by the opportunity it gives of correcting any impression that pilgrimage began with Christian. Little-faith's journey was begun and ended when Christian was telling Hopeful of him as they were leaving the Delectable Mountains behind them. So it comes to light—not by way of explicit statement, which would have been too obtrusive for what seems so much a matter of course the moment it is seen, but in a way as casual as it is unmistakable—that the Dream only draws aside the curtain from sundry recent details of a wonted habit of life among men, and that pilgrimage has an indefinite perspective of backward history. From scattered hints, this might have been inferred before; but now it becomes a part of the texture of the book, and it is Christian

himself who unwittingly disclaims the precedence with
which we might be ready to credit him.

The history of Little-faith resolves itself into the history
of a robbery and its consequences. He had travelled thus
far, it would appear, without any notable mishap befalling
him, and was now in the region between the Delectable
Mountains and Beulah. One day he sat down to rest, and
fell asleep. The spot where he slumbered was near the
opening of a lane notorious for murders, but his rest was
unruffled by the knowledge of so gruesome a circumstance.
This "Dead-man's Lane" led down from a gate which is
worthy of our notice: it was a portal by which the
"Broad Way," the wrong way, communicated freely with
the way that was narrow and right. Down the lane from
this gate, just as the man was bestirring himself to resume
his journey, three robbers, mounted it would seem, spurred
into a gallop upon him, and bullied him with orders to
stand. The three powerful scoundrels were brothers, and
their names were Faint-heart, Mistrust, and Guilt. In so
unexpected a presence, "Little-faith looked as white as a
clout," and had no power either to fight or to flee. Faint-
heart begins business by demanding his purse; Mistrust,
not liking the man's natural hesitation, dashes at his
pocket, and grasps out of it "a bag of silver;" it is the
part of Guilt to fell the poor pilgrim to the ground when
he raises a cry of "Thieves!" The villains hover by
while the battered head of their victim is staining the
road with blood: there may be more that is valuable upon
him. But they hear footsteps somewhere; and in terror
lest they may be those of Great-grace of Good-confidence,
they clatter off up the lane again, and are gone. By-
and-bye, the unlucky traveller recovered consciousness,
"and, getting up, made shift to scrabble on his way."

As he went forward,—so it transpires in the conversation which follows between Christian and Hopeful,—the

poor man's heart was sorer than his head. He had lost the bulk of his "spending-money," and had only "a little odd money left." Happily, "his jewels" were safe. These, however, could not keep him in food; wherefore (if the narrator has not been "misinformed") the man was reduced to begging ere he had got far on his way. His "certificate" for the City was also in his possession still— a fortunate "wonder," which was of necessity much more due to "mere good providence" than to any skilful management of his own. Henceforward, however,—so absorbing was his sense of his loss—he took scarcely any advantage of his document, and for great part of the way had no thought that he possessed such a thing. The recollection of his misfortune continually broke anew upon him with unfading freshness. Christian had been "told that he scattered almost all the rest of the way with nothing but doleful and bitter complaints,—telling also to all that overtook him, or that he overtook on the way as he went, where he was robbed, and how; who they were that did it, and what he lost; how he was wounded, and that he hardly escaped with his life." "It is a wonder," says Christian, "that he did not *die* with grief, poor heart!"

We have already had occasion to admire the magnanimous tenderness which Christian throws into this narrative-description of a brother-pilgrim, and to note with how quick and threatening a glance he holds his shield over this hapless man. It need not be thought that he does all this without solid ground of reason, or that we must discount his good opinion of the man as if it were largely heightened by the abundance of his pity. His compassion depends more upon his good opinion than his good opinion depends upon his compassion. Before he has recalled the full pathos of the story, he twice speaks of him as "a good man;" while, in the course of his relation, he twice returns to the same words. It is only a matter of hearsay to

Christian himself, yet the story has taken an extraordinary hold of his mind. His strong regard for the man seems to found itself most upon his genuineness; and doubtless he has more evidence of this than the story leads him to disclose. He tells us only one fact of his past history: "he dwelt in the town of Sincere." The fact is noteworthy, if only for the new element—that of estimable moral character—which it introduces into the antecedent geography of pilgrims. But its importance, as far as concerns Little-faith, is this—that it shows him to have been, at the worst, a man of sincerity, and one who set forth on pilgrimage out of a life of true intention. We do not know the whereabouts of this native town of his, and possibly he may not have come a longer distance than Hopeful himself had come; but he had got grace grafted on sincerity when he started, and this gracious sincerity had grown richer in him onwards to the day when he was so villanously assailed. He is a man well-appointed in "jewels" of pilgrimage. It is indeed " *his lot* to have but a little faith," yet that little is of excellent quality: so Christian would have us think. To have been without the jewels of gracious character which the robbers had left him, and to have thus been "excluded from an inheritance" in the heavenly City, "would have been worse to him," even by anticipation, "than the appearance and villany of ten thousand thieves." But "as for a *great heart*,"—the words have not yet become personalized,—"Little-faith had none." "Is it meet to think," he asks, "that there should be the strength of an ox in a wren?"—a deep-going question, carrying far down into the philosophy of religious character a whisper of limitations which the most gracious experience is not able to silence. "Some *are strong*, some *are weak;* some *have great faith*, some *have little:* this man was one of the weak, and therefore he went to the wall." His goodness, his weakness, his calamity;—hence

the apologetic delicacy which makes Christian's whole
account of him so much a very study of fine touches of
defence, many of them to be perceived only by careful
attention, and altogether too numerous for us to indicate
here.

We need not look anywhere for further information
about Little-faith than this. Honest adds nothing to our
knowledge by his reference to him—"I feared that you
had been of the company of those that sometime ago did
rob Little-faith of his money,"—except to betoken the
fame his misfortune had won, and to hint at some confusion in the mind of Honest as to the locality of its occur-
rence. Nor is anything added by the incident in which
"there came one running to meet" Great-heart's company,
that they might know how "the robbers"—"the three
that set upon Little-faith heretofore," the guide explains—
were "before" them: only, it must be allowed that it
partially vindicates Honest's alarm, since it happens not
very far past the spot where he slept and awoke to fight
the thieves, who really seem to have become more ubiquitous since Little-faith's days. The sequel also is to be
noted by way of contrast :—"They *came not up* to the
pilgrims," who were evidently enough *too* "ready for them."

Even with the materials we possess, it is easy to make
out, that this first study of pilgrim-infirmity is as distinguishable from the later studies of it as these are from each
other. There are features which recall Feeble-mind, and
there are features which recall Despondency : but the man
could nowhere be mistaken for either. He resembles
them both in the circumstance, that calamity took so cruel
advantage of his feebleness at a certain advanced point of
his journey. He resembles Feeble-mind in the sort of loss
which befell him; he resembles Despondency in the dejec-
tion with which he goes forward ever afterwards. The
ways of Feeble-mind are faintly anticipated by the copious

talk of Little-faith on the subject of his mischance, and by the tendency which his weakness developed, at least after the robbery, of revolving around itself. But the points of difference, in character and in history, are more marked than the points of resemblance in particular. The wonderfully manly tone which Feeble-mind maintained about his loss of money, which seems to have been complete—the real magnanimity of both his speech and his silence on the subject—are a contrast to the manner of Little-faith. But we are bound to give due weight to the consideration, that whereas Feeble-mind and Despondency were rescued by the valour of fellow-pilgrims, and were relieved and cheered by their company all the rest of the way, poor Little-faith had no fellow-pilgrims to come in upon him with surprises of deliverance, and no continuous company to help him to forget his misery by their sympathy or their aid. He had nothing to lighten his retrospect of calamity, and nothing to restrain memory from playing the tyrant with him. Even apart from rescue in the hour of misfortune, Little-faith might have appeared to better advantage if he had fallen in with but one companion, and kept by him. For his solitariness does not seem to have been compelled by the rarity of pilgrims ; we find there were numbers that overtook him, and there were not a few that he himself overtook. This latter fact may be put to his credit in the comparison of him with Feeble-mind, if not with Despondency also, and brings him more into brotherhood with Ready-to-halt. We can guess that he made fair speed, and that he had a better heart for travel than for contest or for loss. It need not have been from fear alone that he gathered himself up so promptly out of the road-way, and went on, with his bleeding wounds unsoothed, towards the City still. We must accept the rumour that he had to beg as he went forward ; but it was going forward that he begged, and what he begged was transformed out of hand into pilgrim-energy and pilgrim-advance. His eyes were often moist with the undying regret that mastered him ; nevertheless they "looked right on," and his dewy "eyelids looked straight before him ; " so that he neither loitered nor swerved. There is something very touching in the picture of this man—weak, but true to the pole of all pilgrims—evermore carrying onward his breastful of sad reminiscence, and scattering his tears upon new ground at every step, and awakening the echoes to his lonely wailings over ever new stretches of the landscape, and pouring his still-remembered woe into ears that met his lips at still advancing stages of his way. Perhaps Feeble-mind or Despondency, in like circumstances, would have shown less steadiness of foot, if also somewhat less heaviness of heart.

Between Little-faith and the later infirm pilgrims who met with calamity, there is both resemblance and difference in regard to the crises in their course which the calamity constituted. None of them was quite the same after it that he was before it. In the case of the later pilgrims it marked a start towards improvement, depending mainly upon the new fellowship which it set agoing with them. In the single instance of Little-faith it seems to mark a change for the worse. His period of comparative brightness would appear to have been the long period which transpired before his misfortune broke upon him : at eventide it was rainy darkness in place of light. The little faith he had would seem to have hitherto proved sufficient for his circumstances, however narrow the margin may at any time have been ; and when the collapse arrived, his long immunity from disaster, instead of bracing him for it when it came, would appear to have only embittered the cup of disappointment with a kind of inconsolable amazedness. He must surely have permitted a quite overgrown regard to gather around that "spending-money" of his while

things were going well with him, and must surely have em-
barked his comfort too entirely upon that alone. His
slender stock of faith was being withdrawn from the funded
verities of a pilgrim's trust, and was fastening itself upon
the more contingent facts and feelings which make up the
more precarious possessions of a pilgrim. It was these that
failed him; and when they were gone, it was not despair
that grasped him, for the verities were with him still; nor
was it despondency that settled on him, for he never lost
touch of the abiding things; but it was a refusing to be
comforted, as if his best had gone beyond recovery, and
had left him without a reason for being happy all his way
henceforward. There is not in his regret a very perceptible
trace of penitence; he turns no blame upon himself, but
keeps it all for his robbers and his fate. As far as we
might gather from him, he thinks of his loss as a stroke of
misfortune crashing in upon him unaccountably from without, like a thunderbolt out of the blue air. From the
doleful hour of his getting to his feet again, he has a
chronic grievance concerning his fortune which is not less
stubborn, and not less self-caressing, than Feeble-mind's
concerning his constitution.

Was he, then, quite blameless about the happening of
the calamity itself?—for, as we have hinted, we cannot
altogether acquit him of blame about the mastery it took
of him afterwards in its aspect of a loss. It seems hard
we should make it a matter against him that he sat
down there and fell asleep; or that we should link his
calamity in any way with the circumstance of his having
slept, and awaked again before the rascals descried him.
Even Honest was so deep in slumber on the wayside, that
those who might have been his robbers had themselves
to set about awakening him; and the fact is not mentioned
anywhere to his discredit, nor did it bring him anything
but good. Honest, however, slept in the Second Part,

and not in the First. Under the severer laws of pilgrim-history which prevailed when Little-faith travelled, sleep was seldom indulged in but to harm. We must fear that Little-faith's hour of repose carries within it the vapours of calamity. The sitting-down means relaxed spiritual energy; the falling-asleep means heedless heaviness of soul; the chosen situation, however unwitting its selection may look, means thoughtless negligence of spirit, and means this negligence with its face in the direction of the world's ways. All this is so compatible with even an exaggerated regard to the mere pocket-money of pilgrimage, that we can imagine this man dropping to sleep with his right hand upon his treasure, while his staff lay on the grass beside him. It was not his sleeping that brought those robbers upon him, but the state of things with him of which his sleeping, and his sleeping in that place, was the symptom. His faith was perhaps less at this moment than ever it had been since he set out, and its scantiness invited the very assault which it made sure would be disastrous if it came. These villains may be said to have been always waiting such an opportunity with him; they are the natural enemies of every Little-faith. They advance together; they are brothers; their successive interference is adjusted beforehand to an ascending climax of attack: in truth, they are shapes projected from the spirit of the pilgrim himself, and mark successive stages in the deepening of the same shadow of eclipse—the shadow which darkens across such a soul in the day when its orbit has been declining too near the old unspiritual interests of an abandoned sphere of things.

Of all this the good heart of Christian makes the very least; nor would we ourselves make of it too much, in presence of the ample penalty which the hapless pilgrim paid for his unguardedness. His deathly dismay when he found himself beset by those unfriendly strangers—the

Faint-heartedness which staggered him as it suggested danger to his dear possessions ; the lapse of Trust in which he felt his possessions snatched from him, and cried into the pitiless air with the courage of his pain ; the blow of Conscience which quenched his cries, and felled him as if he would rise no more, so that he knew not for a while whether he were a pilgrim at all ;—these alone were heavy reprisals. But they were only the first instalments of his retribution. The clouds which gathered over him in that hour were never wholly dispelled till they lifted away before the strong sunshine which suffers no mantling of earthly vapours. He had not faith enough to fetch as much of that sunshine into his way as to melt the clouds as he went. The remaining stages of his pilgrimage were spoiled for him because he had risked the need of more faith than he possessed. His comfort was henceforth gone; his confidence was henceforth irreparably shaken. In the hands of those enemies, he had rapidly doubled back, by reaction, upon the first stage of all—the stage when he was on his way from Sincere to the King's highway; indeed, we might venture to surmise, that his experience was sharper at the mouth of Dead-man's Lane than ever it had been in all his history. Then his thoughts got to be entangled in that most memorable experience, and were held by the past, because he had so little of the faith which stretches forward into the future, and feels its sheet-anchor, after all, to be fixed far-ahead. That pilgrim is ill-fated who fastens much of his trust, and therefore depends for much of his happiness, upon his pocket only, however wellfurnished it may have been, or may be still. Trusting in gathered stores of spiritual memories or emotions, able to be borne about our person and to be lost from it, is but a higher form of laying up for ourselves treasure on earth, where moth and rust corrupt, and thieves steal ; whereas security is found only when treasure and heart are both in heaven. Little-faith's condition was but precarious at the best all the while that it was so with him, and it may have been thus for great part of his way even before his misbap befell him. Would it be heartless to guess, that the King desired him at length to learn how much His sheer grace out of heaven had been doing for him during all the days when his journey had been kept pleasant and bright? But if it was so, the lesson was only indifferently taken, since his gratitude never seems to have struggled itself free from his great burden of comfortlessness.

So it is that our pilgrim vindicates his name. That name, like most of the names in the First Part, describes him in terms of grace rather than of nature. He is the antithesis of Faith-*ful:* nearly all that Faithful was as a pilgrim man, Little-faith is not; and nearly all that Faithful was not as a pilgrim man, Little-faith is. Yet nature does assert itself beneath his name. Even in this earliest pilgrim of all, the place of natural constitution is acknowledged, and by Christian himself is emphatically affirmed. We do not know with how much faith had to contend within this man in whom it was so persistently little. He is not unearnest; pilgrimage is to him the great concern of his life,—if only he had confidence enough, as reposed upon invisible steadfastness, to make it for himself a concern of greater good cheer. Well, sight would be more surprisingly blessed to him when at last it broke upon his glimmering faith. For that faith carried him home. We do not see him in the River, indeed; nor do we strain our ear to catch any of his farewell words. But we have no need to shadow his memory by any faintest doubt, that the day arrived when the name of " Great-grace of Good-confidence," the rumour of whose possible footfall scared the ruffians from his presence that other day, might have become his own name as his tones of wailing changed key once for all into notes of joy.

The last of our Infirm Pilgrims, and the last of all our True Pilgrims together, is among the most infirm, and among the most true, of any of the People of the Pilgrimage. "One Mr FEARING" is a study of Christian character which is remarkable for the precision with which it is conceived, and for the delicacy with which it is elaborated. It is a study for which many a reader of the "Pilgrim" has been deeply grateful, and a study in which many since the days of Christiana have recognised "some semblance" to themselves as they noted the living truthfulness of its touches.

Little-faith's history was the history of a highway-robbery: Fearing's history possesses the advantage, unique among the secondary pilgrims whether feeble or strong, of being the history of a pilgrimage—a "pilgrim's progress" from commencement to close. It is but a conversational sketch, it is true, which Great-heart would take perhaps ten minutes to accomplish; but we see the man vividly through almost every stage of the familiar road, as if we had read a volume about him and his journey. Great-heart made his acquaintance, of course, no earlier than at the Interpreter's House; but he has heard enough of his proceedings from the first to be able to give us a graphic account of even the most of these. We shall need to make free use of the guide's well-condensed narrative while we seek to find our way to the character of his "man."

The character is in its own way a rich one. It is sharply varied, and is set with contrasts which are apt to wear the look of contradictions. As we find with most of the pilgrims of this class, it is not by any means a character of feebleness alone. His infirmity is probably more pronounced and prevailing than that of any other pilgrim; yet none of the infirm brotherhood, not even Ready-to-halt, betrays so much that is admirable behind it.

The sentiment which lies deepest in the breast of Fearing is not fear, but *Self-Depreciation*. He is humble to excess. His lowliness of self-estimation goes beyond reason, and tramples on the skirts of obedience, even where obedience is a matter of life and death. It makes trust an agony of effort which gains nothing of ease by the reiterated success of its exertions. He is not worthy to lay his hand upon anything that is worthy of desire; nay, he is so utterly unworthy, that every new achievement in his progress is a fresh marvel of mercy after it is past. He does not "think of himself more highly than he ought to think," but on the whole more meanly, and "so thinks as " not "to think *soberly*" on the subject. He depresses his own personality almost out of sight, and withdraws it well-nigh out of reach of the gifts which God's grace is holding forth to it as a veritable fact of Divine reckoning and recognition. Therefore he is in danger of becoming unpractical just when his God is most earnestly practical with him, and of becoming impracticable just when his God would have him to be girding himself cheerfully to enter into the abundance of His graciousness.

In all this, however, there was nothing spurious. His Self-Depreciation was true humility, only more; the fault held the virtue within it. If we recall the experience of Christian in the Valley which bore the name of Humility or Humiliation, we shall better appreciate the experience of Fearing there. To Christiana's company, and to Mercy in particular, the Valley was pleasant enough; but to Fearing it was delightful. Descending the Hill on which Christian ominously slipped, " he went down," says his guide, " as well as ever I saw man in my life. . . . Yea, I think there was a kind of sympathy betwixt that Valley and him, for I never saw him better in all his pilgrimage." In the ecstasy of his agreement with the place, " he would lie down, embrace the ground, and kiss the very flowers that

grew in this Valley," and "would now be up every morning by break of day"—(the limits of the Allegory are
stretched to accommodate his emotion)—wandering among
its scenes, and peering about among its nooks, as fondly
as if it were the domain that lay around the revisited home-
stead of his youth. In spirit, indeed, he did find himself
intensely at home. It was more true of him that he had a
Valley of Humiliation "in his mind" than that he had "a
Slough of Despond" there, as Great-heart rather strongly
suggests he had : in this region, the outward precisely answered to the inward, and he throve like an invalid who has
returned from unkindly climes to breathe his native air.
" He cared not how mean he was ;" but this quite under-
states the case with him : not only was it no hardship, no
self-denial, for him to be demeaned in spirit, but it added
a kind of sanction to his own habitual temper, and thrilled
him with a sense of authorised harmony reigning within
and without.

But there are other regions on the road than this tranquil vale of lowliness. There are places where the will
must spur itself into motion, and decision must strike in,
and courage must dare for the sake of duty or of wellbeing.
In the most of such places Fearing was anything but at
home. His self-depression which made a joyous congeniality for him in the Valley, made sore times for him
in many other places which we know, and assumed the
attitude of an all but invincible *Backwardness.* He comes
to the Slough, and it looks as if he would abide there :
" he lay roaring " on the further margin of it " for about a
month together." Others passed him and crossed, but he
could not stir ; some offered him a hand, but he durst not
venture. When at length, " one sunshine morning," he
did mysteriously risk it, and got over without harm, he
found it hard to believe that the thing was actually
managed and past.—He comes to the Gate : for " a good

while " he seems to regard the portal as a matter for his eyes rather than his hands, and has by no means heart enough to knock. The door is opened for many as he hovers near, but he steps aside to let them make their way ; he is not worthy like these. As often as the door is closed again, he is still there in front of it, pitifully " shaking and shrinking." At last, somehow, he hazards "a small rap or two " with the knocker ; the door was immediately opened for him, but he recoiled and could not enter. He who had opened it, departing still further from his wont, went out " after him," demanding of the " trembling man " what was his desire ; whereupon the poor seeker " fell down to the ground." The man of the Gate, touched and wondering, aroused him with cheering words, and got him in— trembling as he went, and ashamed when he found the gate shut safely behind him.—He comes to the House of the Interpreter : " he lay thereabout in the cold a good while before he could adventure to call," and " the nights were long and cold then." This he did, notwithstanding that he carried in his bosom "a note of necessity " to the Master of the House, on the strength of which he should be received and entertained, and granted "a stout and valiant conductor." Others stepped up and knocked and entered, but " he lay up and down thereabouts, till, poor man, he was almost starved." By-and-bye, the guide thinks, he looked out of the window, and " perceiving a man to be up and down about the door," he went out and " asked what he was ; but, poor man, the water stood in his eyes ; *so*," he says, "I perceived what he wanted. I went therefore in and told it in the house, and we showed the thing to our Lord. So *he* sent me out again, to entreat him to come in ; but I dare say I had hard work to do it." —The guide "got him in at the House Beautiful," he thinks, " before he was willing ;" and after he was enjoying himself there, it was a task to get him into the choice company by which the place was so brightened.—Thus he put the drag upon his pilgrimage in the presence of his greatest opportunities, and made it hard for even his friends to help him into the finest spheres of pilgrim-privilege.

The characteristic which gives Fearing his name does not lie so close to this as might seem at first thoughts. His *Fear* was a fear lest " he should come short," as his guide puts it, " of *whither he had a desire to go.*" Fear was a present fact with him, but it fetched itself almost wholly out of the far future. His Backwardness was the fruit of his excess of humility, and had little to do with timorousness; his Fear itself was a fruit of the same tree, and had as little to do with timorousness as his Backwardness had. It was godly fear exaggerating itself into a burden upon godliness. " Let us therefore fear;"—it was a concord with this precept gone so far as to come face to face with a counter-precept of the same writer—" Let us hold fast the confession of our hope that it waver not, for He is faithful that promised." He could not persuade himself of the likelihood of his final success as a pilgrim. Great-heart has to say of him such things as these:— " When we were come to where the three fellows were hanged, he said he doubted that would be *his end* also." " *His* fear was about his *acceptance at last.*" " He cared not how mean he was, so he might be happy *at last.*" Fearing could never make bold to anticipate the issue which Great-heart and Honest together have now to speak of as history—" So he went over—*at last.*" " Then, it seems, he was well—*at last.*" And it was this inability which made him Mr Fearing. It was beyond his power of firm belief that such a man as he was could be safe, with hell and heaven as the alternatives of his fortune. His faith in God was not equal to the strain which his depreciation of himself never ceased to put upon it. Therefore, where a man of no greater faith, and of no greater courage, but of less self-depression, would have been going forward with unhesitating and unfaltering step, Fearing was hanging back in dread, or was magnifying obstacles into tokens of his deserved doom.

Yet this very Fear had no small measure of faith at the root of it, though it was stubborn in its one-sidedness. The man had a clear conception of spiritual and eternal reality. He had a strong apprehension of the enormity of human sin. He was filled with the thought of the desirableness of heaven, and had his eye wide open to the essential excellence of moral purity. But in one splendid department of invisible things his faith was insufficient. He failed to give to the gracious faithfulness of God its due pre-eminence in his spiritual outlook; so that this supreme verity lingered about his eye, without enough of force to penetrate his spirit—at least as a personal verity for himself. And all the while this was the great verity which offered itself less to the gaze of his vision than to the grasp of his trust, that it might nerve him into a holy confidence, and inspire him with a lowly forwardness among the lights and shadows of his way. His faith of the eye was keener than his faith of the hand; and his faith of the hand had special need to be keen, that it might lift him on against the gravitation of his own self-despising habit. Thus it was that his faith did so little to gird him with the readiness and efficiency which his character in other particulars would have made so possible; for the very vividness with which he beheld all that was glorious, and all that was horrible, in the future, only smote him with the greater alarm lest it should never be his own destiny to inherit the one, and to be guided eternally clear of the other. When faith is thus divided against itself, it is apt to prove heavy work just to keep it standing.

This being the unhappy case of our pilgrim, it could not fail to happen, that now and again, even in the company of his "stout and valiant conductor," it would not be hesitancy but terror that would afflict him. As Honest tells us, it was "sin, death, and hell" that he feared, "because he had some doubts of his interest in that celestial country." Whatever, therefore, had on it the light of the "celestial country" was too good for him to enjoy, but whatever had on it the gloom of the nether land was too frightful for him to face. We have seen him in the Earlier Valley, and have smiled with relief to behold him for once in circumstances so grateful to his spirit. But this valley, as we know, led into another. "Death and hell"—it was the Valley in which both of these seem to close in upon the pilgrim with a premature determination to cut off his further journeyings on the spot. Alas for Fearing in such a place, coming so cruelly soon after the days of his unparalleled content! "But when he was come to the *entrance* of the Valley of the Shadow of Death, I *thought I should have lost my man*. . . . He was ready to die for fear. . . . He made such a noise and outcry here, that had they but heard him, it was enough to encourage them to come and fall upon us." It were hard to guess what should have happened with him if the valley had not been "as quiet when he went through it as ever" the guide had known it "before or since."—But there was still, and all along, one other terror awaiting him ; it was the unbridged River :—"There again he was in a heavy case. Now, now, he said, he should be drowned for ever, and *so never see that face with comfort that he had come so many miles to behold*." It was a fine practical comment upon the words, and was the King's own, that "the river was lower at this time than ever" the guide had seen it "in all his life," and that in a little while he was touching the further bank "not much above wet-shod," and in a little while more was "going up to the gate," rejoicing that it was only his Fear that was "drowned for ever."

We have already found ourselves within sight of a
quality in Fearing which must be distinctly claimed for
him: it is *Spiritual Earnestness.* He had no thought of
sparing himself as a pilgrim. His whole soul was in his
pilgrimage, and he followed it strictly as he found it. He
was helplessly dilatory sometimes when he ought to have
pressed forward; but in his utmost straits he never
sought an easier path, and he never went a step back upon
the right one. "The celestial City—he said he should
die if he came not to it;" and he kept his face set for that
City with an unwearying steadfastness which in his peculiar
case had somewhat in it of moral heroism. He would
stand, he would even lie down; but he never sauntered, and
was not over-willing to rest. He was not least in earnest,
by any means, when he was most lingering; indeed, his
pauses were usually occupied by his most intense movements of spiritual desire, and by his most emphatic resolves
to shut his mind against the very idea of returning. At
the Slough,—"He would not *go back* again neither." At
the Gate,—"Nor would he *go back* again." In front of
the Interpreter's porch,—"Yet he would not *go back.*"
Even at the mouth of the dark Valley,—"Not for that he
had any inclination to *go back; that he always abhorred.*"
However dubious might be his prospects, he knew they
were better upon this road in front of him than they could
be elsewhere: the road, anyhow, was the King's own;
and he should perish with his feet going right towards that
presence of His if he perished at all. He should keep the
King's word and the King's way at the worst; this should
not render it less possible that the Ever-Blessed One
should welcome at last such an unworthy man as he.
We might well wish his earnestness to be sunnier; but we
could scarcely wish it to be more absorbing, or more
obedient, or more centred towards the face of the King.
How could he not interpret so earnest an apprehensiveness

itself into conclusive evidence that he had no need of apprehension, the grace of his Lord being simply what he knew it to be? For, one day, he had "seemed glad," and "desired to stay a little to look, and he seemed for a while after to be a little cheery,"—because he was at the Cross and the Sepulchre of his King.

It says all we could desire for the healthy *Conscientiousness* of this man that it went straight towards a habitual *Unselfishness.* "He was, above many, tender of sin." So were others whom we have come to know on this Pilgrimage, but whose Conscience was morbidly self-involved. "He," however, "was so afraid of doing injuries *to others, that he often would deny himself of that which was lawful,* because he would not offend." This was no Feeble-mind: the "uncle" of that good man was a larger Christian than himself, however much shorter he may have been. Nephew and uncle were contradictories of each other in this :—the one, as we saw, had no anxiety about his getting to heaven, but was full of tenderness about himself as he went; the other had much anxiety about his ever getting to heaven, but had nothing of tenderness for himself, though a good deal of it for others, on the way. We are ready to hear that such a man had "no weakness of spirit as to the *practical* part of a pilgrim's life." He set himself under the guidance of Conscience throughout the whole circle of its range, and was able to follow its guidance with all the manly sound-heartedness of a thorough Christian morality. For it was not in outward conduct that this man would display much of feebleness; that was mostly reserved for the inner conduct of his spirit. He may not have been a man to be known as large-hearted, and his benevolent impulses may not have been powerful : perhaps better still, his benevolence, in all the measure of it, took the way through his Conscience, and came forth as a principle of benevolence, at once practical and sure.

This being so, we can have little anxiety about the more rudimentary matters of his uprightness, his fairness, his fidelity, his genuine courtesy; and those who knew not of his distress in the presence of Sloughs and Dark Valleys, or outside the portals of spiritual hospitality, would know him for nothing but a man of unobtrusive righteousness and of most considerate welldoing.

Related to this healthy strength of Conscience, and a more out-going thing than his purely spiritual earnestness, there is to be noticed the *Holy Ardour* of the man. " He was a very zealous man," says Honest, speaking from earliest acquaintance of him. The most remarkable phase of this saintly fervidness, in a character like his, would be a warm Antagonism. There was no lack of this in Fearing. He was unselfish, but (we might say *therefore*) he was not a man of colourless good-nature. Now and again his eye must needs fall upon somewhat which banished his sober benignity, and stirred indignation in him. Folly and falseness discomposed him greatly. Vanity Fair was almost more than he could let alone. " I thought he would have fought with all the men at the Fair," says Great-heart. " I feared *there* we should both have been knocked on the head, so hot was he against their fooleries." In the days of Christian and Faithful, at least as much as this should probably have been their fate—howsoever surprising it might have been to the unthinking to find Mr Fearing a martyr. Yet the annals of pilgrimage have held much more wonderful happenings than this would have been. Righteous anger is a good counteractive to fear of any quality, and not least to that high quality of it which afflicts our Fearings. And is it not so, that almost every estimable element in the character of such men stands right against the spirit of worldliness, and is apt to warm to a glow of indignation when it is compelled to move through the midst of the witless clamour and the bold heartlessness of avowed devotion to the god of this world? And is it not enough to arouse these men to militant ways when they find the very pilgrims to be pestered by the dunnings and audacities of those who have pitched the booths of their trumperies close alongside the King's road? Their humility is confounded by the air of vulgar showiness which surrounds them; their earnestness stands amazed before the organised frivolousness of all they see; their conscientious goodness is disgusted with the disregard of righteousness and goodwill which they witness; their loyalty to the King is struck in the face by this flaunting scene of rebel citizenship; their love of truth and reality is outraged on every hand; their very fear—the fear lest haply they themselves may fail to reach the true City towards which they are toiling—revolts at the blown din of the counterfeit city which would seek to hold them there among its perishing tinsel, or would have them to waste the King's money upon its glittering rubbish,—as if they were fools as well as Fearings. It is a marvel if they so deport themselves that they get past all this with nothing less easy to endure than bad names; and the marvel does not grow less in the proportion in which they find all this godless lightness piercing its way within the very companies of those who bear the name of pilgrims.

Had this phase of Fearing's zeal been all, however, it should have been as one-sided as the zeal of very many is. But his Ardour for Good was as warm as his ardour against evil. In that Happy Valley of his, we see him out by daybreak " tracing and walking to and fro." (Bunyan uses this word " tracing " in both of his references to this Valley in his Second Part: it is evidently a shortened form of " traverse," and has the import of wide-going inspection.) On the Enchanted Ground there is no drowsiness about him : " He was also very wakeful " there. " He always loved good talk : " this was agoing excellently in the House

Beautiful, but his modesty kept him from mingling much with the men and women of the household ; whereupon he did not despise the somewhat undignified device of getting "behind the screen to hear it." We can understand how, when he was nearing the lofty region on which this House stood, and the Hill Difficulty rose steep before him, the man who could hardly be persuaded to enter, and who now shrinks about the place, "made no stick at *that*." There was a reserve of fervent energy in him, which was readily summoned into manifestation wherever the appeal was made to any form of activity that did not let down upon him the weight of his hampering disesteem of himself. But for this very pardonable frailty, we may not conjecture how brilliant a pilgrim this man might have been.

If we were to put the copestone upon his other qualities by naming *Courage* as one of them, it would not now look so very much as if we were sliding into the description of some different character from Fearing. The paradox is simple enough : he was capable of Courage on whatever occasion he was able to be free from himself. Those lions —the chained terrors which tested the nerve of pilgrims as they worked their way to the front of the Palace,—of the like of these Fearing made little account. "Difficulties, lions, or Vanity Fair," as Honest summarises it, "he feared not at all. It was *only* sin, death, and hell that was to him a terror." Truth demands that we should mark the distinction well. To charge such a man with cowardice should be an abuse of words as well as of him. The exaggerated risk of his final unsuccess threw its far shadow over him like a perpetual mantle of embarrassment ; but there was a strong heart, no less than a cordial will, entangled in its folds. The remote hazard daunted him because of the vast magnitude it wore to his self-lowering imagination—a hazard which is only too acutely real in the case of many a man who has not the wisdom to recognise in it any reason at all for concern. Men like our pilgrim are every day misjudged among us, even by Christian eyes. There are Christians, with but half the latent Courage of our Fearings, who carry the look of anything but fear—not because they think more adequately of the grace that saves them, but because they think less extravagantly, let us say, of the task which that grace has in hand with them. And there are those not Christians who would smile at the "chicken-heartedness" of the Fearings of the Church if they knew almost anything of their inner biography, but who themselves would collapse into a heap of helplessness if they were to bear upon them for a day the spiritual pressure which these men and women are bearing upon them from year to year out of the infinitudes of eternal possibility. That pressure doubtless ought not to be borne, and, absolutely speaking, need not be; yet we are entitled to note, that often it is borne by hearts which are brave beneath it, and which should merely *seem* to be braver if it were gone.

Distressful as Fearing's pilgrimage undoubtedly was, he did not meet with any definite calamity, or any real mischance, throughout the whole of his journey. Something of the credit of this result is due to himself. His loyal apprehensiveness kept him watchful, and his watchfulness kept him right. There is not a doubt that some Christians would be safer if they had a little more of Fearing in them. Fear, of a sort that is genuinely manly and most reasonably godly, must always be a living juice in the root of earnest Christian living. If our religion has been rooted well, there is every likelihood that it once had in it, if it has not now, a large infusion of this pungent element of fear; and, indeed, if the root is abiding in vigour, the laws of growth shall not be sweetening this altogether away, nor shall the law of gravity be holding it down from leavening still the topmost branches of our religious being. The Christianity which Bunyan loves, however we may be thought to have outgrown it in some of its features, has at least a closeness of grip upon the soul, and a wholesomeness of vitality within the life, which makes a large proportion of our present-day Christianity look exceedingly feeble. And the feebleness of a man's Christianity is a far fairer subject of censure than the feebleness of the Christian man himself: for it is at once more serious and more clearly within the reach of cure. This less excusable feebleness has usually for one of its symptoms a flippant confidentness in regard to all that comes within the sweep of its present and its future. All is easy-going, because all is shallow. This feebleness blunders on and comes to grief, for it has little anxiety about keeping itself right, and often has not spiritual earnestness enough even to make out very distinctly when it is wrong. There is calamity along the path of those pilgrims, and here and there a lamentable breakdown which makes melancholy comment upon their high attainment of unconcern about sin and spiritual hazard. It is the lack of conscience, of moral touch and integrity, of a steadfast sobriety of righteousness, which sets the worst of feebleness into the heart of so much of the religiousness of our own day—a religiousness which is constantly compelling doubts as to whether it be Christianity at all, since it so nearly despises that holy fear which neither safety nor truth will allow us to separate from religious sentiment amid the conditions of our earthly life.

It must not, however, be affirmed that the credit of Fearing's exemption from calamity was wholly due to himself. Something of it was due to his human friends, and much of it was directly due to his Lord. We have elsewhere seen how the circumstances of pilgrimage temper themselves to gentleness around the footsteps of the infirm travellers to the City. We can see it in no instance so fully and finely as in the instance of Fearing. At every place of rest no less than in the Interpreter's, his hosts "carried it wonderfully lovingly" towards him. Honest and Great-heart had the most brotherly patience with him. Not only this: the Valley of the Shadow was comparatively still, and the River had ebbed to the depth of a rain-pool, when Fearing was in them. A providence with miracle in its hand was going before him on his way. It is all as true as it is beautiful. The heart and hand of the King are in contact with all the Pilgrimage, and the heart and hand of the King are in the hearts and hands of those everywhere who care for pilgrims. Our Fearings, with all their "troublesomeness," appeal most touchingly to the grand benevolence of Him whose eye follows them tenderly as they go, and to the guiding helpfulness of those brethren who reflect that benevolence so visibly here upon the road. "A choice spirit," says Great-heart; "Such a good man," says Honest: that was apology for all their patience. And the King knew Fearing more intimately than ever they could do; and He loved his earnest lealness, his consideration for others all the while that his own trouble was consuming him, still more fervently than they. Therefore it is at the approach of such shrinking heroes that the most threatening enemies between the Wicket-gate and the gate of the City must themselves be made to shrink, and that men must get reason to learn again, if they will, how much the mightiest powers in all the region are under the sceptre of the City's King.

We welcome the hint we have from Great-heart that his "man" gained some little mastery over his weakness as the journey neared its close. "The first string that the musician usually touches," he says, "is the bass, when he intends to put all in tune. God also plays upon this string first, when He sets the soul in tune for Himself. Only, here was the imperfection of Mr Fearing—he could play upon no other music but this, *till towards his latter end.*"[1]

[1] Note Q.

Great-heart would not be "tedious," and he lets us see little of his friend in the later days until the last of all. When his first alarm at sight of the River has spent itself, he is then right content. His guide wishes him a good reception. He answers briefly—"I shall, I shall." It is the characteristic contradiction of his lifelong feeling. He had always been a man "but of few words, only he would sigh aloud:" he is "of few words" still, but the sighing has already fled away.

"Then parted *we* asunder," says Great-heart, giving end to his admirable narrative, "and *I* saw him no more." The words have a tear of farewell in them even now as he speaks. "Yes, yes," he adds hurriedly, like a man under emotion, after the tender remark of Honest; "*I* never had doubt about him." And we find ourselves looking with Great-heart from the nearer bank of that now familiar stream, and our own eye following the figure which once more is solitary—companionless again, but not for long, yet stepping forward whither we cannot go with him, and stepping thither without fear—till we see him safely enfolded within the lustrous haze which is the earthward wing of the light of immortality.

> "He *was* a good man, though much down in spirit ;
> He *is* a good man, and doth life inherit."

For Bunyan too looked after that figure tenderly as it faded into happiness. Unquestionably this man is one of the characters whom he most fondly paints: his quick manly sympathies are stirred by such a character, and his Christian heart goes forth to him for his self-sinking loyalty that is so laden with trouble ;—not to say, that "there was some semblance betwixt this good man and" himself.

We need the aid of all his scattered touches, and we need to give even to these a more pervading significance than the proportions of allegory permit, if we would do

justice to the picture of this man as a man to be met with
in real life.   He is the pensive man of the " Pilgrim," as
his friend Honest might stand for the cheerful one,—more
pensive a great deal than desponding, and more desponding than feeble-minded.   We think of him as a man of
firmer build than his nephew, and with little of the sunken-
eyed decrepitude which bent that lank figure as if with age.
We think of him as a man of more gravity and good-sense
than Little-faith, and without the sparkle in the eye which
bespoke the effervescent spiritedness of Ready-to-halt.   We
see him as a man in love with solitude, yet never sour ; a
man full of earnest feeling and brooding thoughtfulness ; a
man with no narrowness of heart or mind, and with too much
of far-looking sadness for himself to be censorious about
his neighbours ; a man contriving for the welfare of others
though scarcely able to believe in his own ; a man who
fain would feed his sanctified intelligence upon rich
spiritual conversation if he could conquer his disrelish
for company, and who is therefore commonly content
to linger over the voiceless page of his favourite authors ;
a man who enjoys to go back upon the olden past—which
is so quiet now, and yet is so full of God—and to make it
vivid for himself, and cherish reflection from it, and fetch
present truth out of it,—it is so much surer than the future.
Perhaps his Christianity itself has too deep a tinge of the
older economy, and suffers from a too fond loyalty to
antiquity.   He is in church-communion now, but almost
wonders at his own boldness every time he avails himself
of its more sacred privileges.   He may even have accepted
office, but only when his sense of duty became too strong
for his reluctance.   He does not take part in any form of
usefulness which turns men's eyes upon him, yet often
has privately suggested what other men are publicly carrying through.   He has no gift of speech, unless it be when
he prays ; and then, as is remarked by those who hear him,

he shows no such abandonment to deploring confession as is apt to be indulged in by men of less profound reality, and of less delicate regard for those whose sentiments they are uttering as well as their own. Yet it is sometimes told, with respectful amusedness, how he has startled listeners who did not know him well, by some chivalrous outburst of feeling directed against some abuse or injustice, some public wickedness or private wrong, when he rather exceeded than fell short of the limits of prudence, at least for himself. There are periods when his wakeful eyes, as he listens in his pew, are sadder than their wont : it is a sign for his minister or his most intimate Christian friend to seek to get alongside of his trouble, or to handle him out of it with his tenderest patience of persuasiveness. But even when he is pushing you to the verge of your friendly skill to help him, you cannot but feel how fine a man he is, compared with your chattering Christian of self-complacency, who gives you so little trouble save to keep clear of conflict with his conceit of himself and of his easy labours. So this man, by his weakness hardly less than by his strength, rivets himself upon the hearts of the best around him, and sinks deep into his socket in the Church which possesses him ; and when his mortal places miss him at last, there is hushed moistening of eyes at the thought of him for years after his own sadnesses have been sunned away.

But this Fearing of Bunyan's,—we have seen him ford the stream, and he is not any longer in sight. We must return. And we shall not come again to this river-bank with our farewells, for all our True Pilgrims are now at home beyond the further shore.

END OF FIRST SERIES.

NOTES.

NOTES TO FIRST SERIES.

Note A.

" He stuck to his father's craft—that is, to learn the mystery of a country brazier, which indeed is but a small degree from a tinker ; and so he was termed,—the working part being in mending pans, kettles, &c., that the good-wives bring when they come to the market-towns."—" Memoir " appended to the Glasgow Edition (1814) containing the spurious " Third Part."

Note B.

The question as to which of the two contending armies enjoyed the services of Bunyan is not an important one, but it may still be said to hang in the balance. Mr Offor shows good ground for maintaining the view that he served as a Royalist (" Preface " and " Memoir " to Blackie's Edition of the " Whole Works," 1862). " Probability," says Mr Froude, " is on the side of his having been with the Royalists " (" Bunyan," p. 12). Recent evidence, however, chiefly furnished by Mr Brown, goes to strengthen the opposite view (" John Bunyan, his Life and Times," ch. iii.,—henceforth the one biography of Bunyan). This view, as being certainly the more natural one, was that of Macaulay and Carlyle. Macaulay acknowledges no question on the point :—" He enlisted in the Parliamentary army, and served during the decisive campaign of 1645 " (" Biographies," p. 30). Carlyle appears to be more conscious of a possible alternative on the subject :—" John Bunyan, *I believe*, is this night in Leicester ·—not writing his ' Pilgrim's Progress ' upon paper, but acting it on the face of the earth, with a brown matchlock on his shoulder. Or rather, without the matchlock just at present, Leicester and he having been taken the other day." (" Cromwell," Letter xxix.).

Note C.

Mr Brown attaches just importance to a rapid succession of changes which he finds to have taken place in Bunyan's home somewhat less than a year before he entered the army. Within three months there occurred the death of his mother, the death of his sister, and the second marriage of his father. These things, happening together at this period, must have thrown him greatly out of sympathy with his home-life, and must have loosened restraints which had hitherto held him back from ways of open ungodliness.

Note D.

Mr Philip, in his Introductory Essay to "The Greatness of the Soul," etc. (Nelson), finds himself compelled to abandon the common belief about this—"the popular dream," as he rashly calls it—on the strength of the discovery of Doe's chronological catalogue of Bunyan's works. Mr Philip is followed by Dr Black in his "Christian Life" (vol. i. p. 8). Mr Offor strongly maintains the common belief. Mr Brown reconciles the two opinions by supplying valid evidence to show that the First Part of the "Pilgrim" was probably written during Bunyan's imprisonment of six months in the *Town* Jail, after he had been released for three years from his longer imprisonment in the *County* Jail.

In this connection, then, it is still pertinent to refer the reader to some interesting paragraphs in Mr Smiles' volume on "Character" (chap. 12), where he enumerates twenty-five authors who wrote books in prison.

Note E.

Some may be interested to see how Professor Aytoun, with his well-known Cavalier sympathies, regarded Bunyan and his Allegory. The following jottings, taken down from his lips during his last session, are transcribed as we find them :—"The first unlettered author in England : remarkable exception. (The 'Pilgrim') a stupendous literary triumph. By far the finest parable that ever came from a human pen. Admirable plan ; extreme dexterity of the details,—even the number (of them). Style strong and lucid. Natural, homely reality. Great intelligibility : taxes imagination little—so vivid. (He) does not fill up the pictures—outlines. Valley of the Shadow of Death very remarkable. Grim humour in the Second Part. No other work which rose even to mediocrity."

French criticism of Bunyan and the 'Pilgrim,' down to that of M. Taine, has never been chargeable with flattery. We copy a more impartial specimen than usual from the "Biographie Universelle" (Paris, 1854):—"'Voyage du Pélerin, ouvrage allégorique, bizarre, mais plein d'imagination . . . à produire une grande impression sur des esprits simples . . . et il est fort en usage parmi Protestants. . . . C'était un homme sans lettres, mais doué de beaucoup d'imagination et de talent naturel: d'un extérieur grossier, mais d'un caractère doux et de mœurs irréprochables." . . . "D'allégories quelquefois étranges et incohérentes, presque toujours admirable de vigueur, de verve, et de variété."

The latest testimony to the "Pilgrim" that we have seen is more cordial than this. It is from the pen of Mr Walter Besant in the *British Weekly*. He says: "Unquestionably the book which most seized my imagination was the immortal 'Pilgrim's Progress.' It still seems to me the book which has influenced the minds of English-men more than any other outside the covers of the Bible. While it survives, and is read by our boys and girls, two or three great truths will remain deeply burned into the English soul. The first is the personal responsibility of each man; the next is, that Christianity does not want, and cannot have, a priest."

Note F.

"Has not a character which has acquired a place in the minds of mankind as real an existence, even though a creature of imagination merely, as if the person in question had been born with a material body, and had lived a fixed number of years, and had worn clothes and taken his regular meals, and in course of time had died?"— Froude's "Oceana," chap. 2.

Note G.

Some intelligent readers of the "Pilgrim," but readers whose sympathies with the spirit of the work are not profound, have a very natural grudge at Bunyan and his hero for what they deem the heart-lessness of Christian's desertion of his family. We may quote, as an instance, the remarks of Albert Smith, in the encyclopædic little book to which he gives the whimsical title of "The Tin Trumpet." He says—"The hero of this popular and pious allegory, as has been justly observed by Mr Dunlop in his 'History of Fiction,' is a mere negative character, without one good quality to recommend him.

There is little or no display of charity, beneficence, or even benevolence, during the whole course of his pilgrimage.   The sentiments of
Christian are narrow and illiberal, and his struggles and exertions
wholly selfish.   In proof of the latter part of this imputation, mark
with what a heartless indifference to everything but himself he
abandons his wife and family:—'Now he had not run far from his
own home, but his wife and children, perceiving it, began to cry
after him to return, but the man put two fingers into his ears and ran
on, crying, Life, life! eternal life!   So he looked not behind him,
but fled towards the middle of the plain.'   So uniform are the
results of fanaticism, even when engendered by different views of
religion, that a precisely similar trait is related of the Catholic St
Francis Xavier.   'It is well,' says Sir Walter Scott, speaking of
his general character as given by Dryden, 'that our admiration is
qualified by narrations so shocking to humanity as the account of the
saint passing by the house of his ancestors, the abode of his aged
mother, on his road to leave Europe for ever, and conceiving he did
God good service in denying himself the melancholy consolation of a
last farewell.'"

The reader will perceive that the "popular and pious allegory" is
criticised as a novel, or as a biography of real life.   It were waste of
ink to say more than this.

Note II.

Mr Lathrop, in his excellent "Study of Hawthorne" (Boston,
1876), recognises in this passage "almost the motive and the moral of
The Scarlet Letter." (p. 70.)

He tells us that the influence of the "Pilgrim" upon his friend
was great from boyhood onward; and he brings together several
coincidences which he regards as evidence of this.

Note I.

Mr Froude, in his masterly and characteristic sketch of the
"Pilgrim" ("English Men of Letters—'Bunyan,'" pp. 151-172), stays
the rapidity of his movement for a little at Vanity Fair.   He deals but
scanty justice to Faithful.   "Faithful had come to Vanity Fair,"
he tells us, "to make a revolution."   The mere narrative will not
sustain this account of his coming.   He adds—"A prisoner who
admits that he has taught the people that their prince ought to be in
hell, and has called the judge an ungodly villain, cannot complain if

he is accused of preaching rebellion." Again he is pressing the narrative further than is due. He too readily affirms Faithful's admission of the charges brought against him ; and he does not give enough of room for the likelihood that the strong language which Faithful employs at the bar against the Prince and his attendants was flashed from him on the spot by the hopeless indignation which the systematic malice of the proceedings inspired in him. Nor in the narrative does any one "complain," though two very manfully endure.

Note J.

Happily the high authority of Mr Froude need not compel us to accept his almost contemptuous estimate of the Second Part. A more measured criticism had been more likely to rule our opinion. He admits that " of course there are touches of genius." But it vexes him that " the rough simplicity is gone," and that " instead of it there is a tone of sentiment which is almost mawkish. Giants, dragons, and angelic champions carry us into a spurious fairy-land where the knight-errant is a preacher in disguise." As for " Christiana and her children," they "are tolerated for the pilgrim's sake to whom they belong. Had they appealed to our interest on their own merits, we would have been contented to wish them well through their difficulties, and to trouble ourselves no further about them" ("Bunyan," pp. 171, 172). Perhaps the earnestness of Bunyan was none the less lofty, but only the richer, when it proved itself able to embrace more within its sympathies than the earnestness of his accomplished critic seems able to do.

Note K.

It will be noticed that Bunyan complicates his device somewhat, by speaking as if it were needful for him to betake himself in person to the spot on which the pilgrim-history is transacting itself. He must go down "thitherward," and must sleep and dream there, before he can see the story so as to tell it. This no doubt gives a touch of realism to the matter, but it is apt to beget confusion. Dreams, we all suppose, are above conditions of topography. It is good to know that the regions of pilgrimage are regions that a man may verily lodge and dream in ; but it is not good to be expected to assume that a man cannot dream about them except in their midst, or that, being in their midst, he has to dream about them in order to observe what is going on within them. He might have fallen in with

Mr Sagacity in his dream without going to the suburbs of the City of
Destruction to meet him : so that not even this new and happy feature
of his dream-narration is sufficient to give excuse for the inconsistency.
It is an early note of warning that in the Second Part we may look
for still less regard to allegoric consistency than in the First.

Note L.

The names of the four boys are the only literal proper names in the
" Pilgrim." They carry the complexion of the book, however, in
being Bible names ; two from the Old Testament, and two from the
New. The propriety and naturalness of thus naming them are
obvious. It would have been awkward to give them names which
characterised them before character had defined itself in them ; and it
would have been unwise, by individualising them too sharply, to
infringe upon the idea of family collectiveness which it is so well to
maintain. We can hardly imagine the lads going through the story
under such designations as Teachable, Obedient, Grateful, Grace-
begun : even if these names had been individually appropriate, they
would have been severally invidious, and would have been somewhat
absurd in a representation which is really that of a literal household.
Nevertheless, the good-sense of Bunyan here walks safely past a snare
into which some would have fallen.

Note M.

With Bunyan's character of Mercy the reader might compare William
Law's character of MIRANDA in his " Serious Call " (ch. viii.), written
forty years after the publication of Bunyan's Second Part, and written
by a " non-juring minister." The portrait, which is the most elaborate
of the " many " which Gibbon declares to be " not unworthy the pen
of La Bruyère," is drawn from real life. " Under the names of Flavia
and Miranda," says the historian of the " Decline and Fall," " he admirably describes my two aunts, the heathen and the Christian sister."
A few quoted sentences will give the outline of the portrait, which
belongs to a higher social rank than Bunyan's :—
" Her fortune is divided betwixt herself and several other poor
people, and she has only her part of relief from it. . . . As she will
not give a poor man money to go to see a puppet-show, neither will
she allow herself any to spend in the same manner, thinking it very
proper to be as wise herself as she expects poor men should be. . . .
Excepting her victuals, she never spent ten pounds a year upon herself.

If you were to see her, you would wonder what poor body it was that was so scrupulously neat and clean. . . . She seems to be as a guardian angel to those that dwell about her, with her watchings and prayers blessing the places where she dwells, and making intercession with God for those that are asleep. . . . She is either doing something that is necessary for herself, or necessary for others who want to be assisted. There is scarce a poor family in the neighbourhood but wears something or other that has had the labour of her hands. Her wise and pious mind neither wants the amusement, nor can bear with the folly, of idle and impertinent work. . . . To relate her charity would be to relate the history of every day for twenty years. . . . She has set up near twenty poor tradesmen that had failed in their business, and saved as many from failing. She has educated several poor children that were picked up in the streets. . . . If there is any poor man or woman that is more than ordinarily wicked and reprobate, Miranda has her eye upon them. . . . She went the next day and *bought* the three children, that they might not be ruined by living with such wicked parents. They now live with Miranda. . . . Miranda is a constant relief to poor people in their misfortunes and accidents. . . She has a tenderness for old people that are grown past their labour. . . . Miranda never wants compassion, even to common beggars. . . . 'It may be,' says Miranda, 'that I may often give to those that do not deserve it, or that will make an ill use of my alms. But what then?—is not this the very method of Divine goodness?' . . . When she dies, she must shine amongst apostles and saints and martyrs; she must stand amongst the first servants of God, and be glorious amongst those who have fought the good fight, and finished their course with joy."

NOTE N.

The word "honest" had not yet shed very much of the meaning which it wore at the date of our Authorised Version of the Scriptures. In that version we read (Rom. xii. 17)—"Provide things *honest* in the sight of all men:" the Septuagint (Prov. iii. 4) has *kala* in the passage from which Paul is quoting, and he adopts the word as it stands. He had cited the passage in his second letter to the Corinthians (viii. 21), and had employed the same word : the translators again have "honest." In Peter's first letter (ii. 12) we read— "Having your conversation *honest* among the Gentiles:" the word once more is *kalen*. Beza's word in these instances is a Latin equivalent of it : it is *honestus*, the parent of our own word, and but one step from *honour*. In the Book of Acts (vi. 3) we have—"Men of *honest* report" (*marturoumenous*). Our Revisers, in adapting their translation to the modern value of words, have felt the need of rendering these passages thus:—"Take thought for things *honourable* in the sight of all men"—"Take thought for things *honourable*"—"Having your behaviour *seemly* among the Gentiles"—"Men of *good* report," men highly spoken of. King James's translation was published seventy years before Bunyan wrote the Second Part. While this translation was still new, George Herbert was writing *The Temple*, the 47th piece of which ("Constancie") begins with these lines :

> " Who is the *honest* man?
> He that doth still and strongly *good* pursue,
> To *God*, his neighbour, and himself most true;
>   Whom neither force nor fawning can
> Unpinne, or wrench from giving all their due."

The answer which the stanzas give to their opening question has a manifest reference to our modern meaning, but is equally conscious of the higher ideas which the men of the Jerusalem Chamber chose the word to represent, and has especial regard to a noble "constancie." "Now I was," says Bunyan himself ("Grace Abounding," par. 32), "as they said, become godly; now I was become a right *honest man*." Nearly fifty years after Bunyan's death, Pope wrote the line which Burns's quotation of it has made doubly familiar—

> "An honest man 's the noblest work of God." [1]

Unless we have here a very large assertion even for poetry, we must still put something of the old meaning into the word. And indeed a good deal of the older signification, the *honestus* of the Romans and of Beza, lingers among us to this day in such provincial phrases as "an honest fellow" (Burns's own "*honest* men and *bonnie* lasses"); when it is handsomeness, physical and moral, that is being thought of. There is a hint of this, perhaps, in Herbert :

> " His words and works, and *fashion too*,
> *All of a piece*, and all are cleare and straight."

NOTE O.

As was natural it should be, the physical circumstances of the Allegory are essentially those of the North Temperate Zone, and are distinctively those of England, if not simply of Bedfordshire itself.

[1] " Essay on Man," Ep. iv.; "Cottar's Saturday Night," stanza xix.

To Feeble-mind and Honest, and to every pilgrim of them all, "northward" was "off from the sun," and on toward regions of "ice." So local do those cities of Bunyan's appear, that when he speaks with so scrupulous exactness about Stupidity lying 4° to the N. of—Bedford, shall we say?—we in the more boreal province of the kingdom may have reason for uneasiness, seeing that the 4th deg. of lat. N. of the Dreamer's dungeon happens to pass along the further coast of the Firth of Forth. But we shall acquit Bunyan of any purpose to defame us.

This allusion to frigidity of climate, however, gives occasion for a reflection of some importance in regard to the outward imagery of the Allegory. With the faint exception of "the cold" in which Fearing "lay" at the Interpreter's door,—"and the *nights* were long and cold then,"—the Pilgrimage itself has nothing in it of WINTER. It has much of summer, something of autumn, more than hints of spring, but the climate of England from October to March is all but absent from it. Bunyan thus denies himself the use of a good deal that might have well served the purposes of imagery if he had chosen to use it. He employs climatic phenomena effectively enough now and again — the rain-pouring thunder-storm, the drizzling mists, the sunny haze, the sumptuous sunshine : it is surely remarkable that he shuts out of his Allegory the blinding snow-storm, the driving hail, the scowling sleet-showers, the still clear frosts, the short keen days, the long nights of tempestuous darkness; with which from childhood he had been familiar. It is not so with Milton or Danté, or perhaps with any other notable imaginative writer who wrote on religious themes in wintry lands. The omission was probably not the result of deliberate purpose; yet some cause, or cluster of causes, must have been at work with him to keep him off from what should otherwise have been so natural to a genius which appropriated so much else to its holy uses. One or two considerations will suggest themselves :—It is agreeable to the laws of mind, that for the imagination of a man undergoing the rigours of a jail life, the kindlier seasons should have a predominant charm, and the severer season should lie very much out of sight : but this would not apply to the Second Part, except in so far as it might be regulated by the First, and it would only doubtfully apply to the First Part itself if it was written during the half-year's imprisonment which has been brought to light by Mr Brown. That half-year, however, fell in the winter and early spring, when, by a similar law of mind, the kindly summer-time would have all its charm to the imagination. Yet it is of more importance to remember, when it is a literary question concerning Bunyan which is on hand, that in the Book which was nearly library and academy to him, and the Book of which his " Pilgrim " is scarcely more than a lively reflection, Winter has hardly a place : the climate of Palestine is more to him than the climate of England, at least when his imagination is on foot ; and that sub-tropical tract of sky and earth within which the sacred writers wrote is the region that rules the climate and weather of his Allegory, in the midst of all his Engish localisings. Depending somewhat on this circumstance of climate, spiritual deadness is associated with cold in the sacred writings ; and the way of spiritual life, as a separate system of experience, Bunyan instinctively defends, perhaps, against the intrusion of so sinister a complexion of figure as that which wintry scenes and incidents might cast over his story. Therefore he confirms this defence by throwing his hints of Winter back upon the places and times that are prior to pilgrimage, as we have just been finding in the text to which this Note is appended. Taking together all that is valid in these considerations, we may recognise some reason why Bunyan should feel little drawn towards wintry imagery, and even a little repelled from it,—although the revolution of time which the various portions of his Allegory include, upon any calculation, must have brought him opportunity of surrounding his pilgrims with Winter weather if he had been of a mind to do so.

This view is certainly not discountenanced by the part which Winter plays in the " Holy War." The season of dark nights and bitter days which crept over the beleaguered city of Mansoul is very expressive, though little use is made in detail of the peculiar phenomena of Winter such as he knew it in Britain. We cannot forget Bunyan's vision of the mountain in " Grace Abounding ": " I was shivering and shrinking in the cold, afflicted with *frost, snow*, and dark clouds."

The lengthened talk between Wiseman and Attentive about " the life and death of Mr Badman " took place after the noontide of a long summer-day.

NOTE P.

This seafaring simile is interesting as being a figure gathered from the other great sphere and method of human journeyings, and set for illustration of the sphere and method from which the Allegory has actually taken its form. " Sailing upon the seas,"—this also might conceivably supply the materials of an allegory of progress, as it has furnished to classic story the elements of allegorical history ; even in allegorical pilgrimages themselves, we are not without glimpses at least of sails and masts and oars. Of course no question can arise about the wisdom of Bunyan in preferring the form of a pedestrian journey on land, nor would there be much room for the question even if Bunyan had been more conversant with seafaring ways, or had lived in an age when sea-going had become so universal a matter as it is now.

Note Q.

The parenthetical paragraph which follows this passage—a paragraph deprecating criticism of his so musical figures—is instructive as suggesting the sort of censorship under which he was working. He does not detect that the sentence at which he pauses has more need of apology for its confusion than for its freedom. It must be the Divine Hand that "sets in tune" the soul of Fearing by "playing upon this string first;" but when the figure is applied to Fearing, it is "he" himself that "plays." This scarcely interferes, however, with the beauty and truth of the thought.—And it is worth while to notice how Bunyan, here again, has been getting to lose sight of the medium through whom he is speaking, and is so absorbed in the theme as to be unconsciously talking in his own name. The transition is sufficiently marked by the slip which occurs in a paragraph just before : "When he was going up to the gate, *Mr Great-heart* "—of course it is Great-heart who is speaking—" began to take his leave of him " . . .

Turnbull & Spears, Printers, Edinburgh.